The
KATAR LEGACY

by

TOBIN LOSHENTO

NEW LIBRI PRESS

This is a work of fiction. Nothing is in it that has not been imagined.

Copyright © 2012 by Tobin Loshento

Cover design by Arron McArthur, Copyright © 2012 by New Libri Press

ISBN: 978-1-61469-005-4

Published in 2012 by New Libri Press
Mercer Island, WA 98040
www.newlibri.com

New Libri Press is a small independent press dedicated to publishing new authors and independent authors in both eBook and traditional formats.

This book is dedicated to all the usual suspects, including the readers who had the patience to claw their way through early drafts of this book, written years ago and then feigning interest were able to read through the book again in its present form.

Editing is a thankless task and I include Michael in that list of suspects and my wife who let me give up a job that paid more in one year than I will ever make writing. You can't take it with you.

Chapter 1

It was the Festival of Alam, celebrating Harvest: five days and five nights of music, drinking, partying, and forgetting the troubles of Nakana. The raucous symphony of languages swirled with the scents of a thousand foods, libations, and perfumes insinuating themselves into the nose. Just as Tsom became accustomed to the smell, the wind shifted and a new brew manifested itself.

Tsom rubbed his hands together in anticipation of the day's take.

The wharf and its surrounding slums were Tsom's home. He moved through the crowds of outsiders with ease. Farthul, the midday moon rose in the south, signaling a wave of toasts within the sea of people who raised a thousand cups of beer, wine, and stronger drafts into the air. The clinking of so many mugs hitting simultaneously sent a cloud of birds aloft, adding their sound to the chaos. A roar of laughter from the crowd echoed the thunder of wings. Tsom laughed with them, as he pocketed a small money purse obtained during the toast.

Upon the expansive wharf the rich and the poor mingled as they rarely did during the rest of the year. The rich were drunk and careless—so were the poor, but Tsom wasn't interested in them—and the city guards and police were too busy to focus on petty crimes. After three days, he was drunk on his success. Last year's Festival had been good, but not this good.

Tsom was a young thief. In The Cities, thieves were rare, but young ones even rarer. Once caught you did not stay young. The qenar mines, military service, or corporal punishment saw to that. The latter was the worst because it comprised draining of *ka*, the catalytic life energy that formed the basis of civilization. *Ka* loss was on the subconscious thoughts of any criminal. The forced draining of *ka* often led to quick death, the loss of your entire *ka*—the ultimate punishment—meant *true death*. No chance of reincarnation. Ever. The thought tempered Tsom's exhilaration briefly.

He secreted his current take in one of his many caches, all in dark narrow alleys too narrow and filthy for locals—or even the current crowds—to utilize; away from his apartment and prying eyes. There was no time to count, but the weight of the purse combined with the faint rustle of paper was satisfying. If this kept up he would have a year's thieving done in five days.

Gliding back into the crowd, Tsom spied two of the city guard, holding a young light haired woman between them. The woman struggled wildly, fear in her eyes. A dark-haired woman, wearing expensive silk and bright colors from Argn, stood nearby indignantly pointing her finger at the blonde. The guards grabbed a bracelet out of the blonde's pocket and handed it to the rich woman. The crowd avoided getting involved, as did Tsom. His earlier exuberance faded. He didn't know the blonde, but everyone knew there would be punishment.

With habitual care, he wandered the main square at the edge of the docks. The wharf area was huge—serving all six of The Cities it could hold a hundred thousand people—yet with the Festival crowds he felt almost claustrophobic. He scanned for city guards, private guards, and easy targets. Sometimes a floater was left unattended for a few minutes, or a carriage, but for the moment nothing. He moved toward the vendors. Hundreds of them spread out along the wharf, hoping to earn enough to make the rest of the year bearable. No two kiosks were the same. Families passed down their designs from one generation to another, each adding their own story to the tapestries that wrapped the tops of the kiosks like headbands. The fish vendors had colorful renditions of monstrous fish. Madam Mara's whores had a shack where they sold wares that you would not find at their main establishment: perfumes and aphrodisiacs that the rich women paid handsomely for—tittering with scandalous glee at the thought of purchasing something so libertine. Their men avoided the eyes of familiar winking women behind the counter. Festival was a time of celebration, but work for many. Of the millions in Arbeneth, only a few were wealthy enough to enjoy all that the city had to offer, others forgot for a moment they did not have much and still others—the vendors and Tsom—worked.

He loved the thrill of each new conquest. A purse here, a bracelet there, an item from an overstuffed bag. The fear of being caught faded once again. He wandered up to Mara's kiosk, where Turnya was talking to a well-dressed young woman who could not stop blushing as she glanced furtively around. Seeing Tsom, the customer turned scarlet red and made to leave.

"Don't mind him, miss. He's local. Off with you Tsom, you're scaring away the customers." Turnya winked at Tsom while she spoke.

"Perhaps I am a customer today," he replied. The woman blushed again. Turnya laughed, "The day you pay for that is the day the five moons eclipse."

Tsom grinned and slipped Turnya a charm bracelet. Not stolen, but one from a vendor. She smiled again, her eyes crinkling, and gently shooed him on. The blushing woman looking after him with interest.

Tsom's dark hair matched his dark eyes. Dark hair and eyes blended well with the natives of the docks, his favorite corner of the world. He'd roamed much of the city of Arbeneth as a child—this differentiated him from the locals. He had memories of a life elsewhere.

He moved to Karsel's booth, tools and tool repair. Karsel was giving away small wooden anchors for advertising. He knew that no one was interested in work during Festival, but they might remember him later. Tsom picked up one of the anchors, turning it over in his hands.

"Leave it be, Tsom. I don't need to advertise with you."

"You never know, I might take up fishing." They both laughed.

Tsom slid over a bracelet, carefully hidden under a piece of cloth. Karsel casually placed his large calloused hand over the cloth and slid it back, the bracelet falling into his other hand below the counter.

"How much to repair that, Karsel?"

Karsel glanced at it, one eyebrow went high. He quickly wrapped the bracelet in the cloth. "A difficult piece, Tsom."

Tsom nodded. It was high grade steel with jade inlay. The value was both in the metal and that it was probably a talisman. Tsom had not risked trying to activate it. Karsel was an honest fence, so if it was difficult, that meant it would be hard to dispose of.

"I understand, name your price."

"A hundred sintar."

It was worth more in steel and jade alone, but Tsom nodded. Karsel slid one of the wooden toy anchors to Tsom. It was Tsom's turn to raise an eyebrow.

"Careful with those, they have a tendency to break, the inside is hollow."

Tsom grinned and pocketed the toy anchor.

The harbor was a popular destination for other races during Festival. Hrýll, the only artisans capable of making *talismans* mingled with Yanín mercenaries. The occasional Riconé towered over everyone. Yet, even in the port area, the Humans outnumbered the others by a wide margin. Tsom limited his targets to Human. He had seen the results of someone foolish enough to try and steal from a Yanín. He scanned the crowd. No easy targets.

Despite knowing it was going to happen, Tsom jumped with the rest of the crowd as the navy and guard ships, gathered en masse in the harbor, fired off their flame tubes to mark the midday hour. Fifty ships in a semi-circle, with the open end facing the docks, spouted lances of flame as thick as a man two hundred feet into the air, connecting at the center. How much qenar had been used just for that, Tsom wondered.

Tsom watched a Yanín stumble out of the *Lost Mavkin*, a faded carving of the big namesake fish hanging from the front of the tavern. Mavkin were terrible eating, but most at the *Lost Mavkin* were not there to eat. He—by definition a Yanín in public was a he—looked around, confused, and turned into the narrow street Tsom was strategically waiting by. Tsom briefly considered picking his pocket—despite his self-imposed limitation to Humans, but even a drunk Yanín could be dangerous. The seemingly clumsy movements didn't fool him. Tsom eyed the creature that resembled a man covered in loose leather. A second exoskeleton covered the top of its head, making it look like it was wearing a white cap and serving as a fair protective helmet. Yanín had double joints everywhere, allowing them to grab things behind them as if they were in front. Its movements seemed like a badly played marionette, a leg occasionally bending the wrong way, or an arm bending backward. It was tempting. Not many thieves could brag they had picked the pocket of a Yanín. Not many living thieves. Better to wait for an easier target. No rush.

Several hours of patient waiting produced a well-dressed man in his twenties with an attractive woman at his side. On second look, she was beautiful. Tsom gazed at her for a third time, distracted by her elegance. They did not normally belong in this part of town, slumming, as many did, during Festival. Her companion wore a short sword, safety strap unhooked, and the scabbard hung in such a way that his left hand constantly brushed the sword. This gave Tsom a bit of pause. He had lived as a lone thief this long by not being stupid. The man carried himself in an arrogant, self-assured manner, despite being inebriated. Tsom had watched veteran sailors with the same demeanor. This guy might be wealthy, but he was no innocent.

Yet, this mark was too tempting. Drunk, the fool was obviously trying to impress the woman. Tsom could see why. She wore dark royal green that matched her eyes. A green silk scarf pulled her blood red hair back to show off her heart-shaped face. Bright green leather boots peeked and teased from the bottom of her dress. The drunk spoke loudly and did not step aside for anyone. The woman took the man's sword arm into her own, and they started toward Tsom. Tsom decided and made his move.

He stepped into the street and stumbled into the woman, knocking her down. He was careful not to injure her. She smelled of flowers and desire. The scent almost distracted him. Almost.

"Pardon me, Miss! I did not see you there." A slurred voice and a weave for added touch. The inebriate stepped in quickly—for a drunk—and slapped Tsom aside, aiming for true damage instead of simply moving him aside as many would have done. "You disgusting little rat, stand aside." His lips pulled back in a feral manner, his bloodshot eyes narrowed to slits. The sword was halfway out of its scabbard, and then he recovered his composure. Bending, with a slight sway made worse by a puffed out chest, he held out his hand to the woman. "Flana, are you injured?"

"I'm fine, Arlec. You don't need to hit the young man, it was an accident."

He grumbled, touched the hilt of the sword, and glowered at Tsom, but he did not follow as Tsom got up and ran away.

The purse from the pompous drunk with the beautiful woman did not weigh much. Tsom felt very few coins. There was the pleasant sound of paper, which meant some real money. The quality was not bad, albeit made of an ugly red cloth. What bothered him was that despite the heat of the day the purse felt cold, like something he had felt before. Many years ago. He was about to peer inside when he saw a city guard walking toward him. He recognized Tilde. She was a local and knew Tsom's profession, even if she had never caught him. He walked briskly in the opposite direction and turned into an extremely narrow, deserted alley. This alley was not one of his favorites. He went to the southern brick wall, ignoring as best he could the three days of accumulated garbage with rotted fish, vomit, urine, and worse assaulting his nose and lungs. He pulled out a loose brick. He slid the purse in and put the brick back. As he stepped out into the street Tilde grabbed him—he let her.

"Tsom, you handsome young thief, what were you up to in the alley?" She was friendly, but her grip was firm.

"Tilde, I hope you aren't going to arrest me for pissing in public, but with Festival I just didn't think I could make it to the local stall. Besides, the lines are impossible. Oops, better fasten that."

He reached down and buttoned his fly shut, at least made it look that way. Tilde grinned, glanced down the alley for a moment or two, wrinkled her nose, gagged, and sent him on his way. He would get this purse and the other later.

Tsom strolled to the gaming vendors. Without glancing back at Tilde, he knew she was watching him. Here were games of luck and skill, in theory. Tsom knew most of them. They were permanent residents. The games were all rigged, yet he often won—when he played. None of the vendors would let him play for money, but during slow times he would play for fun, or to help demonstrated that the games were not rigged. The tacit agreement was he helped out in this way and they would ignore his occasional theft from the customers who were concentrating on the games. Baldum's knife throwing stand was one of his favorites and he had agreed earlier to periodically stop by. He walked up just as an argument was heating up between Baldum and a disgruntled group of young men.

"The game is rigged. No one can hit anything with these shit knives, not five targets, much less ten in a row in fifteen seconds. I want my money back and the prize I should have won." The large man slammed his fist on the counter, causing his mop of yellow hair to bob up and down. His three companions yelled agreement.

Baldum looked around, Tilde was no longer in sight. He spotted Tsom approaching.

"I run an honest game here. Let me prove it. What about we let this young man try his hand at my simple game of skill? If he can hit the targets you go on your way." He waved Tsom over.

The four men glowered at Tsom, looked him over and noted his clothes. While not ragged, they were local. Dock clothes. One of the three sycophants to the surly leader spoke, nudging one of companions.

"He is a local. Probably can't do anything but load a boat."

"Or scrub the toilets," laughed another.

"Make him hit at least five, Gorth. Don't be too easy on him. Little rat probably is good with knives."

"Fine. Ten knives. Fifteen seconds. He hits at least five targets ." The leader pulled Tsom near and looked down into his eyes. "Think you can do it, wharf rat?" Mop-head laughed.

Tsom managed a smile that held no malice and walked up to the counter. Baldum reached under the counter and handed Tsom ten small throwing knives.

"Wait a minute. He uses the same knives I just used," demanded the yellow mop.

Baldum turned a shade paler. He handed Tsom ten badly balanced knives. This was not part of their prearranged routine. He had never used this set of knives. Yellow mop whispered something to his companions and they loosened their swords. Steel, not bronze. These men were rich or worked for someone with money. Tsom took one knife and quickly felt its imbalance. He picked another, the imbalance was the same. He smiled. *Baldum you old cheat, these are so bad I can't believe you haven't be caught before.*

"Ok. I am ready when you are, Sir." His voice wavered; he tried to sound unsure and nervous. Baldum licked his lips. Tsom gave him a quick wink. He spotted Lita, Baldum's young daughter watching nervously from the side. Lita was fourteen and had a furious crush on Tsom. He tried not to grin at her.

Baldum pressed a button, a weight was released, the gears turned, and the targets sprang to life, moving in seemingly random directions. They were the red circles. Equally random were the orange larger circles that moved near the red circles, sometimes in front of them. Of course there was nothing random about the movement if you knew the pattern. Tsom knew it well.

Tsom threw. He loved knives. His hand was a blur, his eyes seemed unfocused. The knives gave off a solid thunking sound as they hit dead center. The first eight had taken him less than four seconds. Tsom hesitated on the ninth. *Baldum, you old sneak*, he thought to himself. The ninth was balanced perfectly. He adjusted his throw. Hit the target. The tenth was back to the flawed balance of the first eight; he readjusted again and hit the tenth target.

There was a silence from not just the four. A small crowd had gathered. Tsom glanced at his handiwork. A grin washed over his face, disappearing almost before it was finished. Perhaps, he thought, he should have thrown a little less perfectly. Damn. Every one of the targets had been hit dead center. Every one of the blades was exactly parallel to the ground with the orientation of the cutting edges the same. Lita laughed and clapped her hands. Baldum paled.

"The boy's in cahoots with you." Growled mop head, reaching for Tsom, who stepped to the side and melted backwards into the crowd. Fortunately for Baldum, a guard showed up at this point, attracted to the noise and the crowd. Tsom's sigh of relief was cut short. The guardsman was accompanied by a Katar, of all things. Tsom shivered. All the more reason to fade away. Baldum grinned in Tsom's direction and turned to the guard to explain what was going on. The Katar just glowered at everyone, peering at each person until he or she turned away. Tsom felt sick, the way he always did around Katar; sick with fear and hatred. Time to move.

Tsom glided through the crowd easily. He seemed to sense where the opening would be, where it would give way with a little push. He moved almost as fast as if the square were empty. Away from the Katar his stomach calmed down. But, he was still hyped up and jumpy. Not the time to try stealing. Especially with Katar nearby. He made his way to the gnali stand. The sweet pickled fish, coated in spicy batter and deep-fried, was his favorite Festival food. Besides, the stand was run by Shela.

In line, in front of him, was another slummer: a rich woman checking out the docks. She would never venture here during the rest of the year. Her clothes shimmered and changed colors as the light hit at a slightly different angle, a different pattern each time, yet each pattern was elaborate and detailed. She had a cute six or seven-year-old daughter in tow. The girl gazed around, big eyes taking everything in. She had full red lips, which in ten years would cause some problems. Even now, the men walking by smiled and waved at her.

Tsom smiled at her and pulled out a one-sintar coin. He walked it across his fingers on the back of his hand. When it reached the end of his hand, by the small finger, he made it reappear between his thumb and index finger and walked it again. The little girl watched, fascinated.

He tossed the coin up in the air and caught it, clenched his fist and held out the clenched fist to the girl.

She grinned and pointed to his other hand.

Smart girl, he thought, and opened the other hand where the coin now was.

He tossed the coin in the air again and held out both hands. The girl studied them both and then picked the one that he caught the coin with. He signaled for her to hold out her hand and he opened the one she had picked. Onto her hand he dropped a piece of candy.

The little girl giggled. "You know magic."

Before Tsom could answer the mother turned around, sized Tsom up, and pulled the girl away.

"Stay away from the locals dear. They are all thieves and scum."

The smile for the girl frozen on his face, Tsom made an elaborate bow to the woman. "At your service, madam. I pretend to be nothing else, unlike … say a merchant who deals with the Hrýll and cheats them out of talismans." He had guessed at her, or her husband's profession. The clothes she had on were of Hrýll design. He had seen and spoken to Hrýll on the docks over the years. *The Old Ones* as some called them. The Hrýll were the only artisans of talismans, the tools and artifacts that ran The Cities; yet they were treated as servants by many and shunned by others. Their light fur, more of a whisper of hair, gave them a blurry look and made them obviously not Human.

The woman looked shocked and outraged. She pulled her child out of line and pushed her way forcibly through the crowd.

"Madam, you dropped this." Tsom held aloft her money purse. Those nearby might have noted that he never bent down to pick anything up. The woman felt her blouse, blushed deeply, ran back, and grabbed the purse. Moving quickly she pushed into the crowd, the little girl waving to Tsom as she was pulled along.

Shela was working the gnali stand. "Tsom, you are going to piss off somebody important someday." She sounded serious, but she had a twinkle in her eye and handed him a large bag of gnali. Shela was cute—although she ate too many of her own gnali to be called beautiful. Her hair and eyes were dark, marking her as a local. When she smiled dimples appeared that melted his heart. She shook extra salt on them without him asking.

"That'll be half a sintar, Tsom." She held out her hand.

Tsom reached into a pocket and fished out a small coin. He held it up briefly, so Shela could see it and tossed it to her. She caught it, glanced down at the piece of candy she was holding.

"Tsom, get back here." She popped the candy into her mouth, her lips pursed in a kissable manner as she sucked on it. He knew how sweet those lips could be and was tempted to steal a quick kiss, but he laughed, pointed to her cleavage and melted into the crowd.

Shela fished the full sintar coin out of her gnali enhanced bosom, giggled, and went on to help the next customer.

After his meal, Tsom lounged against the corner of the brothel, a lit nart in his hand. The rolled leaves of the slightly narcotic plant gave off a sweet promising smell. *Enough playing time to earn some money.* He rarely inhaled, but it helped him blend in. His father years ago had fretted needlessly that he would stand out, that he would look like his mother, but even as a small child he had the knack for fitting in. Tsom wasn't sure why his father thought he looked different than others. Whenever he asked a friend, they would look closely at him and shrug. "No offense, but you look pretty average in every way." Technically illegal, narts were common on the wharf and cheaper than alcohol. He wriggled his nose to keep from sneezing. A young boy in the crowd caught his eye.

It did not strike him as incongruous to be calling the boy who was sixteen or so 'young.' Tsom was only a few years older, but felt a lifetime of experience and skill between himself and the boy. The boy was obviously a pickpocket. Tsom spotted him from over a hundred feet away. The boy clumsily cut one man's purse and lifted it out of his pocket. Such an amateur. He was going to ignore the boy, but then he saw the boy making his way to a foppishly dressed man who was stumbling along the far side of the street. Idiot. The man was city guard. A plant for Festival. *Look closely, you fool.*

Tsom reached down and picked up a small rock. He hefted it once, and, faster than any of the people around could see, threw it. The rock bounced against the boy's head just as the boy reached the guard. The boy stumbled and almost fell, then staggered to the side of the street, rubbing his head. He looked around, but never saw Tsom.

The rising of three of Nakana's moons warned that soon it would be dark. Festival would go on all night, but the darkness was a welcome security blanket for Tsom. Tilde had finished her shift, and the other guards stayed to the well-lit streets. The cool shine of the Hrýll built glow globes casting circles of artificial light that made the crowds look slightly drunker than they were. Pale luminescence bathed them. Even the very dark skinned northerners look ghostlike. Tsom stifled a yawn and started back to the alley with the loose brick and his stolen purse. It had been a long day and he was anxious to see what was in that purse.

Tsom smiled as he pulled the man's purse out the cubby hole in the wall. He opened the purse, peered in, and nearly dropped it.

It was full of large notes. There could be over several thousand sintar here. Only a very rich man would carry so much around, or a fool. The first wave of adrenalin and excitement quickly faded. Tsom did not excite easily. Excitement led to mistakes. *Think it through.*

This much money all in one purse was disturbing. Wealth meant power. Power meant danger. His stomach sank. He was a petty thief intentionally. Small stuff didn't attract the attention of the authorities. The feeling worsened as he continued the inventory of the purse. There was something else tucked inside the side compartment. He pulled it out. In his hand lay a ring with five small white diamonds set equally apart, with a small black diamond in the center. Tsom hissed with fear. Memories of what had happened to his family rocked him back until he leaned against the wall. The man was Katar. Not just dangerous.

The ring was death.

Chapter 2

"Let's go, Flana. I grow tired of slumming here on the docks," Arlec grabbed her by the elbow and guided her away from the vendor of the scarf she had spotted. The scarf was of Kinel origin. She was sure of it. It was worth one hundred times what the vendor was asking. Flana Showa of the most powerful merchant family in The Cities was not going to let even a Katar of Arlec's standing dictate her every move. She wrestled free of his grip and ran back to the woman. She paid the asking price for the scarf. No time to haggle. Paying she grabbed the scarf and ran back to Arlec before his yell at her was fully formed.

She grabbed his arm and smiling sweetly at him said. "Come, Arlec, let's get you home to a warm bed so you can rest."

Arlec nodded. He was rubbing his bare left hand again. She felt a pang of guilt and glee that he had consented to go out without that dreadful ring on his finger. The looks of loathing that people gave her when they were together and he was in Katar uniform made her stomach knot up. The Showa were respected, not loathed. Arlec seemed to revel in those looks.

As they made their way to the parking areas that only the rich could afford, Flana's mood improved. Having made up her mind how to break it off with Arlec was such a relief that she did not mind missing the rest of the evening of Festival. Maybe she would even sneak back after Arlec dropped her off. She made sure not to let her good mood show as she began to plot how to start the rumors that would further her cause. Maybe the fact that her family came from a long line of daughters. Yes, Devon, Arlec's father would want a grandson to pass on the family power. She had to get Devon to call off his son. Her father had carefully probed if the head of the Karn family would approve of his son marrying a non-Katar, but given that Devon himself had married outside of the Katar, it was no surprise that he did not object. Devon's wife had died early. Flana had no desire to follow in her footsteps.

It was strange how a small incident, like that young man bumping into Arlec, could trigger a train of thought. She would thank that young man if she ever bumped into him again.

Flana's father was surprised to see her at dinner. He looked worried. Before he could open his mouth, Flana leaned over and kissed his forehead.

"Arlec called the evening short, said he had pressing business."

"You didn't do anything to anger him, did you, my dear?" Timon asked.

"Nothing. He was getting drunk and seemed to be enjoying himself, but after a young man bumped into me and caused me to fall—no, no, I'm fine father—he became moody and then when there was an incident later on with some Katar on patrol he became quite panicked, I would say. I know he hated not wearing his ring while out with me. At least he was kind enough to do that for me."

"He does care for you, my dear." Timon helped himself to cold duck, fruits from the north, and a very tall glass of wine. It looked like it wasn't his first.

Flana laughed, bitterly. "Only because he thinks he can't have me. I think he will give up on me soon."

Timon paused in his chewing and raised an eyebrow. A servant came with a new bottle of wine. He swallowed another large quantity of wine before responding.

"Really? A marriage between the Showa and the Karn would be … advantageous."

"For the families, not for me," she snapped. Her father had no sympathy for her dislike of Arlec, all he saw were profits and protection.

"Flana, my dear, really. You must think of the future. Arlec is handsome, strong, and powerful. What is wrong with that? Don't tell me about 'love' … it is too trite, my dear. The rich and powerful do not concern themselves with love."

"Perhaps, but if Arlec loses interest in me, I will hardly shed any tears. For you, or the family. There are other families. Other Katar even."

"If only you had been born a man, my dear."

"If only we lived in Argn," she retorted. By the Sea, she hated custom in Arbeneth.

"You are a strong woman. You could run the business, even here, with a figurehead husband. You have the head for it, when you care to focus."

"Yes, but I find that I value some merchandise," she looked down at her body, "more than others. I will not sell myself to just anyone, Father."

"Even Katar have been known to die and leave widows, my dear."

"Not the Karn. They tend to leave widowers."

Timon frowned and drank more wine. Another bottle appeared as they ate in silence.

Chapter 3

Arlec dropped his exterior calm after Flana. No more pretending to be something that he was not. He breathed deeply inside his floater. The red leather exterior had the Katar insignia on the sides and the Karn ship sigil. Like all floaters, its base was essentially a large rectangle, with black steel and jade inlay in the framing. Both the steel and the jade were worth a fortune. On top rested an ornate carriage, minus the wheels.

By The Sea, he wanted that woman as his own. Not just because of her wealth, although her father owned the majority of the ships in Arbeneth, which explained her fondness for the docks. *Ague, damn that fondness*, he thought to himself. An image of the sea god he had just invoked sinking all of Flana's ships flashed through his mind. Flana's smile flashed before his eyes and the anger toward her burned away. It was his own stupidity and lust, he was forced to acknowledge.

That drunken little snipe must have been the thief. The leather bands securing his purse under his shirt were severed, by a very sharp knife. Soon, he vowed, a dead thief.

Such a loss was inexcusable. He wasn't sure what punishment his father would met out, but Devon was not known for leniency. He thought of his mother and grew cold.

The Katar answered to no one, except themselves.

He could hear the lecture now. The rings were irreplaceable. There were thousands of Katar waiting for the chance to wear one of the rings. The rings made you a true Katar, wielding power over lesser men and women. Even with low birth rates, the Katar families numbered over nine thousand, vying for the five thousand or less rings. Each of the five families controlled one thousand and of those one hundred were family rings. Those were bound to each other.

If he could borrow one of the other rings, he could increase his chances of finding his own. Unless the thief had thrown the ring into the sea. Arlec's stomach roiled at the thought. It was possible, if the thief understood the danger of holding on to the ring. *Perhaps he'll try it on*, Arlec thought. That would simplify matters. The dead body with a Katar ring on it would probably remain untouched and he could collect he ring without incident.

Arlec did not wait for the floater to come to a complete stop before jumping out. The front circle was deserted, no visitors and his sisters were no doubt still enjoying Festival's activities. Just as well, he was not sure he trusted them to help. They were completely under father's thumb. His older sisters. His younger sister Shara was a different matter, but she was up in Argn, receiving her training. Old Devon was going to have a handful when she returned. Arlec shook his head. Devon was too tolerant of his youngest child. He demanded complete obedience from all of his family, immediate and distant, but when it came to Shara, he seemed to go senile. Perhaps when she returned Arlec could use her to manipulate his father a bit. Some of his ideas for change might not be immediately dismissed with her backing.

He snapped his fingers. Later. Now he must move to try and find his ring. Of the family rings, he knew of approximately seventy. Of the seventy, probably fifty were in Arbeneth. Of those ten were worn by his uncles or his father's cousins, another thirty were handpicked by Devon. Ten were on the hands of his own cousins, but most of them would use the loss of his ring to backstab him, or manipulate him. Except for Vard. Vard would help him. Of the entire family, Vard was the only one who had similar ideas as to how the Katar needed to change. How the Karn needed to change. Vard.

Vard was out carousing for Festival. Arlec chaffed at waiting, but he needed one of the family rings and someone to organize a search party in their name instead of his. He would lead the effort at Vard's request. His hunt for the thief would have to wait until morning.

***

"I still can't believe you, you the stealth of the Katar, got taken by a common thief," laughed Vard.

"It's no laughing matter, Vard. You know Devon. He'll make me wish I was dead before giving me another ring," Arlec ran his hand through his thick hair. His eyes showed and felt the lack of sleep and he hadn't bothered to shave this morning. The ring on his left hand felt false, weak, a pale imitation of his own. How did the common Katar stand it, he wondered.

"You sure Sirg won't tell anyone about lending me his ring?" Arlec asked, again.

"Relax, Arlec. He owes me thousands. He keeps his mouth shut and lets you use the ring for a time and we're even. Hell, he probably won't even miss it. Sirg hasn't fought in years."

Vard pulled out his watch. A mechanical, not a talisman. It probably cost more than a talisman, they were so hard to make, but Vard enjoyed the uniqueness. "The others should be here soon. We'll hit the docks first. Put the fear of the Katar into the locals and see if we can flush him out. I'll wander around discreetly with my ring barely activated. If your ring is nearby, it should flare up with resonance."

"What if one of the other family is around?" grumbled Arlec. He hated not being fully in charge. Depending on another.

"Ha, they're all recovering from hangovers. Too bad these don't help with that," laughed Vard. He had an easy laugh. Arlec rarely laughed, but he enjoyed the proximity of Vard's.

Chapter 4

Sleep ended abruptly for Tsom. Mixed with the sounds of early morning Festival was something dark. Tsom staggered to the window of his second story apartment. Below, amongst the vendors setting up and the cleaning crews finished up moved a group of twenty men. Despite the distance Tsom could see they were Katar. Their armbands distinctive, even if he could not make out the sigil of six diamonds.

Two moved off from the group and entered the *Lost Mavkin*, visible from his window. Moments later they came out with the proprietor, Davir, between them. Tsom kept his head low but his ear near the open window. The larger man, Tsom guessed he was the drunk from yesterday, stepped forward and bellowed to the almost deserted docks.

"I am looking for a thief. A young man, about so tall, average looking. Dark hair and dark eyes. He has stolen something of value to the Katar. There is a reward for anyone who turns him in. Twenty thousand sintar. He is a local. If any of you hide his identity," he stopped yelling and with a fast motion grabbed Davir's arm, twisted, and slammed the arm down. The snap was audible from Tsom's window and he winced. "Turn him in by tomorrow morning." The former drunk Katar moved off, leaving five of the Katar behind.

Twenty thousand sintar was a lifetime's wages for some. Tsom backed away from the window. He grabbed his knife, made of steel, not cheaper bronze. If no one turned him in, he had twenty hours.

He went to Karsel, who was sleepily setting up his booth. Karsel took a large swallow from a huge mug that steamed in the morning cool air. He watched Tsom approach with narrowed eyes.

"Tell me it's not you the Katar are after," Karsel said in a low voice, audible only to Tsom.

Tsom nodded.

"I didn't know. Maybe I can get this returned and they will back off?" He held out the purse.

"What's in it?" Karsel took another swig from the mug. The smell of coffee and spices reminded Tsom that he had not eaten. Karsel did not reach for the purse.

"One of their rings."

Karsel set the mug down in a fit of coughing, backing away from Tsom.

"By the Sea, Tsom. You are dead. Do you know who that Katar was, bellowing this morning? Arlec, son of Devon, the Karn family."

He leaned forward, both hands on the counter of the booth, his head hanging low. He continued in a whisper.

"Arlec is heir apparent to the Karn family, as the Karn do not let women rule. He is ruthless, Tsom. He will not accept simple return, he will kill anyone who helps you. I cannot help you." His head hung even lower.

"Tell no one you have the ring. No one. Go about your business for the moment, but you must flee. Best to leave the city altogether."

Tsom rocked back on his feet, glancing around. His life, once again was being destroyed by the Katar. First his parents, now this. He felt the same anger as eight years ago rise up. The need to fight back. Strike at the Katar. Then he was only eleven.

"What of the ring?" Tsom murmured. "Maybe I can break off the diamonds, sell those? Could you get rid of those for me?"

Karsel jumped back, pale. "Tsom, do you know nothing? The rings are talisman, powerful artifacts from before The Cities. You cannot simply break them, it would probably blow up in your face. The rings are what give the Katar their power. Throw it in the river. Never put it on. The rings are death. The expression is real. Death if you put it on, death when wielded by the Katar. Leave, Tsom. Talk to me no more. People will remember you here. Leave."

Karsel turned his back on Tsom. After a moment Tsom moved on, looking at the other vendors. They were watching him uneasily. Several turned away as he approached. Others tensed. A few looked around the open docks, their gaze resting on one of the five Katar moving around. These were his friends. He knew them all. Yet, he feared them and for them.

He left the area and drifted to the food vendors, the gnali stand. Shela was lighting the coals for the grease. She looked up as Tsom approached, her smile warm and unafraid.

"What can I do for you, Tsom," her smile broadening, she leaned forward and looked in his eyes deeply. Tsom longed for a carefree evening with her. A quiet evening.

"I'm in trouble, Shela."

"You're always in trouble, Tsom."

"This time it's the Katar."

Shela's smile faded quickly, but she did not move back. She grabbed his hands. "What can I do? What do you need?"

Tsom squeezed her hand, hard, then let go.

"I need you to not try and protect me when the Katar come. If they question you, tell them I left. That I went to Zethicia."

"Zethicia? You're leaving The Cities?" Her eyes glistened.

"Yes. Yes, tell them I went to Zethicia, or one of the outlying towns. The wilderness. Free of the Katar. I have to. Too many could get hurt." He touched her cheek as he said the latter. She grabbed his hand again and kissed it. Then her eyes went over his shoulder and she hissed. "Katar. Move." She slipped a coin into his hands and turned away from him.

He didn't look behind him. With a fast glide he moved to the alleys and the warehouses. If he was a wharf rat, those were his warren. As he reached the first alley he chanced a glance. A Katar was talking with Shela and she was leaning forward, her ample bosom moving with a distracting motion that kept the Katar focused on her. Tsom wasn't sure if the wink he saw was for him, or the Katar. He faded into his labyrinth, confident that he was safe for the moment. The cold from Arlec's purse reminded him that moment would be all too short.

~~~

Vard yelled and Arlec was the first to join him.

"The ring flared. There was a young man, possibly your thief, talking to that fishmonger. The tasty looking one. I gave chase and the ring just went dead, as if he was never here."

Arlec felt like howling in rage, but that would not look well. Image was important, his father always told him. For instance, breaking the bartender's arm had been necessary. Vard and the other twenty Katar expected an overt show of force. It wasn't that Arlec actually disliked teaching commoners their place, but it always felt too much like something his father would do. He hated imitating his father. He scowled and signaling Vard they strode to the plump young woman's stall. As they neared the woman pulled a tiny crossbow out from behind the stall and shot Vard in the chest. Vard looked down in surprise. His ring flared brightly as did Arlec's. Arlec did not stop for Vard, if his ring was glowing, he was alive. He darted forward, the woman moved in slow motion, but faster than he expected, another bolt was already in the small automatic. "Damn, this inferior ring," he muttered. He knocked the crossbow aside and caught her hand as she pulled a knife out and tried to use it on him. She was strong, but nothing compared to his augmented strength. Without thinking, he broke her wrist and she dropped the knife. Then, she leapt at him and tried to bite him. He pulled her off and knocked her unconscious, deliberately holding back from a death blow. He wanted her alive for questioning.

He raced back to Vard.

"The bitch punctured my lung," yelled Vard.

Arlec ripped back Vard's shirt and examined the wound. Vard had already pulled the tiny quarrel out. He held it up so that Arlec could see it.

"Poison." They said simultaneously.

"Keep your ring active," hissed Arlec.

"That could kill people here."

"That is the price they will have to pay. You can't die, Vard."

"If I did, you could switch rings with me. I'm sure you thought of that."

Arlec had, but didn't want to admit it to his friend and cousin.

"You're too valuable alive. I'm going to get *my own* ring back." He glanced at the unconscious form laying a few feet away. "I have a feeling our young woman here knows more than your average fishmonger."

Chapter 5

Once out of the dock area, Tsom headed north. His memories of childhood rose unbidden and guided him toward the merchant neighborhood he spent his first eleven years. The shops and houses changed from small, worn, and dangerous to prosperous homes and apartments. Here the smell of the sea and river was untainted with centuries of fish guts and boats. A warmth settled over him. The fear, while not gone, retreated to the rear of his consciousness. The wharf was home, but this was something more. Roots. Childhood. Innocence and lost innocence.

He watched several children playing shand against a wall. The game of luck and skill that he had excelled at. He smiled and pulled a coin out from his pocket, ready to toss it against the wall. Glancing down he realized it was the coin Shela had passed him. It was not a legal coin. He looked at it closely. One side had two hands clasping, the other had two swords crossed. He frowned and slowly returned it to his pocket. Where had he seen those symbols before? The boys and shand forgotten, he drifted toward the sound of a parade up the street. One of hundreds going on in The Cities, this one had people dressed up as *daemons*; not the ordinary *daemons* controlled by the Riconé, but the ferocious and deformed *daemons* of myth, said to be the origin of the Riconé *daemons*: the Tarth. Others were dressed as the legendary army that drove them back to Hell. Tsom had never given much thought to the story, said to have occurred more than five thousand years ago, when man was new to the world and the non-humans outnumbered mankind.

Never having traveled outside of The Cities, Tsom found it both easy to believe and impossible to conceive. A world without the teaming millions of The Cities was hard to comprehend. The sailors often told of the lands outside of The Cities as sparsely populated and dangerous; a wilderness with Yanín, Hrýll, Srýll, and the sentient Death Cats. He often daydreamed of traveling with them to the far off and exotic sounding places. Yet, part of him had a hard time believing anything outside of The Cities existed. His knowledge of geography was nonexistent. Truthfully, he did not really know much of the other five cities surrounding Arbeneth. For the first time he realized how ignorant he was. He had been a bright student, before his parents' death, but that was only for a few years.

The parade passed and shaking himself like a mongrel dog, he quit his musing. He patted his inner pocket to make sure the stolen purse was still there. His stomach growled. Food was rising on his list. One of the restaurants now visible across the street had an open window for customers not wishing to sit down. He ordered several buns with meat and nuts baked inside. As he paid, using a few of the coins in the cold cursed purse, he fished out Shela's coin.

"Ever see a coin like this?"

The man's eyes widened and he covered Tsom's hand with his own ample appendage.

"Careful, boy. You don't know who may be watching. You're new here?"

Tsom nodded.

"There's a local operative posing as a beggar, two streets down. Show him the coin. He'll hook you up."

"Thanks, I'll do that."

"Don't flash it around to just anyone, son. The Katar have eyes and ears everywhere."

Tsom managed to not let his excitement show. Shela's smile flashed his mind.

The beggar was easy to spot. He was a member of the Ne Na cult easily identifiable by his clothes. Tsom disliked the Ne Na, a strange group that felt the gods did not deserve worship. They preached that the gods were simply stronger beings that had power that could not be easily comprehended. Any sailor knew that the gods were real. The Ne Na cult was tolerated by the temples, perhaps because they were small in number. Since they had no god, or powerful temple to aid their followers, any money they gathered for their order was through begging or small donations. Normally Tsom would have ignored the beggar, or thrown him a spare sintar, but he had an idea.

Moving forward, Tsom tossed the coin into the beggar's cup and waited.

A breath later the beggar was holding his wrist in a grip that he knew would not break.

"What do you say?" the beggar asked. Up close, the beggar did not look as old and helpless as he had originally.

"I need help."

"Who sent you?"

Tsom hesitated. If he was wrong, this could be bad.

"Shela."

The beggar nodded. "How are Shela's parents doing?"

"They've been dead for three years."

The beggar nodded again, his grip relaxed. In a smooth motion that Tsom found almost impossible to follow the beggar's cape was reversed and he lost his beard. The lean dangerous man now looking at him smiled and gestured that Tsom follow him.

Guiding Tsom through the streets, they soon left the merchant area and approached the gates of an upscale part of town. Tsom knew of the private sub-communities, where the rich paid for a private army and you needed permission to enter. He and other young thieves his age, all who were gone now, had often traded stories of the fabulous wealth they could steal there. They remained stories and speculation, as all of them knew that being caught there was both likely and instant death.

"What do you have there, Lanos?" The smell of old beer and wine wafted over them. A bleary eyed guard stood shakily on his feet, looking unhappy at having to get up from his chair at the gate. His head almost touched the top of the open walled shelter. Truly a rich neighborhood if they cared enough to keep the rain off their guards.

"A thief, whom my master will want to talk to." The guard at the gate laughed, not with much mirth. "Well, I will not look for him on the way out then." He sniffed. A look of disgust crossed his simple face. Tsom felt cold and angry. He would have noted that the guard was no sweet smelling sarra bush himself, but Lanos gestured and he bit off his retort.

The streets were wide, wider than any he had ever seen. They were wide enough for two private floaters to pass each other with room to spare and neither brushed Lanos and Tsom. No stores. Quiet and almost deserted. Most of the estates had walls or bronze fences, some topped with small iron spikes, the latter an ostentatious display of wealth given the rarity of iron. Ornate carvings covered the stone walls depicting the no doubt false heroics of the owner. Tsom tried to focus on one intricate wrought bronze depiction, topping a gate, of a large winged creature being pulled down by a group of men. There was something familiar about the winged creature, like the *daemon* costumes from the parade, but with wings. Lanos pushed him onward.

The estate they arrived at was large, but not as ostentatious on the outside as most they had passed. The tall stone walls were unadorned. The gateway was a simple wrought bronze and copper archway with a double swinging gate. Lanos paused at the gateway to the estate and muttered a few words, inaudible to Tsom. He waited and glanced at the top of the gate, Tsom saw a low glow turn from orange to a blue. Only then did Lanos proceed, pushing him into the main building. There a servant greeted them. Lanos exchanged a few words with him and then guided Tsom out to the garden.

The trees were strategically placed to frame the garden and isolate the area from the fence and the outside noises. Many flowers were of colors he had never seen before, so he could not even describe them. They were probably rare and expensive, but Tsom knew little of flowers so he could not know for sure. A small pond with a fountain at one end accented the small rock garden on the north side of the pond. Entering the garden, Lanos approached something large and prone. He spoke a few words. It took Tsom a moment to realize that he was talking to someone, not just another ornate statue or carving. Tsom's first reaction was to gag. A large man, at least Tsom hoped it was a man, lay in a half prone, half upright position on a chair built for his frame. He had skin the color of white fish belly, which hung loosely and with no small degree of fat. Tsom had heard tales of men who lived in the south, across the sea, where the sun shone weakly. Their skin was supposed to be pale, but surely not like this. The man looked ill. Dying. The red veins on his face shone brightly. Probably an alcoholic. Could this man be alive? One of the folds moved, turning into a mouth. "So, you wish to join the resistance?" said a voice that rumbled from the depths of the earth. It was a surprisingly rich and pleasant voice, which also carried authority. Two small points of light now resolved themselves into eyes.

Tsom's eyes darted around, but no words escaped his lips.

The resistance?

Shit.

Chapter 6

Vard survived, thanks to his ring. They cleared out before the first tourists arrived. Vard wanted to do the interrogations, but Arlec sent him home. "You'll live, but you can't keep the ring active forever. You need to heal naturally now. I'll question the woman."

"Poison, Arlec. She used poison. She's more than hiding the thief. She was expecting something like this."

"Obviously. That poison would have killed most Katar. It would have killed me with this shit ring," Arlec held up his left hand. "She'll talk, Vard."

Torture was not something Arlec enjoyed. A pretty woman such as this should be enjoyed in other ways, not hurt. Not destroyed. But, she had almost killed a Katar and she knew something about the thief.

The Karn compound had jail cells and more, that the extended family used for business. Arlec had Shela in one of the rooms that Devon would not hear about, at least not for some time.

"Listen, Shela. I'm not vindictive, but the young man stole something of mine. I get it back and I let him live."

"Live? You Katar don't let anyone live. We're all dying under the Katar heel." She managed a weak spit in his direction, but it merely ended up as drool down her chin. Arlec felt that tightening in his stomach again. He signaled for the guard to watch her and stepped out of the room for some air. He took a few breaths and returned.

"Leave us," Arlec motioned to the guard. The guard raised an eyebrow and Arlec raised his left hand displaying the ring. The guard paled and hurried out.

Arlec activated the ring with the force of will that all Katar learned. His mind reached out and touched the ring, embraced it. Drew upon its energy. It flared to life and Shela gasped with pain.

"My dear, I just don't have the time. I know you're part of the resistance. You fools tattoo yourselves as a demonstration of your loyalty. No going back, as you say. Is the thief part of the resistance too? Was stealing my ring part of your plan?"

"Your ring?" Shela managed a laugh. "One of the mighty Katar let a common thief steal one of their rings?"

He slapped her, embracing his rage.

"Is the thief part of the resistance? Is this part of a plot?"

"He doesn't know anything. It was a mistake."

"Yes. It was a mistake. Your thief will not die quickly, I promise you. But, if you help me I will let you die. Your *ba,* your soul, will join the Sea and someday you will be reborn."

This time she managed to hit him in the face with her bloody spit.

"You will never catch him, Arlec, son of Devon. The Katar and the Karn will fall."

"Not today. Today you will tell me where he fled. Where is the main cell of resistance in Arbeneth? You would risk rebirth to defend this thief?"

Arlec saw the look in her eyes. It wasn't the resistance she was defending, it was the thief. He could rape her, that might weaken her resolve. Make her understand that the thief would never have her again. He had no stomach for it, but he had to know what she knew and he sensed she was not just some minor player in the resistance.

An hour later, Arlec sat on the table. Shela lay on the ground, naked, bloody, her body and face looked sunken. He had drained an enormous amount of *ka* from her, yet she still lived. She was strong. Was all of the resistance like this? He thought of his mother. She had been strong. He almost retched. He was turning into his father.

"I could have you mind-raped," he said.

She laughed, or he assumed it was a laugh. Her face was facing the floor and the convulsions could have been something else.

"You know we are trained for that. You know what would happen if you, or another, tried."

So the stories were true. He had heard, but this confirmed it. The minds would fuse and she would commit suicide, dragging the other's mind with her. He shuddered. Why hadn't she simply killed herself already? Life is hard to give up, plus physical torture was different. He sighed, driving memories of his mother out of his mind as his ring flared once more.

This young rebel would not be joining the Sea of Souls when she died. She would tell him what he wanted to know.

Hours later, he was sure she had told him everything she could before she died.

***

Arlec hadn't expected much from the thief's apartment, nor was he disappointed. The small room held nothing of value. There was a small picture of a man and a woman holding a baby. It was not simply a drawing, but a *true image*. A three dimensional quality that captured every detail. Not cheap, probably one hundred sintar, a small fortune for someone like this little rat. He put it in his pocket. It could be a clue as to where he was now. The only other items of note were a few books, looking old and worn. So, the little snipe knew how to read also.

He was surprised at how clean the small room was. Cleaner than the hallway. It took him nearly thirty minutes to find the hidden chamber within the bedframe. All it held was a small lock of hair, white-blond, tied with a simple string and a strange medal. The medal was five coins laid flat with their edges fused to one another—forming a pentagon. He held it up and looked closely at the coins. They each had a symbol on them, not common tongue. Hrýll? Yes, he recognized it now. Each coin represented one of the five moons. This was quite valuable, it was from the celebration of the Eclipse of the Five Moons, which occurred every ten thousand years. While the last Eclipse was only twenty years ago, even then only ten thousand of these were made and distributed by the Hrýll. You could not buy them—they chose who received them. *Where did the thief steal this from?* He pocketed it and kept looking, but found nothing of interest. He smashed all the furniture and slashed the bedding in case he had missed something, then strode out in anger and chafed at the lack of progress. It was hours before the planned raid on the rebel cell that Shela had revealed.

Returning to the owner of the disgusting apartment building he made it clear that if Tsom returned, only contact Arlec. By no means should the Katar as a whole be notified, only him. Arlec smiled and the owner shivered and nodded.

In the street the sounds and smells of Festival hit him. With Flana, he had found it amusing. Now the sounds rubbed his nerves raw. Too much noise. Too much happiness. He shouldered aside a street juggler, causing him to drop the burning torches he was juggling. The small crowd made angry noises, which surprised Arlec. He was Katar, how dare they? His armband should have kept them at bay, even if his ring was not visible.

It was Festival. Even the Katar had to show flexibility, when the entire city was supposed to be celebrating, he mused. Arlec sensed that his normal immunity of office would only take him so far. He was not going to accomplish much more here during Festival. People were too drunk and too happy. He returned to his floater and ordered the driver home to prepare for the raid.

The floater arrived at the family compound in less than 30 minutes. Arlec jumped off before it came to a full stop; It really was a bad habit, especially without his ring. The Karn compound was not ostentatious by Katar standards. The guards were few, as it would be suicide to rob or attack a Katar family.

The marble was old, simple, and elegant, paving the walkway and forming the columns of the entrance. The ubiquitous glow lamps told of wealth. The fountain spraying rose-scented water in the air did little to soothe his mood. Keeping his left hand in his pocket, he strode quickly to his private chambers. He had to figure out how to keep his loss secret from his father until he could find the thief and his ring.

Vard was recovering from the poison quickly, but the raid would be under his command, including Vard's forces. They would both benefit from the raid. The resistance had been growing in attacks and boldness, even in their propaganda against the Katar. He would score points over his sisters, for once. Both of his older sisters were senior officers and proud of it. They could not know the second reason for the raid. He had to have the thief in his hands, no one else's. The families needed to believe that the raid was all part of a daring—and successful—plan by Arlec. He would give Vard credit also, but the glory would be his.

Perhaps then his father would listen to his advice on change. If not, then he had another plan, one that would be very private.

Chapter 7

"You're with the Askatasuna?" asked Tsom.

The mound of decaying flesh laughed, rippling the white skin.

"Not all of us are fighters."

"But ..."

"Nor are all who have money with the Katar, child. One can have wealth and resist evil, or tyranny. I do my small part for the cause."

Tsom heard a small snort from Lanos. He glanced behind where Lanos stood relaxed, in the way a cat stays relaxed before a strike.

"I think there must be a mistake. I don't want to join the Askatasuna."

"Then why did you pass us this coin?" The Mound asked, his eyes narrowed. "These coins do not trade hands lightly, boy. Unless you stole it."

"I did not steal it," snapped Tsom. "Shela is a friend of mine."

"So, why did she give it to you?"

"To help me. I am running from the Katar."

"Why?"

"I stole something from one of them."

The Mound settled back into his chair. The effort of sitting forward seemed to have worn him out. He took a sip from an expensive looking glass and exhaling Tsom could smell alcohol. Smokey and sweet with herbs he could not identify.

"Ah," The Mound nodded knowingly, "so you are the thief that Arlec is after. What have you stolen that the Katar have mobilized dozens of their men just for you? Arlec is more than just a Katar, boy. He is Karn. Son of Devon. Only a fool would steal from the Karn family." He paused, sipped, and considered Tsom. "You did not know you were stealing from the Katar. You must be good. Very good. What was it?"

"One of their rings."

Lanos sucked in his breath, but The Mound merely raised an eyebrow.

"Indeed. Pass it here. I assume you have it with you." The Mound casually held out his hand.

"No," Tsom said. "I don't take orders from you, or anyone."

"Yet, you came asking for my help."

"A mistake. I withdraw my request."

The Mound laughed again, although this time there was a hardness to the laugh.

"Lanos, if you please."

Tsom felt a brief stab of pain and suddenly he could not feel anything below the neck. As he sank to the ground, Lanos rifled his body and found the cursed purse. He opened it, ignored the money and pulling out the ring tossed it to The Mound, who surprised Tsom with the dexterity with which he caught the small ring.

"Ah, yes," there was a sigh of satisfaction and at the same time it sounded tremulous. "One of five thousand, but even better, one of the family rings. Very good."

Tsom struggled to speak, but all that occurred was noisy gasps of air.

"Release him, Lanos." Lanos grabbed Tsom's neck and did something that caused pain accompanied by a blissful release.

"Give me that," growled Tsom, glancing at Lanos, who was standing at ease again.

"I am helping you, boy. You wanted to flee the Katar? Yet, you held on to this. They could find you. Trace you. Not instantly, but they would know when this was near."

"It's mine."

"Really, I thought you stole it. If that makes it yours after stealing, then it is now mine. Curious that you refer to the resistance by its traditional name, Askatasuna. Few still know that name from a dead language. I wonder where you learned it?"

The Mound heaved himself forward again to peer at Tsom.

"It is before even your time, Lanos. Did you notice anything unusual about our friend here, when you first encountered him?"

"Unusual? No. He's fast. Angry. Afraid. Nothing unusual."

The Mound began to speak again, but broke into a coughing fit, his rolls of fat undulating with the spasms. Lanos left his side and quickly glided to The Mound, ignoring Tsom as he poured something into the glass next to The Mound and helped him drink it. There was pain on Lanos's face as he watched The Mound fight off the spasm. Tsom briefly thought of fleeing, but recalling both Lanos's speed and the entrance to the compound, he waited.

"So, we return to the question. Will you join the resistance, the Askatasuna? We could use a resourceful young man. A thief who can steal from the Katar is rare."

Tsom's instinct was to spit on the ground and tell The Mound and his man Lanos to slap a Yanín. The resistance were as dangerous as the Katar. Innocent people were killed because of them. It was as much of a death sentence as the Katar. Now that he was rid of the ring, maybe he could flee. Argn to the north, or maybe even Zethicia as he had told Shela. They would never find him now. This mound of flesh stealing the ring may be a blessing. Joining their resistance was simply suicide.

"No. You have the ring. I want nothing more to do with the resistance. The Katar are too strong. They have caused me enough pain."

The Mound pursed his lips. Tsom glanced at Lanos and saw a grim look on his face. Tsom hadn't considered that 'no' was not an option and that it was too late to change his mind.

Chapter 8

Without thinking, he sprang to The Mound's side, pulling his knife out and placed the sharp steel against the gelatinous throat.

"Get back, Lanos. I don't want to hurt anyone, but I have a feeling there aren't too many men alive who have said 'no' to your offer to join the resistance."

They both laughed. Tsom blinked and swallowed. What now?

He landed in a heap next to Lanos, his right wrist numb and the knife lay next to The Mound. Lanos looked at his master, who shook his head.

"Let him live, Lanos. What can he tell them? That he knows of two members of the resistance? Arlec would not spare his life for this information," the impossible old man looked pointedly at Tsom. "We are not quite as ruthless as you suggest, although if I thought you were a danger, you would be already dead. That Shela trusted you with a coin of passage, coupled with the death sentence of the Katar searching for you, is security enough. Be gone. We want only dedicated men and women, not cowardly thieves, with Katar hunting for them."

The Mound reached over to a decanter and poured more of the alcohol into the beautiful cut glass. As the liquid splashed and a new wave of smell wafted over him, Tsom knew what it was. Hrýll brandy. That glass represented a year's wages for most. Memories of his mother and father washed through him. The day his father was injured and his mother had poured this same brandy for him. It was said that the brandy was a liquid talisman. Only the Hrýll could make it. That memory tempted him to change his mind, but it was too late. You don't suddenly change your mind after spitting on an offer like this. It was foolhardy. Safer to run.

The Mound closed his eyes and drank the Hrýll brandy. He kept his eyes closed.

Tsom sagged.

"My knife?"

The Mound reached down exposing his arm with flesh hanging loosely, almost dead, and picked up the knife. With a flick he threw it at Tsom, who caught it by the handle. The Mound chuckled.

"Give him the purse also, Lanos. He will need something to survive. I would flee to Argn, or Zethicia, if I were you, boy." A chill snaked down Tsom's back. Was he that easy to read, or had his thinking been sound and the resistance confirming his idea.

"You could take me past the neighborhood gate. If I am caught inside they'll kill me," Tsom said.

Lanos looked at Alanar, who nodded, all of his loose chins following suit.

At the gate, the guard was surprised to see Lanos, or rather to see Tsom with Lanos.

"I see that your master is in a generous mood."

He grinned at Tsom, a bit of real humor in his voice. "Stay away from this neighborhood, thief, not all are as generous as Alanar." He gripped his sword and rattled it, laughing again.

Tsom took the hint and ran off, tucking the guard's small wallet into the pocket with the purse.

Chapter 9

Alanar stared at the ring in his hand. His breath was wheezing out of his huge decrepit mass. The effort of flipping the boy was more than he had done in years, decades. He continued to sip his morning brandy while he pondered the ring. He concentrated and the five white diamonds glowed, briefly. The effort caused a small bead of sweat to appear on one of the many folds in his forehead and trickle down to his eyes, stinging slightly. After all these years, the thought of the ring both excited him and caused a feeling of dread. It awakened memories.

Indistinct memories of a boy, not much younger than the thief. He died with a look of bewilderment on his face. Alanar was not sure when that was. He was sure he was the reason the boy died. Many had died. All too many. *Never again*, he thought. Not directly from his hand. He reached for his bell. Barthem, ageless in the way that some men over fifty were, appeared. Barthem was more than a servant, he was family. His walk was a strange shuffle hop due to his fused left knee.

"Something stronger. Not sweet."

Barthem nodded, but his lips compressed thin. Alanar knew he recognized these dark depressive moods in his master. He would warn the other servants.

The ring. Several times, he moved his finger toward putting it on; each time he stopped and held it almost touching the finger. His hand trembled. Finally, he sighed and tucked it into a pocket in his loose robe. The garden, his sanctuary, provided no peace today. The boy ... a thief no less. If he could steal a ring of the Katar ... maybe he could be used. The confused memories, from a time so long ago that he could not trust them, again flashed. No, it was unlikely the thief was of any import. He was just a petty thief. Best to let him have a chance at life, brief though it may be. He twirled the ring in his pocket. He should get rid of it. Yes, it was a weapon in the fight against the Katar. But, he had not been lying about the ability to trace them, albeit slowly, or by accident. Best to destroy it, or throw it off of a ship into the ocean, fathoms deep.

He sighed. *Where was that drink?* Trying to take his mind off the ring and his lack of a drink, he turned to his garden.

The garden was a testament to his wealth. There were native plants from all of the remaining non-Human races and even a few from races now extinct. His favorite was a bantri tree from the Hrýll. They took hundreds of years to shape and were passed on, from generation to generation. Some were thousands of years old, and still only a foot or two tall. Special care was needed to nourish them. Rumor had it that this one was so old that it was a survivor from the wars between the Human races and the non-Humans. The gardener bragged to his friends of this tree. It was old when he started working for Alanar and he had heard that the previous gardener had also commented on its age, if it was indeed the same tree—the gardener could not be sure. The tree grew millimeters over the years, while Alanar seemed to grow fatter, but not noticeably older. Of course, he looked so old and close to death, that it would have been hard to look any older, or closer to death. But, he was close, closer than ever before. Did he have enough time to make a difference? Would the resistance carry on and succeed without his backing? Lanos and Larrina were both good leaders. He had to introduce the two. The secrecy would no longer work in their favor if he was dead.

Barthem returned with a large decanter of Hrýll whiskey to replace the brandy. The smell of the constantly blooming flowers in the garden was on the edge of cloying. Alanar sipped the rare distilled spirits, alternating sharp taste with sweet smells. Hrýll whiskey was considered poisonous by some; too much was thought to cause brain damage. Its own sharp scent began to cut through the flowers.

Lanos returned from escorting the thief.

"You are starting early with the hard stuff today."

Any other associate would have never dared such a comment, but Lanos was more than a subordinate. Alanar had saved his life by using his influence when Shenar, the supreme judge, had sentenced him to *true death*. No debt could be larger, yet Alanar had never truly called it in. He had, however, bonded him. Lanos would have served him, regardless, but with the bond he had no choice. Alanar knew that this bothered Lanos more than the debt itself. He would have to drop the bond, Lanos was no longer the new recruit of twenty years ago. He should have dropped it years ago.

"Don't start, Lanos. We didn't have a chance to discuss other news you may have discovered from your spying as a beggar."

"Festival has an edge to it this year. I saw five different parades depicting the final battle with the *daemon* Tarth—five thousand years ago. *Daemons* seem to be on everyone's mind." A slight pause. "The price of imported goods is rising as more caravans and ships are lost and only the goods from the gateways make it here with regularity."

"The gateways are too narrow to provide enough for all of The Cities, even open continuously."

"Obviously. The Cities anger the races by demands of tribute and goods in exchange for added protection. The Hrýll and the Srýll both threaten to withhold talismans altogether rather than pay more."

Alanar nodded. The Old Ones had lost control of the qenar fuel to mankind, but they were the only ones who could fashion the talismans. No talismans meant no floaters, no glow globes, and no modern civilization. The Cities could not support their population without talismans from the Hrýll and food from Zethicia, the largest of the outlying Human settlements. No doubt, the council would give in to the Hrýll and the Srýll—for now. That would be the smart thing to do. How the Katar chafed at not controlling completely the production of talismans. Alanar smiled. Yet, some Humans seemed to be developing minor talents for shaping talismans. Minor for now. His smile faded. That would be the end of the Hrýll.

In the end, it would be the outlying Human settlements that paid. They needed both qenar and the talismans. Alanar shook his head slightly and took another sip of brandy. Lanos interrupted his thinking.

"Are you going to do anything?"

"Such as?" Small burp as punctuation. The slight slur to his speech indicating he must be very drunk indeed.

"Nothing." Lanos turned angrily and left his master alone in the garden.

***

Alanar woke with a start. His right arm hung slack, the cut crystal glass broken. He glanced at the decanter, empty. His mouth was dry and his brain foggy. What had disturbed him?

Barthem came running in. Running. Alanar blinked and struggled to sit up. Barthem didn't run.

"Sir, we are under attack. Katar." His breath came in short gasps. "You must flee."

Katar. Attack. Flee. Alanar shook his head to clear it, but it had no effect. The garden spun wildly. He struggled to stand, the chair creaking as he pushed against the arms. Barthem ran forward and tried to lift him, but his mass was too much for both of them.

"Documents?" whispered Alanar. The garden had stopped spinning for the moment. Damn, the fool thief had not told the entire story. Shela had been seen with Tsom, that was the only explanation for an attack so soon after Tsom left. Alanar groaned with pain, nausea, and sorrow. Shela had been so young.

"Taken care of. Burned."

"How much time before they reach us here?"

"Five, ten minutes at most, Sir. You must escape, the resistance needs you."

"Too late, my old friend. I am near a natural death already, a few months won't make a difference. Lanos and Larrina will finish the job, get word to them."

Barthem reached into Alanar's pocket and pulled out the ring.

"You need to use this, Sir. It's the only option."

"It would kill you, Barthem. The Katar are protected with their own rings, but you are defenseless."

"Exactly. I am dead either way. You have a chance if you use it."

"But, it's true death. I cannot do that to you, my friend. We can kill each other and avoid the true death. Avoid questioning from the Katar.

"How many will die if you do not live?" Barthem slipped the ring onto Alanar's left hand. The diamonds flared to life, indicating the Katar were near, fighting, using their own rings. Barthem gasped and dropped to the ground as the ring drew upon his *ka* for energy.

Alanar felt the surge of energy flow through him. His head cleared. He heaved himself to his feet and grabbed Barthem. Perhaps he could carry Barthem out.

"No, Sir. You need all of the energy. Draw it all. Attack, Sir. Use it all."

Alanar looked down at his friend. The energy from the ring was euphoric. Barthem knew what few did. What the Katar themselves did not. He knew what he was asking, what he was sacrificing and with the energy flowing through his body, Alanar wanted to live. To fight. To finish the job he had spent lifetimes working on. Grabbing Barthem by the neck he leaned forward and kissed him on the forehead. Barthem closed his eyes and smiled. Alanar squeezed and roared in battle rage.

Barthem withered and grew still. The flowers died next, the trees grew black and cracked. Yells of fear and surprise rose from beyond the wall. Alanar laughed, they would taste fear as their rings struggled against his.

Alanar fought to maintain his consciousness as the energy flowed into him. He was filled with rage and ecstasy. He saw now that Barthem had carried his sword with him, hanging unused for decades. He reached down and grabbed it. Momentarily he considered killing them all. The battle rage he hadn't felt in a lifetime was a raging torrent. He glanced down at his fat, flaccid, ancient body. With regret he ran to the wall and using the pruning ladder scaled the tall wall and dropped to the other side, his muscles, even augmented by the energy, were unable to take the fall and he collapsed directly in front of a young Katar.

The Katar was quick to recover, but did not expect the rapid movement from the prone mass at his feet, not with his own ring flaring to augment his own speed.

His muscles protested and he could not match the Katar's speed, but the Katar had no idea how many years of training Alanar had. Ancient muscles still responded with reflexes far older than this man facing him. He hacked the Katar's left hand off; the ring's light faded. The Katar stared with horror as his movements slowed, while the speed of his blood pumping out of his hand seemed to increase. Alanar grabbed him by the throat with his left hand, the ring flared, while his bloody sword in his right was held aloft. The Katar died knowing he would never be reborn, his *ka* was now Alanar's. "A small balance, my old friend," he muttered and the new wave of energy coursed through him. He staggered, knowing he would have to rest soon to digest all this energy.

He fled, hoping he could stay conscious long enough to mourn his old friend another day.

Chapter 10

Tsom still had the wad of sintar from the Katar purse and the small wallet from the guard. At least Alanar had not taken the money, but he was rich enough that he had no use for it. Festival was still going on, providing some opportunity to remain anonymous. Distance was his best defense. Distance from the Katar and from Alanar and the resistance. Keeping an eye out for city guards, police, or worse Katar, Tsom merged with the crowds and made his way north, to Argn.

Argn was the least loyal to the pan city government of the six city-states and had a reputation for flaunting the laws of The Cities. He hoped it was true. With some distance between himself and Alanar's gated neighborhood, he picked up new clothes without incident. With a few careful questions, he was soon on one of the main roads leading north.

With the initial terror gone, he had been thinking constantly of his mother's death. It thrilled him that he had struck a small blow to the Katar. It revived old dreams of revenge upon them, but when his mind danced with revenge, the fear crept back in. He hadn't seen his father die, but the image of his mother's head hanging from a Katar hand impossibly still moving and screaming inside his head for him to run, always generated his mouth to go dry, his heart to race and a raging headache that would not ease until he ran, as if his mother had enthralled him as she died to always fear the Katar. Hate and fear were the combined emotions he felt toward the Katar.

Lanos and Alanar, they were no lovers of the Katar, of that he was sure. The thought of joining the resistance had been tempting, but there was the uncontrollable fear since his mother's death. The need to survive.

Tsom reached a crossroads at dusk. There was a temple to Nu Arr, the god of luck strategically placed at the busy intersection. Tsom hesitated.

Nu Arr was the god for thieves. The temple was a pyramid, with its impossibly balanced ten foot coin on the apex. He had never actually been in a temple. There were small shrines by the docks, but no full-scale temples. The largest shrine on the docks was to Met, the god of weather. With a shrug he approached.

Silence filled the warm fall night. Four of the five moons had risen, providing enough light to see without the need for the public glow globes. Another sign of wealth, all these glow globes on the temple grounds. The temple outskirts were empty. No guards necessary here: robbing the temple would surely be bad luck. Tsom grinned tightly to himself.

A lone robed priest, nodding off at the entrance at the top of a small set of stairs, motioned him in and muttered what sounded like, "It's sometimes hard to tell good luck from bad. Don't assume you know one from the other," followed by a mechanical chuckle. The inside was almost dark. Glow globes were present, but dimmed to save qenar. The fuel for talismans was not cheap and even a rich temple would not waste it. A sign in the antechamber strongly suggested that he buy a "lucky coin" to throw into the wishing well further inside for luck: ten sintars. Heeding the advice Tsom stuffed a ten-sintar note into the box and picked up one of the large coins. Naturally, the cost was ten times its real value; it was merely made of silver. He weighed it in his hand. Too light to be solid silver, he could feel the uneven distribution of weight. He flipped it a few times and watched it wobble in the air. He smiled a bit, remembering the knives not so long ago. He flipped it a few more times and the wobble disappeared. It was not legal coin of The Cities, too large to be useful as currency. It almost covered his smallish palm. He gazed more closely at it. On both of the coin's sides was an etching of a coin and a pyramid, similar to the stone carving he had seen from the outside.

On one side, the etching portrayed the scene of a giant coin fallen on the left of the pyramid with a cloud over the pyramid. On the other side, the etching was the scene of a pyramid with a coin to the right of the pyramid with the sun over the pyramid.

Both sides of the symbolic coin—regardless of which side of the pyramid it sat—was still balanced on edge, and one could just make out an etching on the coin within the coin. It too had a pyramid, with a coin on its right, with what almost seemed like another etching visible. Tsom started squinting at it harder ... he could almost see another layer. It was like a reflection of a mirror in a mirror. His eyes started to water and he stopped staring.

The temple smelled like gambling. That was the only way he could describe it. The mixed smells of sweat, alcohol, food, and greed reminded him of the street gambling that the sailors took part in on the docks.

Tsom knew others did not believe that he could smell—or sense—greed, but he always had been sure he could. When he touched someone, he felt he could tell something about them. The woman he had knocked over had been an innocent. He had felt her innocence for a moment. The man, the Katar, now that he reflected back on it, had the feel of greed. Dangerous greed. This is why he preferred picking pockets to other forms of thievery. If he sensed his target was poor, or an innocent, he left them alone. On occasion he had sensed something after the fact and would pretend that the item he had just stolen had just fallen. Too bad he had not sensed more with the Katar.

Tsom rubbed his face with the palm of his right hand, eyes to mouth. Try to concentrate on the present. He kept moving down the corridor. He could almost hear the dice hitting the stone, but looking around, the hallways were empty. He stuck to the main hallway, which led toward the center of the temple. It seemed that guests were welcome here at night, but it was self-service. Again, he thought how confident they were that no thief would steal from the temple.

The walls were covered with scenes depicting impossible luck, or coincidence, but their craftsmanship was rather inferior—at least to Tsom's eyes. One scene had a man tripping over the root of a tree as two attackers from either side fired arrows that would now kill the opposite attacker. Simultaneously, as the falling man fell, his sword was flying out of his hand and the painting made it clear that the sword would hit a third attacker just as he was swinging an axe behind his own head, where no doubt the axe would fall, cutting a rope that held a horse, and so on, and so on. This was the legend of Dentir, blessed by Nu Arr as he saved his lover from the Tarth, the *daemons* of legend. Tsom smiled and relaxed a bit for the first time since he had picked the Katar's pocket. Almost driven by an inner force, he started flipping the "lucky coin" in the air as he walked. Soon he had it coming up one side, or the other, at will. The dim glow globes cast shadows, and the scenes seemed to have a three dimensional quality to them.

At the center of the temple was a large chamber, with a very wide, but shallow well. It must be the promised wishing well. It held no water, but rather had a pyramid in the center. Dividing the bottom of the well—or more accurately, very large and wide pit—in half was a small wall a foot or two in height with a peaked top ridge. The bottom of the well was full of coins similar to the one he held. He did a quick calculation as to the number of coins, just out of professional curiosity. He did not seriously consider stealing them. He could sense if not see, nor hear, that there were people watching him from the numerous entrances to the chamber. He called this his thieving sense. He knew when he was being watched. On one side of the wall within the well, all the coins were showing the side with the cloud over the pyramid. On the other side of the wall, all the coins were showing the other face: the sunny pyramid. Along various points on the edge of the well were small narrow slides running down toward the point of the pyramid at the center, but ending about halfway there.

It seemed obvious that one was supposed to roll the coin down one of these slides. Tsom put his coin in one of the slides and gave it a small push. The coin rolled down, launched into the air and landed on the point of the pyramid. It then did an amazing thing: it bounced straight up and landed on its edge, on the point of the pyramid and stayed balanced there.

Tsom heard a gasp from off to the side. A priest standing in the shadows came out yelling, "You there, how did you do that?"

Tsom spoke, uneasy. "I just rolled the coin down the slide, as I assumed one was supposed to do?"

"Impossible." His face showed a combination of fear, anger, and almost awe. "Come here boy."

Tsom had enough of being given orders, capture, and questioning. He bolted.

The priest ran after him, calling for help. Tsom laughed as the priest's belt broke and his pants slid down, tripping him. The sleepy priest at the entrance was waiting for him in a crouch. In one hand was a long staff, with both ends of the wood encased in metal, probably bronze. Tsom considered using his knife, but he didn't want to hurt the guy, just get out. Anticipating the staff, Tsom made motions to jump high, but instead slid feet first into the priest, knocking him off his feet. Luckily, the man was no fighter. Tsom rolled up to a run and out into the night air. Without looking back, he chose the right hand road to the north, and the sounds of yelling soon faded.

***

He was moving by dawn. He'd slept near the road, the vast openness between clusters of buildings bothered him. He had heard that much of the area between Argn and Arbeneth was not really city. The popular term The Cities encompassed all the land between the six cities also. Knowing was one thing, seeing it was another. He would stay at an inn tonight, he vowed. The Katar can't have spies everywhere in a population of over twenty million, or was it thirty?

Still, Tsom remained on high alert and watched the roads carefully. The main road teamed with cargo floaters, transporting goods to and fro from the four other cities to the main port of Arbeneth. The massive flat platforms were loaded down so that they hovered only a few inches off the ground. Each floater had the same crew: driver, feeder, and guard. The feeder, tasked with feeding small pieces of qenar laden jade ore to a small dish near the talisman looked as bored as the guard. None of the passing crews paid him any attention. Other traffic consisted primarily of horse drawn vehicles, riders, and a fair number of pedestrians. Keeping his best nonchalant look Tsom walked briskly north.

As a floater, or wagon, slowly passed him, he would listen in to the snatches of conversation.

"Their loss is our gain, I say. If Zethicia can't keep trading with The Cities, we get more for our goods."

"What if it spreads? …" the floater was out of earshot.

"The Katar have gone crazy, I say. Stay out of Arbeneth. They think everyone is part of the rebellion." A stream of fluid landed near Tsom as the speaker, a man not much older than Tsom, spit overboard and then fed qenar to the floater."

"More and more are sympathetic, Wassen. If I were younger …"

Other snatches of conversation were mundane, but one more caught his attention.

"What happens if the Hrýll all die? What then, I ask ya? The Katar squeeze them harder every year."

"They won't kill the sheep that yields the wool, even the Katar aren't that stupid."

"Not so loud, fool. Men have been sent to the mines for less."

"Bah, there's no Katar out here. They're city rats. Hate the exposure. Hate being alone."

"They're desperate I tell you. Squeezing more weapons out of the Hrýll. Look at the Srýll, has anyone seen one in the past decade?"

"Don't mean nothin'. How many Hrýll you seen? Those strange races are always hiding."

"They're dying off, both races. Then what? Civilization needs them …."

By midday it was true countryside. The houses were widely spaced. At each canal crossing there was a small commercial center, usually an inn, a warehouse, some stores, and occasionally a small government building, but little else. Tsom's tension eased.

Now it was all freight traffic with the occasional lone rider. This road was not used much for tourist travelers between The Cities. The occasional passerby greeted him with genuine friendliness—not just emotions enhanced by alcohol; truly different from Arbeneth proper. The distrust that most city dwellers had for each other did not seem to exist here.

By late afternoon, exhausted and not willing to sleep in the streets again, he made his way to an inn that did not look too fancy.

Ann's Place was set back from the road slightly more than other inns. The sign dangled in the light breeze by one hook, the other still intact, beckoning like a crooked finger. No floaters in front, only a wagon and two horses. A sway backed mare turned and looked at him with big, sad, beaten eyes, one hind leg suspended in pain, swollen at the pastern, and unshod. Tsom patted the mare. "Sorry old lady, I don't have anything for you," as she nuzzled his shirt hopefully. Her ears drooped with her head and she turned away.

The interior was a reflection of the exterior. Tsom sat at one of the empty tables, brushing off food from the day, or the day before.

"Do you need a room, or just dinner?"

Maybe it was Ann; she was in the same shape as the sign. Leaning sideways against the bar her varicose veined legs showed at the bottom of her worn skirt. One leg propped on the stool frame, she had moved only her head as he entered. The wrinkles in her face radiated from the dull gray eyes and the corners of her mouth. Her teeth were surprisingly sound. Tsom was reminded of the mare.

"I need a room for one night."

"Three sintar, including dinner. Drinks are extra."

The price seemed steep, given what he saw, but perhaps prices were higher out here. He pulled a note out from within his shirt, not removing the stuffed purse. It was a hundred sintar note.

She looked at the note.

"Where'd you get that? Steel it? Ya got anything smaller?"

Tsom noticed that a number of the customers were looking at him with interest. He shook his head. She held the note up to the dim light and looked at it as if she had never seen one before. Tsom knew the printing process was impossible to forge. She took a beer mug from the bar and slammed it on the note, holding it back up everyone could see the faint glow of the insignia of The Cities, which faded quickly. Something to do with the qenar dust used in the ink.

"Well, it's real," she muttered, sliding between her heavy breasts.

"Did you need a drink?" she asked.

"Beer, just one tankard please." He needed to relax. One beer would take the tension out, but not leave him unable to think. He licked his dry lips.

"Don't forget my change," he called after her, then lowered his head as he realized that this wasn't helping to stay out of sight. He'd never had a problem blending before. It scared him.

She returned with his change, a beer, and a plate. "Room 8," she said without looking at him or waiting for acknowledgment.

Without looking too closely at the food, he ate ravenously, but tucked some bread into his pockets. He watched the other patrons with short glances. He kept his left hand under the table repeatedly palming his knife and returning it to its sheath under his sleeve. He bit his cheek while chewing, drawing blood and cursing softly. Finished, he went outside and gave the old mare the bread and scratched her neck. She looked for more, her soft nose nuzzling his face. Giving her one last pat, he walked back to the inn as one of the diners exited.

Even exhausted and tipsy, Tsom felt the attempt at thievery. Without thinking he stabbed the man in the hand as he tried to lift Tsom's purse. The blood sprayed in a red shower of sparkling garnets as the man shook his right hand.

"Why you little gink." Spittle mixed with blood on his dirty beard as he groped for the sword flopping at his side with his uninjured hand. Tsom folded his legs and rolled backwards. The man's lunge took him too far and he lost his balance. His head hit the hitching post, snapped back, and settled at an impossible angle. Tsom knew he was dead, he had seen that neck angle before, on the docks. Almost out of habit, Tsom rifled the man's clothes—just as the door to the inn opened again.

"Thief! Galin, quick, Cam is down." Noise from within. Tsom turned and bolted into the night, cursing the god of luck once again. He hated having to run when he hadn't done anything.

The stars were not out, making speed difficult. The main road was lit, but he avoided that. Festival was mainly in the cities, with the people from the outskirts flocking to the centers, leaving everything else deserted. The lack of lights and people was disconcerting. A howl. A wolf? Here? No, dogs. Pushing himself, he kept north, tired body protesting, panicked mind pushing.

Tsom thought of his cozy little room back at the port, not bad for a young thief. Never to return. He regretted having to leave behind his picture the most. That and the coins from the Eclipse of the Five Moons. He had been born during the eclipse and the Hrýll had given the coins to his mother as a gift. Maybe once he was safe he could send for the picture and coins. The hotel owner had always treated him well.

The sounds of dogs were gone; perhaps they were never after him. Slowing down to a jog, he started cutting across the small fields instead of sticking to the side roads. Walking, Tsom looked around. The dew on the field gave the grass, or grain, a silver sheen, each blade individually washed and left to dry. Tsom felt alone and exposed in the field. Too soon to head back to the main road. Shaking the dew off himself, he kept going. The last day of Festival, he thought. The big finale. Yet, out here, there seemed to be no one celebrating. He did not know much about rural life, but it seemed quieter than he had imagined; the barking dogs and murderous men notwithstanding.

Finding an old abandoned barn he lay on the musty hay, too tired for even panic to push him any further. *Probably cleaner than Ann's Place*, he thought as he fell asleep.

Chapter 11

Argn, at last.

Increasingly the homes, businesses, and even road signs had become more colorful. Bright. The ubiquitous inn at every major crossroad would be bright green or red or blue depending on if a man or woman owned the establishment. A flag often flew from front, its colored stripes indicating everything from number of children, to how many generations had lived at a home.

At first Tsom looked at every new splash of colors with interest, but soon they faded to the background. He was weary. Panic had long faded with Arbeneth itself, replaced by twisted ankles, false alarms, and sporadic stops at inns. He wasn't running away, he was walking toward. A new life?

As with Arbeneth there was no firm line between city and outlying area, just the steady increase of people. Tsom felt tension ease the higher the population became. As he stood out more and more due to his clothes, he stopped at a premade clothing store. Fast and cheap was what he was looking for.

The purple door with red trim probably meant something to the locals, but to Tsom it was a strange color combination. The store was almost empty and the man behind the counter watched Tsom with a friendly curious gaze.

"Single?" asked the man.

"Yes," replied Tsom. There seemed no harm in that bit of honesty.

"You'll want green for your pants. Profession?"

"Trader," Tsom replied. Thief was probably not something you advertised even in Argn.

"Really? That is more difficult. What do you specialize in?"

Tsom hesitated. He would have said cloth, but that wouldn't fly here in a clothing store.

"Yanín artwork."

The man sputtered for a moment, looking to see if Tsom was joking.

"I've never heard, nor seen, of such a thing. The Yanín have art?"

"It is quite rare. I'm from Arbeneth, as you might have guessed, and I am investigating the market for the art in Argn. I work for a small gallery in Arbeneth that has recently obtained an exclusive source with the Yanín." Tsom was warming to his story, almost believing it himself.

"Well, trade, art, Yanín, Arbeneth … hmm. I would say your shirt should be sea blue, with black trim, and at least one print on it. Floral would be normal, but Yanín art? Well, no matter, floral will work. A black neck tie would be good too."

"Good. Tell me, where would you recommend I go for a few weeks' stay in the city, near where I might make some contacts in the galleries?"

"Certainly near the Tarth river, where the tourists and the rich overlap. It is pricey to stay there," he cocked an eyebrow at Tsom, looking at his current garb and leaving the rest unsaid.

"Ah, yes, well perhaps I will stay nearby, but not directly in the area. We are a new gallery, I would not want to waste my employer's resources."

The man nodded approvingly.

"That is a good attitude to have with an employer's money."

The store had a dressing room and with his old clothes stuffed in a shopping bag, Tsom stepped out of the store in what he hoped was acceptable garb.

The proprietor's information was sound. He scouted the area and then went for the newspapers. He wanted something near this area, where strangers did not stand out, but cheap enough that he need not worry about money for some time.

Tsom picked up one of the small newspapers at a small colorful kiosk. Color. The mixes almost gave him a headache. The meanings were complex. A couple of inquiries told him that the bright red tops with the brown in this neighborhood had something to do with who owned them all and possibly the protection they received.

The latter in his mind, he paid for the paper. He had thought of simply stealing it. He had to get out of the petty thievery mentality. He dug out the appropriate coin and tossed it to the vendor with a smile. The vendor smiled back. People always seemed to smile back at him when he smiled and tried to make them feel friendly, but in Argn they smiled more than Arbeneth.

Stepping across the busy street full of clusters of brightly dressed people, Tsom leaned against the railing of the boardwalk, as others were doing. He absorbed their habits and mannerisms. He already was able to imitate the Argn accent well enough that one or two vendors seemed to think he was a longtime resident. Not born here, but not new. He noticed the men avoided greens for shirts and the women avoided blues, other than that there seemed to be no discernible pattern. There were enough from the other city-states that with some effort he blended in. He was only one of many.

The papers were full of news. He had read the old papers on the docks, thirsty for knowledge outside of his small world, but now he was interested in any hints of the Katar chasing him and the resistance. There was an article on the resistance, their reign of terror on common citizens and how the Katar were making progress in fighting them, including a recent raid in Arbeneth where the leader of the resistance had been operating.

Alanar. He read the article in detail. While the leader had not been captured, the base had been destroyed, with over one hundred local terrorists killed or captured. Tsom wondered if that was an exaggeration, or if that meant outside of Alanar's compound. He would have guessed twenty at most at the compound. The financial blow was large. According to the paper over ten million sintar in property had been seized. Ten million was a number Tsom could not even process. Alanar had been richer than he thought.

What of Shela? He scanned the entire paper, but no mention of the resistance from the dock area. Still, how had they found Alanar? Shela's round face floated on the pages of the paper as he worried about her. He was glad he had not joined the resistance. If he had, he would have been one of the hundred. Was Lanos one of those captured? They both had told Tsom to flee to Argn or Zethicia, but he had not confirmed his plans, so they could not tell the Katar much.

In Zethicia, where he had seriously considered fleeing, there were reports of large raids, disruptions to trade, and wild stories of Tarth, the extinct *daemons*, leading the attacks. Tsom shook his head in disbelief. The memories of the Festival parades flashed through his mind. The Tarth seemed to be on everyone's mind.

He flipped to the apartment and rooms for rent section. There were enough sintar in his purse to cover the cost of a moderately priced apartment for a long time, with some left over for additional brightly colored clothes that would fit in.

He found a suitable simple, but furnished, apartment without incident and in time for a nap.

***

He awoke drenched in sweat. The same nightmare had been plaguing him since the Katar started chasing him. His mother's head, severed, dripping blood held by a hand with a glowing ring. His mother's head impossibly screaming, "Run, Tsom. Run. Always run from the Katar. RUN." The last an explosion in his head, waking him.

He looked out the window, it was near dinner and his stomach reminded him that he had not had a real food in over a day. He dried off his face and went in search of food.

Nothing fancy, but after his time on the road, he was ready for a nice meal.

51

He was clean and rested—despite the nightmare—but ravenous. He wanted a meal he could look at while he ate. A few inquiries and he headed toward a likely spot, a pleasant looking outdoor café, with a view of the river and the evening sun blocked by a bright blue and yellow awning. The chatter of the diners sounded inviting and the smell drifting over caused a small rumble in his stomach. He picked up his pace scanning for an open table.

Three Katar, all women, were sitting at the outdoor café laughing. He suppressed the instinct to flee, his recent nightmare scream echoing in his head. Katar: women or men, they were all killers. The familiar panic, that only the Katar could trigger, was countered by a flash of anger. He realized that although he had no confirmation, he assumed Shela was one of the hundred rebels captured and he was angry.

He should leave, blend with the crowd and disappear. He doubted they were looking for him specifically, but they might have heard something. *Run*, ran through his head multiple times. *They will know you. They will kill you as they killed your mother.* He fought it down. This flight instinct was as dangerous as anything. Instead, he walked toward them and smiled. Damn if he was going to be like a cowardly Hrýll and run from the Katar forever. The rebellion had that part right, he decided.

"Good evening, ladies."

They stopped, looking shocked. The oldest coughed a bit, taking a quick sip of water from her glass.

"I'm new in Argn. Is the food here good?" Small talk was never his forte. He kept his new accent, hoping they would not place him from Arbeneth and that they would buy his color scheme.

The youngest, about a year or two older than him, smiled. All three had the look of Arbeneth, but she had the look of someone trying to blend in. Her cheekbones were high, a bit too prominent, but with her smile gave her a heart shaped look.

"Why yes, it is. Care to join us?"

The other two women looked at her in astonishment equal to their reaction to his initial greeting. The oldest then smiled a bit knowingly.

"Well, Piea and I need to go. Why don't you stay and have dinner with …." She looked expectantly at him.

Well, why not risk giving his name and find out what they knew.

"Tsom."

No reaction. Mentally, he began to breathe again.

"Mine is Shara." The youngest again spoke, gesturing for him to sit as the other two left.

Shara was the type of woman that many would call very attractive, but some would not find desirable. Tsom studied her with a practiced eye. His knowledge of women was primarily from the brothel near where he lived, not from frequenting it often, but from having been raised—for a few years—by the women there. The women had grown so used to him that they talked openly of their clients and what they did. While he was not well practiced in all the arts of love making and other techniques that had less to do with love, he was well versed in the theoretical knowledge. One of the things he had learned very early was not to judge a woman on initial looks, or even conversation.

He looked at Shara, trying to see past the initial impression of a tall, well-muscled, lean young woman who had big eyes and a slightly too large mouth and a button nose. Her hair was too short, a soldier's cut. Her mouth was made for smiling, which he found disconcerting in a Katar. She chatted about Argn and what sights he should see and how to interpret the colors of clothes and buildings. He listened and nodded and tried to remember to say something at the proper times.

He found that despite his inherent hatred of the Katar, he enjoyed the company of Shara. His eyes kept straying to her mouth as she smiled and the way her eyes remained large and open when she both smiled and laughed.

"Tsom, I am delighted you joined me. Too many are fearful of the Katar."

"With reason," he could not help saying.

She raised her eyebrows, but kept smiling.

"I, for one, regret the rift between the Katar and the citizens. We are guardians of The Cities, here to protect. To serve, in a sense, yet over the centuries we have taken our role as elite guardians a bit too far."

Tsom didn't want to get pulled into an argument, but she seemed so reasonable. She seemed to believe what she was saying.

"A bit? No offense, but the Katar rule with an iron fist, not tolerating any dissent. The only group they don't control are the priesthoods."

Shara shook her head sadly.

"The actions of a few rub off on all of us. Not all Katar act in that manner."

"The very act of wearing those rings," he nodded to her left hand, "is an act of oppression. They drain the very *ka* of those nearby—whether you activate them or not."

She blinked in surprise and looked at Tsom more closely. Had he gone too far?

"You know more than most, Tsom," she said cautiously.

"Or more know more than you think."

She took a long sip of wine, then nodded.

"I agree with you, to some extent. Think of it as a tax. Only a tiny part of your average citizen's *ka* is taken. Isn't that worth the protection we offer?"

"Protection from what? The enemies of mankind have been defeated long ago. The Tarth, even the Yanín have not been at war with man for thousands of years. The Hrýll are almost a slave race. What do the Katar protect us from."

"The rebels who terrorize The Cities. That and if we did not exist, then the Yanín would fight. And if the rumors from Zethicia are to be believed, the Tarth are not as extinct as we thought. The Katar are needed. Don't you think it is a small price to pay for peace and protection?"

"If the price was voluntary. It is not with the Katar," he growled, not quite containing the venom on the last word.

Shara nodded. This interesting woman was again surprising him.

"I agree. We should change with the times. I think people will still want us, but it should be with open cooperation with the people, with civilian leaders of The Cities."

"Like Zethicia? They survive without the Katar ruling them," said Tsom.

"Only because they know we are here in case of emergency, but yes, perhaps something like that."

"The Katar will never allow it. You're an idealist."

"You're wrong, Tsom. My generation—others—are different. We are trying to change the Katar. Some families are changing."

"Is yours?" Tsom took his own large sip of wine. The alcohol was making him a bit bold, loose tongued, but he enjoyed talking with Shara. She was real, she seemed to care. An exception, he thought cooling with recollection of his nightmare.

"Not as quickly as I would like. My sisters are more flexible than some. My father is a traditionalist. But, the Katar here, in Argn, have changed the most. Among other things, they allow women to rule the families here."

"But, you aren't from Argn, you are from Arbeneth, aren't you?"

She nodded.

"Enough politics for now. What about you, Tsom? What are you doing in Argn?"

She reached for a small light roll and poured more wine for both of them. Her hands were small, strong and capable looking. Yet, they seemed soft.

"I just moved here. No plans yet."

"Oh, a man of independent means? You don't need to work?"

He thought back to his mother's shop, her trading with the Hrýll for exotic cloth.

"I trade with the Hrýll, and Argn is closer to their lands."

"Ah, that explains your comment on Hrýll as slaves. So you like the Hrýll? They are so strange. So … non-human."

"They are like us. They feel, they love, they die, they dream, they want freedom," he said, repeating he realized something his mother had said years ago, scolding some of his friends.

"Freedom. Are any of us free to do what we want? I wonder," Shara drank some more. She was getting tipsy faster than he was. More relaxed. It grew dark enough that the café's glow globes went on. One of the staff lit a few additional lanterns to augment their light. In the flickering light Shara's eyes danced and her lips were darker and fuller. He could almost forget she was Katar.

Chapter 12

Arlec had kept his name out of the papers, after the raid on Alanar Tonshon's estate. Even the Katar could not completely quiet the press. If Tsom had joined the resistance, as it seemed he had, then he would flee to one of the other centers of operation. Argn would be his guess.

His father, Devon, had been pleased, in his own way.

"I didn't think you had it in you, Arlec," said Devon. "You generally don't have the stomach for getting answers from prisoners. For taking decisive action. But, you let the leader get away. This Alanar is key. Our information is that he is a key member, possibly their leader. Do you think you can handle tracking him down and getting more of these terrorist rebels? We've wounded them, but a hundred out of thousands is only an injury. By the Sea, Arlec, we need to cut the head off of this rebellion. It is organized, not a bunch of small loose cells. We need to go in for the kill. Do you have the stomach for it?"

Arlec bit back his initial reply.

"I'll succeed, Father. These rebels grow too bold. They are making mistakes."

Devon grunted from behind his huge desk in the study, his large frame fitting well. Under black hair with the faintest of white sprinkles his face was unwrinkled, the effects of the ring and the Katar blood.

"Good. I'll leave it to you. I have to deal with the governors of The Cities and this crisis in Zethicia. Don't tarnish the Karn name, Arlec."

By, for instance, losing one of the family rings? Arlec thought.

"The rumors abound on Zethicia. Which of them are true?" he said aloud.

Devon leaned back, a puzzled look on his face.

"It seems as if there is something to the wild stories of Tarth." Devon raised his hand to the unspoken. "Something, but I am not sure what. Still, they are disturbing. The Katar have not dealt with an enemy such as the Tarth in millennia, but we have resources for war, if necessary. You deal with these terrorists. Quickly."

Arlec met his sisters in one of the family rooms. He wanted the meeting to be private.

Larra and Piea had just returned from Argn, celebrating their youngest sister's gradua-tion from the academy. Shara was a fully trained Katar, wearing one of the family rings, not one of the feeble imitations that was on his own left hand.

Despite the three of them vying for power with Devon, he had a fondness and respect for his sisters. If they could be reined in and follow his lead, they would be valuable. They too felt it was time for the Katar to change, not in the way foolish Shara wanted, but for the Karn family to assert its place as true head of all the Katar, and by extension The Cities. Devon was stuck in his ways. Tradition. Balance of power. Arlec almost spit as he paced the floor waiting for his sisters.

Larra and Piea came in without knocking. Larra locked the door behind her. Larra was almost as tall as Arlec, had the Karn family hair color and her hair was tied back with an expensive Hrýll scarf, the colors changing and shim-mering with the slightest movement. Her blouse was open enough that even a brother could admire the exposed cleavage with a certain clinical interest.

Piea, much shorter and almost plump, sat down. She picked an apple from the bowl next to the chair and took a bite.

"Nice raid, Brother," Piea said, between crunches.

"Too bad the leader got away," Larra chimed in, sitting in another of the comfortable chairs. Arlec felt too energized and continued his pacing.

"Yes, that's stating the obvious. I think he fled to Argn. Our intelligence indicates that there is a major cell there."

"Intelligence?" chuckled Larra. "You took prisoners from the raid. I would have thought they wouldn't talk that easily, or know enough."

"I used a mind scan on them."

Piea coughed. Larra's smile changed, but did not disappear. "Really, a mind rape? Who did you get to do that? Or did you do it yourself?" Larra asked.

Arlec managed to look shocked and offended. A mind scan was almost as dangerous to the scanner as it was to the subject. Larra was needling him and he would not rise to the bait.

"Father wouldn't approve," Piea crunched the last of the apple.

"Father needs to change," muttered Arlec. Larra nodded in agreement.

"The rebels are terrorists. They need to be controlled. People are starting to question the strength of the Katar. We need to crush them. Completely." Arlec stopped his pacing.

"I need you to help me with this Alanar. I need you to use your influence in Argn."

"Of course, Dear Brother," Larra came up to him and put a hand on his arm. "But, there's more, isn't there. I can see it in your tension. You really want to crush these rebels personally."

He hesitated, looking from Larra to Piea. Then he held up his left hand, ring facing Larra. She squinted her left eye, then both eyes went wide.

"Oh dear. Father doesn't know, does he?"

Arlec shook his head.

"What?" demanded Piea. She jumped up and looked at his hand. "What?"

"Dear, dear. The thief that stole something from one of the Katar on the docks? A rebel?"

"What?" Piea stamped her foot.

"Don't be dense. Arlec has lost his ring. He is wearing a common Katar ring, not one of the family rings. The thief we heard about is Arlec's thief and he has one of the Karn family rings. And Father mustn't know. Not when things are going your way, eh, Brother?" Larra smiled and it carried both sarcasm and genuine care. Arlec felt some of his muscles along his neck relax.

Larra and Piea were both more understanding than he had anticipated. At first, he was suspicious of their motivations. Larra did most of the talking.

"Arlec, we understand the need to feel normal. Taking the ring off was insane, of course, but we understand." Piea nodded in agreement. "Of course you men always think with your groin, but it is not as if we have not had our moments." Now Piea blushed a bit, looking down, her high cheekbones accentuated at that angle. Arlec wondered at those moments she referred to and why Piea was blushing, but given that it was his sister speaking, he was not sure he really wanted to know the details. He knew that most men considered both of them attractive. Even in uniform, their hips were just wide enough to draw attention when they walked. Not the stunning beauty of Flana, but even he had to admit that they were attractive. Larra, the eldest, had the look of command about her. She was father's trusted one and while he resented it, he knew that she had earned it.

Larra snapped her fingers to regain his attention. "You must wear gloves as much as possible."

Piea chimed in.

"Don't get into any fights until you get the ring back."

"He is not an idiot Piea. But, she is right. Just don't pick any fights for now Arlie. Keep that temper of yours in check. And By the Sea, don't piss off father for a while."

He hated when she used her childhood name for him, but this time he kept his mouth shut.

"I just hope the Katar are not called upon to help the guard, due to all the losses in trade. There are rumors that only one out of ten caravans is making it through from the plains surrounding Zethicia. The Hrýll and the few Srýll, when they come to trade, speak of *daemons* from the past walking the land

again. The merchants are all complaining to the council that this is important enough for the Katar to be used." Larra paused and spat on the ground.
"Guarding merchants!"

All three of them looked glum at the prospect.

"Give us a description of this thief."

"I had a true image made."

"How? Oh. You are getting bold, Arlec," Larra purred, rubbing his arm.
"I think we should thank this thief when we find him, Piea. He has forced a
change upon our indolent brother."

"As long as you kill him after thanking him," replied Arlec.

Businesslike again, Larra indicated to Piea that they should leave. The well-
oiled door made no noise as they opened it.

"Send Shara my love in Argn." Arlec called to the closing door.

Chapter 13

Lord Priest Farlam came to view the still balanced coin. He had not visited the minor temple in Arbeneth in years. The fool priest, Cern, who ran this temple followed obsequiously behind Lord Priest.

"A trick of some sort, my Lord. He was a commoner, in dirty clothes and of no importance. Or perhaps he influenced the coin somehow?"

Cern smelled of sweat, a common problem when Farlam visited the backwaters.

"Silence. I will be the judge of the events."

He examined the coin without touching it. He moved his staff of office near the coin, staring at the diamond on the handle as he did so. "No *ka* residual."

The fawning one grew pale. Farlam kept his composure, but he knew the same questions were racing through both their minds. What did it mean? For centuries, they were told to look for this event, but no hint of its meaning had ever been passed on. Was this good or bad?

"I will retire to the prayer chamber now."

"Yes, Lord, follow me."

The prayer chamber for priests was where all prayer chambers were in the temples of the god of luck, underneath the pyramid that worshipers tossed their coins at. Underneath the pyramid that now had a coin still balanced on the top. To be underneath that coin bothered the Lord Priest, yet he let himself be led. No time to ignore protocol, even if he was in a panic. Once inside the stark chamber, alone, he sank to his knees and holding his staff began to pray. Not the prayers of the commoners, but a prayer known only to a few of the high priests. An important prayer. A prayer where he used his own *ka* channeled to his staff. His mind cried out at the loss. He was giving up years of his life, but he knew how important this was. It was years of his life now, or potentially his entire life later.

The diamond on the staff began to glow. Sweat ran in rivulets down his face and creases formed around his eyes. Across from him, a gateway began to form—still not fully corporeal. Those who were rich enough to use the gateways between the cities, or even to the far away trading centers, would recognize a gateway such as this. Those city gates were formed long ago as giant artifacts shaped by *ka,* but powered day-to-day with qenar ore. This one was not some pre-formed gate. He created it now, without a talisman. No living man had seen such a thing before, nor done such a thing. The Lord Priest had not even been sure it would work. Lord Priests had, for centuries, been taught how, but none had ever tried—as far as he knew. After all, *ka* was irreplaceable and talking face to face with your god was different from communication via prayer staff.

He was prepared intellectually for what happened next, yet he dropped the gateway and sagged to the ground at his own success. He had summoned his god. Summoned. This was no vision through a prayer staff. This was no image projected to the council of priests. This was his god in the flesh. The sight of his god was overwhelming—he had hoped for success and feared success. All priests knew the gods were real. They drew *ka* from their worshippers. They directly intervened on the behalf of a few lucky worshippers every year. They communicated with their priests, but the gods rarely showed themselves. It had been lifetimes. Success already had its cost, the Lord Priest felt ten years older. He could smell his own fear.

Nu Arr strode through the gateway. A tall man. His eyes were black, no visible iris or cornea, just black. He was obviously not pleased, but the displeasure was not focused on his high priest.

"My Lord, I have uttered the prayer of calling as I have been instructed to do when someone has passed the test of the coin."

Nu Arr nodded. Lord Priest was sure that he was mistaken, but in a mortal it would have been fear he saw. Not for the first time blasphemous thoughts raced through his head. Why would the gods need to be told of such an important event? Because they were not all powerful and certainly not all knowing. They were, however, still powerful, he reminded himself.

"The Eclipse. I had *hoped* that the few who had been born had all died."

Lord Priest remembered for two or three years after the eclipse of the Five Moons many newborn and young children died of strange accidents. He suppressed a small shiver and listened, prostrate from fear and fatigue.

Nu Arr continued. "His existence imperils ...."

The Lord Priest looked more directly at his god. The emotions of a god were hard to read. He quickly looked down once again.

"... the delicate balance of this plane. You must find the young man and destroy him. Do it quickly. You will be rewarded, for I am a generous god."

To emphasize the last statement Nu Arr grabbed the staff of his priest and allowed some of his own *ka* to flow through it. The Lord Priest writhed in agony and pleasure as the energy coursed through him. All his aches and pains disappeared. He was young again, younger than before the gateway. Healthier than he had ever felt. Powerful. He felt the power of many men within him. He bowed down. "We will find him, Lord Nu Arr."

Nu Arr fished a talisman from his pocket and a gateway formed. He stepped through and it closed up behind him, like a mouth snapping shut, leaving the priest alone with his plans of glory and death and wondering why a god had to use a talisman to form a gate.

Chapter 14

All five moons were out, bathing Tsom and Shara in a spectrum of diffuse light that mixed well with the glow globes, mellowing the cacophony of colors omnipresent in Argn. The pleasant warmth of fall added to the feeling of relaxation. Argn was a bit warmer than Tsom was used to, being further away from the ocean's cooling effect, but it allowed for a late evening without a jacket. His initial focus on information gathering drifted to simple enjoyment of her company. It was hard to believe *she* was Katar. Yet, he did not forget the initial reason for his boldness. He kept wine flowing with the dinner, distracting her with idle chatter that was foreign to his nature while pouring slightly more in her glass than his own each time. This, combined with his own natural defense, had the desired effect.

He felt he was taking advantage of Shara, by using alcohol. She was an adult, but he recalled a recent incident with the women at the brothel in his neighborhood in Arbeneth. His former neighborhood, he reminded himself. His sisters—as he called them since the time they took him in when first fleeing the death of his mother—decided to throw a party and get him drunk. Soon, all the women were drunk, but Tsom remained sober. Tarina laughed and said "I suppose it is only fair. After a few drinks we become as foolish as a man, thus allowing equal footing once in a while." The more he drank with them the drunker his companions got. Tarina, twice his age, grabbed Tsom and stared deeply into his eyes. "You're a dangerous man Tsom. Drinking with you is like drinking and smoking nart at the same time. It is a good thing I am twenty years older than you, or I would quit this place and make you mine."

As the alcohol had its effect on Shara, he pushed forward with information gathering.

"Is it forbidden for a non-Katar to wear the ring?"

"Not only forbidden, but death. The rings are attuned to the Katar families. Only those of Katar blood may wear the ring. Anyone else would suffer true death." She dropped her voice slightly at the last two words, it was not polite to discuss such things in public, at a restaurant.

Tsom paled slightly, but feigned nonchalance, nodding his head with as little expression as possible. He believed, as most did, that as long as some *ka* remained at death that one's soul returned to the Ocean of Souls via the River of Death to recover its *ka* lost during life, to be reborn via the River of Life. True death was the total loss of *ka*.

"Do the Katar make the rings?"

"No, no, they're ancient." She tilted her head back, with her eyes half closed. "They are from the wars between the Humans and the Old Ones. It is said, this was before the gods existed. Back when Humans knew how to shape *ka* into talismans. One of the original Katar was such a person. He, or *she*." She paused, looking a bit proud to be both Katar and a woman. "The Tarth started a great war with mankind, fearful that we would grow in population and destroy all the other races. The Tarth were truly *daemons*, invincible, destroying thousands for each of their own. The first of the Katar formed an army from those who had the talent to shape *ka*. Five thousand of the best warriors, men and women. He, or she, taught the first how to shape and bind *ka* to diamonds. They defeated the Tarth and old races allied with the Tarth; only the Hrýll, the Srýll, and the Riconé survived. Mankind was in chaos and many bands of Humans formed independent armies and kingdoms, but the Katar unified The Cities, building a civilization that has lasted at least five thousand years."

Tsom tilted his head to the side, frowning.

"What about Yanín?"

"They are not as old. I suppose that war with the Yanín, over the course of time, is inevitable, but they fight amongst themselves enough to keep their population in check."

Tsom had heard something similar from sailors on the docks, but never the part about the rings. Hard to believe the now placid and obedient Hrýll were ever at war with anyone. Let alone their cousins the Srýll, who some said were already extinct. Still, she was not telling him something. What was the power of these rings to help defeat the old races? After all, it was the remaining Old Ones that Humans depended on still for talismans. Only they seemed capable of creating talismans. He poured Shara some more wine while looking her in the eyes. He felt he had to know all about these rings, that had brought him so much trouble.

She blinked and leaned forward. "There is something strange about your eyes … the color changes … your whites …" She gazed thoughtfully at him while reaching for the wine. "No, it is gone." Her movements were slightly slower than before and she spoke with a thickened tongue. Tsom smiled at her and she smiled back, a genuine smile. A smile with a trace of lust and longing in it. Her large mouth was the perfect size when she smiled and her lips remained full. He would have to be careful not to let his feelings get away. He did not want to take advantage of her, beyond information.

He laughed to himself—take advantage, once she sobered up she could have him killed, or kill him herself. Did any of the Katar ever leave the families? The military order that defined them? No time for daydreaming.

"It is hard to believe that five thousand could defeat the combined forces of eight or more races."

He wished that he did not have to use her. The faint scent of cinnamon that she wore was distracting as were her lips as she pursed them in thought. She was Katar, the enemy, he reminded himself.

Shara looked sad and seemed about to change the topic of conversation or worse, to leave. He leaned closer and placed his hand on her left hand, her ring hand. The covered ring seemed warm, but he ignored it and covered it completely, hiding it from her sight. He felt a rush at touching her and an equal rush that she did not pull away. She really was pretty. The slight cinnamon smell was intoxicating. Afraid that she might consider leaving he concentrated on her staying, as if willing her to stay would make it so. For a second it seemed that there was only the two of them, alone in the world. Tsom held on to the feeling. Let nothing interrupt them, he thought.

The waiter bringing a new bottle of wine to Tsom and Shara's table grabbed an exceedingly rare vintage, instead of the table wine Tsom had requested. Shara stopped hesitating in her speech, looked at Tsom's eyes again, blinked, left her hand within Tsom's and continued.

"Enough about history. We'll have to get together again if you want more history. I do feel quite tipsy." She giggled. "You know, I really never cared for most of the Katar men my own age. It's nice to finally meet a man who is not planning his next step in Katar hierarchy. Tell me, Tsom," she said squeezing his hand, "what do you find attractive in a woman?"

He eyed Shara's hand for its beauty and the ring she was wearing and to avoid staring into her eyes and answering her question right away. Dangerous ground, he thought. He saw the diamonds on her ring glowing and dropped her hand. Staring he saw he was wrong. To cover up the abrupt dropping of her hand, he poured some more wine.

Argn certainly had better wine than he was used to. Shara sipped hers and, tasting it, drank more deeply. Her upper lip grew a deeper red and she unconsciously licked the wine off of her lip. Tsom found this very appealing.

"I find a woman's lips, her smile, extremely attractive," he replied. She rewarded him with an inviting one, causing him to feel a bit of the wine for the first time.

The night progressed and Shara and Tsom left the café. As they walked along the Tarth river, much smaller than Darnen river in Arbeneth, Shara stumbled and grabbed onto Tsom for support. Regaining her footing, she kept her hands on his arm. His hand intertwined with hers, her ring hand.

Chapter 15

Devon ran both hands across his face and through his hair. He was tired. The Katar weren't supposed to get tired, he told himself. He reviewed the summary reports again. The raids on all caravans had increased. Outlying farms and small towns were destroyed, most near Zethicia. The gateway between The Cities and Zethicia was constantly packed, despite the huge cost to use it. While the Katar, who owned the gateway, were enjoying the increased profits, they too were becoming concerned. *Daemons*. That was what everyone kept calling the raiders. Not the tame *daemons* of the Riconé, that were used to mine iron deep within the *Web of God,* the massive mountain chain to the North. The Riconé *daemons* were not malevolent, simply incredibly good at finding iron, long lived, and superb tool makers, but rather limited in intelligence. Devon wished the Katar had some hold over the elusive Riconé and their iron. *Someday*, he thought. No these *daemons* were from myth and legend. These were, if the reports were to be trusted, the *daemons* that the Katar themselves had helped banish thousands of years ago. Back to wreak revenge, the survivors said. The Katar kept reassuring the citizens that it was all foolishness. Talk of dead races returning from out of time was nonsense. But as the casualties mounted, even the Katar had a hard time ignoring the rumors.

Devon set down the first stack and drank deeply of his tsunon tea. The stimulant effect was fading, he had to get some rest soon. He arched his back, stretched, and grabbed the next report. A knock interrupted his reading. With a jerk of his head, he realized it had interrupted his sleeping. He grunted an 'enter.' His advisor, Brontriste, strode in and gave him a cursory bow.

"Sir, the Council of Cities has called a special meeting of all five Katar families and all six city governors."

"By the Sea, don't they know we are busy? Is it the Zethicia situation? Is it worse?"

"Yes, but it's worse. The priesthoods are now involved. They are all clamoring for Katar intervention. Zethicia and the *daemons* …" Brontriste saw Devon's expression, "… the unknown raiders, the rebels, and the priesthood of Nu

Arr in particular is claiming that one of the rebels is very dangerous and part of prophesy."

Devon scowled. Prophesy. Prophesies came true because people believed in them, nothing more. Damn the priests and their worthless false gods. One day the Katar would have to deal with them. One day. He sighed heavily, glanced at the stack of paper, nodded as he got up.

"I suppose the meeting is now?"

"Yes, Sir. You're leading it."

***

Devon, head of the Karn clan, was the only Katar normally at a council meeting. While the council members were in theory the government of The Cities, everybody knew that the Katar were the military and police power. Devon was all that was normally needed to represent that power. The Council must want something he would not approve of.

The chamber was circular, with a raised dais in the center, where Devon stood. Glow globes kept the chamber well lit; a large one with a lens focusing the light over the dais. The chamber was normally only used for the council of six and their servants, so the addition of four more dignitaries and their guard made for a crowded room. Of the over thirty present, only three were women, all from Argn. Devon briefly wished the tradition of Arbeneth allowed him to use his own daughters more openly. He raised his hand for attention.

"The Lord Priest of Nu Arr has been to see the Council. He has indicated that the god of luck has paid him a visit." He paused to let this sink in. The clans were no superstitious peons, believing that the gods were all powerful, but they were not naïve either. A visit by one of the gods was rare, even within the priesthoods. No one denied a god's power, when they chose to use it.

"Nu Arr feels that the barriers between the planes have weakened, allowing the Tarth to return from Hell."

He paused. Devon still had a hard time believing in Tarth.

"There is a man, more a boy, foretold would arise amongst us centuries ago, born on the Eclipse of the Five Moons. According to the priest, this man is a catalyst and may be the cause of all of this, indirectly, or merely a symptom, but the priesthood is set on destroying this man, Tsom. Some have assumed that any special importance to the event was mere superstition, but others give it more import."

Several of the clan leaders nodded. Nu Arr was a major god, so most were familiar with the test of the coin. The council members looked shocked, they had assumed the rumors of the Tarth were simply rumors. The planes were real, everyone knew that, but the movement between planes was an abstract. Even the gods did not move between planes.

"This young man—the priests tell us—is the nexus of chaos, of wild unpredictable change. He must be destroyed, before he causes barriers between Hell and the other planes to break. That is what Nu Arr, or his priests, predict will happen—is happening. The old *daemons* will return and wreak revenge upon mankind. Our Katar ancestors fought the Tarth in the past, but it was a close battle. Without the forces we had allied with us then, we do not hold certain victory."

Devon's voice held the doom he felt. His cleared his voice, which was about to crack. He did not want to go on. Revealing the next piece would be a huge blow to his reputation and image, but he knew under the circumstances that it was important. He also knew that by now one or more of the other families was aware. Best to appear open and honest.

"I have reason to believe that this man, a young thief, is in possession of a Katar ring."

Before he could continue, cries of outrage from the clansmen drowned out his next words.

"Who could have been so foolish?"

"It must be recovered."

"This hasn't happened for centuries."

"He obviously has not put it on, or we would have heard of the disaster." This last was Jern, head of the Tanec family of Argn speaking. Jern had the fiery red hair of the north, as did his two daughters flanking him, with the third woman, a cousin, behind. The Tanec family once had women leading them and it looked as if they would again. Only in Argn, thought Devon.

Devon raised his hand for silence. It was a testament to his power that it was granted.

"Yes, we have been lucky in that respect, although at least that would have probably killed the thief too. I must shamefully admit that the ring is my son Arlec's ring—one of the family rings."

Silence as the Katar families digested the news. He could see the plots forming in their heads. They would use this against him. Against his family. The Karn family had held power over the other Katar for too long. Yet, given the crisis, he had to inform them, before the news leaked from other sources. His fool son had hoped to hide it from him, as had his sisters. His spies and informers told him of the sloppy network Arlec had employed to find the ring and the way Larra and Piea had tried to ask around in Argn, all under the guise of crushing the rebellion.

They should know better than to trust fellow Katar in something like this.

No doubt Jern knew all about it too. The thief was supposed to be somewhere in his city. Jern and his daughters usually knew more than they let on.

"It is possible, as you know, that if he still has the ring with him, that even without trying it on he is using some of its power. Certainly if Nu Arr is correct, this young man is not ordinary. He must be a *ka* shaper without knowing it, to be the type of catalyst that Nu Arr is proposing."

"Is he Kinel?" whispered several of the Katar.

The same thought had crossed Devon's mind. Most thought that the Kinel had been exterminated, but Devon suspected that some survived. A Kinel with the power to change probability would be extremely dangerous. More so than even most of the Katar realized. The Kinel were hated by all, but few actually knew why. Devon would keep that secret. He ignored the whisper, but Jern interrupted next.

"There is the possibility that this thief is part of the resistance, isn't there, Devon?"

May his ba *rot in the Sea*, Devon thought. *I knew he knew more.*

"It is a possibility. Would you care to let us know what else you may know, my Friend?" Devon glared at Jern.

"As I'm sure Commander Devon was about to tell us, the rebels have three primary centers, one in Arbeneth—which may have been partially neutralized, one in Argn, where the thief and the remnants of the Arbeneth rebel command may have fled, and one in Qenaril. Now that the cell in Arbeneth has been attacked, the other cells will be on high alert."

Devon flinched at the rarely used military title. Jern was trying to remind the Council that Devon was the Katar representative and that he should be held responsible.

"I accept the responsibility of my son's carelessness, but the real issue is that we must mobilize the entire Katar to find this man, on the off chance that the priests are correct. The rebellion will try and use him, and certainly the rebellion will try and use the ring."

"I know you have a hard time with your offspring, my dear Commander." The smile Jern gave Devon held danger. "But, it is not just your son that concerns the Katar of Argn. Our information indicates that your daughter, Shara, has been seen multiple times with the thief we are searching for. I'm sure that she is unaware of the connection to the lost ring and that it is all an unfortunate coincidence. Still, as you say this thief must be caught and destroyed. I just hope that your daughter is not caught in the crossfire, that would be most unfortunate."

Devon did not hear the outcries that ensued after Jern's revelation. Could it be true? Jern would not dare to play games without something to back it up.

A member of the council, Korrell, spoke up.

"But, this is just one man. All this fuss over one young man?"

Jern spoke.

"One man can tip the balance, Korrell." Jern smiled and stood looking at the entire group. "I was just a child, before most of you were born. One of the Katar went rogue. Turned on the families. Tried to form his own power base." He looked at Devon for confirmation. Devon nodded. "This single individual gathered support. He killed twenty Katar, destroyed two artifacts, and the town of Bla-ne was wiped out. That was a single individual, with a ring of the Katar. If this boy can use the ring, or anyone of the rebellion, then we must act now. Quickly. Before it is too late."

"But, I thought only Katar could use the rings?" ask Korrell.

"Come now, Korrell. You are a handsome man, with power. Are you sure you don't have any bastards out there? Or if you are pure, was your father? Your grandfather?"

Korrell flushed.

There was no real debate. With Zethicia on one side and the rebels on the other and now the priesthood throwing fuel onto the fire it was agreed that significant action was warranted. Jern was designated the commander for destroying the terrorist rebels and in particular finding the thief and the ring. The council and families also agreed that Telem, head of the Sho family in Qenaril, should lead all forces associated with the defense of Zethicia. Devon ground his teeth but did not argue. Jern had outmaneuvered him and Telem had been prepared. The gateway between The Cities and Zethicia was in Qenaril, leaving Telem the obvious choice.

It had been many years since Devon felt out of control. The sensation was not pleasant.

Chapter 16

Tsom spent the next week performing petty thievery for both money and to mingle with the crowds and gather information. He did not need the money. There was still plenty left over from the purse. By selling his take to the local black market he became plugged into the network of gossip that was better than any other. By the end of the week, he knew that far from having found safety in Argn he was hunted in all directions. He grew a beard. Despite living on society's fringes all his life, he had always tried to look his best. Some half memory of his mother's voice came back, *Tsom there is nothing arrogant about looking good. If you don't care for yourself then you show no respect for others.*

Convincing himself that he needed more information on the Katar, despite the risk, he managed to see Shara multiple times. She was due to return to Arbeneth soon and although he had no logical reason to see her again he sent her a note by courier, a simple trade's courier, not those used by nobles.

That the courier was a for trade was evident by the bright yellow and purple colors she wore. A noble would have used a courier that wore bright orange and purple. Tsom continued to marvel at how every color combination had a meaning in Argn. The courier had been reluctant to bring a message to a Katar, but a large tip in advance with promise of another after delivery convinced her. That and a smile. A smile always helped.

They met at a small tavern not too far from the café where they first met. A marine tavern, on the shores of the Tarth River, frequented by both street and river traffic. Tsom missed the docks of Arbeneth and found it peaceful here. He watched her from across the street, blending into the shadow of a narrow alley, somehow making himself smaller looking. She had not been followed.

"Tsom, you need to shave, you look—" she paused, not wanting to hurt his feelings, but seeing that he was grinning she continued "—like a scruffy little thief."

He winced. Not the look he was going for. Hopefully, his beard would even out in time. She looked even more appealing in the brighter light of day than by the moonlight of a few nights ago. Each time he saw her, she grew prettier.

"Do all Katar women smell like cinnamon?"

She giggled, a slight flush to her cheeks. "No, I really should stop wearing that perfume, now that I am a Katar junior officer. It is from the Hrýll. My brother gave it to me just before I came to Argn for training. He knew it was a favorite of my mother's."

"If more Katar smelled like you, perhaps your average citizen would not fear them so much. You say was? Your mother?"

The sadness on Shara's face broke his heart.

"She died giving birth."

"Oh. I'm sorry. I thought all Katar … I mean …."

"My mother wasn't Katar. My father broke all tradition and married a commoner. He loved her, but …" She turned her face away, surreptitiously wiping a tear. The other customers lowered their eyes. A Katar crying was something they were not accustomed to.

"I sometimes wish I had not been born into the Katar." She looked at Tsom and grabbed his hand. "I know you hate us." She waved around the restaurant dining area. "But you know, sometimes I hate the Katar too."

"What?" Whispered Tsom.

"My mother wasn't Katar. What if she hadn't married my father, she might still be alive."

He started trembling, the image of his own mother's head hanging from the hand of the Katar, her mouth moving silently even though she had died, telling him to run. Run from the Katar. Fear them. Never look back. Run.

"She lived with the Katar. We always wear our rings." She held up her left hand. "So many Katar, all in one household. She slept next to him, even when he was injured. The rings take their toll. Even servants only serve a short time in a Katar household, but my mother never left. I killed her. My father killed her. My family killed her. She had no strength left. Her *ka* was too weak. You see, Tsom. I am sympathetic to the cost of Katar rule."

Tsom placed his hand over hers, forcing himself to touch her ring.

"Yet, you accept these? You accept it?"

"I … oh, Tsom, I fear life without it. Mankind needs protection, order, peace. The Katar provide that for a price." Tsom heard the doubt in her voice.

"The Katar killed my family, Shara."

She looked up, eyes wide, pulling her hand back, but he held on tightly.

"I was ten. Playing games, shand, with friends. The clock tower rang and I knew I was going to be late, again. I helped in my parent's shop. We sold Hrýll cloth and other items from the Hrýll. My mother knew the Hrýll.

When I entered the shop, my father was already dead. There were three of them. Three Katar. My mother tried to pretend I was a stranger. To warn me, but the Katar knew. So my mother fought them. She killed one. I wounded one, but those rings."

He rubbed her ring as she stared horrified into his eyes.

"Those rings were as bright as small suns. One of the Katar severed my mother's head completely off as she screamed at me to run. Even detached from her body I heard the scream, as if it were in my head. Run. It was like a compulsion. I ran and somehow they never caught me.

Now, now you know why I feel the way I do."

Tears were streaming down both of their faces. The customers in the restaurant were carefully leaving and the owner was standing off to the side twisting a towel in his hands.

"Tsom, how can you stand to be with me?"

"You're different. You aren't like them."

"But, why? Why would the Katar kill your family?"

"I don't know. I've asked myself that every day. I just don't know."

They kissed without thought to the people around them. The shocked looks were quickly averted. The proprietor twisted his towel more fiercely and began to scrub the same spot on the bar over and over.

Coming to their senses they left the eating establishment and walked along the river. No words, just holding hands tightly, both thinking that tomorrow Shara would return to Arbeneth.

"Take me for a boat ride," she suddenly said, pulling him toward a tourist rental shop.

"I'd rather not. I don't know how to swim," he admitted.

She pouted, causing Tsom to once again marvel how something as small and insignificant as a lip could be so attractive.

He left a few sintar as security and took her out on the river. The Tarth River was not swift here and he didn't have to exert himself to move slowly upstream. It gave Tsom a chance to watch Shara while he rowed. He watched her as she studied the swirls that his oars left. The starboard side swirled clockwise, the port counter clockwise. Suddenly, the swirls seemed to disintegrate into many random currents. Then, she looked up over his shoulders, her face tensing. The progress of the skiff suddenly slowed. Tsom looked back. Behind the skiff the currents converged and a large whirlpool formed. He began to paddle harder, but the vortex spun faster, the current increased. He fought the current to a standstill, but he couldn't maintain the effort for long.

He suddenly spun the skiff around.

"Tsom, what are you doing? It will sink us, row away!"

He ignored her plea. He was tired of running from everything. He aimed the skiff at the center and focused. The whirlpool should not be there. Part of him knew this and focused on it. As the skiff hit the maelstrom, it parted into two smaller swirls. As he passed between them, they matched his oars and disappeared into the normal minute whirls of each stroke he made.

"What just happened?" Shara was standing, staring at the water. She released her hands, cramping from clenching the gunnels, and glancing down at the left one caught the end glow of her ring. "My ring. It should only be glowing if I am using it or another Katar nearby is using their ring." She scanned the banks of the river, but did not see anything. "I wonder if I somehow tapped the ring's power to destroy the vortex?"

"You must have, I have no such power."

"But, what about the original vortex? I surely did not do that."

Tsom shrugged, heading back to the tavern's dock. He had had enough of rowing for one day. Approaching the dock, they both spotted the priest, with two Katar women flanking him. As this was Argn, it was not unusual that the Katar were women. A priest, that was more unusual. All priests looked the same from a distance. Too bad they did not follow the Argn color codes. If it were a priest of Nu Arr then it was clear whom they were waiting for. It might also explain the recent events in the river. Tsom slowed down, hesitating. Shara looked from the dock to Tsom.

"Are you in some sort of trouble?"

"Yes," he hissed. "I'm sorry you are getting dragged into this, Shara. Stay out of it and hopefully you can plead ignorance."

Tsom did not like the odds. Three to one. He could jump ship and swim for it. The distance was short enough that his lack of swimming ability might not drown him. By the Sea, he wished he had taken up those offers on swimming lessons from his sailor friends.

The Katar on the dock rested their hands on sword hilts, smiles twitching their faces. Tsom could see the slight glow of the rings on both of them. He was fast, but he knew they must be faster with the rings. He raised his hands up in the air. "It's me you want, I surrender."

Shara's lower lip stood out as she squinted at the three.

The taller and older of the two Katar, a lean looking woman and slightly graying hair, pulled out her sword, some sort of rapier, and held it ready— pointing at Tsom, the ring glowing more fiercely. Tsom felt a momentary weakness, but this passed almost immediately. He felt Shara's hand on his arm. Had she stopped the weakness?

"You are draining him!" Shara yelled in shock. Tsom frowned, he did not feel different. The weakness had been momentary.

"Stand aside *cappa*."

Shara stiffened. "I received full commission last week. I am fourth of the Karn. What right do you have to attack this man!"

Karn? Shara had told him her name was Darnee. Shara Darnee. Karn was the family of Arlec. She was Arlec's sister! Tsom pushed aside the torrent of thoughts and concentrated on the issue at hand.

The older woman frowned.

"Do you know who you are harboring, Sar Karn?"

Using the honorific address, but not acknowledging any military, or family rank. Safe, but almost insulting. "I will assume not, or your father would punish you himself. This is a thief, a rebel, extremely dangerous and wanted by the temple of Nu Arr, the Katar, the Council of Governors, and your father. He stole your very brother's ring! We have orders to kill on sight and recover the ring."

Tsom and Shara looked at each other shocked and dismayed. Shedding his momentary paralysis he struck Shara with a blow just below the sternum, going upward slightly. She let out a rush of air and doubled over semi-conscious. "I'm sorry," he whispered, not wondering that he had been able to hit Shara at all. He grabbed her left hand and tugged on the ring. No need to let her use her powers on him, she had a guilty conscience already. It resisted, then glowed slightly and slid off her finger. He then pulled her rapier out, pushed her back, and turned to face the dock. The two Katar were running to the edge of the dock to jump toward the skiff, which had drifted away in the current.

"Stop using your rings, she is no longer wearing hers," he held up Shara's ring. The women looked shocked, but the glow on their hands did not diminish. Shara gasped and fell back in pain. Damn, the Katar were hurting their own. The ring must be protecting him even though he wasn't wearing it.

The priest, who had been silent and immobile to this point, reached out and pushed both the Katar sharply in the middle of their backs. They stumbled and fell into the water, their light armor and swords hampering swimming even with the aid of the rings. While the current was not strong, they were soon pulled down stream, to the right. Tsom kept even with the dock with a mere stroke or two.

The priest pulled back his cowl. It was Lanos, grinning he yelled, "Throw the girl overboard and paddle here. They will try and save her."

Tsom shook his head, they had just insulted her and used their rings when she had no protection, they would not save her.

Rowing just enough to stay even with the dock, he watched the two Katar drift further downstream. They would make not make shore quickly, but they didn't look like they would drown. He then nosed up to Lanos.

Lanos jumped in and Tsom aimed for the opposite bank of the river.

Neither Tsom, nor Lanos had forgotten about Shara, lying still, but obviously conscious at the back of the skiff. She glowered at both of them. "Is this one of your thieving friends?"

Lanos grinned. "Quiet, *cappa*."

She rubbed her hand where her ring should have been. "How did you manage to take my ring off? Only I should be able to take it off." Tsom shrugged, as he continued to row. The small splash of the oars was the only sound in the middle of the river.

"Well, give it back to me," she sounded less angry and hopeful.

"I don't think so. You would use it to kill me."

"Do you really think that, Tsom?" She whispered. Lanos looked back and forth between them and grinned again.

This seemed to hurt her, but he didn't trust her reaction. She would side with her family and her compatriots first. He was now nothing but a thief, the thief who stole from her brother, from her. Atem's luck again. Of all the Katar for her to be related to!

"You told me your name was Darnee," he snapped.

"That was my mother's name. It is acceptable custom in Arn to use your mother's name."

"Karn," Tsom shook his head and kept paddling.

"I told you that you should have thrown her overboard. Now what do you plan on doing with her?"

"I have no reason to trust you, so my plans are my own. What were you doing disguised as a priest hanging out with Katar?"

"Alanar has decided to help you. You are in more trouble than you realize."

"He was such a big help last time."

"Granted. Yet, you should not throw away an offer from Alanar for help. It is rarely given. He is more powerful than you might guess and he can help you. Do you know how much trouble you're in?"

"I heard from those two a moment ago."

The skiff approached the riverbank. Both Tsom and Lanos stopped and scanned the bank for trouble. This side of the Tarth was less crowded and they had drifted down stream a bit, but the Katar might have some additional groups looking for them already. Glancing across the river, he could see the two climbing onto the shore downstream. There was a bridge less than a five marks away from the dock they had left. On foot a considerable distance, but on horse not too far. Their bank was clear and Tsom aimed for one of the many public mooring spots.

"I know that both the Katar and the priesthood of Nu Arr are after me, although the latter makes no sense."

"You have met a test of their prophesy."

"That coin? It was just a trick, it's like anything I throw, you get the balance and it works. There is nothing prophetic about it. I could do it a hundred times."

"Word has it that their god himself has declared you a danger."

"Damn, prophesies shouldn't be based on some stupid trick."

Shara looked at Tsom with concern and interest, mingled with fear. He caught her gaze and she quickly looked back at the dock with feigned interest. Lanos noted the interplay, but continued.

"Her father is of the Karn clan, not some minor Katar family, but one of the five. In fact the most powerful of the five. He will not rest until you are dead. Devon takes his status very seriously. No doubt knowing that you have now kidnapped his daughter will endear you to him even more."

Lanos sent Shara a withering gaze, but again his lips twitched at their corners. The skiff bumped against the dock and Lanos leapt onto the dock and tied the boat to the supporting pile. Pulling the oars in, Tsom followed suit. Shara stayed in the boat. Was she still weak from the blow and the Katar rings?

"Well, what are you going to do with her? Are you going to accept Alanar's offer or battle gods, priests, and the Katar, all on your own?" Lanos alternated his gaze from Shara to scanning the docks and the nearby road.

"We can't leave her here, she'll be punished for losing her ring and I won't give it back to her, just yet. I will not give up this ring as easily as the last. Do I have your word that Alanar will not try and take this one from me?"

Lanos hesitated. Tsom had guessed correctly that Lanos did not give his word lightly. "I give you my word that I will not take it."

Tsom held out his hand to Shara, which, surprisingly, she accepted. She leapt lightly to the dock, not showing any signs of being hit earlier.

"So, you are the famous Lanos?" She asked.

"Famous?" Lanos and Tsom said simultaneously.

"Alanar's left hand. Slayer of women, former captain of the Qenarelian Guard, head of the rebel spy network."

Lanos hissed, his sword in his hand. Tsom grabbed his arm.

"She wouldn't be telling you this if she didn't have something else to say."

Shara smiled at Tsom and he almost forgot she was now his enemy.

"The Hrýll brandy tastes like piss today."

Lanos froze, his mouth slowly dropped open, then just as slowly closed.

"Probably because it is piss," he whispered.

"In that case, I'll have a refill," she replied.

Lanos held out his left hand and Shara grasped it with her left. He held out his sword with his right and Shara drew her short blade with her own right and crossed blades with Lanos.

"Well, this changes things," smiled Lanos.

"It does? What in the Sea was that all about?"

"Shara is my primary source of information into the Katar. Until this moment, her identity was secret even from me. Give her the ring back."

"No."

Lanos and Shara both raised their eyebrows. Shara looked hurt, sad, and angry all at the same time.

Lanos looked around.

"We don't have time for this. Give her the ring, she may need it."

"What, so she drains us when she is in trouble? No. Isn't it a bit convenient that she is the one with me? Do you trust her?"

"No one else could know the signals."

"Really, the Katar would never torture someone for information?"

"Enough," said Shara, placing a hand on Tsom. He did not flinch away. Her hand felt good. "I see Tsom's point. Let's discuss this later. My sisters-in-arms will be here soon."

The walked briskly away from the Tarth River, Lanos taking the lead. Lanos and Shara spoke while they walked, all but ignoring Tsom.

"The Katar and the priesthood are both after him," Lanos jerked his head to Tsom. "They assume he is with the resistance and the priests seem to think he is special. Something about being born on the Eclipse of the Five Moons."

Shara looked at Tsom, question in her eyes. He nodded.

"What of Zethicia? Have you heard anything from your network?" Shara asked.

"It's bad. The rumors are true. Tarth. Actual *daemons*. Alanar seems to think they can be used by the rebellion, but I'm not sure that's wise." Lanos hesitated at an intersection, looking left and right several moments, as if he did not trust the almost empty streets.

"Alanar survived the raid my brother led?"

"Yes. At least I think so. He hasn't been heard from since. We suspect he will link up with our command center here. That's where we are heading now."

"Is that wise?" Tsom interrupted, nodding to Shara.

"She risked her life for the cause for years, Thief. You have risked yours only accidently. I trust her more than you."

Chagrined, Tsom bit back an angry retort.

Shara looked back at Tsom and smiled, cooling his anger.

"He just doesn't trust anyone yet, Lanos. He has reason to hate the Katar. All Katar."

"If the Katar want him so much and are worried about him, then we help him. He does seem to have a knack for getting rings," Lanos grinned.

"Yes. How does he do that?" Shara rubbed her left hand.

"Hey. I'm here," muttered Tsom.

Several of the passersby looked curiously at the young Katar with two men on either side of her. None noticed the lack of a ring on her left hand.

Lanos's hand guided Shara around a pothole in the road, one he seemed to see without even looking down during his talk. He kept a sharp eye out on the people in the street, guiding them down side streets seemingly for no reason, until once Tsom spotted a priest deep in the crowd far ahead. Lanos seemed to be aware of everything in all directions.

They rounded the corner and there stood ten Katar. The lead was the tall woman from the dock. They all had their rapiers drawn and each of their rings glowed with death.

Chapter 17

While Tsom did not fight often, he'd witnessed enough combat to know that hand-to-hand combat tends to occur very quickly. Even the best swordsmen can last only ten, maybe twenty seconds before one lands a blow that incapacitates the other, or somebody tires out. Tsom had seen a few knife fights and one or two sword fights on the docks. Yarm, his dead friend and mentor had taught him the basics of swordplay, but he knew, as he drew his sword, that he did not stand a chance.

By the time his sword had cleared its scabbard the Katar engaged. Shara almost instantly managed to knock one down and wrest the sword from the fallen Katar. Lanos, as the first time Tsom had met him, moved almost too fast to see. Tsom had a vague idea from peripheral vision that he had killed one Katar and injured another. Four Katar focused on him. He parried one or two blows, surprising them that a commoner had any skill at all. As they fell back into trained formation for a real attack Tsom pulled his ever-ready knife and targeting the leader threw with focused concentration. Everyone was too busy to notice all the rings flare simultaneously, nor to hear the cries of pain in the buildings nearby.

The knife struck true, entering the Katar's heart, killing her almost instantly. Her look of surprise was of anyone dying suddenly and that of someone who has never lost. The other three Katar attacked in synchronized formation, their trained reflexes taking over for the loss of their comrade.

Yarm had always told him to get to the edge of a group, not to ever let himself be cornered. Tsom pushed his panic into a mad adrenalin rush and instead of defending pushed, dodged, and slashed his way to the edge. For a moment he thought he had been entirely successful, until he felt the warmth spreading down his left leg.

It must have been only muscle as he was still walking. Part of him cried at the future pain he was going to feel.

His new position gave him the full battle perspective. Lanos had amazingly killed three Katar. Shara was down, but Lanos was defending her from the two not focused on Tsom. Both Katar were injured, but so was Lanos. The three turning to Tsom were unscathed.

He had no recollection of the next few seconds. Tsom was surprised to still be alive. He was standing and had injured one of the three. But, he was tiring and losing a lot of blood, from his right forearm, left shoulder, and another wound to the left leg. They had him and knew it, simply keeping him moving until he keeled over.

He was not going to give them the satisfaction.

He found the ring in his pocket with his left hand. He managed to get it on partially and pulled out his hand and pushed it on all the way as the three closed on him. As they saw what he was doing their eyes widened. One mouthed, "You fool, you're simply killing innocent people. We will survive." Then she started moving very, very, slowly.

Everyone was moving very, very, slowly. He limped over to Lanos and Shara. Lanos had killed one more and looked like he was about to kill the last of his assailants. Shara was lying at his feet, a bad stomach wound and sliced hand. Tsom tried grabbing Lanos. The instant Tsom touched him Lanos's strike completed, his sword entering the Katar below the sternum. Tsom winced both at the kill and the barely checked strike Lanos aimed at him.

"What ...?"

Tsom lifted his hand with the ring, causing Lanos to cringe. Then he looked at Tsom, staring at his eyes. "Grab the girl."

"No, I think if I do she will move normally again, like you."

"So?"

"So, look at her stomach wound. Maybe if you can carry her, she will stay slowed down and we can save her."

Lanos nodded, scooping up Shara, ignoring his own wounds. "Let's go, that ring must be draining *ka* from somewhere and either you are hurting people, or it will drop soon as it runs out of *ka,* or you're draining mine and I just don't know it! Follow me, but tie a fast tourniquet on that leg or you won't make it a hundred feet."

Tsom was thinking the same. He slashed a piece of clothing off the nearest dead Katar and tied a fast, tight tourniquet. Killing the rest of the Katar would take too much time, this slowness could stop at any moment. Limping behind Lanos they entered the main street. They were still close to the river, but this was the residential riverbank. The merchants who had business near the river or in the main town lived here. Everyone on the street was moving slowly also. Lanos headed for a covered carriage tied up nearby. Tsom followed, each step more painful and clumsy as the adrenalin wore off and his leg lost its feeling. Lanos pulled open the door and half dropped Shara inside the carriage. He grabbed Tsom and guided him to the horse. *I like horses,* he smiled. He let Lanos put his hand on the horse. *Why does he want me to pet the horse?* He would prefer to sleep. He leaned against the horse. The horse turned its head and sniffed him, moving normally. Lanos pulled him up and guided him to the door and pushed him in.

Lanos then loosened the tourniquet. The pain revived Tsom momentarily. Lanos leaned over Shara and ripped the bottom of her shirt open. He examined the wound. Tsom saw his mouth tighten. He then put his hand on the side of Shara's cheek and held it there momentarily. "Not bad fighting for a little *cappa.*" He turned to Tsom.

"You must stay conscious until I get this carriage away from here, then you have to take off that ring. Who knows what it is doing to you, to all of us. Then you have to retie the tourniquet, but loosely on top of the wound itself. I loosened just for a moment so that it won't kill your leg. Can you do that?"

Tsom nodded. "She won't make it will she?" He was feeling cold. He had killed her. She was dying because she had tried to save him. He started to shiver. The image of the Katar woman he had killed and Shara we blurring together.

"No. We don't have time to find a healer, besides any healer would cause attention. The intestines are cut. She has only a short time left. I am sorry Tsom, I can tell you cared for her. She is unconscious, she won't feel anything."

Chapter 18

Lanos banged on the carriage wall. "OK, take off the ring." Nothing happened. He banged again. Hopefully the boy was not in shock and unconscious. Suddenly, the people around them started moving normally. Lanos kept driving for an hour, not daring to stop even to check on Tsom. Shara was dead by now. Lanos rubbed his eyes. She knew the risks. It was her cause too. So young. War always hit the young the hardest.

He reached his destination, a house that had been only an address until now. The less contact the rebellion had with each other the safer, but things were moving rapidly. If Alanar was anywhere, it would be here. Pulling up to the small barn at the side he stepped off slowly. His wounds were minor compared to Tsom's, but they were hurting and stiffening up.

Inside the carriage he found Tsom with his left hand on Shara's stomach, face down on the seat. She was pale but breathing steadily. Her wound was closed and partially healed. Lanos rolled Tsom up, off of her and pulled his hand back sharply, sucking in his breath.

Tsom had aged at least two years. He now looked more like a tired young man than the almost boy of just a few hours ago. The ring was off, inside his tightly clenched right fist. Tsom's injuries had not healed, only Shara's.

The house was colorful, as most houses in Argn were. Bright reds and yellows adorned the trim, with one side having a mural. This was also fairly common. The small bantri tree incorporated into the mural was one of the signals that the house was part of Alanar's network.

An woman stepped out of the house. She had practical cloths on: pants instead of a dress, and a tight fitting blouse—not to show off her still attractive body, but to keep any loose flapping material out of the way. She looked like she was in her mid-40s, but she had looked like that when Lanos first met her, twenty years ago, at Alanar's compound. Her dark red hair and pale skin would make her native of Arbeneth, but Lanos knew that was an illusion of sorts, At least that was what Alanar had told him one evening over drinks. He had never seen what she really looked like. Larrina was part Kinel, maybe even full blooded, who lived much longer than Humans. Interbreeding between Human and Kinel was rarely successful and also illegal, but there was some Kinel blood still surviving after their genocide by the Katar. Some sort of chameleon effect that she and her kind had. Her warm smile faded as she saw Lanos's injuries, already dried and crusted. She immediately got down to business.

"Others?"

He nodded, pointing to the carriage inside the barn.

"Dead?"

"No, amazingly both are alive. One man, one woman. The woman is Katar, but she is one of us and defended us against ten of her comrades. Treat her well. The man is the thief everyone is looking for, Tsom. Seven Katar are dead."

An arched eyebrow for a response. She assessed Lanos's injuries quickly. "You'll live. You carry the man, I will take the woman."

Both did their best to make sure that no one was watching the house before carrying the two bodies. She examined Shara's wounds and opted for a two-armed cradling carry. Lanos slung Tsom over his shoulder, staggered a bit and followed her.

***

Lanos sat at the kitchen table with Larrina, sipping an herb tea that she had brewed. His sore muscles relaxed and a slight lightheadedness came over him. The strange colors of the kitchen, different from the exterior, swam a bit. To Larrina the purples and violets splashed across the cabinets were probably soothing. After a few more sips of tea, they were soothing to him also. The smell of the tea reminded him of violets, or the colors triggered the smell, he was not sure which.

"Thank you Larrina, I was fading fast. One of these days you will have to tell me what is in your teas."

She smiled, the warm smile she had started when he first arrived. "If I told you the recipe you would have no excuse to visit again."

"Now that I see you again, I need no tea for an excuse."

"I am well past the age of blushing, but sometimes you get me close. What of the boy? Has he joined us? He looks older than I heard."

"He was two or three years younger before the battle. He did something with one of the rings. He wore it." Lanos filled her in on the battle and the aftermath.

Larrina's eyes narrowed and her lips slightly pursed.

"I saw nothing when I looked at him. Yet—So Alanar simply let him go on the first encounter?"

"He seemed a common thief, with the misfortune of stealing from the Katar.

He refused to join the resistance and Alanar felt he was safer away from Arbeneth and told him to run to Argn or Zethicia."

"How did Alanar escape? Last I heard he could scarcely make it from the garden to the toilet. Rumor had it that he was so drunk most of the time that you were handling Arbeneth on your own." Larrina reached out and held his hand, looked into his eyes and let his hand go.

"He is dying, Larrina. Nightmares, constant drinking, with only moments of lucid thought. I owe him my life, but I fear that his leadership of the resistance is over. He must have had help escaping, or the Katar are feeding our intelligence lies."

"Alanar dying, it is hard to believe, Lanos. Harder than you might guess. I have known Alanar a very, very long time. He swore this time he would let himself die, but if he escaped …."

"Let himself die?"

Larrina shook her head, but did not respond. She stared unfocused over Lanos' shoulder.

"How old *are* you Larrina?"

She was startled at his question, but regained her composure. She took his left hand between both of hers again. He could feel how warm they were. He smelled spices, or perfume, or her. He noticed that her grip was firm and there were no wrinkles on her slim hands.

"I am older than you think and I know you are guessing that I am quite old based on our last meeting twenty years ago. You were so young then, Lanos. Now, you are a man."

"I was a man then. In my thirties. Now I am past my prime and slowing down."

"Perhaps, but your thoughts are finally mature."

Larrina squeezed his hand and stood up. Again he admired how fit she looked. The minute wrinkles around her eyes were more from habit then age. As she went to fill her teacup he admired her from behind.

"You're staring at my ass, Lanos."

He looked up, her head was tilted sideways, a smile pulling her mouth. She turned and sat back down.

"What were we talking about," she asked.

He was tempted to say something about her ass.

"Alanar. You have known him even longer than I. How long?"

She shook her head.

"That is for Alanar to tell you, if he chooses. Suffice to say, he is older than he looks, and I know he looks very old."

Lanos was no longer listening. His head nodded forward. She got up and softly kissed him on the eyes.

"I feel young around you, Lanos," she murmured in his dream. Carefully, with only a small grunt, she lifted him up and carried him to a bedroom. No woman could do that he thought, it is only a dream. She checked the dressings on his wounds, then went out.

Chapter 19

Hallam relaxed in her hot pool. The scents of flowers and honey drifted off the surface. Her breasts half floated in the water as she leaned back and concentrated momentarily. Soon the sound of several song birds wafted to her and she smiled with satisfaction. She was just entering that state between wakefulness and sleep when the voices of protest reached her.

"My lord you cannot enter! My lady is bathing and does not wish to be disturbed."

"She'll see me."

A young serving woman came running in. "Lady, it is the Lord Nu Arr. I tried to tell him that you could not be disturbed. I tried locking all the doors, but the latches all seem broken."

"Of course they are. Don't worry. Go fetch me something to wear." She leaned back in the water again and concentrated more. The steam rose off the pool a little more, obscuring her breasts. A large eagle landed on the tree overhanging the pool.

"Lady Hallam, I pardon the interruption, but I must speak with you." Nu Arr's black on black eyes ran quickly over her submerged body. He showed no embarrassment.

"I had heard that you were visiting some of the gods. You seem to be in a panic about some boy."

"Panic is a little strong. Prudent is the way I view it. I'm simply ensuring he is eliminated. Already he has escaped a number of times, once from a group of ten Katar."

"Really, a single boy took on ten Katar? They must be slipping in their training." She sat up, ignoring the fact that her servant had not yet arrived with clothes. "So tell me, is he truly a *catalyst*? Does he have some of your power?" She smiled wickedly at Nu Arr.

"I am sure of it."

"Jealous?" She stood up and strode toward the running servant. Quickly, without rushing, she slipped the loose dress robe on and tied it at the waist. A warm breeze stirred, speeding the drying and keeping her warm. She gestured to the chairs by the pool. "Sit." Half invitation, half command.

He scowled, but sat. She beckoned to the waiting woman. "I will have a glass of Srýll honey wine. He will have … I think a glass of Kinel whiskey." She smiled an evil smile at her little joke. If Nu Arr hated any race, any group, it was the Kinel. His luck just never seemed to hold around them. The Srýll, well she had been their downfall.

"You know that jealousy has nothing to do with it. Change is already afoot and his influence could be catastrophic."

"Just as yours was?"

"I make no pardons for my choices. The Old Ones had their chances. We warned them that Humans would overwhelm them. They could have accepted our help, instead they snubbed us. It was inevitable."

"Lucky for us, Humans are so in need of someone to worship, or our power would not have been enough, even with your influence on events. Of course, we might never have banded together without your influence. You are like a tornado; you draw us in, but destroy along the way." She laid one leg over the other, letting the dress slide back, exposing most of her long legs. Nu Arr looked longingly at her legs, the breeze shifted and blew the dress up even further. She laughed, as she smoothed the dress down.

"Careful, here even your luck is limited. I have been influencing these grounds for centuries." The eagle screeched. A cougar wandered into sight and curled up under the same tree as the eagle.

"Lady of Nature, I would never presume."

"You always presumed. I acknowledge your role in making us all gods, those many years ago. You no doubt want my help in finding and killing the boy. Very well, my priests will join the hunt. So will the birds and beasts that I control. How many of us have you enlisted in this hunt for one mere mortal?"

"With you, nine. Pé is unreachable. He stays by the rivers of Life and Death, where only he can go. I have also enlisted the Katar, but that was easy as the boy has stolen one of their rings. This mere mortal already has drawn powerful friends to his aid."

"Who?"

"I don't know, but those seven Katar killed were not killed by a thief who has no control over his powers. The resistance. Those rebels that try to over-throw the Katar." Their drinks arrived. Nu Arr paused and assessed the servant woman.

"Not with my servants, Luck."

The cougar growled to emphasize her words.

"If he is with the rebels, you should be happy. The Katar are hardly allies to our priesthoods. They steal *ka* as we do."

"We've lived with the Katar for five thousand years. It's a balance of power both sides understand."

"What of the raids? My priests in Zethicia have been calling for my help constantly. Entire villages have been destroyed. Do you think the Tarth have returned? Do you think your thief is somehow part of that?" asked Hallam.

"I don't know. I would call it a coincidence, but ..."

"Yes, it is hard for the god of luck to believe in coincidences isn't it?"

"I am a catalyst, but that does not mean I can make the impossible happen. I can just influence the possible, sometimes. When great events are occurring, than that small influence can be crucial. I feel great things are occurring and we cannot have this additional influence on the wrong side."

She was silent. She enjoyed being a god, all these years, but of late she had felt guilty at the cost imposed on her worshipers. She was not as powerful as the other gods, not receiving as much prayer, nor siphoning off as much *ka* as the others. Her advantage was that of all the gods, she could tap the *ka* of animals and plants. This source was much weaker than Human *ka*, but none-theless a diversified source. Humans perhaps deserved better. Maybe the Ne Na cult, who called the gods parasites, were correct. Yet, she did not want to give up her powers. To survive amongst the gods she needed the combined *ka* of both Humans and other living things.

A catalyst could change everything—but perhaps her special diversity could be leveraged. Maybe *this* catalyst would shift the power toward her. If the Humans' population shrank, or better still the gods suffered a loss of faith, then she would be the only god who could tap *ka,* with the possible exception of Pé. But, Pé did not matter, all he did was play with his rivers. He had not been seen for centuries. Some thought he was dead. The cougar began to purr.

"I will do everything in my power to help you Luck, you can count on me also." She smiled and let the breeze stir her robe once again.

Chapter 20

Devon sat in the library with his children. Larra and Piea on the left side of the desk, Arlec on the right. Arlec felt worn and drawn, still feeling the forced mind probe that his own father had ordered. A crime punishable by death, and his father seemed oblivious to his pain. Arlec knew his father was tough, cold, and calculating, but a mind probe? For the first time Arlec not just resented the old man, he hated him. I could have suffered brain damage, he thought and Devon had simply taken that risk. Because of the ring? He would risk his own son for a ring. We are the Karn family, he thought. Surely, being the most powerful family of the Katar had some benefit. Arlec glanced at his sisters across the desk. Were they part of it? Was Devon going to break all tradition and give the reins of power to women. By the Sea, he thought, I will never let that happen.

Devon looked worried, frown lines on his face, crow's feet standing out around his eyes. The short verbal silence as they settled into their chairs, surrounding their father in a semi-circle, was emphasized by the sharp crack of the fireplace. The fire was hardly necessary given the year round warmth of The Cities, but Devon always had one burning in his study. Arlec had never seen the fire go out. It was a fixture. The glow globes were tastefully placed where they were not obvious, but still provided ample light.

"I called you here with bad tidings. Shara has been killed or kidnapped—by that thief that you let steal your ring." Arlec clenched his jaw, his face white. He cast his eyes downward. Devon continued. "Some of the families suspect Shara was a spy, working for the resistance." He held up his hands as Piea and Larra opened their mouths to defend their sister.

Ah, thought Arlec. You don't trust any of us. Had both his sisters been mind-raped too?

"Seven Katar are dead. Survivors of a group of ten that had the thief trapped. The survivors say that Shara was fighting on the thief's side. I of course refuted that. My daughter would die before turning on the Katar for any reason."

With the last statement he pounded the desk for emphasis.

"I know that one of the rebels you were supposed to have captured killed four of the Katar by himself."

He paused, raised his hand to prevent the questions forming on their lips. He saw the disbelief and concern on their faces.

"Let me finish. The Karn family influence is in danger. Jern is in charge of the rebel destruction now, because you didn't finish the job."

"We were close, we needed more time," Larra said.

Arlec nodded. You can only squeeze information out of prisoners so fast and after the one attack the rebels leaders had all gone into hiding. Simultaneously, the attacks by rebels and even common citizens had increased. Cries for independence from the Katar were heard in all of The Cities.

"The respect and fear that the citizens give the Katar is in jeopardy by the actions of this thief and his allies. Nine major temples have sent priests stressing the urgency of finding and killing this thief. Our family name is being tainted …" a glare at Arlec "… so if by some cruel twist of fate Shara is mixed up with this and not a prisoner, she must be killed. We will tell the families that she was a prisoner and killed by the thief. Silence Piea, I am not done.

"We must finish this business with the thief and the rebels quickly. The raids in Zethicia are now more than raids. Full scale siege of the main city has started. Fortunately, we have the main gateway between here and there and control both ends. We have not allowed many refugees through to keep the panic down, but twenty-five hundred of the Katar have gone through to aid in the battle; as many of the city guard have also gone through. We have even been able to obtain the services of a thousand Yanín, at no small expense. The distraction of the thief and this Alanar with his revolution comes at a crucial time. We have to keep the remaining Katar in The Cities to prevent panic and unrest—dividing our forces. In a few short days this has gone from a stupid mistake," again the pointed look at Arlec, "to full scale rebellion in the cities and all-out war in Zethicia. We can't afford to lose either."

Arlec saw true fear in his father's face. He had never seen him afraid of anything. He also knew his father never exaggerated. His own spies had confirmed that it was indeed Tarth attacking Zethicia. It seemed hard to believe they were actually Tarth, but his father was acting as if they were. The entire Katar elite were being mobilized. Five thousand with rings and many more without, with half of the ring wielders now in Zethicia, stretching their hold on The Cities. War. Arlec found his heart racing. War, including civil war, was opportunity. People died in wars, others gained. He would gain. He would make sure of it.

"I know you love your sister and want to work to aid her, but I cannot trust you will do the right thing if she should be involved. I am sending all three of you to aid in Zethicia." Devon finally allowed Piea to speak.

"Father, we must be allowed to avenge our sister!" She paused, aware that her voice had an edge of hysteria to it. "The thief is in Argn then you know that the women are better suited to finding him there. All female Katar are familiar with Argn. I was a squad leader for training there for five years. Who better to lead the efforts in finding Shara?"

"No, I thought of that, but you love your sister too much. If she is alive then she must be working with them—or the families will assume it. You know that she has too many idealist tendencies. She has never been comfortable with the price of power. I had hoped that the training and discipline of the guard would change her. It is too late to save her and we must ensure that the Karn family does not lose further prestige and standing. No, I have placed key personnel with the Katar in Argn who know what to do when the time comes—if it comes. I truly hope that she is already dead, for the good of the Katar and the Karn family."

Larra placed a comforting arm around her sister and pulled her toward the door. Arlec still sat, ashen faced, wracked with guilt and fury. "Father, how can I help in Zethicia like this?" He held up his left hand, the band of untanned white making a ghost of a ring.

Devon stood up and went to the fireplace.

"You know I had to know for sure that you had not betrayed the Katar, Arlec. You are the heir to the Karn. There are things I should show you. Teach you. This is one."

He rolled up his right sleeve and reached into the flames, pulling out a box hidden behind a hidden door in the flames. His flesh was unharmed

"A talisman I picked up years ago when visiting the Hrýll during negotiations. Not quite an illusion. Anyone not wearing the matching talisman," he patted his chest "would burn. No metal, wood, or other substance can survive past what looks like the fire. The fire burns with or without logs, but the logs keep the illusion real."

He opened the box and withdrew a ring; a duplicate of the one Arlec had lost. Arlec peered into the open box, but Devon snapped the lid shut and returned it to its hiding spot in the fireplace.

"Needless to say Arlec, if you lose this one, there will be more than a small intrusion into your mind to pay."

Arlec slipped on the ring wordlessly. No, he would not pay any price again to his father. He rubbed his temple hoping to keep the pain that had haunted him since the *small intrusion* into his mind. Then he rubbed his new ring. A family ring, not some inferior. Yes, war and revolution simultaneously was definitely an opportunity. Already, one of his sisters had shown that women were too weak to lead. Devon was past his time. Arlec got up to leave, giving a short bow to his father. As he turned, his gaze rested momentarily on the fireplace. What else lay in there?

Chapter 21

Alanar stayed on foot as he made his way to Argn. It would be good to see Larrina again after all these years. He went alone, as most would not expect a rich man to be either on foot, or alone. Few who had known him recently would recognize him. He was just slightly beefy at this point, a scant ten days, a full week, since the garden incident. The lost weight did not lead to flaps of loose skin. The color had returned to his face. He had not had a drink since then. This last was almost as big a burden as his conscience. He licked his lips thinking of a nice brandy.

He had been ready to die in peace this time. He'd promised Larrina. Fund the revolution, organize it, but he had made sure that he was not the only head, nor heart of the group. He had made sure that the right people would know more in the event of death, which for many years he felt was coming and had welcomed. Once again, he was cheated out of his own demise.

It had taken seven days in hiding before he felt strong enough for the trek to Argn. He posed as an old homeless beggar, which no one had trouble believing the first few days. The guise helped him keep in touch with the news and gossip; no one bothered to keep quiet around a beggar.

The thief, Tsom, was becoming key. He should have seen something in the boy, but he had been too drunk, or too feeble. More than once as his strength returned he mourned the loss of his old friend and servant.

He had never paid much attention to the superstition surrounding the Eclipse of the Five Moons. He had assumed it was some game that Nu Arr or his priesthood had been playing. That too had been short sighted, Nu Arr was no fool.

Alanar's route was similar to Tsom's. He stayed at better inns, but the well-traveled road was so busy that he did not stand out in any way. When floaters approached, he respectfully got out of their way. There were no Katar on the roads, only police and guards. Most of the guard were patrolling trade routes or had gone through the gateway to Zethicia to fight. Occasionally, he had to avoid a priest, but he guessed that they were not after him, but looking for Tsom.

The fourth day, one day out of Argn, Alanar stopped at an already colorful inn. The large quantity of green indicated that the establishment was run by a man, and thus was likely to have more male customers. This suited Alanar as he did not want to stand out. Walking into the well-lit common room, he noticed five priests of Gakko Sama, the moon goddess. Given that Nakana had five moons, it was not surprising that she was considered a major deity throughout the land and not just in one city as many of the other gods. Her priesthood was generally benevolent, which made Alanar wonder how the orders to hunt down and kill a young man must have gone over. He sat down close to the priests, but not so close as to attract attention. His hearing was good and he was adept at filtering out background noise. After a while his patience panned out.

"There are rumors that the boy was born on the Fivefold Eclipse."

"What of it? Hundreds were born that night, maybe thousands. All received the blessings of the temple. We lost track of many of them, but not all died of *accidents*."

"What if he was born exactly during the eclipse? Wouldn't that make him the one from prophesy?"

"You make too much of prophesy. The Nu Arr temple made that up centuries ago, knowing that it would sound impressive when the eclipse occurred. We had charts even then. We knew when it was going to occur. Do you remember how many worshipers we gained that year? How much money? Don't be gullible."

"Still, it does not seem right to be trying to kill someone born on the Fivefold Eclipse. It just doesn't feel right."

"Nonsense. We will simply say that the birth was an ill omen, not a positive one. Why should the birth be a positive event? Maybe it portends great evil, not good."

"That sounds reasonable."

"May Pé bless his soul when we send it his way."

"You have not heard? We are to make sure he is true deathed. We have a talisman that when placed on the body will destroy the last of his *ka*. No one wants him to be reborn again. He is bad luck."

"I don't like it. The Fivefold eclipse and true death."

The last statement was followed by the oldest of the priests tilting his head back and swallowing his drink. Alanar could smell the whiskey. Not a bad blend. His mouth watered slightly and his stomach growled. He took a mouthful of food, trying to control the trembling of his hand.

***

He arrived at Larrina's midday. He paused to gaze at the mural with the small bantri tree. The sight caused a mixed flood of emotions. As if sensing his presence, Larrina came out the front door and watched him. She did not seem astonished at his loss of weight. As he walked up to her he smiled. This too would have surprised those who knew him recently. It was not one of his usual smiles, laced with irony, sardonic, or a touch of meanness. Warmth lit up his face as he reached and pulled her into his arms and gave her a familiar kiss on the lips. She did not struggle.

"Alanar, it has been too long." She pushed back a bit, staying in his arms and looking carefully into his eyes. She seemed satisfied with what she saw. He noticed that her nose dilated briefly. *Yes*, he thought, *I am sober.*

"Yes, Lar. Ten, fifteen years?"

"Try twenty."

They strode into the house, arm in arm, where Lanos was sitting at the table finishing a meal. He dropped his fork and reached for his sword, then stopped. "Alanar?"

"Yes. Yes, I know. I look different," he grinned

His smile faded, thinking of the cost.

The last of the beefiness was fading. His high cheekbones were showing. His chin, without the reams of fat, was strong, yet not too broad. His hair was still white, but the roots were already showing an inky black, almost-blue, the way a raven's feather reflects a black then blue sheen. His skin had darkened, as if he had a deep tan. He stepped forward and clasped arms with Lanos. His grip was iron strong.

"Where are the thief and the woman?"

"The woman is fussing over Tsom, who is up in the bedroom. He is … older."

"The Katar?"

"No, I think he did this to himself. He healed the woman. She was past saving; her guts were slit open and spilled inside of her. That and he slowed time around us, as near as I can tell."

"The ring?"

"Yes. Larrina hinted that you might still be alive. And changed."

Alanar looked questioningly at Larrina. She smiled and untangled her arm from his. Lanos rose and stood behind Larrina, placing a hand on her shoulder; which did not go unnoticed. She could take whomever she wanted as a lover, he thought.

She continued, "The boy is currently a pawn, being pursued by everyone for their own interests. What are your plans for him? Is he to have any free choice, or is it to die; to be used by us?"

Alanar stopped the flow of questions with a look, one that they both knew well.

"Get the boy … Tsom," he ordered, "and we shall see. Even a pawn can win a game if used properly."

"Used being the operative word," muttered Lanos as he went to fetch Tsom.

Chapter 22

"They'll both be down in a minute. Tsom is stronger, but Shara keeps fussing over him," said Lanos. He joined Larrina and Alanar at the large kitchen table made of ironwood. Lanos admired the dark sheen and gazed at Larrina's reflection directly across the table. Her lithe movements and gentle smile continued to stir dormant partitions of his mind. He found the smell of cinnamon that followed her everywhere distracting, more so than the similar perfume Shara wore. On Larrina it held a musty overtone and carried with it a feeling of wellbeing; was it Hrýll as Shara's perfume was? Forcing his gaze to the left, where Alanar sat at the head of the table, he waited for an opening in the conversation.

Alanar's change was more than physical. He smiled as he spoke with Larrina and chit-chatted about unimportant things. Alanar chit-chatting, Lanos mentally shook his head at the impossibility. The voice and the eyes were the same, but this man was a shadow of the fat, flaccid bitter old man that he had been serving for so many years.

The aging Tsom had undergone reminded Lanos of his own narrowly avoided fate, years ago. Damn the Katar and their gods, he thought. Leeches. Parasites. We need to defeat them. He pounded his fist on the table in anger.

Lanos and Larrina stopped their conversation and looked questioningly at Lanos. He felt a small flush of embarrassment. Might as well speak now.

"We've been plotting and planning against the Katar for years. You kept telling me that there was a was a weapon the Katar had that could be used against them, if you only had a way of getting it. Stealing it."

Alanar frowned and rubbed his temples.

"Memory?"

"Yes. It's all mixed up. Chaos. Pieces missing."

Larrina nodded, stood and walked behind Alanar's chair. She placed her hands on his head and pushed gently forward until his head was bowed. Then she started massaging his head in a pattern that Lanos had a hard time following.

"There is only one such weapon that I can think of. The Sphere of Banishment," said Larrina. "I have volunteered countless times to steal it, but Alanar always refuses to let me go. It is somewhere in the Karn family compound."

Lanos was surprised, but tried to not let it show. Larrina as a thief? Why did she think she had a chance where others would not?

Alanar rubbed a hand over his face looking almost confused, then his expression hardened and he leaned forward, his hands clasped in front, on the table. Lanos could see the beads of sweat on his forehead. Was it the lack of drink? He hadn't seen Alanar drink anything since he arrived. He seemed to be constantly fighting for control.

"Lanos, I have been battling the Katar for longer than you imagine. You are an important lieutenant, but I can't tell you everything. You know more than anyone, save Larrina, of my plans."

Lanos nodded. This was probably true. He was in charge of coordinating between the cells of resistance. Yet, often the orders Alanar gave made no sense.

"You … you never do anything just to spite them. Everything is planned with you. I don't always know your plans, but I know you always have a plan. A scheme. Or multiple schemes. You are a puppet master, never participating due to your health."

Of course that was before this change. Lanos had not seen Alanar leave his compound. Even when he intervened to stay Lanos' execution by *ka* draining, he had done so from afar.

"So, what is your plan now, Alanar? If ever the time was ripe for action, this is it. The Katar are split between Zethicia and The Cities."

"Yes, what exactly is your plan for me," said Tsom.

They all turned toward the doorway, where Tsom stood, with Shara, the Katar woman behind him, a worried look on her face.

Larrina smiled and gestured to the empty chairs at the table and went to fetch tea. Larrina was always brewing tea and each seemed to have the desired effect on the drinker: healing, relaxing, waking, or sleeping. She set a cup in front of Tsom, who sniffed it suspiciously, took a sip, then smiled back at her. Lanos knew the feeling. It was hard not to smile at Larrina. Especially after her tea.

Alanar rubbed his face again.

"I … we, have need of a thief. A special thief," said Alanar.

Tsom's eyes narrowed.

"I won't ask what happened to you, physically. Was the fat man an elaborate disguise? Is that how you fooled me into acting like an idiot? So, suddenly you need me? After casting me out to the Katar, like chum from a fishing boat?" He made a spitting noise, but did not actually spit on the floor. "Why, by the Sea, would I do anything to help you?"

"Because we did, in the end, help you. You hate the Katar. They killed your parents. Your mother."

Tsom's eyes opened wide, he glared at Shara who shook her head. This was the first Lanos had heard of this.

"They killed your mother for the same reason they would kill Larrina if they had a chance."

"Because she was a traitor? A rebel like us?" asked Shara, who had remained standing by the door.

"I suppose all Kinel are traitors and rebels now. We are dead, as a race, because of the genocidal parasites, the Katar," Larrina said it softly, but her tone was icy hard.

She gestured and her face changed. Her skin darkened, except her face. From her chin to her forehead the dark skin drew to a peak, leaving her cheeks and eyes pale. Her hair suddenly turned pure white. Not the white of age, which was the lack of color, but an actual white pigment.

The effect, combined with her look of cool anger made Lanos draw back. She was beautiful, but alien. Kinel. He had never seen Larrina undisguised. The Katar said they were evil, that they stole your *ka* while you slept. He knew that it was just a story spread by the Katar, yet he still instinctively drew back seeing her like this; but part of him was drawn toward her.

Shara let out a small shriek, backing out of the room a step. She seemed genuinely frightened. Her hand dropped to where her sword would have hung and she held up her left hand, now bereft of its ring as if to ward off Larrina. Larrina laughed, her face softened, and as suddenly as it had appeared, her visage disappeared and she became the light skinned woman with red hair again.

Tsom had not leapt back. Rather he looked almost as if he were going to breakdown and cry.

"Once, when my mother did not know I was watching her, she sat in front of mirror and suddenly looked as you did. She touched her hair and cheeks and wept. I never let her know I saw her like that," Tsom said.

Larrina nodded with understanding. She reached across the table and touched Tsom's cheek. "You are part Kinel, yet I do not see through your chameleon effect. You are very strong, or the Kinel blood is weak in your veins—just as it is with the Katar."

There was a sharp intake of breath from Shara.

"What are you saying? That is a lie," she strode forward, anger in her eyes as she again reached for the non-existent sword.

Larrina smiled with pity. She looked to Alanar. "May I?" she asked, holding out her hand. He pulled a string from around his neck up. Arlec's ring was tied to it. He tossed it to Larrina. Shara looked greedily at the ring, but did not try and take it. Larrina held up her hand and slipped it on. Shara cringed with her eyes half closed, then opened them wide. Nothing had happened. No death. No devastation.

"Yes, Dear," Larrina said holding her ringed hand toward Shara, "the Katar are of Kinel blood. Very dilute. Very weak. The Katar hate us because they are us, in a way. You hate us because you fear we are stronger than you. You don't even have the power to use these properly, you use them only as weapons, as a drain upon all who are unfortunate to be nearby. The Katar know only one thing, how to destroy."

"Can you teach me how to use it in different ways? Do you know how to use it?"

"Like this?" The ring on Larrina's finger glowed brightly and Shara leapt back in fear. Lanos was about to, but then noticed Alanar sitting back smiling. Lanos knew the weakness one felt around the Katar when their rings were active. Sometimes it was subtle, but he knew it well and he was not feeling it now. Somehow, Larrina was activating the ring without hurting them. He calmed himself and waited for the interplay to continue.

Shara must have sensed that she was in no danger also. She relaxed and leaned forward.

"The rings were made for Kinel. Full blooded Kinel. What you do is only for battle in extreme situations … what we did was use our own *ka*, not others. It amplifies. Real Kinel can shape *ka* as no others can, not even the Srýll. We cannot create talisman, that is true, but we are independent. She gestured with her hand and a feeling of energy swept through Lanos. He felt rested as he had never felt before. Whole. All aches and pains were gone. He looked at the others and they all felt it, except perhaps Alanar. He appeared to be either making a show of not feeling the effect, or was indeed impervious to it.

Shara staggered back. "It is … wonderful. How …? Teach me?" She stopped and Lanos could see her absorbing her own words, grappling with the implication that Larrina spoke the truth. The Katar were architects of genocide over their very own kin. She sat down and buried her mouth in her hands and simply watched Larrina and the others. Then she looked to Tsom. The others did too.

"Which brings us back to you, doesn't it Tsom?" said Larrina. The ring flared and for an instant Tsom visage changed. His skin turned dark, almost black, except for the cheeks and forehead. As with Larrina a peak of dark skin reached up on top of pale cheeks and eyes. His eyes were golden and his hair bright white. As suddenly as his visage changed it reverted back. Larrina gasped in pain and pulled off the ring which had flared brightly. "Stop, Tsom! You're not in danger. Stop. She covered the ring with her hand. Lanos felt momentarily weak and then it faded. Alanar was nodding in a satisfied manner. Shara was looking ill.

Alanar held out his hand and Larrina tossed the ring back to him. In a flash it disappeared back around his neck.

"You see, Larrina?" Alanar asked.

She nodded, tears in her eyes. Happiness or fear, Lanos could not tell.

"Once I heard the story of your battle from Larrina and Lanos, I guessed on your past. It was the same story for most Kinel. I asked Larrina to test my theory. Tsom, you are the purest Kinel I have seen ... in a very, very long time,"

Alanar looked again to Larrina for confirmation, which she gave.

"You are strong, but in a way that is hard to pin down. Larrina did not feel your strength, which is rare. Kinel can usually sense each other's strength. It is how the Katar were able to hunt them down so easily. Your strength seems to be in staying hidden, or blending in. Helpful in surviving, or in thieving. A perfect thief to steal from the Katar. To steal from the Karn family."

Again a noise from Shara. She is not good at hiding her emotions, thought Lanos.

"What is it that is so important?" Shara asked.

"Lanos reminded me of a weapon. An artifact from centuries ago ..." Alanar stopped and rubbed his temples as if fighting a headache, or thinking.

"It was used to banish the Tarth thousands of years ago," finished Larrina.

Lanos rocked back in his chair. Banish. If it kept the Katar away for thousands years, that was as good as wiping them out.

"I'm guessing this weapon is not used on one person at a time?"

"No. No it is not a subtle weapon. All living beings, not plants but all other living beings within a radius of the sphere is banished," said Larrina. She pushed a cup of tea to Alanar and motioned for him to drink.

"Then we use it on the Katar and Tarth at the same time," said Lanos. Get them to join in battle near Zethicia and use it.

"We don't have it yet, Lanos," muttered Alanar. His eyes were haunted. Something was bothering him. Lanos had never seen him so troubled. So indecisive.

"Assuming we get it. We get the resistance to stop for the time being, allowing the Katar to send more of their forces to Zethicia, then we destroy the gateway and strike. Strike the Katar and Tarth with this sphere and strike hard in The Cities. Against five thousand Katar armed with rings, we were out classed, but a thousand, spread across all The Cities, we can take that many."

"What about the city guards?" asked Tsom.

"Assume as many as eleven thousand city guards," said Lanos.

"That's a lot," said Tsom.

Lanos smiled, tasting victory.

"There are twenty thousand in the resistance. If all out fighting broke out, I'll wager another twenty thousand would join us."

"It's a good plan," said Alanar, also smiling. "We need to ensure that even without the sphere, it'll work.

"With or without the sphere, we let the Tarth weaken the Katar, possibly cripple them. Then, we use the sphere, or if there is no sphere, we come to Zethicia's aid," Alanar finished

Lanos glanced at Larrina, across from him. It was hard not to see her real image superimposed upon what he was looking at. She was shaking her head, hopefully for the same reason he was about to voice.

"We can't do that, Alanar. Even you would not sacrifice so many innocents that lie between the Katar and the Tarth. Thousands could die, if the reports of their initial attacks are accurate. Tens of thousands. They burn entire villages and towns to the ground. No mercy, just destruction. We can't allow that. If word got out that we waited and let that happen we end up being as evil as the Katar," Lanos gestured toward Shara who scowled deeply, her normally too large lips narrowed and pursed in anger. He had not meant to include her in the broad brush of all Katar.

Alanar shook his head, but his face showed pain.

"We must weaken the Katar, lower their numbers. There are five thousand of them with rings …"

"The Tarth are the first force in millennia that can actually destroy the Katar. We let them break the Katar, then we come to the rescue."

"And become the next Katar?" asked Shara.

"No, we destroy the rings so that there will never be another Katar. It is bad enough that the gods leech *ka* off of fool worshippers. But, those worshippers do it willingly, if in ignorance. With the Katar, they have no choice. There will be no more Katar. No more true death in the name of order." Alanar banged the table. Lanos was astonished to see a crack in the wood where his fist hand landed. Ironwood did not crack. What exactly had happened to Alanar? He was stronger, but seemed almost ruthlessly cold now.

Larrina seemed to be thinking the same thing, but she seemed to understand something that he did not.

"Either way we need the artifact. The Sphere of Banishment, the *San Par'eh Shante*. We agree that the Katar should not have it. In fact, they probably do not know what it is. Devon, your father," she nodded to Shara, "has kept it and other artifacts hidden for centuries from the other Katar. He feels it is good to have resources that others don't know about."

Shara nodded reluctant acknowledgement.

"That sounds like my father, but I have no idea where he might have hidden it, or any other artifact. The Katar do have Hrýll weapons, as you know. The flame cannons used on ships are also mounted on floaters. The Katar are hardly defenseless against the Tarth."

"The Tarth are immune to fire and heat," said Alanar, leaning back with a strangely satisfied look on his face. "If the Katar remember their legends, they will remember that."

"Oh," Shara looked shocked as she considered. "Fire is the main mass weapon of all the armies."

"Indeed. The Tarth were not defeated, my girl. They were banished. Banished because they could not be defeated. Even by five thousand Katar who knew how to use those rings in ways that the Katar today do not. Even with the Kinel aiding the half-blood Katar." Shara paled slightly at the reminder of her blood and looked at Larrina and Tsom.

"The artifact will be important. Without it … things will get messy."

"We can continue the argument as to when to use the artifact later, but we need to find out if Tsom is with us, or not," said Larrina. She rose to fill everyone's tea cups and to wipe the spilled tea from Alanar's pounding fist. Lanos noticed that the cinnamon scent had returned. He wasn't sure when it had disappeared, but the return accented that it had been gone and everyone seemed to relax ever so slightly. While Larrina moved smoothly around the table, the rest turned to Tsom. Lanos noted that the added years in physical age seemed to be matched by a maturity and calmness in manner too. The young thief, in a few short weeks, was no longer so young. He had killed. He had aged. He had found a connection to the rebels in Larrina. Would he join their cause now, after the initial hesitation?

Shara walked behind Tsom and rested her hands on his shoulders.

"Tsom," she said softly, but they could all hear, "we need you. I need you. The Askatasuna needs you."

Tsom reached up and touched Shara's hand and held on.

"I've been running my whole life from the Katar. I have always seen them as a single evil entity. Knowing that they are not all alike," his eyes flashed toward Shara, who flushed lightly, "and that they are actually of the same blood as me," Shara shook her head in disbelief, "changes things. If I help, you have to swear you will use the artifact to aid Zethicia as quickly as possible. Larrina and Lanos are right, we cannot become like … most of the Katar." Again, the look toward Shara.

"I cannot do that, son," said Alanar. "But, I can promise that we will debate it further and I will listen to what Larrina and Lanos have to say. We will do what is best for mankind in the long run and I can promise that I have no aspirations to rule, in any form, let alone as the Katar do. After this is over. After the Katar are crushed, the people will rule themselves, however foolishly they decide to do that."

Tsom frowned, obviously not liking the reply. He looked to Larrina, who smiled back and nodded. He glanced at Shara, who also nodded her head. He ignored Alanar and Lanos.

"If someone like Larrina and Shara trusts you, then so do I. For now. Tell me what I have to do." He leaned back and sipped his tea, looking relaxed and at peace with his decision. Lanos had enough experience with soldiers to know that look. He was wound up tighter than a catapult rope and it was not clear if the rope was going to break or simply let loose. Lanos agreed with the statement, he would trust Tsom. For now.

Chapter 23

Barnus stood on one of the old guard towers of Zethicia proper, gazing West through a Disc of Seeing. The height of the tower, over fifteen stories, combined with the old talisman allowed him to see almost two hundred marks to the west as if it were just below. It was a scene that caused the old warrior's stomach to clench as if someone had reached in and curled a fist around it. He would have preferred to avert his gaze, but he needed to know the full nature of their foe.

He was gazing at a small town, Vel perhaps. There were so many small towns surrounding Zethicia, which stood on the edge of the Muglanth Plains. The city was the hub of a giant wheel of agriculture. Small towns, trading centers, were scattered along the spokes and rim. Zethicia referred to both the city and the entire wheel. There were a few hundred thousand scattered on the wheel and almost a million in the city. Still, this made Zethicia small in population when compared to The Cities. The tower was born of early conflict and the lack of natural defenses, but Zethicia had not fought in a real war for a thousand years. The small town was burning.

He understood loot and burn as a tactic, but this was burn to kill. The enemy force had the small town surrounded and simply kept lobbing huge balls of fire from the trebuchets. The range of these was incredible, further indication of the strength of those using them. As the villagers fled they were torn apart by huge dogs, the size of small ponies. Torn apart and eaten. He moved the Disc away from that and focused on the army surrounding the village. The Disc was at its maximum magnification, but some details were hard to make out. There seemed to be two races in the army, neither were familiar to him, but he knew the leaders were said to be Tarth. *Daemons.*

The leaders were large Humanoid figures that wore almost no armor, or even clothes for that matter. Their skin had a pink, almost red tinge to it, as if they were southerners and had a bad sunburn. All had white blond hair. He might have guessed that they were albino, but even at this distance he could tell that was not the case. Although these red giants were the leaders, it was they who were manning the trebuchets. They lifted boulders that must have weighed over a ton to the leather pouch on one side of the lever. Hauling the weights up they then combined the counter weight with their incredible strength to send the balls of flame and stone flying.

The smaller men outnumbered the giants by ten to one. They were covered in light fur. Not skins, but their own fur. Barnus was reminded of apes, but the fur was like a short haired dog and their faces were very Human like. They wore armor. Many were swordsmen, with a few spearman and archers. He wished the Disc could somehow provide sound, but no doubt he would not understand the language.

The village destruction did not tell him as much as he had hoped. There was no fighting, it was simply a slaughter. It showed coordination and cruel intelligence of the group, but did not show how well they fought hand to hand. Given their discipline and strength, he guessed it was better than his own men. Ignoring the carnage visible through the Disc he carefully did his best to count the enemy. His estimate was 8,000 give or take a few hundred. A clearing of a throat at his rear startled him.

"Sir, the Katar are arriving from The Cities through the gateway. Their commander wishes to speak to you and refuses to put any of the Katar under our command."

"Damn arrogant sons of Yanín. No doubt they want special quarters also."

It had not been a serious question, but the look on his captain's face showed that this was indeed true. Well, they were doomed without the skill, expertise, and special powers of the Katar. Much as he hated having them in Zethicia, he was relieved that they were arriving. The Katar and the council must have realized that ultimately the destruction of Zethicia was dangerous to The Cities also. That huge teaming mass of civilization that thought the world centered around them. They could not even grow enough to feed themselves. If it were not for the qenar and their Katar .... He let the thought disappear. He knew that he, just as the rest of the world, resented the power The Cities had. For over a thousand year they were the center of power on Nakana and even the gods favored them. Zethicia had only one real priesthood, the god of weather. The Cities had all ten major gods represented. Their own single god did not seem disposed to helping them now. Certainly the prayers of the village he had been watching had not been answered.

He instructed the captain to keep watching through the Disc and take notes. Gathering all of his manners and politeness, but leaving his pride behind, he went to greet the Katar.

Chapter 24

Be Na Tarth, First of the Tarth, watched the village burn with small satisfaction. He hated all Humans, but took no real pleasure in their suffering. He knew most of his army did. Their hatred, like his, could never be satiated, but they took glee in sending in the Maite dogs to kill and eat. Many laughed at the occasional Human who was still breathing as the dogs ate them. If it were completely his choice, he would have killed them swiftly. Yes, they were only Human and descendants of those who had banished the *daemon* lords eons ago. But, he wished them only exterminated, nothing more. Of course their *ka* as they died would prove useful in the future.

To date the Humans had offered little resistance. His men had been worried that their tiny force would be overwhelmed by the combined forces of Humans, Hrýll, Srýll, Riconé, Kinel, and Yanín. Their initial delight was hard to contain when they found out that the Kinel had been utterly destroyed and only remnants of the other races remained. The stories that the Human prisoners—before they died—told were hard to believe. Humans had grown in numbers that were impossible; tens of millions in what used to be small cities near the qenar mines of the Hrýll and Srýll, who had been driven completely out of the area, and were now virtually slave races doomed to make talismans for the Humans. Hundreds of thousands scattered in other cities, all paying tribute in one way or another to the population center called "The Cities." The sheer number of Humans was initially daunting. This area called Zethicia had been a small village when the Tarth were banished.

His apprehension at those numbers was partially assuaged after the first few encounters on the plains. The Humans were pitiful fighters, worse than at the time of the War of Banishment. They must have grown soft after defeating all the old races. His small army of nine thousand was all he had and most of those were Chimi, their slaves.

Two thousand were on reconnaissance missions, with orders to hit and run, but never to fully engage. His escape portal from the 95th plane, which both he and the Humans referred to as Hell, had lasted only a short time. Thousands of his troops were still stuck on Hell, with no way to get here and he no longer had the power to open a portal. He fingered the jade medallion on his huge, bare, red chest. So much *ka* had been required and only nine thousand had made it through. The Humans were rich in *ka*. Soon, enough will have died to power another portal. The added bonus was that those who died would not be reborn to bother the *daemon* lords again. The Humans referred to this as true death, yet the deaths on Hell had all been true. Let them taste their own punishment. Only on this plane were you reborn. Did the Humans know? Would they have acted any differently? It did not matter. Not now.

Be Na Tarth ground his teeth thinking of Hell and all those left behind. So little was known of the planes. Even he had been surprised at the time differential. Many thousands of years had passed here. Humans had forgotten what battle with the Tarth was like; this was a huge advantage, but the Human capacity to reproduce was astounding. It would be hard to wipe them all out. It would take time. But, he had time. Now that he understood the time difference, the desperation to open another portal quickly was lessened. They could take their time reaping the *ka* of mankind for years, and only a short time would have passed for his race stuck on Hell.

He leaned his head back and let the warmth of the sun he had missed so much bath his face.

It was good to be home. Soon, the Humans would remember what it was like to face the Tarth. This time, there would be no mercy, no treaties, no betrayal.

Chapter 25

Shara sat on the edge of her bed on the second floor of Larrina's home. She didn't trust Alanar. Lanos, whom she had known for years without actually meeting, she trusted. Alanar was out to utterly destroy the Katar at any cost. The end justifies the means. Shara wanted the Katar give up rule, but utter destruction wasn't necessary. She would have to watch Alanar carefully.

She struggled with the knowledge that Larrina and Tsom were Kinel. The prejudices of a lifetime of stories conflicted with what she saw and knew. When Larrina had put on the ring the feeling of peace, wellbeing and happiness was powerful. During that time she had felt drawn toward Tsom as if he were part of her. It was as if the power of the ring were a drug, more powerful than anything she had felt. This could not come from something evil. From the Kinel of myth and stories she'd heard. If Alanar and Larrina were to believed, she had Kinel blood flowing through her veins also. This didn't frighten her, but it made the actions and teachings of the Katar harder to take.

Her task, up here alone, was to think of where her father would hide valuable old talismans. Artifacts. The Sphere of Banishment.

Planning to rob her father, her family, seemed like a bigger betrayal than the information she had been feeding Lanos for years. Stupid, she thought. I would be executed for either offense. Yet, it hurt. She had a hard time concentrating.

A knock interrupted her.

Tsom entered.

"Yes," she tried to keep any warmth out of her voice.

"Here," Tsom held out her ring, his hand trembling. He looked so … mature now. The aging fit him well, it matched the way she thought of him. Still, the loss of enough *ka* to cause visible aging … she rubbed her stomach in sympathetic pain.

She stood and closed the distance between them. She placed her left hand on top of his extended hand, her right underneath it.

"Are you sure? It seems you can use it more effectively than I can, if Larrina is correct." She stared into his eyes, trying to see past the chameleon effect she now knew he had. She could almost see flashes of gold in his eyes.

He returned her gaze and pulled her closer.

"I. I don't want any harm to come to you. The ring will help protect you."

She pulled him lower and gave him a kiss. It was intended as a thank you kiss, but it turned to something else as he responded with amazing strength and passion.

The ring fell to the floor, forgotten.

***

Shara lay looking at Tsom, asleep beside her. His passion had exhausted him utterly in a way she had never seen with a man. Was it the loss of *ka*, or something else? When he had peaked, his chameleon effect had dropped and she had found it exciting and tender at the same time. In that moment he had been completely vulnerable and she had cried out in pleasure with him.

She hesitated a moment before performing the cleansing meditation that all Katar women knew. She did not want to get pregnant, not now. She gazed at him a moment longer and then closed her eyes and looked within, felt for any stirrings of life within her. She winced with sadness as she felt that the egg within her was alive, fertilized. Steeling herself, she willed it loose, to flow free. It took only a few moments, yet felt longer.

Tsom stirred in his sleep, a small groan escaped his lips and then he was still again. She opened her eyes and wiped a single tear away. She put on a robe, bent down and picked up the ring, slipped it on her hand and went to the bathroom down the hall.

Chapter 26

Tsom was growing to like this new Alanar. Alanar trained with him daily and would occasionally compliment him on his natural speed or even on a trick or two Tsom had picked up.

"Your eye-hand coordination is exceptional, Tsom. Are you sure you're not tapping your *ka* to speed yourself up? It's dangerous and a waste to do so."

Alanar glanced at Larrina, who shook her head. Lanos, standing next to her, also shook his head, but in amazement—although Tsom was not sure if it was at Alanar, or himself. The practice was thrice daily, and at the end of each he would drop in exhaustion. He was not fully recovered from his injuries and Alanar was pushing him hard. The desire to move quickly was tempered by the knowledge that Tsom needed to be in top form if he was to succeed in stealing the Sphere from the Karn compound.

As he trained, Tsom probed Alanar for more information on the Kinel, his own powers, and the history of the Katar.

"Why do you think I must have some power related to my hands?" He presented his side to make himself a smaller target and bent his knees to give himself more balance.

"The way you caught the knife the first time we met."

Alanar attacked with the wooden sword, demonstrating what they had discussed before this session.

"I simply caught it."

He slapped the blade to the side and jumped a step back.

"Downward." Hissed Alanar. Tsom nodded at the mistake. He had struck the blade too flatly, the edge could have been turned to cut him. Suddenly, not prearranged, Alanar's free hand whipped forward, a long knife in his hand flying the short distance. Just as suddenly, Tsom found himself holding it, blade first.

"Look at your hand." Alanar commanded.

Tsom looked at the hand with the knife.

"Yeah?"

"No blood. No cut. I held nothing back on that throw. It's a double-edged blade, very sharp. I'm fast. Yet you now hold the blade without a scratch. Your hands act on their own. Remember that. Don't force them, let them act. That is part of *your* natural Kinel talent."

Often there would be a similar lesson, or test, in their training. Occasionally, Tsom would be injured and Alanar would seem surprised and simultaneously oddly concerned. Without discussing it, neither of them ever mentioned the injuries to Larrina if she wasn't present.

Tsom guessed that he was growing fond of Alanar partially due to Larrina. She obviously liked Alanar and had known him for a long time. There was an easy camaraderie between her and Alanar. With her, Alanar was less intense, less obsessed with revenge, less in charge, and more Human. Tsom still thought of himself as "Human" and the expression held regardless as to whether he was a half-breed or not.

Larrina felt like a combination of mother, sister, and one of the "sisters" from the brothel. She exuded sexuality, which he noticed and felt, but he still did not feel strongly drawn to her sexually. He admitted there was an attraction, but she was too old. Plus, he found his mind wandering to Shara more often than he liked to admit.

When thinking of Larrina he thought of tea. She was always brewing. Her teas were somehow different for each person, even when poured from the same pot. Lanos would comment on the citrus smell and how they soothed his aching muscles and relaxed him. Alanar said the smell reminded him of Hrýll brandy and his eyes would close and he would inhale deeply. The slight shake that affected Alanar less and less each day, would disappear completely when he drank tea with them. To Tsom the tea smelled like cinnamon, vaguely like Shara's perfume and he would stop worrying about his powers and the upcoming task he must perform. Shara seemed the least affected by it, but her tight mouth and tense eyes would relax when sipping. Once she commented that it smelled lightly of apple blossoms.

Dinners were simple, but tasteful meals that Larrina prepared. Of the group she was the only one that did not practice fighting. Even Shara joined in the practices at Alanar's request. Tsom suspected that he was trying to get Shara to show them some of the Katar training that Shara had received. His suspicions were confirmed during one practice between Alanar and Shara. She pressed him with a standard attack and he growled something about holding back. She shook her head in a negative, but then he attacked with an unusual set of strokes that in a standard sword fight would have been disastrous, except if one had extreme speed. Suddenly, Alanar demonstrated such extreme speed that Tsom's eyes could not follow. Shara responded instinctively with unusual micro movements of her own sword that indicated she knew exactly what the strokes were even if she could not fully follow them and then she countered with her own set of unusual strokes. Tsom caught the look of astonishment in her eyes and the respect at his speed.

Tsom asked Alanar why Larrina never practiced.

"Will she not be fighting at all in the revolution? Is Larrina more of a sidelines person?"

Alanar looked at him puzzled for a moment, then roared with laughter. He laughed until tears came to his eyes. Lanos and Larrina came from inside the house to see what was happening. Wiping tears from his eyes Alanar looked up and saw Larrina. He called out.

"Tsom is afraid that you cannot fight since you never practice." He convulsed into laughter again. Larrina scowled at them both and spun around and returned to the house. Lanos looked puzzled. Between gasps of air Alanar said, "Trust me, Tsom, if you see Larrina wielding a sword, you do not want to be the target." Lanos' eyebrows went up and he glanced at the doorway where Larrina had just slammed the door.

Two weeks went by quickly. One evening Alanar looked up from his tea in the sitting room at Shara and Tsom.

"You leave tomorrow. We simply don't have any more time. Our intelligence indicates that the main battle between the Tarth and Zethicia will occur in just over two weeks. The Katar will have to move most of their forces over the next two weeks and we are keeping the resistance in check. Tsom, you have two weeks to get the artifact and get back here. If I am not here, Larrina will know what to do."

Shara and Tsom sat next to each other and she squeezed his hand. They had dropped any pretense of their growing relationship over a week ago and Shara now shared Tsom's bedroom.

The next day Shara and Tsom were off to Arbeneth. With some practice and guidance from Larrina, Tsom was now able to alter the appearance of his own image more. He enhanced the appearance of age, easier due to his recent physical aging. His beard looked fuller than it really was and his skin was paler, that of a noble from the south. They went by boat, along the river, rather than the roads. Less chance encounters that way. Larrina drove them to the docks, as both Lanos and Alanar were known. There were flyers in all the cities with fairly accurate likenesses of both Lanos and Alanar. Although those of Alanar were of the fat version, the drawing captured something about him that was still visible.

As they parted at the ferry docks, Larrina embraced Shara and looked into her eyes, her face very close. Shara started to look away, but then held her gaze.

"Loyalty to what is right is stronger than loyalty to family. You do not choose your family, but you do choose your actions. Think before you act and you will do the right thing." She kissed Shara on the forehead, leaving a pink set of lip marks that slowly faded.

Chapter 27

Lanos was good; he knew he was one of the best living swordsman in The Cities and had no false modesty about it. Yet, he had not beaten Alanar in recent practice sessions. Before his 'change' Alanar would have been exhausted after a minute, but this new man was stronger every day. Fatigue would not be the route to success as they sparred, it was time to try another tactic.

"A hot day like today, I look forward to a cool beer when we are done," Lanos said.

A flicker in Alanar's advance, Lanos was able to beat the saber and try a counter-parry.

"A day like today Larrina will no doubt want to go for a swim later," Alanar replied.

Alanar disengaged the counter-parry. He tried a glaze, his blade sliding along Lanos's, several sparks flying.

"I noticed that she keeps exotic liquor in her cabinet. The Hrýll brandy last night was excellent."

Lanos tried a cut-over, passing over the tip of Alanar's sword and did a double feint followed by a fast direct. Alanar licked his lips momentarily.

"Larrina enjoys swimming in the nude. She is not ashamed of her body, which is still exquisite after all these years isn't it?"

Alanar enveloped Lanos's blade, in a forceful sweep, then slammed body-to-body knocking Lanos backwards, causing a small stumble.

"We spent most of our time talking before you made it here."

Lanos tried to erase the image of Larrina diving nude into the water from his mind. He used his stumble to feint a wild moulinet, then lunged forward with a reprise, using his first attack, but turning to the right at the same time.

"Really? Larrina and I never seemed to have much time for talking."

Alanar ignored the feint, and switched sword hands. Using the left hand holding the sword, he slammed down Lanos's blade, spun to stay facing with his blade now on the inside, and poked Lanos firmly on his armored chest—winning the practice. "I have always found talking to be dangerous."

Larrina walked out to the yard, two cool teas in her hands. She looked at both of them with a frank assessment. She seemed to find the smell of workout enjoyable, breathing deeply through her nose—stretching her blouse—and exhaling slowly. Seeing that Alanar had won yet another practice, she teasingly asked, "Are you teaching Lanos anything new?"

"I think he has learned at least one lesson for the day."

***

"Smell the air, Lanos. Free of the stench of The Cities, free of the sins of Humanity and its gods." Alanar sat upon a mottled brown gelding, just over 15 hands. He had picked the horse out of a large collection that they had viewed, the owner surprised at his choice. Lanos rode a larger black gelding, with a blaze and two front stockings, 16 hands and muscular looking. He thought that Alanar would have problems keeping up with him, but the small brown was all stamina. Additionally, as the they got off the maintained roads of The Cities, his own gelding seemed to stumble more often than the brown.

He did smell the change. The air was cooler as they entered the forest and very slowly increased in elevation. They were headed west-northwest nearing the massive *Web of God*. "Not the 'gods'," Lanos noted out loud to Alanar, who shrugged. "The mountain range was named by the Hrýll and the Srýll long before the 'gods' were around. They do not worship any god, yet that is the name they used. I have heard them talk of an 'unknown god', which may be what they are referring to."

"Why the 'Web?'"

"It is said that the mountains exist on many planes and the planes are connected in a complex web. If you know how to walk the web you can travel between the planes."

Lanos pondered this story. He had a rough belief in other planes, the Sea of Souls was said to simply be another plane. Reincarnation was strongly believed by most, but given that this belief was encouraged by the 'gods—and he knew them to be less than godlike—it was hard for him to fully buy into all of the other myths and stories. Alanar spoke as if it were fact, so he did not press the matter. They agreed on politics, best not to delve too deeply into religion and myth. Of course the Tarth, the *daemons* by Zethicia had also once been part of myth.

The firs and the pines intermingled with smells he could not identify, but spoke of humidity, fecundity, and animal life. His gelding was nervous at the latter smells, and again Alanar's choice seemed the better one. The smaller brown swiveled his ears continuously, but moved at a steady mile eating pace. His own gelding ended up being the follower.

"How long have we known each other Lanos?"

Lanos considered. "Over twenty one years."

"Really? I cannot remember."

Lanos took a moment to consider what he meant. Alanar had been acting strangely since his change. Larrina had warned him that his memory would be worse as he became more of this new, fit and healthy, person.

"Do you mean in a normal sense, the way I cannot remember if something occurred ten, or eleven years ago?"

"No. It is gone. I remember ghosts of memories. I know you. I trust you. I don't remember much. Why do you follow me? I feel that whatever debt you owed me is long repaid, but I do not know."

Remembering was painful for Lanos. Did Alanar really not remember?

"So you feel the debt is repaid? I owe you nothing?"

Alanar turned to consider him. "I am sure of it." He said softly, a look of compassion in his eyes.

"Then swear it. Proclaim it in the tongue you used when you first rescued me. I do not know the meaning of those words, but I felt the power then. Proclaim me free."

"I know not of what you speak, what language?"

"I thought so," he tried to keep the bitterness out of his voice.

Silence. They continued with Lanos staring at Alanar's back.

Softly a noise began to drift from Alanar. Strange noises, impossible from the throat of man. It was Alanar. It was that tongue from years ago. The forest grew quiet and both horses stopped. The hairs on Lanos's scalp rose. The sounds grew and Lanos felt the energy tingling him. His bones resonated. His head hurt. Suddenly, a feeling of something ripped from his being. He felt weak. The sounds from Alanar stopped. Alanar bowed his head and spoke so softly that if it were not for the silence Lanos would not have heard him. "It should have been done long ago. I wonder why I did not." Alanar's horse moved forward of its own accord.

***

"I still do not feel we can trust the Srýll and Hrýll," Lanos muttered. They had been on the road for days without meeting anyone. The road had once been wide and well maintained, but the lack of traffic over the years was showing. Narrows, washed out sections hastily repaired, weeds growing in the center. The Hrýll were dying out and the road testified. Lanos was sore, tired, and although he hated to admit it, he was nervous. No one *just visited* the Hrýll and he thought the Srýll exterminated, which certainly did not endear Humans to either race. Their only hope was that they hated the Katar as much as Lanos.

The Katar controlled the trade of talismans with the Hrýll. Of course dealing directly with the Hrýll was also a death sentence from the Katar, but what was one more death sentence from the Katar? Lanos smiled to himself.

"Trust and need are two different things. They no doubt think they cannot trust us as well. They will not trust me ... for good reason, I think."

"Then why not let me go on my own?"

"One must face one's past. There is unfinished business with the Hrýll, even if I cannot remember it all, or most of it. As my past vanishes from my memory, I have the feeling that I must come to terms with it. The Hrýll are part of my past."

Lanos continued to look around nervously. The horse kept stopping and snorting. It would then lunge forward a few steps and then wheel around. He was making his horse nervous, or the horse was making him nervous, either way it was a cycle that needed to be broken.

The section of the road looked well-traveled, compared to the rest. This added to his unease. Casual traveling was rare. This far out floaters would be rare too. Horses and wagons would be the norm. There should have been a steady trickle of them, but the road had been empty for a day. For the first time the intelligence reports they had been getting for over a month felt real and personal. Thievery was up, the Tarth were causing mayhem to the Northeast and the ripples were being felt all the way here.

Lanos tried to remember what he had heard about the Hrýll, sometimes known as the Old Ones. They had no love of The Cities and its iron control of qenar. That, and Humans were just plain afraid of the old races, or any non-Human race for that matter. Lanos was a city man and despite knowing that it was illogical, he was getting apprehensive as they drew closer to the strange civilization. Not normally very talkative, he had queried Alanar repeatedly over the past week on the Hrýll and their ways, but Alanar would only repeat "You will see that when we get there."

Their only warning of attack was Alanar's brown's nose dilating suddenly. Alanar had his sword out as multiple quarrels hit both horses and men. The armor they both wore under their clothes proved worthy, but Lanos had one bolt in his left thigh, Alanar one in his right shoulder. Repeating crossbows, thought Lanos. Terrible accuracy made up for in volume. Probably three or four of them, plus normal bows. The horses were too injured to run far, but in a panic tried. No doubt their retreat backwards was blocked also. Almost simultaneously both Alanar and Lanos forced the horses to fall and slit their throats. Lanos was surprised at the look of sadness on Alanar's face. This new Alanar seemed much more compassionate than the one he was familiar with.

A number of additional quarrels hit the horses as both of them hid behind the bodies.

"Any ideas?" Alanar asked.

Lanos had none. "You?" He asked.

Two or three arrows hit the horses. They were probably reloading the repeating crossbows. "How many do you think are there?" Lanos asked.

"Large group. Twelve at least. Four repeaters, four longbows, the rest are probably swordsmen and possible a grunt or two."

"How do you know?" He was surprised; the guess was more than his own.

"I saw ten; I am guessing that I missed two further away."

He *saw* ten? Lanos had not seen anyone, just guessed by the quantity of arrows and the direction of the attacks. No doubt if they were ambushing caravans, then twelve was a small enough number of bandits. Still, twelve or 100, they were seriously outnumbered and the lack of a chance for hand to hand reduced their odds. Both of them were swordsman first. Lanos pulled the bolt out of his leg; a small groan escaped his lips. Alanar had already done the same with the one in his shoulder. The quarrel must not have hit a major artery as the amount of blood on his shoulder was not bad. Alanar held his hand over Lanos's leg and the blood loss lessened. Lanos raised an eyebrow. "I have a small talent in healing skills, but not enough to truly heal it." More surprises from a man he had known for over 20 years. Lanos bound the wound quickly with a piece of his shirt, not so tightly that the blood would not flow to the rest of his leg.

After some time, they heard quiet talking to the north of them. Then silence.

"They are going to try and force us to show ourselves with one person, then shoot us as we deal with him. They were arguing over who has to try." How could he know that, Lanos wondered?

"I will deal with him; you keep your head down." Lanos nodded. He was no coward, but the practices that they had been holding every day confirmed that right now Alanar was the superior fighter. Certainly his ears had improved.

Shortly they heard the swinging of a sword near the horses. Alanar waited. Suddenly, his head momentarily crested the horse corpse, a knife left his hand, and a man fell face down between them. Alanar pulled the knife from the man's eye socket and cleaned it. They then waited for the next move. Sunset was still hours away.

The sweet smell of fresh blood was beginning to change to a rotten stench and sicken Lanos. Flies were beginning to discover the corpses and the buzzing further nauseated him. He was going to push the dead man further away, but Alanar just stacked the body in a strategic place, covering a gap between the two horses. At least he had the decency to point the single eyed face in the opposite direction.

More whispered conversation to the north. Alanar tilted his head, holding up his hand for silence from Lanos. "They don't want to give us the cover of darkness. They are going to send four men in with swords. I did not catch all of the conversation, but one of the repeaters is not working and they don't want to risk the inaccuracy of multiple shots on the others, so they are depending on the longbows." He paused, considering. "We rush to the north as they attack. Go for fast kills, even if you might get injured. The goal is speed while they are still around us. Their horses are to the north. As they follow us, we should be able to stay in the woods on horseback and evade." *If we are not pin cushions by then,* thought Lanos.

On Alanar's signal, they leapt up, just as the four men were about to leap over the horses. Alanar killed one with the previously used knife, pushed the body into the other and, charging at the same time, sliced the man's hand off as he used his comrade as a shield. Lanos killed the closest one also, but his sword got stuck in the man's ribs. The person to the side of this was a woman, which gave Lanos only the slightest of pauses. He dropped the stuck sword and began what seemed like a wild charge. The woman smiled and set herself in a strike position. At the last second Lanos folded his front leg into a self-tripping roll. He glanced back as he got up and continued his charge to the trees; the woman was staring in surprise at an arrow in her stomach.

Alanar beat Lanos to the trees. He pointed toward where he thought the horses were and tossed Lanos his sword. Without protesting, Lanos kept it and they ran to the horses. He was surprised that the wound in his leg did not bother him more and hoped that the partial healing would hold. Still, he could not keep up with Alanar.

Arrows and now quarrels smacked into trees near him as he ran. Alanar was already on one horse and held the reins of another. One body lay nearby. Lanos glanced at the other horses as he mounted. "No time." Yelled Alanar. The horse galloped dangerously in the woods, as shouts and more arrows struck dirt and wood. Lanos noted Alanar's horse was the more sure footed and faster mount.

***

Pain and the after effects of shock and adrenalin coursed through Lanos's body. The horses were not doing well either. The smell of drying horse sweat kept reminding his nose of the dead horses and having to lie among the bodies. Blood dripped from a hundred scratches on both horse and man; neither had the strength to swat the flies. Finally, Alanar called a halt. He dropped down of his horse, giving a minor stumble. *So he has some limits too*, thought Lanos. Alanar rested his hands on his mount and stood there for a few moments, then did the same on Lanos's mount. Both horses perked up and the glaze went out of their eyes. Without a word, Alanar slowly pulled himself back on his horse and motioned forward. The fatigue was now fully evident on his face.

Lanos did not know much about manipulating *ka* without a talisman, but he wondered how much of this healing Alanar could do in one day. Bringing a sick one to a healer in The Cities was extremely expensive and they used a talisman, shaped by the Hrýll, to aid in their healing. Even then, they would only deal with one very sick client in a week. Alanar had helped both him and two horses. Did a horse take more *ka* to heal than a man? Wearily he moved his horse after Alanar.

***

For two days they continued without rest. Four more times Alanar had worked on the horses, each time the effect was weaker and Alanar looked more exhausted. Not older, as Lanos had seen with Tsom healing Shara, just drained. He looked like he was deathly tired. He had seen prisoners worked until they died and Alanar had that look. Lanos had protested that they all needed rest, but Alanar reminded him that their enemy had ten horses and could use two or three men and keep trading off the horses. In their current state, even their combined skill with weapons would not save them. They kept on.

The fifth time Alanar attempted to resuscitate the horse it did not perk up. Alanar leaned on the horse and the horse looked like it would have a hard time supporting this extra weight. Alanar tried to remount, but fell down. He did not get back up. From where he lay, he pointed to the saddles on the horses. Lanos slid off his mount and fell to his knees. His legs no longer worked properly. His knees were painfully sore from riding so much and his partially healed wound was beyond pain; it was simply without feeling. Numbness in a wound was dangerous, he thought to himself, but couldn't summon the energy to get nervous. He pulled himself to his feet by the stirrups. He uncinched the saddles and let them fall next to the horses. Both horses had sores from the continuous use of the saddles, but they were partially healed already, no doubt due to Alanar. Both of them crawled next to the saddles. They made wonderful pillows.

***

Lanos opened his eyes slowly. He had heard voices. He opened them fully. Surrounding them were not bandits, but either Hrýll or Srýll, he could never really tell them apart. They were Humanoid, but covered in a fine light fur, or hair. Not heavy or shaggy, but still enough to protect the skin somewhat. Most had brownish hair, but there was a variety of colors was analogous to hair color of Humans. They wore extensive jewelry, both the men and the women, and Lanos had heard rumors that much of the jewelry were also talismans. A vague recollection that the Srýll never mixed sexes in public made him think these must be Hrýll, for several of the over 20 were female.

An older Hrýll noticed that Lanos was awake. While he was bent slightly with age and emaciated due to atrophy of muscles, his eyes were alert and showed no signs that his mind was deteriorating with the body. Much of his hair was silver. He spoke in common tongue, which was the language used in The Cities. All people and races spoke common tongue, due to the influence of The Cities throughout Nakana. His accent was faint and he was easy to understand.

"Your friend is drained. He will not awaken soon. You flee the bandits, yes?"

Lanos nodded. His throat was dry and he did not trust speaking immediately until he could get his saliva flowing. He glanced at the horses. Both were being tended to by two Hrýll and seemed to be recovering well. He noticed the slight smell of cinnamon, similar to the perfume Shara used and tea that Larrina brewed. He wondered how Tsom and Shara were faring, as by now they should have succeeded, or failed, at stealing her father's old talisman.

The old Hrýll motioned to one of the others, who bent and picked up Alanar like a heavy sack of grain. Then started walking. The two with the horses also started walking.

"Can you walk? The horses are too weak for anything but themselves, but we can carry you too."

Lanos did not feel like being treated as a sack of grain. He struggled to his feet, surprised that the pain in his leg was not worse. The Hrýll noticed, "We continued the healing process as best as we could. The rest is up to your body. You will need food, as the healing drains not only the healer, but the healed." Lanos discovered he was ravenous and accepted the dried meat and water passed to him. After a long swallow he felt that his throat would not betray him.

"What is your name? Mine is Lanos."

"Mine is Unchya, translated to common tongue as 'First of the Tea Family.' You may find it easier to call me Oonie."

"Oonie, why are you helping us? Or *are* you helping us?"

"Bandits are bad for both of us. We have no reason to let you fall into their hands. Besides, he …" Oonie nodded toward the vanishing form of Alanar, "… should not die, just yet. Can you walk?"

"Yes."

"Good. We can talk as we move. The bandits are not that far behind you."

Lanos noticed that two more Hrýll were carrying the saddles, giving the horses even more of a break. They traveled straight north, which was almost perpendicular to the road and ostensibly away from their destination. Yet, their destination was to contact the Hrýll for help; at least Lanos assumed it was help, Alanar had not shared his plan. *Contact had been made*, he thought. *Now what?*

Oonie asked many questions as to what was happening in The Cities and in Zethicia. He seemed to know most of the answers, but was ensuring that there were no gaps in his knowledge. He was particularly interested in the brewing war in Zethicia. What did Lanos know of the current state of invading army? Very little, as Alanar's network, while extensive, did not use the gateways and thus was slow in gathering intelligence and they had been on the road for days, adding to the lag time. The gateways were too well monitored and only for the rich and the politically well connected. The carrier pigeons had a tendency to die en route. Oonie seemed to know more than him on Zethicia. He chewed on the spiced meat he was given, enjoying the peppery, orange flavor, while they walked. He listened to Ooni's version of what was happening.

"The army is small but powerful. There can be no doubt that the army has the banished *daemons* among them. The Tarth." The Tarth was also the name of the river that flowed through Argn, he suddenly remembered. The naming of the river was a bit of history that he had never heard, what was the connection? "The Tarth are powerful beyond the memories of mankind, who were instrumental in their banishment. If they succeed in their initial conquests, then they may be able to bring more armies to Nakana."

"Why can't we banish them again?"

"It is not as easy as it sounds. Back then Humans were allied with the Kinel. The Kinel could shape *ka* on their own. With qenar they could boost their power. By cooperating as a group they could boost it even more. All this was also aided by an old talisman of the Hrýll and the Srýll. The Talisman of Planes. It is how we first came to Nakana." More history that he had never heard before. Was this the same talisman that Alanar had sent Tsom for? It must be. Of course the Hrýll and Srýll were called the Old Ones for a reason. They had been around for longer than Humans. *I wonder if they know where we—Humans—come from?* His thoughts were disrupted as Oonie continued.

"The man of death knows this. That is why he came here." Oonie had waved toward the still immobile body of Alanar, bouncing lightly off of the back of the Hrýll carrying him. Lanos interrupted.

"You mean Alanar? Do you know him?"

"We know of him. He is in many of our legends."

Legends? Lanos's mind went down too many paths simultaneously, causing a pause in his speech. He pulled himself together.

"But have you met him before?"

"No … not in this life. He is easy to recognize, to a Hrýll or a Srýll."

No more was forthcoming, despite a number of other questions. All the answers were obtuse and referred to legend and the past. How old was Alanar? Lanos mused, not listening too closely anymore to Oonie. Then something he said caught his ear.

"Those reborn do not always have to die."

"Reincarnation?" It just now occurred to him that he did not know what the other races believed in.

"You distrust."

"What I know of reincarnation comes from the priesthoods." Lanos turned his head to the left and looked down on the last word.

"Truth can come from untrustworthy sources."

"Then tell me the truth, so I can hear it from a trustworthy source." The corners of his lips turned up slightly, but he was attentive.

"The Sea of Souls existed before mankind, or its gods, and will exist afterwards."

Silence from Lanos, one eyebrow slightly raised. He swerved around a fallen branch; lifting his injured leg was too painful to hop over.

"If there is *ka* left when you die, you will return to the Sea."

"For how long?"

"As long as is necessary."

"That is evasion. How do you *know* that reincarnation takes place?" Lanos was shaking his head. "What is the purpose?"

"I know because I remember." Oonie nodded toward Alanar again.

"You remember your past life?"

"After much reflection, some of it has returned."

"I suppose you were a king in your past life?" The corners of his smile were pulled back firmly, lips almost pursed. When speaking with enlisted men, years ago, they all joked that they were reincarnated kings, or nobles, and this life as a soldier was just a phase. With a laugh they would all down their drinks and toast the dead kings.

Oonie seemed not to notice. "King? The Hrýll do not have kings."

"So what was your past life?"

"The one I remember involves him. Do you not think it strange that of all my past lives, I remember this one? It puzzles me."

"And you were a Hrýll?"

"This is true. I am Hrýll, so it is not surprising that I was Hrýll."

"No, not surprising at all. So all the teaming millions of Humans were Humans before, even though the population of mankind was only in the hundreds of thousands not long ago?" Well, not long from the way Oonie was speaking.

"Not all who are born were born before. That is why we all end up in the Sea of Souls. To heal. To create more souls."

They rested for a time, and as they rose Lanos' leg gave out. Oonie called to one of the other Hrýll and moments later it returned with a strange horse.

"You had other horses and you let me walk?"

"You were able to before. Now you can ride." He gestured to the large mottled stallion; Lanos noted that he was not neutered. Great, he thought, now I have to deal with the energy of a stallion. But, the horse was remarkably well behaved.

They continued, with the old Hrýll having no problem keeping up.

Lanos tensed his right leg straight, pressed with his left, the horse turned right and avoided the hole in the path.

"You work well with the horse. You understand each other."

Lanos nodded. "I have been riding many years."

"No, you understand each other. This is also true with you and … Alanar."

Lanos looked at his master. Master was not quite the right word, he knew, now that the strange bond Alanar had placed years ago on him had been lifted, but he still felt connected to him. Oonie continued.

"The horse obeys you, but you are not really its master."

"Back to the subject we started off on."

"Yes?"

"What did you mean, 'those reborn do not always have to die?'"

"I meant him."

"So, when you said you remember him, you meant it was really him, as he his now?"

"I am not sure that he is the same"

"But you just said—"

"Alanar, as you call him, has been reborn many times, but has never died."

"You have lost me. Again."

"His physical body has never been destroyed. He has not returned to the Sea of Souls."

"So by what you have told me he cannot have been reborn; reincarnated."

"Yet, he has been."

"What does that mean?"

"He has changed. He changes each time. Perhaps this time …"

Lanos waited. He was not going to be the one constantly prying out every word. He gave up. "This time what? And *how* do you *know* this?"

"It is strange how a dog, or a horse, will do what their master asks. Even when in the past, the experience has not always been a pleasant one."

This was as far as Lanos got. The only other response he got was variations of "He has changed has he not?"

He pondered this new information on his companion and master for 20 years. They continued toward their destination, which Lanos learned was a smaller town on the outskirts of the Hrýll civilization. Their original destination had been the center of the Hrýll lands, but this new one would have to do for now. Alanar would need to heal and this was where Oonie was determined to go.

The next two days brought no new information and Lanos felt hopelessly lost as they stayed off any roads and made their way through dense forest. Alanar remained in a deep sleep, or coma, the entire time, but Oonie did not seem concerned. The old Hrýll seemed to not worry about anything. He was tough and always at peace with his actions. The other Hrýll gave him deep respect. He would suggest an action and they would follow without question. It was Lanos who was worn out each night.

Their food was extremely simple, mainly dried venison flavored as the first pieces of meat he had received, various vegetables—many which he did not recognize, and water or tea. Each evening it was Oonie who prepared the tea, in almost a ritual manner. The tea relaxed his tired muscles and he always slept well. He was reminded of Larrina's splendid brews as he inhaled the strange spices in his cup. The memory made him warm and he smiled into his cup. Oonie, watching him drink over the lip of his own cup—the steam framing his face—commented.

"You have the look of a man thinking of a woman."

Startled, Lanos stopped smiling. "Why do you say that?"

"Mankind and Hrýll are not so different. I recognize the look. Is she very beautiful?"

"Beautiful is perhaps not the right word, but she has an attractiveness that I am drawn toward."

"So you are not yet lovers?" Oonie seemed unaware that he was asking very personal questions.

"Not yet."

"Optimistic aren't you?" The voice behind him was weak. Alanar was awake.

Chapter 28

Barnus strode into the meeting room, already full of Katar officers. It was a sparse and functional room, not full of comfortable seats and other amenities. The governor of Zethicia, Courie Marcone, was squirming in her chair, not used to so many men, military, and lack of servants. Her gray hair was tied back, but wisps were straying loose into her eyes, which showed a lack of sleep. Barnus knew she had been coordinating refugees and emergency building of defenses. She handled the bureaucracy that he found impossible to deal with. Barnus recognized Jern, head of the Tanec family, as one of the Katar. A good indicator, he thought, that one of the actual heads of the families has come. Jern was the one who spoke.

"Commander Barnus, sorry to pull you away from your reconnaissance of the invaders, but I felt you need to be in on our discussions and can give us the best briefing of the situation." Jern spoke without looking up from his papers. Barnus nodded and sat down to Jern's left. Jern continued, "Fully half of the Katar guard are here to help you. I will personally command them. I am happy to be able to provide twenty of my officers to assist you with your own men."

The corners of Barnus's mouth pulled back, tightening his lips. Governor Courie shot him a look, blowing a lock of hair out of her eyes. He managed to bite back the initial response. "Of course, we welcome the expertise of the Katar. Zethicia has not had experience in military matters in many years. Yes, it's fortunate that to preserve the peace over the years the Katar have remained so proficient in military matters."

"The Katar are always ready to serve," Jern smiled, looking Barnus in the eyes. They both knew what the other thought, the exchange was simply a dance for the other men, and the governor.

"What of the Yanín?" asked Courie. Both men looked uncomfortable at the mention of the mercenaries. Courie continued, "I do not want them roaming the streets, uncontrolled. Tales of the destruction caused by a drunken Yanín are well known to all. The citizens are very uneasy with their presence. They must either camp outside the main city or stay in the military barracks with your men."

Jern sighed. "I will assign one of my men to work with the Yanín commander. I would recommend that you make sure that none of your men provoke any of the Yanín, Barnus. It would simply lead to the death of your men and bad feelings all around. They may look almost Human, but they do not think like us. Anything can set them off and fighting is like breathing to them. No, more like sex. They enjoy it. The battle is lust for them. I have a man experienced in their ways."

Courie looked, and Barnus felt, relieved.

"Barnus, what can you tell me of the invaders? To date all we have are courier reports, many of them conflicting, and the fact that fewer and fewer trade caravans make it between The Cities and Zethicia. Survivors are always viewing from a distance."

Barnus strode to the wall were his aids had already hung large sheets of paper for writing. "The forces are two races. One race, larger than Human, seem to be the leaders. Incredibly strong. We have no credible witnesses as to their fighting capability hand to hand, but the rumors are that their skin is thick and dense, like hardened leather, and hard to penetrate. They use trebuchets for their raids on smaller towns, with incredible efficiency and from incredible distances, making it impossible for the towns they strike to fight back with longbow, crossbow, or even our own siege weapons—such as we have. As the townspeople flee, the enemy always let their huge dogs loose on them. The only survivors we have talked to were people who were already outside of the towns when the attack occurred. Those were few and far between as the dogs are set on those also, and they are evidently good trackers."

"Numbers?"

"Five to ten thousand. I know that is a large variance, but it is the best we can do. We understand that it is the same composition of forces attacking the caravans; scouting parties that destroy what they come across, but do not engage with any large groups. Some heavily guarded trade is making it through, but it is rare. Without the gateway we would be nearly cut off. Thankfully, they have no ships."

"Have you tried sending out any forces to engage them when they attack the towns?"

"Yes, once." Barnus would not meet Jern's or the governor's eyes. "It was a total rout. Again, no accurate reports, but the large ones—*daemons* for want of a better word—didn't even bother to draw their own weapons. Those that were not killed by the dogs and the stones from the trebuchets were brushed aside like pesky ants. My men reported that heads were smashed with fists, arms literally ripped from sockets, and similar destruction." Barnus looked slightly ill. His voice caught and he swallowed, mad at himself for seeming like a coward in front of the Katar. "We sent two thousand against them as a test, with the intent of retreating quickly. Over nineteen hundred died."

The briefing continued for another hour. Jern listened well and took terse notes. The other Katar also paid close attention and occasionally asked questions, most were intelligent and well thought out. Barnus was surprised that many of the best questions came from female Katar. He knew that the Katar of Argn allowed women to fight, but it was obvious that Jern respected their opinions and advice as much as, if not more, those of his men. At the end the sun was setting and glow globes were activated. Jern turned to the governor.

"Now there is the uncomfortable matter of needing some payment for supplies and other necessities. We of course come to the aid of our friends in Zethicia, but cannot bear the entire cost ourselves."

"Naturally, we would have insisted on compensating our friends, the Katar." Governor Courie moved her chair forward. The Katar were moving in, taking over Zethicia as much as the Tarth, the *deamons* and their minions. *At least the Katar are Human*, Barnus thought.

Chapter 29

The Karn family compound was silent at three in the morning. While ostensibly the most powerful Katar family, the Karn philosophy was to separate family from governance. This was not just for an escape from work, but for practical purposes. It was easier to guard a smaller space that has less people coming and going.

Arlec's ears strained for the slightest sound as he made his way to his father's room. He knew that Marin, the old watchman, would be asleep. The assumption was that an intruder would be caught long before he—or she—made it into the main building. There had not been anyone foolish to break into the compound in Arlec's lifetime. A night watchman indoors was out of ancient custom, nothing more. Marin had been with the family all of his life. Interior watchman was his retirement reward. Arlec paused outside his father's door, the glow globes on the walls, all set on low, seemed like eerie will-o-wisps floating in nothingness. He listened. The sound of his father's gentle snore made it to his stressed auditory senses.

The door opened without a sound. Devon always insisted that the compound be kept in perfect order, down to well-oiled hinges. Arlec's eyes blinked at the unexpected light. The room was fully illuminated. He panicked, momentarily, but then saw the book fallen from his father's hand. Reading late again. He was always reading, planning, criticizing. A man of inaction; not willing to let his son step in and make things happen. Always consulting his daughters and listening to their chatter. What did they know? Warped by the attitudes of Argn women. Devon's time had come and gone. A new leader of the Karn family was needed.

Arlec did not hesitate, he slid the long knife that he had taken from the thief's room deep into his father's right eye and swirled quickly. No gasp escaped Devon's lips. Arlec would have liked to have used his ring while killing him; drawing the *ka* from his father as he died and causing true death. It would have been one small bit of extra satisfaction, but, of course, his father slept with his own ring on, removing that opportunity. Death had to be quick if he were to avoid any alarm.

The small medallion was around his neck, as Arlec had expected. It was made of intricately carved jade, gold, and a black metal that he did not recognize. He removed it and the ring off his father's left hand. Slipping the medallion over his neck and tucking it under his shirt he left as quietly as he had come. Turning back, he gazed for a moment at his work. The knife sticking up out of his father's face looked like a small cross from a distance. The ancient sign of victory. Except for the absence of snoring and the rise and fall of his chest, Devon could have been asleep.

The library was locked with an ancient combination lock. No simple key would open this door. Family members learned the combination once they finished officer training. The library was the repository of the entire Karn history, said to go back over four thousand years. Until now, Arlec had never had much interest in history. He wanted the tools he was sure his father had been keeping hidden. The stories the Katar children exchanged told of incredible powers the Karn wielded ages ago. Talismans with unheard of powers. His father had laughed the stories off when pressed by his children, but Arlec was certain that the medallion and fireplace held the secrets. Power. Unused power. His power. He needed to get whatever was hidden before his sisters interfered. Anything missing could be blamed on the thief. If his sisters even knew of the fireplace cache. If not, so much the better.

The omnipresent fire burned in the fireplace. Reaching into the flames, a bit cautiously, he felt only a slight warmth. Deep behind the flames he found the small box. Inside he was astonished to find only a simple glass sphere along with five rings of Katar. He cursed. Rings and one single sphere? It had no obvious switch or control, as glow globes and floaters had. He turned it over in his hands, the glass feeling cold despite coming from a box sitting in flames. He dropped it in his pocket, with the rings. He returned the empty box to its place in the flames and returned to his room and wait for the rest of his plan to unfold.

***

The young man wondered at his strange assignment. It was 3:30 in the morning. Two moons had already set. He scaled the Karn compound wall. He had been told to scale it in this precise location, at this precise time, wearing a very specific set of clothes. Then, to wait for the guard to walk by and drop to the ground noisily, run into the guard, knock him out after a brief fight, drop a true image of a couple with a small boy that had been given to him, then run. Obviously, his employer had something in mind with all this, but he didn't really care to know the details. He had been paid well and assured that the guard would not put up much of a fight. He spat on the ground. Assurances from the Katar were like water captured by a sieve; he had two friends waiting in the landscaped bushes near this spot. The guard would not accidentally win the fight through some failed promise of the Katar.

Chapter 30

The *Bindi* plowed downstream swiftly, outracing the current with qenar fueled power, focused by the talisman on the bridge. Their speed kept a breeze washing across the ship, preventing the small angry clouds of insects from settling onboard. The shore was never completely without buildings: small docks, gazebo or pergola sprouting out from the deep green of vegetation covering both banks. The occasional massive tree stood out, the patriarch guarding his domain. In his mind Tsom pictured the population of The Cities merged together from above like five dough balls left to rise too long. The entire riverbank between Argn and Arbeneth had been settled by millions of Humans, the other races driven out or destroyed. Tsom wondered what wilderness must be like. He had heard stories that most of Nakana was without Human habitation, no people for thousands of marks, with Humanity exploding only in the cities, Zethicia, and small towns, ranches, and fiefdoms in between. It was hard to imagine. Frightening. He did well around people, crowds. It was his environment. The tales of strange creatures that roamed Nakana were bad enough in abstract; the thought of a personal encounter sent a small shiver down his back. He did not envy Lanos and Alanar's journey, despite his own sojourn leading to its own danger.

The workings of the small ship were fascinating. Growing up in the dock area, he had still only observed ships from shore. He watched every movement by the small crew. There was plenty of time; Shara had been deep in thought and depressed at the thought of so personally betraying her family, so he explored on his own.

Those who were interested received a short tour of the bridge the second day. The most fascinating part to Tsom was the talisman that powered the ship. It was a jade inlaid circle on a flat slanted surface in front of the bow-facing window. In the circle was a set of lines, making the entire inlay similar to a wagon wheel with 16 crossing lines forming the 32 spokes. A small black sphere rested on the spoke that would have been north on a map. Tsom leaned closer to the talisman. The sphere was a black diamond, surrounded by glass, making it appear larger than it was. Black diamonds must have some significance as talisman, he thought, thinking of his stolen Katar ring. The diamond was approximately one third of the way from the center to the perimeter. Tsom's guess this told the ship how fast to go. He turned back to the captain, who had paused his monologue and was staring at Tsom. The captain resumed talking once Tsom looked at him.

The self-important captain had a hard time talking and keeping his chest expanded at the same time. A balloon slowly losing air as he spoke, he explained that the ball controlled the direction and amount of thrust. To add to this method of steering was another wheel that connected to a tiller. They all got permission to touch the talisman's edge and examine it more closely, but the watchful eye of the quiet Second-in-Command made sure no one touched the sphere. Tsom touched the jade inlay, running his fingers along the perimeter. He wondered how fast the ship could go if this was only one-third speed. Suddenly, the ship surged forward, throwing passengers to the deck. Tsom stumbled, but his instinctive reflexes kicked in and he maintained balance. The completely deflated captain cut the tour short and ushered them out of the bridge. His Second was already at the talisman adjusting it, a puzzled expression on his face.

The press of strangers on all sides ignited his innate thieving nature. The woman in front of him obviously did not realize that her intricate gold bracelet's clasp was easy to open in less than a second. The large man next to her, smelling of expensive booze, had a bulge in his pocket that spoke of a large roll of sintars. Temptation all around. He moved away from the crowd, the wolf leaving the sheep unharmed. He wandered the deck considering the warning that Larrina had given him the day they left, in private. It had been cryptic. "Love does not conquer all. Don't trust love." Love, he wasn't sure he knew what love was. He looked for Shara. He would be content with trust.

He wondered how Alanar and Lanos were making out on their mission. At least they could depend on each other, even if there was a bit of jealousy over Larrina. As the sun set, the three winter moons rose as a group; forming a triangle.

As they neared Arbeneth, he sought Shara out. She had been subdued during the trip, no doubt thinking of the betrayal she was about to do. He had comforted her as best as he knew how. Their lovemaking had grown from wild passion to quiet intensity, with Shara waking in the middle of the night needing more. Today she had drifted away, to be alone, and Tsom had respected her wishes.

Most of the passengers were on the main deck, enjoying the pastoral scene rolling by, with the occasional mansion near the riverbank. The warm breeze stirred Shara's hair as she leaned on the starboard railing and stared into the side wake. Her eyes flicked to the side as he approached, then returned to the water. Tsom watched her, a small furrow in his brow. He looked down at his own hands, careful not to concentrate too hard and accidentally reveal his true visage. Looking back at Shara, he gripped the railing more tightly. A fellow passenger stepped up next to him, an older woman, dressed in the wild colors of Argn, the predominance of purple indicating that she was a widow, but available. She smiled at Tsom. "Would you believe that I have never been to Arbeneth?"

"It is the largest of The Cities, or so I have heard. I have not been to all of them." He glanced over to see if Shara was listening.

"I am visiting my daughter there. Her husband has been called away to the conflict in Zethicia and I will help her around the bookstore."

The implied question hung in the air. Before it could grow too ripe, another voice chimed in. "We are visiting my father, a dye merchant." Shara had stepped in.

The two of them spoke animatedly about dyes and how it was such a pity that Arbeneth did not utilize the bright colors of Argn and how confusing this would be for the women from Argn. Colors with no meaning, she shook her head in disbelief. She told Shara how worried she was that she would not be able to cope and would commit some terrible social blunder. Shara assured her she had nothing to worry about.

The *Bindi* docked with a light bump. Tsom came next to Shara, that light spice scent that he associated with her caressing his nose. "Thank you for saying the right thing to that woman." She looked at him for a long moment before replying.

"You know, Larrina says that all Katar have some Kinel blood in them."

He kept silent. This did not really need a reply.

"When we kill—killed—the Kinel, we exterminated our own past, our own shame at being half breeds, neither Human, nor Kinel." She reached out and touched Tsom's cheek. "You are so pure. Larrina said she has not seen such strong Kinel blood in centuries."

"I am a half breed, just as you are. My father was Human."

"Tsom, now that we are here, away from Alanar, Lanos … and Larrina, let's forget about their wild plan. The Katar are too powerful. Let's … let's run away together. To the frontier, the outskirts of Zethicia."

They had reached the walkway. An excited young crewman was holding a newspaper and talking to one of the passenger crew in loud animated tones. The words drifted up to Tsom and Shara.

"The old man Devon, of the Karn clan, has been murdered by a young thief, who stole his *ring*! His son Arlec has called for an all-out hunt for the killer and posted a 10,000 sintar reward for his capture, or death. The paper has an etching of his likeness here! Just think of what one could do with 10,000 sintar! That thief is short of this world. The entire city is looking for him. 10,000 sintar, I could retire with that much."

Tsom held Shara's elbow as she briefly stumbled. Blood drained from her face. For the first time Tsom saw the faintest of markings on her face indicating her Kinel blood; a flash of the teardrop coloring from forehead to shoulders. Maybe it was his imagination, since he now knew of the Kinel connection to the Katar. She recovered quickly. She looked from the likeness of Tsom in the paper to him quickly, a smile that held no happiness was frozen on her face as they left the ship and conferred away from the ferry crowd.

"Your new look is safe. I would not recognize you as the person in the picture."

"I am so sorry Shara. You know I had nothing to do with it."

"Yes. But, who is trying to frame you? Why kill my father? I should contact my sisters!"

"No, Shara. You can't. This could mean they know about you if they are trying to frame me."

"We can't steal this talisman that Alanar thinks is so important now. The compound will be impregnable. Everyone is on the lookout for you. Even with your illusion, or whatever it is that hides the way you look, you could be recognized, or questioned, or caught."

"What choice do we have? Do I have? We need this weapon. The Katar must not even know they have it—or they would use it before endangering so many in battle. This is the resistance's chance."

Tsom felt his passion rising. It was not until now, with the possibility of Shara backing out, that he realized how strongly he felt. It was time. Time to finally break the Katar's back. Shara had to see that. She had been in the resistance for years. She couldn't back down now.

He palmed his knife, the one in his arm sheath, with nervous energy. Shara was looking at him, eyes wide and full of trust. The knife disappeared again. He thought of his dead mother and father. Of Yarm, his mentor, friend, and fellow thief. He thought of his friends on the wharf, probably all dead. He thought of Shela, and looking into Shara's eyes he saw echoes of Shela.

"Shara, I hope we do not end up on opposite sides, but family is important. You do what you have to do." He pulled her gently and kissed her very lightly on the lips. Both of their eyes stayed open. "I have to end this hold that the Katar have over me ... and The Cities. I may not fully trust Alanar, but I trust

Larrina and maybe Lanos … and you. I will contact you soon, but for now you must go to your family, if you think it's safe."

"My family would never hurt me and I must make sure they are safe. I won't betray you, my Tsom. I am still part of the resistance, but with this we must separate. Neither of us can be seen with the other. I will put an ad in the paper, for Argn silks. You know the Argn colors well enough to figure out the meaning when you see it."

He turned swiftly, blinking at the dust in his eyes. He felt alone and wished he could melt into the crowd, and without thinking he did.

Tsom made his way to the Karn compound. It was very near Alanar's former residence. A few weeks ago the rich area of Arbeneth would have been intimidating. He made a short detour to swing by Alanar's place. He stopped near the guard entrance to the neighborhood. Time to try the techniques that Alanar and Larrina had taught him on disguise. Somewhere between an illusion and guiding the way a person thinks, nudging them to make a mistake in perception. Larrina knew more about Kinel powers than Alanar, yet Tsom still felt that Alanar was connected to the Kinel race in some way. She had come to Tsom's room the night before they left, after Shara was asleep, and signaled for him to join her in the living room. It had been a long conversation, but he ran through the important parts in his head.

You have the ability to manipulate ka *directly, indicating the strength of your Kinel blood. For subtle things, this will not cost you significantly. The Kinel were the only race that manipulated* ka *this way. The Hrýll and Srýll could shape and bind it to talismans, which could be used over and over again with qenar as fuel. Humans use it even more subtly, where the great craftsmen are really using some of their own* ka *to achieve their results. What you call true images is an example. The healers and mind readers are the same. Your true skill is hidden to me. I cannot help you there, but the small things that all Kinel know, I can guide you with. Blending in, not being noticed, moving swiftly, having an instinct which person to rob, these are all related, but stem from abilities Kinel all have. You have instinctively blended in all your life, but if you try you can be more proactive in your appearance. You cannot appear to be a rock, or a horse, or something that is unbelievable, but if you focus, you can build on what is there. People believe what they want to believe and you can touch on that. When all else fails experiment. Many Kinel have some minor power in more than one direction—experiment.*

Tsom slid the Katar ring onto his left hand, in open view. He concentrated on a feeling of arrogance and entitlement. He *was* Katar. All who met him would see Katar. He strode up to the guarded gateway to the rich section of the city, not even glancing at the guards.

The same guard that had laughed at him as Lanos dragged him through was there. This time he nodded politely at Tsom and stood up a bit straighter. Tsom ignored him as best he could, a smile tugging very hard at the corners of his lips. He thought about sniffing loudly and curling his nose, but there was enough fate to tempt today.

Alanar's compound was a wasteland. The walls were crumbled, the buildings burned. Obviously unwatched for some time, Tsom wandered into the remains of the garden thinking thoughts that he belonged here, he was Katar, hoping to influence any who might see him here.

Nothing lived. He poked around the dead plants and broken furniture. Out of all the blackened vegetation a small microcosm of green stood out. Tsom brushed the debris aside. A broken miniature tree lay smashed on the ground. At first glance it was totally crushed. The branches were broken, bent and twisted. Yet, amongst the blackened vegetation of the garden, the small shoot of green at its base stood out, its tiny nascent needles unfurling valiantly. On a whim, Tsom bent and wrapped a scrap of cloth around its roots and tucked it into his coat. The Karn family estate was not far.

"I have a message from Arlec's sisters, which is of a sensitive nature." Tsom looked directly at the compound guards, willing himself to appear Katar and self-confident. He patted his breast pocket, as if something were in it. Pretending to be Katar was easier this second time and of course the Katar knew that only one of their own could wear the ring. The guard nodded. "He is in the briefing room. Ask the doorman for directions." He looked disinterested and bored. He waved Tsom in.

As soon as he was out of sight he moved quickly. He did not know if it would help, but he thought of himself as a shadow and hard to see. Concentrating on the task he did not notice the ring on his left hand glow ever so slightly. He felt very hungry, despite having eaten well not long ago.

He made it to a second story window, by climbing to the roof and then dropping to the narrow sill below. His original thought was to go in on the first floor, but something drew him to this window. Shara had not told him where she thought the talisman would be, but people were people, even Katar. Something that valuable, even if well hidden, would be on the second floor he reasoned. Just that much harder to get to. Shara had spoken of the hours her father spent reading and gazing out of the second story window of the library. This window looked like it had the best view. Remembering the safety features of Alanar's compound the first time he had entered, he looked around for any strange lights, or inlays, or talismans. None. The window wasn't even locked and opened with ease. He slid in noiselessly.

Looking around, he was in some sort of study. A fire burned in the fireplace, despite the warmth of the season. He walked straight to the fireplace. He was almost always right about where things were hidden, even if in the past his theft was petty compared to what he was after now. He ran his hands over the mantle looking for a flaw. He tried tugging and pushing on various parts, remembering stories he heard as a kid of moving fireplaces or bookshelves.

Tsom wondered where Shara's room was in relation to the study. She was probably here, comforting her family. Would she abandon her loyalty to the resistance? He felt guilty attempting the theft now, instead of waiting for Shara as they had planned, but this was safer for her, possibly for him. No one would expect a break in the moment Shara arrived.

Stumped he crouched and stared into the flames. Strange how regular the flames were. Normally the dance between the flames varied in a manner that was unpredictable; one swallowing another, a new one born, a change of mood, loss of energy, and then flaring up. These flames were like two new dancers. The steps were right, but there was no passion, no life. A few moments of continued gazing confirmed this. The flames were not right. He waved his hand near the flames. Definitely hot, so hot that his hand blistered just from the wave.

Somewhere must be a talisman generating these flames—probably within the flames itself. Where was the qenar fueling this, he wondered. He tried moving the logs with a poker. The log moved, but the flames did not. He moved all the logs and the fire grate. The flames stayed where they were. Now a small door was visible just beyond the flames, on the floor. A very complex latch held the door. The latch needed finger manipulation he could see, impossible to open with anything else. Every instinct screamed that this was the hiding place.

Voices from one of the other rooms drifted over to him from the open window. Shara, he recognized her voice instantly. Would she guess that he had come so soon to steal? He wanted to leave her out of this. He would leave her to her grief and she would not have to make the decision between loyalty to family and the resistance—and what decision would he make, if forced to choose between Shara and the resistance?

The voices were near, the approach slow due to some sort of argument.

Not much time. He had to act fast. Not time to think this through, or finesse. If he was going to do this before Shara moved the item, or warned the Karn family he had to act now.

Clenching his teeth he said to himself, 'It won't hurt, it won't hurt, it's just an illusion." He willed it to be true.

The pain was unbelievable. The damage was much worse than any normal fire. The smell of burning meat was overwhelming and combined with the sickening sound of searing and bubbling was almost worse than the pain. The pain faded to an abstraction as his brain could no longer deal with it, but somehow he did not make a sound. The Katar ring glowed fiercely on his left hand and a commotion seemed to be occurring within the compound. Men yelling something about a Katar in need nearby, servants crying in pain. Somehow he got the door open and pulled out the small box inside before his right hand became totally useless. It was almost as if his fingers had a mind of their own, as if through the pain he could feel the latch. Using his good left hand he tucked it inside his tunic and ran for the window. Refusing to look at his burned hand, he used his good hand as he swung over the edge and let himself drop the rest of the way.

He rolled with the fall, hitting the burned hand several times. The pain was there, but again it was as if he were observing something too terrible to process fully. Shock, he thought. Thank the Sea for shock. He started for the gate. Now he had to look at his right hand, or he would not know how to focus his visage. He threw up.

The hand was not really there. A charred skeleton with small bits of burned flesh clinging to it was all that remained. He had no idea how he had been able to actually manipulate the small latch and lift the box out, but there was no fooling anyone with the hand. If Larrina was right the illusion that he was able to pull off was based on what actually existed. It was more like a chameleon ability. He could not appear smaller or larger than he was. He could not make a hand that wasn't there appear to be there. He clenched his teeth and shoved his right stump into his pants pocket. Wiping the tears and sweat off of his face he proceeded to the gate.

The guards were tense. "What's happening in the compound?" Asked the closer one.

"Arlec's sister, Shara, is making quite a scene. Has the whole house in an uproar. She is screaming and yelling at Arlec. I felt I had best leave and not intrude on the family at this difficult time." Tsom did his best to keep his voice steady. He hoped that any tremulous intonations would be attributed to the factors cited in his lie.

Both guards seemed to buy it. The spokesman for the two noted, "We thought there was something more dangerous, with all the Katar seeming to run toward the main house at the same time, as if some sort of signal had gone off."

"Everyone is just on edge, with the recent happenings. Keep your eyes open." He lifted his left hand and waved a goodbye and kept going.

***

Later, staring inside the empty box, Tsom wept softly to himself.

Chapter 31

The village contained no more than a few hundred Hrýll. What first struck Lanos was that there were very few young adults. A few children and many older adults. Not all were very old, but very few were eighteen to thirty five, child bearing years. Despite its small size the village was hardly primitive. The buildings were mainly wood, but looked like they were quite old and elaborate—if not very large. Each doorway was hand carved and inlaid with jade. The roofs were steep and had small chimneys poking out near the center; making the street a row of umbrellas made of wood and tile, or perhaps mushrooms. The roads cobbled with worn wooden pavers that interlocked in strange patterns were better than most Alanar had seen in The Cities; ironwood, or some wood even harder that showed no signs of rot.

The townspeople stopped and stared. Humans were not a common occurrence. Oonie stopped in front of a house that, while no larger than the rest, had an air of importance about it. The street in front was slightly more worn, the jade inlay had a diamond or two in it and a single sapphire. There was a female Hrýll standing in the doorway. Oonie greeted her affectionately and introduced her to Lanos and Alanar.

"Tiar, my what you would call *wife*. We do not use the term, but it is close enough."

Although alien, with her light fur, she was attractive. Her lips were full and her smile made Lanos want to smile back. She was leaner than most Human women, although this seemed the norm for the Hrýll he had seen. Her breasts were held in place by some sort of bra, but it was obviously meant as an external garment. He guessed she wore this for practical purposes, as they were larger than the uncovered breasts of the other female Hrýll—he found that Tiar's garb drew his eyes to her chest more than if she had been bare breasted. Maybe she wore it for more than practical purposes. Her lower garb accented modest hips and she had an almost Human sway to her walk. Her light red fur showed no signs of age, but her face had lines of experience on it. She smiled welcomingly to them.

"Death and his companion return to the Hrýll," Tiar addressed Alanar.

"Madam, do I know you?" Alanar dropped a bit ungracefully off the horse, not quite stumbling. He was tired, but no worse for the wear and tear of the past days with the Hrýll.

"No, not in this lifetime. Yet, you are unchanged … physically. Do you remember a Nelsa from your past?"

The name had a surprising effect on Alanar. Fragments of memories assaulted him. Evil, cruel memories. Visions of slaughtering women and children and a young Hrýll woman. She had been raped and left to die … had he done it … no, but somehow he was responsible.

"I … you … no … I did not mean to … did it really happen?" Alanar seemed to be in a waking nightmare, unsure of his memories, or reaction.

Tiar seemed a bit surprised at his reaction. Oonie placed a hand on her shoulder. "He does not truly remember. Lanos told me some of what has transpired in the past month. He already had problems remembering before the past month. He is reborn without going to the Sea of Souls. It is a change that occurs suddenly, as Lanos described it. My guess is each time he 'changes' his mind is partially reborn." Tiar looked skeptical, but waved them both in. Oonie took their horses himself, not delegating the task to another.

Alanar had been fighting a constant headache since the change. His emotions always seemed to be in flux and his memories ephemeral. He would try and concentrate on something and his headache would get worse. Larrina had been an anchor, and now that anchor was gone. His memories of her were strong and just being with her and drinking her teas had kept that portion of his brain steady. The battle with the bandits had been almost a relief, but it had taken its own toll. Instinct had taken over and he didn't need to think. Act. Move. Act. Move. Then, the exhausted sleep. He thought he had just passed out for a moment, until he awoke amongst the Hrýll party. Almost immediately the headache had returned. Strange fragments of memories upon seeing the Hrýll and yet he could not even remember why he was here. The more he needed to heal, the more he got lost in memories.

They sat in a comfortable room, lit by a combination of glow globes and skylights. The glow globes were elaborate and mimicked the outdoor light. In The Cities these would be worth a small treasure, but the Hrýll were—after all—the creators of glow globes. Oonie served tea, while Tiar sat with the guests. She grilled Lanos on how long he knew Alanar and what his relationship was to him. She constantly nodded and smiled as if she had been expecting his response. She had rather openly loosened her tunic that held her breasts firmly against her chest, embarrassing Lanos. It seemed to be a natural action, based solely on her comfort. Alanar concentrated on her face and remained silent. Something about her face was making his head worse. It was as if she were out of focus, blurry.

Oonie returned and sat next to Tiar, his hand slipping comfortably into her lap. "You have come to request something of us, of the Hrýll."

Not a question, but a statement and an invitation to explain.

Alanar spoke. "I had intended on making it to Farnlaran, to meet with your leader there."

"While I do not speak for all of the Hrýll, I can speak with knowledge of how any request may be received," Oonie responded.

Alanar hesitated, sipping his tea. Apple flavors, not sweet, with flowers he could not identify. These two Hrýll were so familiar. That name, Nelsa, kept stirring memories, making it hard to think. *Death, she had called him. Death. He was young. Distant past—an unknown number of years. Death. They had escaped. They, who had been with him? They had to fight for their foothold. The qenar was life and they had to fight for it. The Hrýll had foolishly resisted. Battle lust. He had not meant to kill so many. So much power back then. He sipped his tea and tried to focus. When? When had he been young?* He spoke.

"The Katar rule mankind, subtly and not so subtly. Through mankind they have ruled the races of Nakana for millennia. While man's numbers grow, each individual is also growing weaker due to the parasitic drain of the Katar. An opportunity exists to change that. To overthrow the Katar. This is an opportunity for both mankind and the old races. The Hrýll have a chance, perhaps the Srýll too."

Tiar shook her head. "You know it is more than the Katar. The gods of man are the ones truly draining mankind of its essence. You know this more than any man. Do you propose to overthrow both gods and Katar?"

So much power. It had been impossible not to use it. Glory. Victory. Death. Even his friends had called him Death. He had saved them and they had shunned him. He closed down the flood of thoughts. It was chaos and he could not make sense of them right now. If only he could remember, yet the more he tried to remember the faster the half memories fled. He replied.

"The gods are cowards. They will try and use their worshippers to aid the Katar, but they and the Katar are busy battling the new threat, the Tarth back from Hell." He hesitated. How had he known the Tarth had been banished to Hell, the name he somehow knew was given to the 95th plane. He rubbed his temples. 95th … how many planes were there? Ninety-nine sprang to mind. He shook his head and continued speaking. "With the aid of the Hrýll and Srýll we could strike when they are the weakest. You would have access to qenar again, without the restrictions that the Katar place on you."

"Why should we risk ourselves? The *daemons* will probably do the work for us. If they succeed in coming through full-force, mankind will be unable to keep them back, even if the gods come to their aid. Hrýll and Srýll lived in peace with the *daemons* in the past and we could do so again. They know that we had nothing to do with their banishment."

"Perhaps, but then your races controlled the qenar. Also, that was many millennia ago. From their perspective, the weapons used against them now are Hrýll weapons; made by you for the Katar. If the *daemons* wipe out mankind, then they may decide to keep the qenar for themselves. They may also remove the last threat to their dominance."

Alanar wished he had a brandy. It would help clear his head. Too many disjointed images, memories—less than memories, intruded. He pushed forward, playing his final cards.

"One of our group is a catalyst, born on the five moon eclipse. I believe he is full blooded Kinel. By now he has the talisman of banishment, which can be used to open the gateway to Hell long enough for the full force of *daemons* to come through. Or, to banish the force already here back to Hell. With this artifact we will be able to turn back the Tarth. Wouldn't you rather, after they are turned back, that mankind owed you a favor and had reason to see that they, through the Katar, have treated your race badly?"

Oonie looked sorrowful. "A Kinel. So few remain. They made the mistake of trusting mankind themselves and look where they are. Extinct, except for a few half-breeds and perhaps this one and Larrina. Man destroys those he does not understand, or resemble. Why are you trying to help them now, after all these years?"

Alanar raised his hand. He opened his mouth to reply and then shut it. The short silence was rich with expectancy. He couldn't think through his headache. He had helped them before, hadn't he? He saw Lanos watching him.

"I stood by too long. For a period I forgot to care. I have missed opportunities before." The latter was almost a question. Lanos nodded his head imperceptibly. "This opportunity cannot be ignored. It is history repeating itself, but this time I won't ..." He clutched his head and finished in a whisper "... it would be easier not to make the same mistakes if I could just remember more. This time mankind will share what it has with the Hrýll and Srýll as equals. The Katar and their rings will go and their gods will follow. If you don't help, and mankind does beat back both the Katar and Tarth, where does that leave you?" Alanar waited a moment. Was this persuasive to the Hrýll? Mankind had not been generous to the Hrýll in the past. "I can see what the demands of the Katar are doing to you. You are all aging prematurely. You will go the way of the Kinel. I am offering you a chance to return to equal footing with mankind. Nothing more."

144

Oonie sat back, satisfied. "I cannot speak for the few remaining Srýll, but the Hrýll will help, after some discussion. The Katar will be demanding talismans to aid in their fight against the *daemons* from Hell. They will be surprised when they give out at crucial times. We are few and we are not warriors, but we will travel to Argn and help the resistance when the time comes," he sipped his glass of tea and then leaned forward looking at Alanar's eyes.

"The Talisman of Banishment is an ancient device. It is from Before. If it still exists and you have it, then we have a chance, but misused it could have an effect opposite from that which is intended. If it has survived in the Katar hands all this time, I am surprised we have not heard of its misuse. I hope for our sake that your Kinel thief has indeed found it, or if not that the Katar do not misuse it. But, you are right, it is time, my old friend and old enemy."

Tiar did not look satisfied. "Perhaps you have changed, perhaps you have simply forgotten enough to live with yourself again. Perhaps." She touched Oonie lightly. "I do not remember as much of my past incarnations as my mate, but I *know* you. You are a double edged sword." She stopped to take a breath. So much talking in common tongue seemed taxing to her and she switched to Hrýll, the Old Tongue. "10,000 years since the last catalyst influenced the world's events, if our legends and recorded history is accurate." Another pause. She was looking inward, considering what he had told her. "A Kinel born on the Eclipse. That is an interesting twist. He will have to learn quickly his own powers to survive being a nexus of change. If he is pure Kinel he must be careful not to burn himself out. The ability of the Kinel was always strong, but they lacked control." Oonie and Alanar nodded in agreement. Lanos turned from one to the other, a vaguely confused look on his face.

Chapter 32

Be Na Tarth, Lord of the *Daemons*, strode through the smoking remains of the village. His given name, Carnel, was rarely used since his rise he occasionally didn't think of himself as anything but Be Na Tarth. The smell of burnt wood, flesh, and a mixture of smaller sundries was strong. He inhaled deeply, smelling a portion of revenge. The jade sphere hung at his throat, constantly reminding him of how empty it was. The *ka* of many more were needed before it would be full again. The Humans had so little *ka* compared with the Tarth. Each death did little to add to the power of the sphere. He was loath to attempt an attack against the large city of Zethicia so soon. A few more villages would help. More Human souls destroyed, never to trouble his people again, their pitiful *ka* fueling the future destruction of their own kind.

He stood within a still smoldering structure. The heat did not bother him, although he knew that the Chimi, the companions of the Tarth, would be uncomfortable. Bending down he picked up the charred remains of an infant. *So like us when you see them like this*. He thought of how many of his own children had perished in the harshness of the Hell, the 95th plane. *At least we will not subject them to that. Simple death. Simple, but they would never be reborn, never to plague Nakana again.*

A clearing of a throat. One of the Chimi scouts. "Yes?"

"Lord, the Katar have started to arrive at Zethicia."

"Then the real fight begins soon." Things had changed since the Tarth last roamed Nakana. There had been no gate between Zethicia, a small town then, and The Cities. The interrogated prisoners claimed that five thousand years had passed since the banishment. To him it had been a mere one hundred. They had guessed that time was different between the planes, but nothing so radical. Much had changed here. Mankind was much more populous. They had destroyed many of the old races. The Tarth would avenge them also. These Humans were a pestilence that needed eradicating.

Be Na Tarth crushed the child's skull to dust and let the dust sift through his fingers.

***

The battle between the Tarth and the forces of Zethicia had not gone well. Carnel had expected real resistance, but had hoped the Katar, after five thousand years, had grown soft. Yet, they had managed to beat back the Tarth at the hastily constructed walls surrounding the core of the city.

The Chimi fell before the Katar. However, most had separated from the Tarth before the battle, circling to engage the Humans. The Katar had concentrated on only the Tarth, ignoring the Chimi—as they had expected. This left the Humans and the Chimi to battle largely on their own.

At the nexus of the battle stood Be Na Tarth. His red skin glowed with exertion and rage. Five Katar had him surrounded. They moved quickly, but soon discovered that he moved as fast as they did. Their rings glowed, but he was immune to the affects. He grinned with satisfaction as he severed the head of one Katar. He felt the flow of *ka* from the jade sphere around his neck provide the fuel for the Katar instead of his own *ka,* a terrible waste, but better than his own. He could not stop the rings from draining *ka,* but that they were gaining their power from the *ka* of the already dead villagers provided him some satisfaction. He regretted the loss, but there were plenty more Humans to fuel the gate later on.

One of the Katar came too close; his sword hit Be Na Tarth, but only nicked his dense flesh. The *daemon* grabbed the sword arm with one hand, clenching the arm, it broke as he pulled the man closer, and snapped his neck with the other hand. He then threw the body at one of the other Katar. Not waiting to see if he hit, he leapt backwards at the Katar he knew was there. His massive weight knocked his opponent down and a fast kick to the windpipe finished him.

After ten Katar died at Be Na Tarth's hands, they backed off, keeping him occupied but not closing. The arrows began to fly. Most he swatted in mid-air but a few found their mark. Of those only a few penetrated his dense skin and flesh, but eventually those had an effect. They did not penetrate deeply, but now he had hundreds of small wounds covering his body. *Cowards*. Between the physical wounds and the vanishing *ka* from the jade sphere, he knew it was time to leave. His companions would not have the protection he did and while their *ka* was stronger than any Human, they would be tiring.

He called out in a strangely melodic voice. The expected response of howling and barking was returned. The Katar had been told of the Maite dogs, but had not seen them during the battle. While they fended off the giant battle dogs, Be Na Tarth moved quickly away. The screams of Humans mixed with the dogs. He had to survive. Without his leadership, the gateway would never be opened. His people would die on Hell and curse his failure. For their sake he retreated, leaving a swath of destruction in his path. The Katar's rings would have no effect on the Maite dogs. They were not truly sentient. He knew the power and limitations of those rings, perhaps better than the Katar of this time did.

The Katar had, in the end, saved the day for Zethicia at great sacrifice to their numbers. Their rings glowing, they moved with inconceivable speed, several attacking a single Tarth. The unfortunate soldier who wandered too near during the attack found out why orders had been given to stay separate from the Katar. It had been centuries since the Katar had fought in force. The legends of their destructive power were no longer clear. Civilians and soldiers alike fell not by sword, but were dying of old age. Withered before their time, as if punished by the prisons of The Cities en masse. The Katar as a group were an indiscriminate weapon, but effective.

Of the two thousand Tarth and six thousand Chimi, over five hundred Tarth had died in the battle, and three thousand Chimi. Most of the Maite dogs had also perished. Reports indicated that over one thousand of the Katar had been killed, with over five hundred of their rings collected. The Humans had done better than Be Na Tarth had expected. They had killed only seven thousand of them. He moved his forces further away. Another frontal attack was not yet possible. They would no doubt be sending more Katar in through the gateway between Zethicia and The Cities. He had reduced the ring wielding Katar by over a fifth, at a cost of over a fourth of his own Tarth. A different strategy was in order. If only he had his full forces here. Then the Katar would be no more. He growled in rage, his massive neck muscles tight. He hoped there were a few prisoners to question.

Chapter 33

The alley provided comforting obscurity from crowds. Tsom leaned against the dirty brick wall and allowed himself a moment to breathe. The foul smells familiar to a wharf rat, as Tsom sometimes thought of himself. He knew how to stay to the alleys and avoid confrontation with its denizens. His tired and dazed mind struggled with pain while nothing but questions rolled around as dice in his head, always coming up with small faces as the pips: Larrina, Shara, Lanos, Arlec, Alanar. Different combinations, same faces. Why hide an empty box? An elaborate trap? Arlec had already framed him for a break in and murder, why this? He would have had to know that it was a target? It must be coincidence. Had it been moved ages ago? Just bad luck—what was luck? Luck couldn't be the whole story. Could Shara have betrayed him by mistake? His thinking was far from clear as the throbbing of his ruined right hand increased. Luck. Was he really doomed to have bad luck all the time? Was this balance to his 'good' luck as a thief? Questions, but no answers. Each question just generated its own set of children. There would be no answers if he did not survive.

His breath was coming hard and he blinked and looked around. A large rat stopped its progress along the far wall and stared at him, its nose twitching. As if to say, 'follow me' it turned its head, looked back at Tsom and then darted into a crack along the wall. Tsom nodded and pushed himself to a full stand. He had to move. It had been a mistake to come back here along the wharf. The Katar were sure to be looking here, or their spies. The dice in his head came up two Larrinas.

Born on the eclipse of the five moons. His mother had said it in hushed tones. It was never to be mentioned. They celebrated his birthday two weeks later. He had almost forgotten his real birthdate. The shock over finding out he was Kinel, or part Kinel, had not been jarring once he had time to digest it and his memories filled in pieces he had long forgotten. His mother had always been the more powerful of his parents, his memories of his father more vague. She had told him to concentrate on not drawing attention to himself. 'Concentrate, you are just like everyone else, believe it, know it.'

He had been drawn to Larrina immediately because she reminded him of his mother. Kinel. He was Kinel. Now he understood why the Katar had gone after his mother. He did not hate them less, but finally there was a reason. The intolerance of the Katar. Their fear. Their hatred. He had seen people mistreat the Hrýll and other races. He understood prejudice, people feared and hated what they did not understand and what was different. He was the one different now. He was the race everyone hated, because the Katar had taught them to hate. The fuel of pain made him hate the Katar even more.

Tsom looked out of the alley into the street. He kept what remained of his right hand tucked into his jacket. Could he afford seeking medical attention? No. He had the address of another in the resistance memorized. It was his rendezvous point with the sphere. He had no sphere, but he was one of Alanar's troops now. Lanos had said, 'Once you are in, we take care of our own.' Hopefully they were as skilled in healing as Larrina was. He had no choice. He had to get word to Larrina and Alanar that he had failed them.

The street was crowded. Normally a good thing for blending in and picking pockets, but Tsom was worried he wouldn't have the energy to navigate the crowd. He pulled his burned right arm stump out from his jacket and examined it carefully. From the wrist onward there was necrotized flesh where his hand had been. He felt phantom pain in the hand, where no nerves existed. It was almost as if he could flex his hand. What could a healer do? The rest of his arm did not appear to be infected. No healer would try to regenerate a limb, unless forced, due to risk to their own life. Full limb regeneration was rare, dangerous, and both the healer and the injured were likely to die. From what he had heard, it had to be done in the first few hours after the injury and somehow he thought that this injury was far from normal. It was a loss. He would never have a right hand again.

Whether it was shock or he was simply getting used to the bizarre and unexpected, Tsom could not find it in himself to dwell on his injury. He had to move on and survive. His escape from the Katar compound was a temporary respite, he had to keep moving. For now he was alive.

The smell of his own charred flesh was starting to sicken and distract his thinking. He went to the edge of a nearby dumpster. He clenched his teeth and focused his gaze on a single point. He swung his right arm down. There was snapping noise and the pain made him double over, hugging himself and moaning. He forced himself up and looked at his right arm. At the wrist ended a pink and purple stump which looked like it was partially healed over. The blacked hand was gone. Glancing he noticed it had fallen neatly into the dumpster. He smiled grimly. His thieving days were over, finally reformed.

Larrina believed that the reason he had survived so long as a thief was twofold: one he was plain good at it, with skill that was probably *ka* enhanced over the years and two that his luck, being born on the Eclipse, had worked in conjunction with his natural skills. For example whenever he broke into a house that he thought was empty, it really was. If he chose his mark for picking a pocket assuming that the person was distracted, they really were distracted. Skill combined with luck. Luck alone would not save him. It may have helped him in the past—but maybe the bill was past due. He pulled a handkerchief out of his pocket and managed to tie it around his right stump. The Katar and city guards would be looking for a thief. No one knew that he had lost a hand, might as well make use of that. Make it obvious he had no hand. As he went in search of the rendezvous safe house he tried to recall something from his talks with Larrina.

Larrina had tried to cram a lifetime of Kinel teaching and history into a few days. They had talked for hours over his life, analyzing it.

As he got older, she felt that these small events would continue to pile up and provide the opportunity for big things. From Larrina's viewpoint, Arlec would have probably taken his ring off sometime and it was the catalyst, Tsom's *luck*, that brought him to the docks. Tsom could have ignored Arlec. The choice was still his. The drunk Yanín might have had a purse full of sintar too and picking his pocket might have had no consequences. The choices were still his and the consequences of those choices were real, but the potential in each of those choices would continue to increase with time. Something big occurred the longer a catalyst lived. Or a catalyst died a strange and spectacular death. This was the legend of those born on the Eclipse.

She did not claim to know everything, but her insights rang true. Both Larrina and Alanar had knowledge that spanned many of his lifetimes.

He glanced into the street again. The crowd had thinned and he felt a trifle more energized. Time to move. He went through the chameleon effect thought exercise. He thought of himself as merchant's assistant. He *was* a merchant's assistant. One did not need two hands to be useful to a merchant. He stood up straight and sauntered into the street.

As he made his way to the rendezvous point he thought of what role he could play now. He had failed as a thief, but he could still help. If Alanar and Larrina were right, he had value simply in existing and being on their side. He would fight, as best as he could, as long as the Katar existed, for as long as they did Larrina was in danger. Alanar needed to succeed and maybe he could help. If he survived long enough. If he was really a catalyst. The young merchant's assistant made his way through Argn to a neighborhood he had only heard of, but had never been to.

The neighborhood was unsavory even by Tsom's old wharf standards. Given Alanar and Larrina's homes he had expected something different for his contact. He looked at the address plate once again, rubbing off some of the dirt. '*Herbalist, Taxidermy, Embalming, and Exotic Foods—Second Floor.*' His stomach turned at the latter. What sort of exotic foods would be available considering the rest? The bell on the door was broken. He opened the door to the dark stairway. Even with the door open very little of the bright sun filtered in. Someone had made the mistake of carpeting the stairs, a long time ago. The mold assaulted his nose and he repressed a sneeze. A mouse darted into the darker gloom under the bottom stair. He unconsciously flexed for his right hand knife. It almost felt as if his hand were there. Trying to breathe only through his mouth he mounted the stairs.

The door at the top was made of thick oak, old but still true. He rapped with his left hand, letting the ring hit the wood for emphasis.

"Yeah. It's open."

The smoothness of the door's movement was incongruous to the decay all around. Tsom strode in.

"So the little wharf rat continues to run errands for his master."

Tsom was already rolling as the blow hit him on the side of the head. Not enough to knock him out, but he was dazed. He tried focusing on the ring. It began to glow as he was slammed into the wall. As he blacked out he saw Arlec's grinning face behind the two men attached to massive metal covered fists descending on his face.

***

Kenavar brownies. Warm sweet spicy smell. And milk. His mother had not baked those in such a long time. He chewed the warm brownie and sipped the milk. Some dribbled down his chin. The milk was warm. Salty.

Tsom opened his eyes. The blood dripped off of his chin. A torch sputtered to the side and he focused on it. Or tried to. Slowly his eyes focused. He rubbed his eyes with his left hand and screamed.

They had cut off his *other* hand. The bloody left stump was crudely bandaged and soaked in blood. He passed out.

Chapter 34

Shara awoke. Her pillow was wet with drool and smelled sour. She turned her head and the room swam, spinning in the direction she turned her head. Repressing a gag she pushed herself up. It was her room. Daylight. She was naked and stank of urine. Her throat was dry and harsh. The nightstand had a glass full of water, which she desperately filled her mouth with.

She quickly spat out the water and sniffed the glass. Fenbar. She recognized it from her training. A powerful drug, it was used for questioning of suspects and keeping them calm and cooperative. Large quantities would render one unconscious. Not quite a truth serum, but close.

Her brother.

He had not been overjoyed to see her—no surprise, there was no love lost between Arlec and his sisters. The fact he called her an accomplice to murdering her father had been a surprise. That he dared to take action using other Katar had been shocking. The other Katar present had been reluctant, but she remembered being forced to drink. Alcohol and Fenbar. Her own brother. Her own clan. She turned her head and threw up, managing to keep it off of the bed.

The forced drinking of the Fenbar cocktail was the last she remembered.

She didn't have much time. She stood up quickly ... then picked herself off the floor where she had found herself immediately. Sounds outside. She tossed the contents of the glass of tainted water into her bed, with the urine, then quickly filled the glass with fresh water from the pitcher, spilling a little. No time to mop up the spill, she hoped it would go unnoticed in the general mess of the room. She jumped into her bed and pulled the covers back over herself.

"There's the high and mighty princess." She kept her eyes shut and her breathing slow and steady. "Time for your medicine you little tramp." An arm slid under her neck and roughly lifted her up. The glass pushed against her lips and the water was poured down quickly and sloppily. She couldn't avoid a cough or two, but that seemed normal to whomever was pouring.

She felt the covers pulled back and managed not to move. A rough hand ran itself over her breasts and crotch. "No time *today* sweetheart. Maybe tomorrow." A chuckle as the hand probed her then the hand was gone. The door opened and closed.

The rage helped clear her head, but she managed to remain still with her eyes shut. She would remember that voice.

Chapter 35

He was not sure how long he was out the second time, not that he had any concept how long the first time had been. The bloody left stump was crusting over when he regained consciousness. Tsom sat and stared at both of his arms. His brain refused to fully accept that in the space of one day he had lost two hands. Twice he reached to rub his eyes with an open hand, hitting the traumatized ends of his right arm against his chin and face. It was as if hands were real and not figments of his imagination. The pain was real. For a time he focused on the pain. Intentionally bumping both stumps against his head several times to force the knowledge in. The pain of the left arm was greater than the right.

Slowly the sounds, smells, and dim sights of the room sank through the shock. He tried standing, reaching out with his hand to get to his feet. More pain, as he yet again relearned the lesson that he had no hand to reach out with. No hands—no balance. The strange part was how much both of his hands hurt. Phantom pain. He had heard of it. It sure felt real. Better to stay on his knees. He thought *hands* and knees for a second and had to catch himself. Just knees.

He crawled over to the wall, turned, leaning against the wall, and looked at his cell. Thankfully, it was lit, not a dark cell. No furniture. A small drain in the center of the eight-by-eight room. The sputtering torch was on the other side of the door which was comprised of bars and let some light in.

A thief with no hands. An ancient punishment, before they switched to draining *ka* as punishment. Useless. Useless to himself. Useless to overthrowing the Katar. Useless to saving Larrina from the fate of his mother, useless to Shara. He pounded his stumps on the ground ignoring the pain shooting up both arms, lighting them on fire. The left one began to bleed again. Eventually, he passed out for a third time.

Time to wake up Tsumi. My little Tsumi you will be late for school. You were out late playing again, time to wake up. He opened his eyes. *Mom?* It was not his mother shaking him. The large guard stepped back.

"I thought you might be dead. Lord Arlec wanted to make sure you were alive. No simple death for you. True death for the likes of you, murderer." A small kick at his kidneys, enough to hurt dully through his fog of existing pain. He rolled up to a sitting posture, avoiding his two stumps by using his elbows. The extended time of unconsciousness allowed him to process the fact that he had no hands. At least his reactions took it into account. He had always reacted fast to physical stimulus, but he was not sure that would be a great help now. The left one was newly bandaged and only lightly soaked. The right one was left as is, the burned and puckered skin looking inflamed, but not bloody.

A tin of water and a plate of something resembling food was near him. The guard was already locking the door and walking away. *I guess I'm not much fun to taunt.*

He drank, holding the tin carefully between his forearms. Despite being hungry, he could not quite force himself to eat the smelly, moldy, indeterminate mess on the plate. He would have had to shove his face into it to eat and the thought of it made him gag.

He smelled himself and realized that they had let him soil himself several times. There was no way to untie his pants. Tears of frustration ran down his crusted face.

He crawled to the door and looked down the hallway. Several other doors, all ajar. It seemed his was the only occupied cell. *I must be privileged.* The crawl back to the wall exhausted him. He dozed off. Not quite passing out this time, but falling into a fitful sleep.

***

He had fallen asleep on his hand again. Sometimes after playing late at night he was so exhausted he slept in weird positions. His mother worried that he was staying out too late rather than studying. She said he was almost old enough to learn important new things, but that he had to show he was ready. 'Wake up, your arm will fall off if you sleep on it like that.' That tingling feeling mixed with pain was annoying. Tsom awoke with a start. The pain was real. Two feet away a rat was gnawing on his bandaged left hand. Disgust and rage. He wanted to crush the rat. Kill it. He desperately reached out with his non-existent hand and tried to strangle it. Suddenly he *felt* the rat in his grip. The hand was not there, but he felt it. He squeezed—hard. The rat struggled in the air a few inches from the end of his stump. It was in obvious pain. It bit at whatever was grabbing it, but nothing was there. Surprised, Tsom's rage disappeared. The rat scurried away.

He lifted his bloody stump and stared at it. He willed the bandages to move. Nothing happened. He moved his right arm, with its burned stump near his left arm. He concentrated on grabbing his left arm with the hand of his imagination, the hand that had grasped the rat. He jumped when he felt the pressure—both with his *hand* and on his arm.

***

Time lost meaning. His main worry was that they would come for his execution before he mastered his new *hands*. When he was able to maintain consciousness he kept concentrating and practicing. The problem was the longer he used his invisible hands the more tired he became. Fatigue was both his enemy and his friend. The fatigue kept him from dwelling on his plight, on his loss. All he could do was focus. Practice with his new found power. He had a fever too. Either that or it was very hot down here in his prison. Each time he slipped into unconsciousness it was worse. The rats were gnawing on his wounds when he was under. He killed two. If he had the energy he would have been more revolted. If he had the energy he would have killed more of them.

Eventually he knew it was time to try out his idea. It had occurred to him during one of the many semi-conscious bouts. He knew he had to succeed in escaping soon, or he would not wake up after one of his exhausted sleeps. He dragged himself to the door. Concentrating he moved the end of his right hand stump to the lock. He reached inside the lock with his *hand*. He thought of these invisible things as his *hands*. There was no other word for them. He could feel the lock mechanism, just as he had two years ago.

He had broken into the shipping company's main office. The sailor had been so frightened of returning to sea. He had told Tsom of the papers that forced him to work for another five years for the company: debt to a healer for his young daughter. Normally he took stories of sailors with a grain of salt, but this young man was only a year or two older than Tsom. His fear was so tangible that Tsom had shivered with him. That night, after the sailor lay passed out at the bar while Tsom remained sober, he had gone to the shipping company office. He just wanted to prove what a good thief he was. No other reason. He hardly knew the young sailor.

The office had been easy, but the safe was not. He was not used to major break ins and had only a vague idea as to how to break into a safe. He had spun the dial and then listened. He had concentrated so hard that his fingers had started to hurt, then it was as if he could feel the lock mechanism. Tumblers moving, gears, small shafts with springs, he could feel it all. A light in the outer office. He concentrated and the safe opened. He scanned the contents in the light filtering in from outside. A box full of papers. Thanking his ability to read, he realized the entire box was conscript papers. Without bothering to sort them he closed the safe. Moments later the guard stuck his head in the office, the expensive glow lantern in one hand.

The sensation of feeling inside a lock had never happened again and soon he had forgotten about it. It was during one of his fitful sleeping spells that he had recalled the incident from a lifetime ago.

Fighting to stay conscious he manipulated the lock. It was as he recalled, but this time there was no external hand mimicking the motions of what was occurring inside the lock. It was a simple enough mechanism, not easy to pick without the proper tools, but nothing complex. The thought that this was the first time he was trying to break *out* of someplace, rather than in, crossed his mind. *Times have changed*, he thought.

The lock complained, but gave way. He dropped his hand manifestation, exhausted and barely able to focus. He forced himself to a stand and staggered to the hallway door. It was unlocked, but he had to manifest a hand to open it. It had a lever on the outside. If many more doors were in his way, he would not make it.

The stairs up were dark. This prison, or personal dungeon of Arlec, did not warrant expensive glow globes down here. The sputtering torch was giving off as much smoke as light. He coughed lightly, his arm coming up to cover his mouth with his hand … which he stopped in mid movement. His already adjusted eyes could make out the outlines of the stairs, but not much else. Another door. Another exhausting effort. Each manifestation cost him dearly, the actual process of calling up *hands* seeming faster and slightly easier than before, but there were no reserves of energy left. He noticed he clenched his teeth with the effort now, his jaws ached.

The upper hallway was deserted and dark. It was obviously not a prison that he was in, but something else. His guess was that he was back at the Karn compound, given the comments by the guard earlier. How many days ago was that? Arlec must have wanted to enjoy the punishment before bringing him to public execution and true death. Tsom shuddered, even through his fog of exhaustion he felt fear. He wanted to believe in rebirth. If true, it was possible some age later to reunite with his mother and father again, especially his mother. She had always protected him. He had always felt there was something special about her. More than the normal feeling a son had. Now he understood some of that. She was Kinel, and so was he. She had been special. But, he did not want to be special. He had wanted revenge, but now he would trade it for freedom. He had been more free when he had not known that he was Kinel. Free to fight his small battles and thieve just enough to survive. Freedom. He focused on the thought.

He walked and slid down the hallway; his right shoulder scraping the sides as he staggered. The inevitable occurred. He heard voices approaching. His leg muscles were twitching in a mindless seizure. There was a side door five feet away and it looked impossible. One step. Rest. One step. Rest. The voices came closer. He was at the door.

It was locked. Given time and energy it would have not posed a problem. He had neither.

"Corl, who's that?" There were three of them. Tsom had no idea which one had spoken.

He had to dig deep to find fear within the exhaustion. He needed the fear. He stood and prepared to meet the three on the other side of the door.

Chapter 36

Hallam stretched—as a large cat would—she leaned forward over the table and reached past the edge, her back went concave then arched convex as she went up on her toes and her fingers curled at the end. She sighed contentedly and walked slowly around her pool, listening to her spies as they came and went.

Her spies—the birds, rodents, and other small creatures she had sent into The Cities and Zethicia—gave her a steady trickle of news. Some she passed on to Luck, some she did not, as it suited her. The boy, Tsom was his name, was indeed Kinel. The animals did not see his chameleon effect. They had no expectations and thus were not fooled by the illusion. She recalled when the Kinel had no such power. Once they became hunted by the Katar they had developed it as a race, adaptation. Under stress they were amazingly fast learners, but they always went too far. They used up their *ka* needlessly, tried too much too quickly. The Kinel were racially predisposed risk takers. It had been their downfall. It would probably be this boy's downfall. Still, of all the races, the gods feared, or had feared, only the Kinel. That glorious power to shape *ka* directly and in so many ways. So flexible, so useful, so dangerous to the myth of gods dominion over mankind. Little disturbed the gods any more, but this last of the Kinel had rattled them all.

It's that stupid prophesy of Nu Arr's. Why did they believe him? Because of his lover. That damned Kinel woman. Luck had thought he would be able to breed with her, to create an heir. Fool. The Kinel had used him as much as he had them, so long ago. Now the gods were on edge. The gods were afraid of a boy and the memories of a dead race. She shook her head and laughed. Most of the gods were on edge. She paused and popped a grape into her mouth, slowly chewing it as she walked to the steps leading into the pool. The temperature was perfect, as it should be after millennia of fiddling with the natural streams of hot spring water. She settled into the natural marble chair polished smooth and shaped for her body and let the warm water further relax her.

No, the boy did not worry her, but she was with the rest of the gods when it came to the Katar. The Katar and those damnable rings. Their ability to slow time and drain *ka* was dangerous. Combined with their unity and they could not be defeated by any one god, or even two. Too bad the gods could not show never show such unity. She smiled at her joke: Her plot to let the Katar, the *daemons*, and mankind all destroy each other would hardly be considered an act of unity. They couldn't tap the *ka* of animals; only she could do that. She smiled as an eagle landed on the tree limb overhanging the pool and opened its mind to hers with a view of Zethicia. Without humans she would be the only god with power, she and perhaps Pé. Pé did not matter, he did not crave power and would hide by his rivers of life and death—perhaps he had already perished. It had been centuries since he had answered a call to his temples, or shown up for one of their conclaves.

She stretched again and almost purred. An owl dropped a rat at the edge of the pool. Gazing into the rat's eyes she saw what the rat had seen in the prison. She sat up, frowning. *Fool*, she thought, *you're killing yourself even faster than your ancestors*. She sighed. The Kinel boy was needed for a time, then he could burn himself out, or get himself killed by the Katar. She would have to interfere again. Fortunately gods, mankind, and the races always ignored animals.

She concentrated and a white cat appeared, strolling slowly into her garden. She picked it up and gazed into its eyes and then fastened a collar around its neck. Dropping the cat to the ground the eagle swooped down and plucked it up. The cat did not struggle and the eagle kept its talons loose enough not to pierce the skin nor break the cat's back. Soon they were a mere speck in the sky.

Chapter 37

Tsom watched the three guards cautiously approach. The largest had his short sword out.

"Corl, is that the thief? He's got no hands. Lord Arlec cut them off? 'E looks half dead, why do three of us have ta come fetch 'im?"

"Viton, do you think he let himself out? Look sharp, there must be an accomplice somewhere nearby, go sound an alarm," the leader replied.

"Fuck that Corl, we stay together. We was told to get the thief, that's all. We can sound the alarm when we get him to Lord Arlec."

"He's not a Lord, he's a Chief," muttered the third.

"Bug off, Kimt," said Viton.

"Hard to believe this half dead rat killed Lord Devon," said Kimt, stepping forward and grabbing Tsom by one arm. Kimt was the shortest of the three and had a large beard, while the other two were clean shaven. Corl motioned for Viton to grab Tsom's other arm. He kept his sword out and briefly inspected the lock on Tsom's cell.

"No signs of force, he must have someone inside the house helping him."

"Who would help a murderer?" asked Viton.

"One of the other families, the rebels, any number of enemies of the Karn." Kimt nodded.

"Let's get 'im to Arlec before he dies on us, although it might be mercy. I hear it's going to be true death for you, thief."

"You can put your weapon away, Corl. Or are you afraid of a thief with no hands?" Viton laughed. Tsom slumped in their arms as they started carrying him, letting them take his full weight, such as it was. Standing, let alone walking, was simply too hard.

"Look at his eyes, he's not normal. I saw a death cat with eyes like that once. We had him treed after five days. The cat was more dead than alive, but it found reserves of fury that killed three dogs and one man," said Corl.

"Well this cat's been declawed," laughed Viton, waving Tsom's left arm stump. The blood rushing to the wound sent pain shooting up Tsom's arm.

"Bryl's arse Corl, he reeks of shit and piss," Viton complained as they maneuvered through the door they had recently come through.

Tsom was exhausted. He began to silently weep. Damn the Katar. Arlec not only cut off his hand, but now he was going to drain him, kill him forever, no rebirth. Mixed with his fear was despair, not at his death, but that he had not wreaked revenge for his mother, had failed her, Larrina, and the cause. The Katar had won again. He was feverish from his wounds, he knew, his mind kept slipping back and forth from memory to the present, the difference between them blurred. The memories of his mother's death had come often in his cell. Other memories of her drifted in as he fought to remain conscious. *Her*, was *her* his mother or Larrina, he could not remember ....

~~~

He asked his mother if she needed help in the shop. There was always something to do, or some lesson to be learned, so he was surprised when she replied, '*Someday Tsumi you will have to learn about your heritage. In a few years. No lessons today. No work. Enjoy being a child my little Tsumi. Enjoy life and its opportunities. Go play.*'

And he had.

At the end of the day he ran back to their shop to help with closing. The bright colors of *B'lama's Fabric* leapt out as he rounded the last corner. Oranges, shades of pomegranate, and blue that put the sky to shame. The shop was primarily a textile store, although other items were also for sale. Cloth from Argn, some from the Hrýll lands and even strange weaves from the Yanín. Tsom's mom, B'lama, did not deal in ordinary material. A few yards of some of her wares could cost a year's wages of an average worker.

Tsom burst into the shop, intending to make a hurried and dramatic entrance. He had his story all ready to spill forth between gasps of air.

Five men turned as he entered. He spotted their armbands immediately. Five small solid white circles arranged in a pentagon around a solid black circle, on a red background. Katar.

"Who are you?" growled one. He was standing nearest Tsom's mother, holding her arm tightly with his left hand. He was the largest of the group, with black curly hair, a broad face and a frog nose. The large ring on his left hand— five white diamonds surrounding a central black diamond—was visible. It was glowing. He could see that his mom's hand was turning pale as the blood struggled to flow past the barrier.

He opened his mouth to demand the same of this man hurting his mother. Katar or not, he did not have the right to do that. His mother's voice interrupted his thought.

"Keep quiet. You do not know me. Pretend you are an errand boy."

Tsom blinked. It was his mother's voice, but her mouth had remained shut. The voice was in his head. This was new.

"I, uh, I'm Ilianas, here to pick up the order for Lady Megwin."

The man holding his mother glared at him, never loosening his grip. He glanced at Tsom's mom and then back to Tsom, comparing them.

"Come back tomorrow." This was another of the men, with eyebrows that merged together in the center of his frowning forehead. His voice was calm but his eyes were dancing. "The order is not ready."

"Go." The voice in his head said. "Go now, Tsom."

Tsom backed toward the doorway. As he turned to dart out the door, he glanced down the aisle of dark blue, almost black, silks. The cloth in that one aisle was worth a fortune. At the end of the aisle was a foot. A foot attached to someone on the ground. He knew that foot. He knew that shoe. It was father's. As if pulled by a rope he stepped toward the foot.

"GO!"

The voice in his head screamed. It was commanding. He felt as if he had to obey, but some part of his mind fought off the command. It hurt his head, as if a small hammer rang his skull from the inside. His ears registered a small sob from his mother. Still, he was drawn to the foot.

The smallest of the men spoke. He looked uncomfortable. He was maybe eighteen. His voice was high, almost an alto.

"Leave, boy. We are Katar. This is none of your business."

The voice was pleading. Warning. Afraid. Afraid for him. Tsom ignored it. If he could ignore that command in his head, he could ignore this trembling alto voice.

He walked to the end of the aisle and looked upon his father; what remained of him. His face was a ruin. He had taken multiple punches. The impression of five small red marks surrounding a center red mark was visible on his forehead, on a relatively un-damaged section of skin. The pool of blood was not from the face. It was from the cavity where father's stomach should have been. Tsom felt like throwing up, but he didn't. His head rang again with his mother's command.

"GO. YOU WILL NOT RESIST. LEAVE."

He ignored the command, despite the ache in his head and the pull on his body toward the door. The pull was physical, but somehow he fought it off. He pushed everything but his rage aside. This he embraced. He reached for the nearby shears. Grabbing them like a knife he charged the five men.

"The kid was lying. He must be her son. Look at his face. He has the mark."

Three of the men pulled out short swords. The youngest of the five looked ill and turned away. The man with his left hand on mom grabbed her by the throat with his right.

"Filthy Kinel, you tricked us."

Everything sped up. All five of the men's rings were glowing and Eyebrows was grinning as he moved incredibly fast to grab Tsom.

Then, Eyebrows' head exploded.

Everybody was moving normally.

Alto started screaming, looking pale and scared. Katar weren't supposed to get scared.

"She killed Krelic." He screamed as he pulled frantically on his sword. It was sticking in its scabbard. "Our rings, they're not working. She's doing something. Kill her. Kill her." The alto voice cracked and almost made soprano.

Tsom acted without thinking. He pulled his arm back and for a moment he felt the shears as if they were alive. He sensed every part of it. He could feel the flaw on the one blade, the loose screw, the heavy imbalance of the handles. As he flung the shears his hand knew what to do to adjust for the balance. They did not go end over end. The heavy shears landed in Alto's throat. He never got his sword out of the scabbard.

"RUN" The voice in Tsom's head echoed the audible yell his mother gave. The audible command was tangible. It carried energy. Eyebrows stepped back, fear evident on his face. Eyebrows' ring was on fire.

Tsom felt the urge to run countered by a flow of energy. The white diamonds on Eyebrows' ring exploded and Tsom felt the tidal wave of force in his mom's command. It was irresistible this time. His will was no longer his own. Rage turned to fear. The single word run carried with it an emotional message. Eyebrows screamed in fear and ran. Tsom ran. He ran, but even in fear he looked back. Part of him wished he had not.

One of the remaining two Katar was standing, his eyes and ears pouring out blood. His head had not completely exploded, it was just leaking. It was not the large man holding his mother. He wished it had been. That one slid a sword through his mother's throat and twisted. His mother's head was hanging free of her body. Her eyes moved and focused on him.

"RUN. HIDE. RUN."

The voice commanded as she died and he was compelled.

He had no choice, he would later tell himself. She had made him run away. He could not have done anything against two Katar. He had no choice.

He had been running from the Katar for ten years.

~~~

He fought back his consciousness to the present. His non-existent hands burned with fiery pain. He seized upon the pain and added it to the rage and his memories. He stoked the rage with visions of Shela being raped, or worse, and killed, and heaped on the death of his mother again and again. Momentarily the exhaustion was gone. The two guards sensed the change in their load, belatedly. He concentrated on those *hands* of his. He could feel them, his hands of pain. Phantom pain that continued to fuel his rage. Pain caused by the Katar. Pain caused by these two. He reached. He stretched his hands. He reached inside each of the guards chests and squeezed. He could feel their hearts pulsing in his pain filled hands. He thought of the rat gnawing on his bloody stump and he squeezed. He thought of Arlec cutting off his hand and he squeezed. He thought of how Shara must have betrayed their meeting place and squeezed. *I loved you Shara.* Squeeze. *Feel my pain.*

Both of them died at the same time. He had not so much ripped their hearts out as simply ripped the insides of the hearts as his grip had given way. The rage was gone. No energy left. A small part of his brain hoped they had not felt too much pain. Too much pain already existed.

Corl's voice soft, shocked of all force, from behind, "Shit."

Tsom had no reflexes left, he sank to his knees. No physical strength, he managed to keep his *hands* manifested. The pain in his head was causing his ears to ring. His eyesight was blurring. Using both of his *hands* he grasped the sword of one of the fallen guards and turned on his knees—too weak to stand.

Corl's eyes were wide at the sight of the sword floating between the two stumps of arms, or perhaps still wide from shock at seeing both of his companions drop dead. He backed a step.

"Those eyes of yours. Golden. That means Kinel. I have heard stories of Kinel. Lord Arlec should have been more cautious. He should have warned us, damn him."

Corl did not come any closer, his eyes fixated on the floating sword as if it were alive and ready to bite.

"Your element of surprise is gone. I will not get near those invisible hands of yours. Drop your weapon and stay out of reach."

Better to die a real death fighting, than a true death for Arlec's pleasure. "Come and get me," Tsom croaked.

"I know what you're trying to do. If you fight, I won't kill you. You'll still have to face Lord Arlec's punishment." Corl sounded a bit regretful. Perhaps admiring Tsom's fight, or perhaps simply not wishing true death upon anyone. Or perhaps not wanting to fight those strange invisible hands.

Tsom could not take the fight to him and he knew it was only a matter of time before he had to drop his *hands*. Already the sword was wobbling. He reversed the short sword, placing the tip against his sternum and resting the hilt against the ground. *So much left to do.* "Fuck me," Corl yelled, rushing forward.

Chapter 38

Lanos chafed at the personal inactivity. He knew, despite the general plan being incredibly simple, numerous details needed to be articulated between Alanar and Oonie. Alanar excelled at this. Lanos knew that Alanar was both a strategist and a tactician, while his own skill lay in fighting the actual battle. Now that they had finally decided to move against the Katar, he was anxious to get at it. He worried that Larrina was vulnerable, now that the network was out in the open. He was worried about Shara. What if she was discovered? What if she were a double agent? The excess time was driving him to paranoia.

Word of the Tarth battle on the outskirts of Zethicia reached them along with the demands from the Katar that the Hrýll to supply key talismans for the war effort. That fit their plans well. The more the Katar depended on the Hrýll talismans the better.

There were only a thousand Hrýll that could help with actual fighting. So few. Hrýll were not part of The Cities and ostensibly not under Katar rule, but in reality their existence was controlled by the Katar and their numbers had been decimated over the centuries. Revolution. Lanos rolled the sound of the word around his head. Finally. If Alanar's web of spies and influence was correct, it would explode into a full revolution quickly. He had been part of the resistance effort for decades. The Katar had bled too many dry too fast in the past fifty years. They could fan this quickly. The added help of the Hrýll would be useful, but only a thousand? But the five thousand ring-bearing Katar were now split between Zethicia and The Cities. A thousand would help indeed.

Walking Oonie's village day after day, he absorbed the Hrýll condition. *We don't think about how even a talisman fueled by qenar needed ka for its initial shaping.* The slow to procreate Hrýll population had aged through overuse of *ka.* Low population and too few healthy, younger Hrýll. *We have destroyed them,* he thought. *Not just the Katar, but our greed for talismans. Our population growth. We are only the lesser of two evils to the Hrýll.*

The Srýll were worse off. Rumors of their extinction were all but true. They were the cousin race to the Hrýll, often thought of as part of the Hrýll. Only women Srýll were able to shape talisman. There were no females left to bear children. In fifty years or so they would be completely extinct, unless they interbred with the Hrýll or some miracle occurred. *Another race dead at the hands of Katar—and mankind's general greed.* Like the Kinel, he grudgingly acknowledged to himself. At least the Kinel blood survived by crossbreeding with Humans, no such salvation for the Hrýll and Srýll.

Lanos and Oonie had time to continue their personal conversations when Alanar and the other Hrýll plotted. Oonie seemed to be the spokesman for the Hrýll in many respects, but unconcerned with the details of what was being planned. Yet, whenever some detail was mentioned in passing, Oonie seemed completely aware of it and its ramifications. As usual their conversation took place over the spiced tea that never failed to remind him of Larrina. Oonie responded to Lanos's angry outburst over the Hrýll plight of aging and potential extinction.

"It may simply be that mankind and their gods are destined to cover all of Nakana."

"If you believe that, then why resist at all? Why help Alanar in his scheme to destroy the Katar?"

"I do not believe, I speculate. I fight because I can, whether it is fruitless or not. I fight to save my race. The Katar will destroy all races, or enslave them, eventually. Mankind may do the same on its own, or it may not. The Katar are a known. We all do what we can within the scheme of things. The Kinel did what they could and almost succeeded. Perhaps, if this young thief is what many think he is, then ultimately it will have been the Kinel who won—albeit too late to preserve the Kinel race. We will do what we can. My reasons are both personal and greater than myself. I know Alanar's reasons, even if he does not remember them all. What of you, my friend? Why do you risk your life in this struggle?"

Lanos let his chin sink as he stared unfocused at the ground. He owed Alanar his life. Lanos, already one of the best fighters in all The Cities, had been headstrong and full of himself back then, decades ago. The girl had not been seriously injured, he could have walked away. No one challenged a Katar to a duel—and lived. Until that day. Despite the witnesses that it had been a fair fight he had been sentenced to *true death*. Alanar had pulled strings and paid for his release. He never found out the payment. Nothing with Alanar was free though. Yet, he had recently freed Lanos from his bond. He was now free to choose. Why did he choose to stay and help? Because he hated the Katar. All of them. But, did he hate them enough to risk the entire Human race to the Tarth? That question was nagging, worming its way to the forefront of his thinking. Yes, it was worth fighting for freedom and dying, but that fight could occur after the Tarth were killed, or driven away again. And now, for the first time in a long time, he regretted the possibility of his own death. There might be something worth living for.

"I see that woman in your eyes again, my friend. She is part Kinel, is she not?"

Lanos nodded.

"Your youth is over, but your tolerance for injustice is not."

"But is destroying the Katar, when Nakana faces its old threat from the Tarth, justice?"

"Your struggle is harder than mine. I have no love of Humans, who too have destroyed the Hrýll and the Srýll. I do not hate them all. Your race simply multiplies and consumes. The Katar are more overt. They abuse their power, a power they did not even shape themselves. Even if we succeed we, Humans and Hrýll, will have to live with the Katar legacy of rule."

He paused and smiled at Lanos.

"But, the Tarth are not the threat to my race that they are to yours. We have lived together in the past. The Tarth and Hrýll were here before all other races. You call us the Old Ones, but the Tarth are just as old, simply more warlike. I would regret seeing the Tarth perish as a race. They are not evil, just different. They have been wronged as much as we have."

Another long pause.

"In an armed struggle, some innocent will always die. A trite truism to be sure, but true nonetheless. I believe the risk and the lives are worth the outcome. I grieve for those that will die in this plot, but believe that in this case the price is worth it. You need to believe the same, my friend. You should only fight for what you believe in."

Chapter 39

Alone in her room, Shara tried to put out of her mind the touch she had endured. That any man would dare to touch a Katar woman in such a way shocked her. Had her brother so debased the household in such a short time? It seemed impossible. Was this the new chief of the Karn clan? Surely the other families would not allow it.

Despite the precious time it took, she wiped herself clean as best she could. She slipped on practical clothes along with the slim dagger that they had not bothered to remove from her closet. They had not searched very hard, or knew she would be drugged the entire time. She rubbed her left ring finger, missing her ring. She would be subject to the power of the other rings now. Naked again. How long had she been unconscious? She had to meet Tsom and warn him that Arlec suspected something and that he had to abandon plans of stealing the artifact.

She was sure, now, that her brother had killed their father and was framing Tsom. It was clever. The families would go from disdain that Arlec had lost a ring, to fear and revenge against a murderer and thief that could wield the power of a ring. She rubbed her left hand again. Bastard Katar were not uncommon, but usually they were incorporated into the clans as minor members. To them Tsom would be just a Katar bastard gone rogue.

There would be no asking Arlec about the talisman, the artifact, that Alanar had sent Tsom to steal. What did Arlec know of it? Father had always entrusted her older sisters with important information, not Arlec nor Shara. Would he have told Arlec about this? Or had Devon been ignorant of its power? She would not be talking to her brother again, unless it was at a Katar trial for treason. His or hers, she wondered. Despite his unpardonable actions, she would be labeled the traitor too. Would her sisters understand? At least they will rule with some compassion. They were not murderous. When the time came, she would stand trial with her brother, she knew, but only after he was exposed. Until then, she had to be free. She had to fulfill her promise to Tsom and somehow also help mankind against the Tarth. If the Katar were weakened enough she could persuade her sisters to change. To rule with more justice. If she could do that, then it would not matter if she and Arlec were executed.

She listened at the door and opened it. No guard. A drugged woman was not worth guarding. Stepping into the hallway, she had no plan other than to get out. Maybe he was already at the meeting place Larrina had told them about. She prayed to the gods she knew were not real that he was alright. That he had not tried anything without. He was so headstrong and acted before thinking. Ironically, that was the way Arlec was.

If she couldn't find Tsom, then back to Argn and Larrina, or perhaps one of the local safe houses. But first she had to get out of here.

A noise. She paused. Nothing. No. A cat. A white cat. A beautiful white cat. It stood in the hallway and meowed loudly.

"Shhh," she whispered moving toward it. It let her get closer. She then noticed the thin leather collar. With … a ring on it. A Katar ring.

"Come here kitty. Come here."

It strolled away, not too fast, but at a fast walk, or kitty trot.

She followed as it led her to the first floor. All was quiet. It was late at night from the way the glow globes were set on low. The cat waited patiently when she fell behind. Several times she almost had it, then it meowed and walked away.

To the lower levels. The door was ajar and the cat slipped through. She rarely went to the lower levels. This side of the compound they led to the old prison, unused for hundreds of years. The city took in all the prisoners now, but at one time the Katar took and interrogated their own prisoners. She was glad those days were over.

Down here no expensive glow globes were used. But someone had been down here very recently. A lantern was already lit and hanging. The smell tickled her nose and she almost sneezed. Cheap oil. *We can afford better than this*, she thought. Listening, she heard voices on the other side of the door at the end of the hallway. She stopped and pulled out her dagger. The cat stood by the door. Then sat and started to groom itself.

Atem's luck she cursed to herself. She wanted that ring. Quickly and quietly she approached the cat. "Kitty, much as I hate to do it, you run away and you are a dead cat." She whispered, holding her dagger in a throwing position. The cat purred.

As she bent down to take off the collar, the voices on the other side of the door became audible.

"I know what you are trying to do. If you fight, I won't kill you. You will still have to face Lord Arlec's punishment."

She yanked the collar off the cat, which yowled in displeasure, but did not scratch her. Slipping on the ring, she yanked open the door.

Shara took in the scene instantly. She seized onto the power of the ring faster than she had ever done before causing a wrenching pain in her head. The guard rushing forward stumbled as the ring drew upon his *ka*. Their movements slowed as the ring did its work. Calls from throughout the compound would no doubt be starting up as her fellow Katar saw their own rings flare with protection against her draw of power, but she did not think of these things.

The sword was already piercing Tsom's skin as she kicked him sideways. The guard was upon them both, then unconscious as she quickly dispatched him. The ring gave her strength that she knew was short lived, if she didn't want to kill Tsom with its use so close. She rolled Tsom over and looked at the wound. He was alive. Then the rest of him finally registered as a sharp blow; *goddess of mercy what have they done to him?*

No time to let all this soak in. She heaved his body over her shoulder, still staggering under the weight and her drug flaccid muscles. She took a moment to grab the guard's sword and then stagger-ran out to the compound. She desperately longed to draw upon the power of her ring, but Tsom could not take even the smallest of drain she reasoned.

Running to a side gate she knew of, she rounded the tall shrubbery and nearly collided with one of the outside guards. His name escaped her. She was about to drop Tsom to properly fight when a streak of white hit the man in the face. He fell screaming and grabbing at the cat that fought with fury and intelligence. "Good kitty," she muttered as she stepped forward and knocked him out. He was inept, but he was Katar. She pulled off his ring and quickly slid it over the toe of one of his bare, filth encrusted, feet.

Now, she pulled on the ring's power as never before, causing the pain from the temples to move all the way to the back of her neck. The unprotected servants in the house would be paying for her energy, as would the entire neighborhood. An image of the cook, her childhood friend, doubled over in pain came to her. *I hope she is away for some reason.*

She tried the gate; It was locked.

She began to hack at the lock with her sword. Tears ran down her cheeks, flying out in drops with her manic swings. More power, she demanded of the ring. More power. The ring glowed brilliantly. The guard behind her screamed in agony, waking and falling back unconscious from the pain. *I will not be drugged and molested again!* The sword bit deep into the lock. *You will not harm Tsom anymore!* The lock gave way. She pulled Tsom back onto her shoulders. The movement on the street was slow—the ring still exerting its influence. A late night passerby took one look at her and fled. She could feel her face was red with veins standing out as if they ran on her head's surface. The ring on her hand glowed brilliantly and her hand and part of her forearm were completely white as if cold frozen. Her eyes were bloodshot to the point of drops of blood forming. Her lips were curled back exposing her teeth.

With a heave she threw Tsom onto a horse, knocking the drunk rider off, and leapt on behind him. The horse suddenly found itself moving faster than everything around it, with two bloody Humans on its back that were not there a moment before. It bolted—which suited Shara.

***

The horse gave out about the same time as she did. They were still in Arbeneth, but on the northern outskirts of the city. She turned the horse down smaller and smaller roads, with buildings further and further apart. This was the area where one of the safe houses for the resistance was, but she was unfamiliar with the details and too tired to search every street. Finally, the horse stumbled and dropped to the ground. It was dead. It had given all it had. She patted its still neck and not for the first time thought about how Humans asked for so much, but rarely returned. The ring had stopped glowing and her energy level was fading rapidly. She scanned the nearby area. A horse left dead in the road was going to be noticed. Tsom's wound had to be attended to. She would not last much longer either.

An old couple entered the street on horseback and stopped. Shara drew her sword. "I don't want to hurt you. This is Katar business. I need your help." She held up her left hand displaying the ring. The man frowned and his hand dropped, but the woman grabbed it. "That's her! The one Larrina told us about. And the other must be the thief, Tsom."

The woman turned to Shara. "Its ok, Shara, we know who you are. Barin, we need to get rid of the horse." He rode over and using the cinch from the dead horse managed to tie a loop around a leg and his own saddle. He then slowly dragged the horse off the road and into the trees and bushes nearby. It would do for now.

"My name is Kaylee. That is my husband Barin. We are part of Askatasuna. Word of your escape traveled fast and all of us have been looking for signs of someone draining *ka*. Come with us, we should get as far away from here as possible. Most likely you were seen."

Shara knelt next to Tsom, ripping open his shirt. The skin wound was not bad, primarily the muscle over the ribs. Her kick had caused the blade to hang up on his ribs, saving him. She lifted his arms gingerly. She lightly stroked his right arm and shook her head. Kaylee was next to them. "I thought the thief was a boy, a young man?"

"He is." Shara whispered. Unconscious, weak, and injured his chameleon effect was gone. His face was drawn tight and he looked at least thirty, a worn thirty. She rested a hand on his forehead. He was burning up with fever. She unwrapped the bandages on the left arm. It was bad. No gangrene yet, but she could tell it was infected. Swollen and angry looking it must be painful.

Barin returned. "You take the … man … I'll take the girl." He dropped off the horse and bent down to grab Tsom. Shara pushed him aside. "I'll do it." She bent, struggled, heaved and got Tsom over her shoulder. Two steps and over the horse's back. She then sank to the ground. Kaylee stepped in and secured Tsom and turned to Barin.

"Take the ring off of her. I don't trust any Katar with one of those on, even if she is part of the resistance and has been imprisoned by her own kind." Barin nodded and pulled off the ring as Shara sank into unconsciousness.

Chapter 40

The Chimi scouts returned with two prisoners. Human females. Be Na Tarth disliked dealing with Human prisoners. Too often they reminded him of young Tarth. Weaker of course, but they were so similar looking. He often wondered why so many races were similar and some could even interbreed. The Tarth could not interbreed with Humans or any of the other races on Nakana. Usually, this made him feel that they were a superior race. It was the Tarth history that they were the first and original inhabitants of Nakana and that all other races came through holes connecting the planes, even the Hrýll. The interconnections in the Web of God. Tarth did not believe in gods and yet they had adopted the Hrýll name. The connections were real, his standing here now was testament to that, but they were not stable, nor easy to use.

There were so few Tarth, and the Humans bred so fast. He was starting to feel it would be more advantageous for survival to be able to interbreed. Even the Kinel had interbred—but at what cost. They were simply mongrel Humans now. Katar. Without the advantage of faster breeding, the Tarth could win all the battles and still lose control of Nakana. Unless the Humans were completely eliminated, down to the last child. One had to be cold hearted about this war. It was survival. Kill or be killed. A lesson all Tarth learned well on Hell. Repeatedly.

He was surprised to see that the new prisoners were Katar. To take two Katar must have cost the Chimi dearly. Instinctively, he glanced at their hands. Both were missing their ring fingers, the wound burned closed. Good, the rings had been removed. The Chimi scout stepped forward, understanding the glance, and dropped two rings into his hand. At least he had had the good sense to dispose of the fingers first.

"We surprised them near Argn. They were patrolling the route between Argn and the Hrýll. We managed to knock one out immediately and the other was so busy defending her that we were able to overwhelm her with minimal injury. They were not expecting us so close to The Cities."

Be Na Tarth nodded. Switching to common tongue he addressed them.

"What families are you from?"

The two women looked at each other confused. He realized that his common tongue must be archaic to them, given the time differential since he had been here last. He repeated himself and waited. They understood this time.

Finally, the older one shrugged. "We are Karn. Direct in line to the head of the Karn. Set us free and we will show some mercy when the time comes."

Be Na Tarth could not help a small smile. Certainly brave enough, and arrogant. Karn, so at least some of the families remained the same. Karn had been the most powerful family during the first war. Good. It seemed only right that his revenge remain personal with the same families who had banished the Tarth so long ago.

"How many Katar exist?"

This time neither answered. He knew enough about torture to know how inaccurate a tool it was. It might be worth it to make the Karn family feel pain, a small portion of the pain his own family had felt, but he did not want to lower himself to the Human level. Better to simply kill them. Yet, they might be useful as tools if they were actually direct in line to succession.

He rose from the table with the maps spread across. His huge size caused both of the Katar to shrink back a bit. He strode one long stride to stand over them. Grabbing one by the arm he lifted her effortlessly to eye level. She bit her lip and tears ran down, but she did not say anything.

"Tell me Karn woman. What are your names? Simple enough request. No games. No torture. Tell me or I kill both of you. Now."

"Larra and Piea. I am Larra."

He dropped her to the ground. Her sister rushed to her side. The arm was broken.

He turned to the Chimi scout. In Tarth he said "They live, for now. I have a meeting with a woman who calls herself a goddess. Let them stew over their fate until later."

Chapter 41

Hundreds of years of peace had not prepared Zethicia for war. Yes, the various towns occasionally fought amongst themselves, and the Zethician militia would enforce peace, but no real war in centuries. Barnus pounded his fist into his hand. The Katar had *protected* them for so long that they were suffering from stupid mistakes. His son now lay among the dead. The defense of Zethicia was on his shoulders and he was failing. He should have studied military history, now it was too late.

Sad and angrily he walked from the armory toward the temporary command headquarters. So angrily that he ran straight into a Yanín without seeing it. So angrily that he did not care. He just kept going. The Yanín reversed his arms and legs, walking backwards as fast as forwards. It reached out and grabbed Barnus by the arm.

"Human, you are exceedingly clumsy today." Its grip tightened.

Barnus knew he should simply apologize and let the Yanín have its pride. But at that moment he hated all non-Humans. He hated the Tarth, he hated the Hrýll that they depended on for their talismans, he hated the Yanín that fought for money, he hated them all. He spun and pulled his dagger out. Moving faster than he thought his worn and tired body could handle, he managed to get the dagger tip behind the Yanín's ear, one of the few vulnerable spots on their body. "Let me go mercenary. I am Barnus, commander of the Zethician army, and the one who authorizes your pay and that of your fellow mercenaries. You might be able to kill me as you die, but I will kill you if you don't let go—now."

The Yanín's grip tightened. It moved its head close to Barnus's and stared into his eyes. Suddenly, it let go and a strange gasping hissing noise came from its mouth. Finally, it stopped the noise and slammed its solid leathery arm onto his shoulder and spoke. "Thssshth hssshth, you are a good one. Hssshtht, I will remember you." With that it walked away. It took Barnus a few moments to realize the hissing and gasping was laughter.

There was very little laughter in the armory. Arrows and quarrels were in short supply. Swords and lances were broken and also in short supply. Iron was always in short supply, due to the small deposits on Nakana. Gold was almost cheaper. In a few short weeks the war had depleted all metal caches and every scrap was being recycled. The heat from the forges was stifling, the smell of superheated metal, coal, and coke mixing with sweat and days without bathing for most.

Barnus consulted with the foreman. "How soon before we are fully equipped again?" The foreman was a woman, the daughter of the original foreman, who had died two days ago. Not from wounds, but a broken heart. Both of his sons had perished in the major battle with the Tarth. Three more souls on his head, thought Barnus. Sreena was as large as her father, easily over six feet, with arms that were used to swinging a large hammer all day. She had stepped into the position of managing the other smiths and craftsmen easily. Despite her strength and size most men found her attractive, in a massive sort of way. Her long hair, tied tightly behind her now, was black coal. Her skin a dark coffee with cream and no natural blemishes just the occasional scar from a stray ember. It was usually her voice that melted them: a small choir within her ample chest.

"With the current rate of supplies? Weeks." She saw his expression. "I know, we don't have weeks. Do you have any idea when the Tarth will attack—in earnest?"

"No. We took the battle to them this time ..." He did not finish. She knew too well the disastrous results. "The Tarth are regrouping within sight of Zethicia, but are keeping raiding parties of their Chimi active. If not for the gateway to The Cities, we would be totally cut off from supplies."

She nodded. "I hate being dependent on those damn arrogant Cities and their Katar." She pounded her fist on the table—which jumped and made a cracking noise, but held. Barnus knew she spoke for most of the citizens of Zethicia. Even winning this war was going to be a huge loss of independence from The Cities. Zethicia had just been getting something of an even footing over the past century and now it was lost.

"Focus on getting me long distance weapons within a week. Ignore the armor, it is useless against the Tarth in hand to hand. In fact it slows us down. Better to be agile than hope that armor will slow down any of their blows."

"What about those Maite dogs as I have heard them called?"

"We killed a great deal of them in the last battle. Granted armor slows them down, but only long enough for a Chimi or Tarth to finish the job. Ignore the armor."

Sreena grimly nodded. She went back to coordinating her teams and even in his exhausted, depressed state he admired the curves of her from behind. Smiling grimly to himself he prepared for yet another meeting with the Katar.

Convening with the Katar went no better. Jern had been called away for a council with the other families, leaving the sons of Telem and Wara in charge.

Barnus preferred Jern and his two daughters, the least offensive of the Katar. Niik, Telem's son was supremely arrogant and felt his brief battles with Saman, a decade ago, made him more qualified than Barnus. *Perhaps he was right*, Barnus ruefully thought. *But I will not cede all of Zethicia over to this young Katar just because he crushed a minor rebellion by a backward starving group of people in the mountains.*

Niik lashed into him the minute they were assembled. "Your tactics nearly cost us the war Barnus! Next time we do it my way."

Biting back his full thoughts he replied. "The tactics were jointly developed between me and Jern. Do you feel that he also knows nothing about planning a battle?"

Niik obviously did, but was not going to be baited into saying so out loud in front of other Katar.

"*We* have a shipment of Hrýll weapon talismans coming in soon. With the *proper* use of those I think we can turn the tide."

More non-Human devices. I don't trust this dependence on talismans. He kept these thoughts to himself. The Katar used talismans freely. They were even willing to use Human *ka* to fuel them. Barnus knew too well the number of lives that the gateway had cost. The Katar on one side and the Tarth on the other with Zethicia right in the middle.

The Hrýll weapons did indeed sound like something that could turn the tide. Explosive spheres with a delay on them when activated. Lances of flame. Even the Tarth would not be immune to these, the heat was said to melt stone. The first shipment was due in a less than a week, through the gateway—yet another talisman they were now dependent on. They had to hold back any attacks for a week and not launch any foolish attacks of their own. On this, even Niik agreed. One week and perhaps this hell they found themselves in would be over.

Chapter 42

Nu Arr felt for the first time in many centuries a sense of panic. The other gods also felt it. They had felt their power waning for years. The Humans were not worshipping as much as they used to and even with population growth, the flow of *ka* was diminishing. Now the Tarth were back and would need to be dealt with, sooner or later. A war should have brought mankind flocking to the temples, praying, the wonderful prayer that fed them all. How could mankind expect the gods to help them if they did not pray? *We need ka*, he thought, *all except that bitch Hallam.* She had no need for worshippers. Why she, of all the gods, gained power from animals remained a mystery.

He paced the garden of his sanctuary. A Hrýll brandy would be nice, to calm his nerves. He glanced around and spotted a decanter on the small carved marble table. This did not surprise him. If asked a servant would say he simply had taken the decanter there this morning on a whim, by mistake, or something similar. This was Nu Arr's power. It worked well with little things, but large events were more difficult and though he would not admit it to the others, even minor events no longer bent to his needs as often as they had in the past.

His priests told him the thief who had triggered the omen in the temple was safely imprisoned by the Katar. The Karn clan. He knew the family well. Old Devon, so like his ancestor of the same name, had died; leaving his son to rule the greater family. Arlec would be more easy to influence than Devon. The old man never liked the priesthoods and was willing to risk the wrath of the gods, but Arlec. He was not just greedy, but in a hurry. Arlec could be useful, but Arlec needed to make sure that the thief was killed.

Nu Arr knew, better than anyone, that imprisoned was not the same as dead. He wanted that thief dead. True death. No rebirth some centuries later to worry about. Perhaps Pé could catch the soul before it made it to the Sea of Souls, should the thief die a normal death. He would have to ask Pé that, next time the arrogant bastard showed up to one of the conclaves. If he made an appearance. No, Nu Arr could not depend on Pé.

So much *ka* in the Sea, if only there was a way to tap that source. Even Pé could not touch the Sea itself. There was power. Literally an ocean of it. To be able to tap that power would make any of the gods invincible. He had tried to follow Pé to the twin rivers that spilled into the Sea of Souls, but had never succeeded. From his subtle enquiries it was clear the other gods had tried the same. None of the gods wanted to risk learning the method of traveling as Pé had and simply following him was not sufficient. No god had attempted traveling since Krisl had failed to return, three thousand years ago. Traveling between planes was something the Tarth could do, or even Hrýll, or … he refused to think of him, their old companion. Yet, it was denied to the gods. Nu Arr took a large swallow of the brandy. So much was denied them, he thought gazing into the smoky substance. Even this wonderful liquor was something they could not make on their own. He sighed and finished the glass, letting the warmth spread. Time to spur the others to action. They hid their panic in indolence. Game playing in the Chamber of Seeing.

Ague and Met, the sea god and weather god, were enjoying a small game as Luck entered. The Chamber always caused some vertigo when first entered. It was a room that acted as a huge talisman. The gods had contracted with the Hrýll eons ago to have it constructed. When not activated it was a thirty foot by thirty foot room made of granite and jade. Jade imbued with qenar. The scene of focus superimposed on the Chamber was sometimes hard for the brain to process. Especially this scene, which was the sea with two ships enjoined in battle. One was obviously filled with worshippers of Ague, the other with worshippers of Met. They took turns *helping* their worshippers. First Sea then Weather.

"Your worshippers are idiots Ague. They pray for the stupidest things! You will lose the bet soon."

"I am afraid you are right. They deserve to die for such stupid requests." In a fit of petulance he smacked his hand down within the image of water and concentrated. They all felt the *ka* flow. A large wave washed over the ship of Ague, swamping it. Met shook his head and laughed. "You are such a poor loser. Pay up!"

Ague grabbed Met's wrist. His eyes glazed over for a second, or two. He let go, looking slightly tired. Met had a euphoric, drunken look on his face. He looked up seeing Nu Arr for the first time. In a cheerful voice he called out.

"Luck, you missed all the fun." The sea scene faded away.

"So I see. Wasting *ka* on bets again."

"Don't be pissy, Luck. You're just angry that no one gambles with you anymore."

"What news of war and your thief?" asked Ague, recovering from his transfer of *ka* to Met.

"My priests have given me the same information as your own. Be Na Tarth has a device that drains all the *ka* of those they kill. Worse, every time we try and influence anything nearby, the *ka* is siphoned into the device. No doubt making him stronger. It is like beating ourselves over the head to attack him using our powers."

Met's euphoria wore off. "I have tried lightning strikes from above, out of the influence of their device. The damn Tarth are virtually immune to lightning. We should have killed them off rather than banish them."

"Who knew they would survive in Hell?" Ague asked, rubbing his bearded chin with his slightly webbed fingers. "It seemed certain death. It was all we could do while allied with the Katar."

All three nodded. "The Katar," muttered Met. "The Katar, again. We cannot seem to shake off their power and influence. Then and now."

"A pity our power does not extend to the crafting of talismans. Even the Human ability in that regard seems to be growing, if ever so slightly," Ague said.

"Enough bemoaning. What are we going to *do?*" asked Nu Arr. *Must he always be the catalyst for these lazy gods?*

"I think the situation is worse than you think."

Inlas, goddess of illusions, spoke from the entrance. As always, she overdid her appearance. The color of her hair was red and orange and yellow. Her eyes changed with each blink. Her dress was shear, but you could not quite make out her body underneath as the dress kept shimmering and shifting and swirling around. Hints and promises of what lay beneath the cloth, but nothing truly revealed.

Nu Arr did not turn around, he could see her effect on the other two. Without looking he called out. "Tone it down Inlas, you give me a headache whenever I look at you."

She pouted but the dress shifted to a solid color, not quite shear anymore. Her eyes settled to a dark green. Ague licked his lips. He had lusted after Inlas for centuries, to no avail. He watched her hungrily as she settled down amongst them.

"Alright woman, out with it." Nu Arr was not in the mood for games and he knew Inlas loved them.

"Alanar," she said.

Nothing. No reaction. She smiled. Nu Arr kicked her lightly, which made her smile more. "Talanas." She waited. Nu Arr remembered first.

"He is dead."

"Hardly. I saw him not long ago."

The other two looked puzzled. Nu Arr glared at them. "Idiots, don't you two

182

remember anything? Death by any other name is still Death, we used to say. He changed his name more often than she changes appearance."

He turned back to Inlas. "So he is alive. What is he doing? And how did you find out when we did not?"

Inlas smiled. They were now looking at an attractive Hrýll female.

"My *husband*, Oonie, has a long history with Alanar. Long indeed."

Chapter 43

Lanos and Alanar were packing their horses when the messenger arrived. Lanos watched as the messenger and Alanar conferred. His horse nipped at him as he tightened the cinch. Lanos pushed its head back absently while concentrating on the interplay between Alanar and the messenger. Bad news. Most people's eyes narrowed with anger or similar emotion. Alanar's would always widen, as if surprised that he could be hearing such bad news. The angrier he got the wider his eyes. They were wide now.

Lanos walked up, leading his horse. "Trouble?"

"Tsom failed. Worse he's been captured by the Katar. Arlec, the idiot son of Devon. It seems he has murdered his father and has laid the blame on Tsom."

"What of Shara?"

Alanar's eyes narrowed. "She betrayed us."

"I don't believe it, she has been helping us for years and is in love with Tsom—as anyone could see."

"I did not say she did it willingly. Tsom was captured at a safe house location that only a few knew about. Several other safe houses have been raided. Tsom would not know of those. Worse, Arlec has the Sphere. We have some contingency plans in play, but they may not be enough." Alanar shook his head, his wide eyes staring off unseeing.

"The boy is no doubt dead by now. Shara may also be dead, if Arlec is head of the Karn now. I had grown fond of both of them during our time with Larrina. We must go on without them," Alanar said.

Lanos had started to think Shara would come through. She was young enough and rebellious enough and tough enough. Her willingness to change her own people had been infectious.

"We need to find out if they live and if there is anything we can do."

"More important, how can we get the talisman that Devon had hidden?" Alanar countered.

"The boy is important. We pulled him in! We must do something to save him if we can."

The anger in Lanos's voice was undisguised. Didn't Alanar care about any individual? Was everything about his revenge on the Katar? His revenge on the gods themselves?

Alanar grabbed the reins from Lanos. The horse was getting agitated at his anger.

"Calm down. Larrina has already mobilized the network. *We* cannot do anything, but if anyone can—she can. She motivates the network, I just fund it. You know that she cares for them both. We need to move to Zethicia. The key Katar will be there soon. We have our mission in Zethicia. When the time is right we will strike there and in The Cities. Hopefully that fool Arlec will neither figure out the talisman, nor destroy half The Cities learning how to use it. Trust Larrina, Lanos. She's no fool. She will figure a way to trap the Katar in Zethicia. Tsom was a bonus, not our only hope."

At least now the Tarth would be taken care of, Lanos thought, *if, as Alanar said, Arlec didn't destroy half The Cities with the Sphere.*

Chapter 44

Arlec convened a meeting of the families. As the new chief—he liked the sound of that: 'chief'—of the Karn family it was his right. The war with the Tarth was not going as well as most had hoped. Most did not include Arlec, who saw opportunity.

He had been busy the past few days. Finally, things were going as they should. His father was no longer in the way to keep him from his rightful place as head of the family. His sisters were no longer the trusted advisors. The thief was soon to be executed, with the priesthoods' blessings and rewards. And, best of all, he had his father's secret talisman. His investigations there had proved interesting. Devon's library had some vague reference to the old spherical talisman, but nothing of use. Technically, an artifact, or *iribansu* in Hrýll. The Sphere of Banishment it had been called in one book, again with a Hrýll reference, *San Par'eh Shante*. The actual use of the talisman was rather cryptically referred to.

Some experimentation had been necessary. This girl in front of him was servant number four. A plain looking thing from the kitchens, probably seventeen years old. Arlec gave a reassuring smile as he gave directions to the slow witted girl.

"Turn the top and bottom of the sphere in opposite directions," Arlec called. They were in the library, which was extremely quiet and isolated from the rest of the compound. Arlec suspected his father had done many things here that required privacy. No one would ever interrupt him here, old Devon's tradition lived on.

She nervously did as instructed. Her hands shook slightly and sweat dripped off of her brow. Other servants had accompanied Arlec to the library and had not returned. She twisted the two halves a fraction. Nothing happened. The girl started to let her breath out and began a tentative smile.

Arlec noticed his ring glowing. He commanded the young woman to stay where she was. Soon the area around the woman, a small spherical area, seemed to shift and blur. A jungle scene replaced the study. Arlec backed up a step, he was all too close to the edge of the changed scene. His servant girl looked around nervously and started to run. Arlec opened his mouth to order her to stay, but it was unnecessary. The sphere of jungle suddenly shrank and disappeared—along with the woman. The talisman remained. Good, good. That had almost been as planned. The loss of the girl was to be expected.

Some additional experimentation, with the regrettable loss of five more servants, gave Arlec many of the parameters on the use the talisman. After the first older woman, he made sure that the other servants did not have any close living relatives. It was such a bother to have to explain that their beloved had disappeared permanently.

The more one turned the two halves, the larger the sphere. There did not seem to be an upper limit on size, but Arlec stopped after a hundred feet in diameter. The delay in the sphere's shutting down and pulling all animal life could be altered also, that had taken a test subject or two. All breathing things within the sphere disappeared. Transported, as far as he could tell, to the jungle area that was always visible. The sphere could be hidden inside of something, or even buried. The result was the same. He even dug up the earth to see if the effect was indeed a full sphere: no earth worms, bugs, rodents in the ground, rock did not stop it, nor water.

That the Tarth were not easily defeated, even by coordinated Katar, fit his plans. He could help defeat the Tarth with The Sphere; the old Hrýll name was too hard to pronounce. He would make the Karn family the most powerful of Katar. The families would have to acknowledge his saving the Katar and mankind. His father had been a fool to not use this power earlier. Old Devon had been content as the Karn representative on the Council of Five. Arlec would change that. It was time for the Katar to be led by a single family and sweep aside any semblance of civil power within The Cities. The council was already weak and dependent on the Katar, why pretend that the council had any say in ruling The Cities. Then, of course, Zethicia. Later, the distant colonies and the last of the old races. He had read of such power, the ruler was called a king. Or emperor. Emperor Arlec, the First.

He smiled as the families filed in to the meeting room. The perfumed smell of the women of Argn, which normally annoyed him, smelled like victory. For the first time their garish colors did not bother him. Maybe he would choose an Argn woman as his wife later, to emphasize that the Karn family was in charge and no woman should be leading any of the families, even as advisors, as Jern's daughters did.

Jern was the first to speak, ignoring the formalities of a full conclave of the Katar families. It should have been Arlec, as the one who had called the meeting, to first address them all. No matter. Later there would be time to remember this insult. As Jern stood Arlec looked at the old man. Of the family heads, Arlec was by far the youngest, but Jern was showing his age. The toll of fighting in Zethicia was showing. His two daughters, Crissa and Mia stood by his side, each resting a hand on his shoulder. Despite his disdain for women leaders Arlec knew that these two were the best fighters in all of Argn. He would keep comments as to their inappropriateness to himself. Things would change.

"Arlec, why have you called a full meeting of the families? We've all heard that you captured the thief that murdered your father and who is wanted by the priesthoods. This is good news, but we are at war and this hardly constitutes a reason for a conclave."

Thankfully, he let the part about Arlec's loss of the ring go unvoiced, one mark in Jern's favor.

"With that threat out of the way, the families should be focusing on the Tarth. Maybe the damned priesthoods will get off their asses and join in the war. They stand to lose as much as we do," said Telem Sho. His city was suffering due to lost trade while the Karn family had the ports and the war was increasing trade by sea as overland trade suffered. Arlec understood his anger, almost relished it; best not to let the latter show.

Arlec scowled. Damn spies everywhere, even amongst the Katar. He wanted to spring the capture of Tsom on the meeting as part of his general display of success. He tried his father's trick of raising his hand for silence. Telem, who controlled the Katar in both Qenaril and Vranin, ignored him.

"You should have already killed him Arlec. You know the priests are adamant that he is a threat by his very existence. As long as he lives large events are likely, which rarely is good for the status quo."

True, you powerful bastard, but my rise to power is a large event. I would like to see him alive until my power is solidified. Arlec's scowl deepened. He decided to speak rather than wait for silence.

"The thief will die soon enough. He poses no real harm any more, I have removed his hands so that he cannot wear a ring. What your internal *information sources* did not tell you is that he is pureblood Kinel." He let that sink in. He had their full attention now. "I have also learned, from my own sources, that there is an entire underground of Kinel half breeds still alive and plotting our downfall along with a group of disillusioned traitors that have fallen prey to their lies." He pushed the vision of his drugged sister from his mind. She was a traitor. She deserved no pity.

The Katar heads started murmuring, but now when Arlec raised his hand, they shut up quickly. Better, much better. They would learn.

"Worse than that, the Hrýll and the remaining Srýll are betraying us."

Jern, the leader of the war effort looked shocked, but he was too damn smart and recovered quickly. He nodded and dared to interrupt him, again. "Of course, our demands for weapons talismans, they are tainted." Wara of the Terrel family and Jahone of the Katir family looked puzzled. Telem also nodded. "The next offensive depends on the additional weapons. They are crucial to tipping the balance decisively with the Tarth. What manner of sabotage have they used Arlec?"

Damn them, they were not reacting the way he wanted them to. Too calm and fast. These men were not quite the fools he had assumed they were. Jern and Telem would have to go, soon. They were too smart. They saw patterns too quickly, making him seem like simply an information source and nothing more.

"You're correct. The talismans will backfire when used for any length of time. I have done some testing." Jern looked disgusted, guessing at how the testing was done. This was war, some sacrifices had to be made. Arlec ignored the look and sipped his glass of water. He let Wara and Jahone catch up in their thinking. He turned to Jern, "Do you think that without the talismans you—we—can defeat the Tarth?"

Jern considered. "With the Yanín and all of the Katar … probably. But, we have never had all of the Katar out of The Cities. Even during the Riconé extermination we had a thousand Katar to keep the Cities in line. During the Hrýll uprising we had five hundred left and there was the uprising in The Cities then. We almost lost control. If not for the aid of the priesthoods then we would have. I would not recommend it. We might have to let Zethicia fall and then attack."

Telem followed up. "The gods and their priests are not to be trusted. They resent the Katar's continued power. This time I would not depend on the priests helping the Katar in The Cities. Better to get their aid in the battlefield."

Arlec let them discuss various tactics for a time. Finally, at an opportune time, he raised his hand again. With a slight clearing of his throat they were silenced. Arlec wondered if he looked like his father with his hand raised and the attention of the families focused on him.

"I have something that may be of use to us. My father entrusted its knowledge to me. The Sphere of Banishment, *San Par'eh Shante,"* he managed to not slaughter the pronunciation. Even Jern and Telem were silent this time. Strangely, it was Jahone that spoke. Jahone was an idiot.

"The Sphere still exists? I thought it destroyed in the original banishment of the Tarth, five thousand years ago?"

"It exists and still works," Arlec replied with a smile.

Questions from all four came simultaneously. How did it work? Was it a talisman of old, or did it need qenar as all the Hrýll and Srýll talismans?

"Fortuitous that Devon had this talisman of old within his arsenal. What other talismans do you have that we should know about Arlec?" Asked Jern.

Arlec considered Jern's statement, despite the sarcasm. It was fortuitous. Certainly the Tarth wars were an important event in history, but why was it that this was the only special talisman that Devon had hidden. The thought that the thief really could influence these events somehow no longer seemed so unbelievable. Yet, there must be more that Devon had hidden. He would have to tear apart the library and study later. The old man had been a crafty one.

"My father told me that this was a weapon that could be used against any of the enemies of the Karn ... and the Katar, not just the Tarth." The distinction between the family and the Katar as a whole was not lost on any of them. No doubt they all had variations of the same vision of major portions of any of their families simply disappearing. Jern, of them all, looked unafraid. His look was more of assessment. The same look that he had when looking at a map with troop positions and numbers. His daughters showed frank looks of disgust. Damn Argn women.

Telem spoke, putting into words what they all were thinking. "I think that unlike Devon, we can expect a willingness on your part to use this talisman. What do you need to help you use it *properly*?"

Arlec smiled. They understood.

Chapter 45

'What have you done? Even I felt the ka flow. You are aged!' He held his wife's hand with concern.

'I have passed it on. The legacy of the family. He may be the one. If not, than his child may be the one. It is the eclipse of the five moons, an omen—either good or bad—that Tsom will be an agent of change in this world.' She lay back exhausted from the birth. Her Kinel colorings visible for the first time in many years. Her Human husband picked up the child. His child's eyes were gold on gold. His already thick hair white, contrasting with its chocolate brown skin—except for parts of his chest and face which were pale. *'How will we hide him, my love? He is so Kinel, almost like a pureblood.'*

'Don't worry. He will blend in more than you can imagine.'

Tsom awoke in a strange bed. "Father?" he whispered. He would have leapt up, but he was too weak. He had been dreaming of his mother again, but this time it felt as if he were inside of his father's head. He had loved his father, but it was always his mother that he felt a visceral connection to. She had had such high hopes for him, he often felt like his survival as a thief had betrayed her dream, yet it had been her that drove him away from her murder, from the Katar. He tried to rub his eyes and started as his arms encountered no resistance, which in turn caused him to throw his arms out and bang his stumps on the bed, causing some pain and considerable anger.

Using his elbows and forearms, he clumsily pushed his bed covers off and sat up. He was clean and dressed in comfortable bed clothes. The sunlight streamed in the window. A few birds chirped in the tree outside, the sound carried by the warm but not too warm fall breeze. Except for the fact that the room was spinning, it was a pleasant scene. He waited until his head stopped pounding.

The bandages on his left hand were clean. None were needed on his right. The scar tissue was already well formed. How long had he been out? How had he gotten here? Someone had kicked him. He almost could remember who it was. Someone he knew. He felt that he was safe here, but did not trust that feeling.

He got up and found clothes that fit him placed on the table nearby. Putting them on was the challenge. In frustration he resorted to manifesting his virtual hands, despite the cost in energy, both real and less tangible. He was not going to go walking around in bed clothes, a helpless child. The effort weakened him, but he felt that this time he had used significantly less energy than the first time, with the lock in the cell.

Expending more energy he opened the door. The speed of manifesting and dropping his hands was increasing, but it was still quite tiring as long as he had them up.

Shara bumped into him as he opened the door. She smiled a huge smile and hugged him. "You are up and about! You probably shouldn't be, but I won't be the one to try and keep you in bed." She stepped back to look at him, giving him an opportunity to see her. She looked like crap.

Her eyes were bloodshot and baggy. Broken blood vessels crisscrossed her face, neck, and arms. What the hell had happened to her?

"You're the one who kicked me."

She grinned. "Yes indeed. And none too soon."

He considered. His initial rage at betrayal was gone. Staring at her, he felt the surge of love and knew if it had been her that had betrayed him then it had been through torture. He could not deny his feelings, nor the fact that she had saved him and was here now.

"How did you get your clothes on?"

He reached out and manifested a hand and brushed back a stray strand of hair from her face. She jumped back with a yelp. Then grabbed his arm and guided it to her face. He touched it. He could feel it through the pain. He could also feel the veins and arteries on her face. He could feel the damage. Concentrating he touched deeper. The burst vessels faded and her lightly tanned skin showed where he had touched her. The effort exhausted him and he dropped his hands.

She raised her hand to her cheek.

"What did you do? The pain is gone!" she said.

He smiled and leaned against the wall to hold himself up. At least someone's pain was gone.

"Kaylee come help me!"

"I'm OK, just give me a moment."

"I don't think so."

Kaylee appeared, grabbed one arm and Shara grabbed the other. They guided him back into the bedroom, but allowed him to sit in a chair instead of forcing him back into bed.

Kaylee looked at Shara's cheek and listened to her explain about Tsom's hands. She then looked at Tsom, checked his bandaged arm. Finally, she spoke.

"I am not Kinel, or part Kinel, as both of you are."

Kaylee paused and looked pointedly at Shara. They had obviously been discussing this before. Shara shook her head slightly, still dealing with the knowledge.

"But, I know something of the Kinel. You"—Kaylee pointed her finger at Tsom—"must be very careful you do not burn yourself out playing with your new found powers. The Kinel were famous for the magnificent things they could do. They were also famous for dying early by over using the powers they discovered. Larrina has told me some of the less known history of the Kinel. She has known me since I was a little girl and I remember many of her stories. Each family was known for a special skill."

She lifted one of Tsom's arms and held a hand where his hand should be.

"This may be part of your special skill, or it may be something new. Only the Kinel, of all the races, were ever able to directly manipulate ka in an improvised manner. This always cost them dearly, until they mastered the skill, or died."

She stopped her lecture and waited to see if it was sinking in. Tsom nodded, as it seemed it was expected of him. Shara looked worriedly at Tsom, as if seeing something that he did not know about.

Shara went to the washroom and came back with a small mirror. She held it in front of his face.

The reflection resembled him. But, it was no boy, or even young man. The man looking back was thirty or more. No eighteen year old. He leaned back heavily. Despite the shock of the image in the mirror, he yawned. He fell asleep as the two women moved him to the bed and tucked him in.

Both women protesting, Tsom was back on his feet in a few hours. They went downstairs to discuss next moves. Kaylee made tea, but it lacked the revitalizing quality of Larrina's. He turned to Kaylee.

"I have failed in retrieving the talisman that Alanar felt was so important."

"So we assumed when word came of your and Shara's capture."

Tsom looked at Shara with a raised eyebrow. Shara looked away. Kaylee watched them both.

"She was drugged and tortured by her brother. Any secrets she gave away were out of her control. That the Katar would treat one of their own that way …" Kaylee made a spitting noise.

Shara still refused to meet Tsom's eyes. He turned back to Kaylee.

"Can the resistance succeed without the talisman?" he asked.

"We have to try. We are out in the open, as never before. Alanar has made his move, committed the resistance to full open rebellion. There is no turning back. We have to leverage the war with the Tarth and the separated Katar forces."

"Can't the Hrýll make a new talisman, a new sphere?"

Kaylee looked vaguely amused.

"They did not tell you much about the Sphere, did they?" She did not wait for the acknowledgment. "The Sphere of Banishment is from the time of the old races. Before mankind. It does not require qenar. It was shaped by the Hrýll, the Kinel, the Riconé, and possibly the Lost Ones, and others—all combined. There is no way to combine that power again."

"The Lost Ones?" Shara interrupted.

"I know very little about these. Larrina spoke of them occasionally. They were legend to her also. From what I gather they were the precursor to mankind. Mankind would not exist without them, yet they were not what we would call Human. Some say the gods are the Lost Ones. Some say the gods also came from the Lost Ones. They may be legend and the talisman may have only been created by the other three races."

"Which leaves us—me—where?" Tsom said with some bitterness.

"Alanar will head to Zethicia, hopefully with Hrýll as allies. Larrina is aware that you have failed." Tsom winced at the word and nodded bitterly. "She is mobilizing the resistance and by now has fled her home as the Katar may have traced movements to her."

Shara looked worried and glanced at Tsom and placed a hand on his forearm.

Kaylee nodded in understanding.

"Don't worry, Shara, this safe house is a well-guarded secret. Only Larrina knows who we are. Even the information given to you, to get to us, was false. We looked for you where you were told to go, but that was simply a false location that will not be used again."

Shara stroked his forearm gently. Kaylee continued.

"The rest of the resistance will do their part, fight once the signal is given, but we have our own mission. We must disable the gateway between Zethicia and The Cities. Cut the Katar in two. Trap the Sphere in Zethicia, while we gain control of The Cities and destroy the Katar here." Kaylee stopped, both she and Tsom looked at Shara.

She met their gazes and leaned forward.

"I am with you, I am a traitor to my people, my families, but not to mankind. I have not betrayed you," she looked pointedly at Tsom, " and I will die for the cause. I had hoped to influence my family, but that hope is gone."

Tsom saw the hurt and revulsion in her eyes. What had Arlec done to her?

"I will do what I can to make sure that mankind, and the Kinel," she looked at Tsom closely, "do not utterly destroy the Katar out of revenge. The goal is to remove their power and rule over Nakana, not to wipe them out."

She rubbed her empty ring finger and looked at Kaylee hopefully, then finished. "Without our rings, unity, and ability to cause fear, we have no more power than any other group."

Kaylee nodded.

"I can speak for a large portion of the resistance. We are not out for revenge, just freedom. There will be some who are not willing to focus on the ultimate goal, so your fears are not completely without merit."

"What about Alanar, do you speak for him?" Barin asked as he strode into the room. He had something tucked under his arm, which he set down on the kitchen table. Two strange looking wooden and metal devices, with leather straps and metal cables. Barin looked at Tsom. "I made you some hands."

Kaylee answered the question. "Unfortunately, no one speaks for Alanar. Not even Larrina."

Chapter 46

The head priests for all the major gods, ten in all, were in the same room. It had taken a week of negotiating just to get agreement where to meet. While Djarn, the Lord Priest of Nu Arr, felt it was his place to host the meeting, the other priesthoods did not trust each other and refused a meeting on another's ground. The priestesses of Hallam, not a major priesthood, finally prevailed. Their argument that she was the most neutral, because she had the least to lose, swayed the other priests. Hallam, while powerful, had very few worshippers and almost no temples, except in the small towns of great Zethicia, or the wilderness colonies.

They met in the large outdoor amphitheater temple on the outskirts of Bronin. This took an extra three days for the priests as there was no gateway between The Cities themselves—only between the city of Qenaril and Zethicia—thus, well-guarded, high-speed floaters were used to bring in the scattered lesser priests for the conclave.

The amphitheater glowed with hundreds of high intensity glow globes. Cost was not an issue for such an important event. Lord and Lady Priests, with their entourages, gathered in groups, gossiping, plotting, waiting for the meeting to start. Their staffs of power were never out of their hands; conduits to their gods and the siphoned *ka* of many worshipers. Owls and bats circled overhead, which all took as a good sign that the Priestesses of Hallam were watching over the entire area. The various food tables were frequented often, once the lower priests had tested food and wine for poisons. If not for the grave reasons for the meeting, it would have been a party atmosphere. But everybody was nervous with the Katar forces so concentrated in Zethicia and the rebellion out in the open. If the Katar could be challenged, so could the priesthoods.

Djarn sampled the food with little appetite. He had been on edge since his meeting with his god. Too many things were happening. The thief was on the loose again and his god's reaction disturbing. At least this could not be blamed on him. But, he had not succeeded in capturing the thief either, which would have been well rewarded. None of the priesthoods had been successful. A few dozen revolutionaries had been found and dealt with, but the thief was invisible. No one had seen him, or could even describe him. The true image that the Katar had passed out had led to some initial avenues, but soon that image seemed to have no relation to their quarry, who seemed to change his looks at will.

His junior priests hovered, ready to fulfill his every command. Normally, this pleased him.

"Lord do you need more wine?" one asked.

"Leave me. The meeting will start soon. I need no distractions." He waved the lackey away.

Djarn joined the other nine Lord Priests on the dais. The hundred or so lower priests gathered more closely. Another fifty guards manned the various entrances. They had discussed between themselves what they would say. The need to mobilize the priesthoods with the right message was clear. They could not let the underlings know that the gods were powerless against the Tarth. A united message was necessary.

Tian, high priestess of Hallam, signaled for silence. The birds overhead all screamed simultaneously to emphasize her.

"While the goddess, Hallam, has been chosen to host this event, as a neutral party, it is Nu Arr and his voice, Djarn, that will be addressing you. May the gods bless our conclave." With that she bowed her head briefly and stepped aside for Djarn.

"The gods have spoken to each of us", began Djarn nodding to his fellow high priests, "mankind is being tested by the gods. Those worthy will be rewarded in this life and in the return. Those unworthy will never make it to the Sea of Souls. Pé will cast his net and discard forever those who do not live up to the challenge! Strong prayer and strong deeds in the holy battle against the Tarth is necessary. Do not expect miracles from the gods without mankind's sacrifice first."

The other lord priests nodded and called out in assent. Lord Priest of Ague, god of the seas, and Lord Priest of Met, the weather god, stepped forward and reinforced the message.

"Nor will these rebels be tolerated. Rebels who declare the Katar and gods are parasites on mankind! We, who protect man, know better. Prayer is necessary. Pray with your prayer sticks to the gods. Pray with all your might and those who are worthy will be rewarded. Tell the faithful to pray deeply, though it may hurt, they will be rewarded in the end. Mankind must pray. The gods must feel the *ka* before they will join together to defeat the enemies of man.

"The gods have spoken. Those who fight in the holy war against the Tarth will be rewarded with noble incarnation in the next life. Death in the holy war is a blessing. Carry forth the message! Call forth the faithful and the masses! We will be victorious in our battle against the Tarth!"

The staffs of power all glowed and the lower priests felt the call. They believed. They knew this was what the gods wanted and it was mankind's destiny. The call went up. "Carry forth the message! Pray! We will be victorious!"

***

The white cat sat atop the horizontal pole holding a glow globe that illuminated the small amphitheater where the priests were now yelling in unison. The pole was attached to a vertical post over thirty feet tall. The priests were all crying and chanting together below. She purred and licked herself. Looking up she spied a large owl, which swooped down and braked in the air, its massive wings back beating, its talons extended. She stood and arched her back, but did not move to avoid the owl. She was gently picked up by the owl and it flew off silently into the night.

Chapter 47

The chameleon effect was something all the half breeds knew, all the ones that survived. After a while simply not wanting to stand out triggered it. Larrina did not even have to think about it. It was like breathing. These days it took an effort to drop the effect. Thinking of Tsom, she did so and stared in the mirror. It had been a relief to look at another Kinel, uncloaked, after so many years. Tsom had power, more than he knew. Undefined power. He felt like a true blood.

She hated that he was so young. It seemed unfair that he had no time to enjoy life before being thrust in the middle of their struggle. Yet, struggle he must, or his life was worthless. The Katar would see to that. Still, she felt like the resistance was using him. She knew they were. *We all get used. Even Alanar,* she thought. *We use his hatred and revenge. We are not blind to his faults and we use them.*

She changed into traveling clothes while whistling an ancient tune. A love song concerning a Kinel woman and a hero named Tadai, who appeared from nowhere and helped the Kinel beat back the Tarth *daemons.* Not the story, or legend, the Katar told, but that was before the Katar. Before the rings. Before mankind. The Tarth had always been battling the races for Nakana. Not that she really blamed the Tarth, they were at least as old as the Hrýll and saw all races as invaders, even the Kinel. She hoped Alanar was right, that eliminating the Katar would bring at least a period of freedom to the races and allow them all to flourish for a time. Neither she, nor Alanar, believed it would be forever. Some group always wanted to rule. Just a breather. Time for rebalancing.

She stopped with her shirt off and looked at herself in the mirror. Despite the light cords of muscle and no fat, gravity could not be denied. She cupped her breasts upward and examined herself that way. She smiled ruefully. The image of Lanos and Alanar fencing flashed briefly and brought a flush to her face. She pushed the image back and let her breasts fall their short distance. She put on a breast band. Not for show. Practical. A fighting outfit. It was time. At long last, action. She regretted it and embraced it simultaneously. Alanar knew her too well. Even a century of no combat and she was ready to embrace that again, despite the risk to her healing powers. *One cannot be a healer and a killer at the same time*, she thought.

Where are you now, Tsom, my fellow Kinel? If you had been older, if you had not already been in love, maybe I would have bonded with you. Then, at least I would know if you were alive. I would sense you. Feel you all these marks away.

She cast her mind and emotions out. She had not bonded with another for a century, but until that person died, there was always a connection.

Alanar lived.

If he lived Lanos did, too. She smiled. Would Alanar be jealous if she had slept with Lanos? Bonded with him? She shook her head. It had been even more than a century since she had made love to a Human and joined her emotions with one. They die so easily, they live such short lives. *I am too old*, she thought. *It is time for rebellion to rise up and fight and I don't need the pain of feeling the others die. Now we must all fight and prepare to die. Even I must think of death now, not healing.*

Larrina finished her small travel bag. She stood for a moment, looking at her bedroom, her home for over fifty years. She would miss it. She went to the window and looked out. The garden was beautiful, but she stared at one tree, the small bantri in the southwest corner. A tear ran down her cheek. No time to dig it up. No place to take it. She let only one tear fall before turning away from the window.

She went to the closet and pulled out the object wrapped in Hrýll cloth, setting it on the bed. There was no turning back. If the Katar were to be beaten, this was the time. All of them must fight. All of them. *We are all expendable.*

She unrolled the cloth. The short black scabbard was new looking. She grasped the jeweled handle and pulled it out. The black blade was polished and reflected the light. Momentarily her eyes flashed gold and her chameleon effect dropped again. I hope you live, my brethren, but if not, many Katar will pay for your death, before I join you. Her smile was grim as she sheathed the blade and strapped it to her back.

The man had been following her for too long to be a coincidence. Larrina increased her pace and made her way to the less crowded blocks. Soon she was in an industrial area. It was past normal waking hours, few people were about. She stepped into an alley.

The man entered with his sword drawn. He was expecting some sort of a trap and moved cautiously. The Katar ring on his left hand glowed lightly. The black jeweled blade in Larrina's hand echoed the glow. *Why is it that people never look up*, she thought as she dropped onto him, severing his carotid artery and snapping his neck. She pulled off his ring, wiped her sword on his chest and sheathed the blade as she was rounding the corner of the alley back onto the street. One less Katar. Not a sound was made.

The rebel cell that she initially planned connecting with had been discovered by the Guardians of Nu Arr, the warrior priests, after neighbors turned them in. She had missed them by hours. She had heard of a rash of incidents in just the past few days; citizen turning on citizen, proclaiming that they would be blessed by the gods. The priesthoods and their gods were making a play for power. Demonstrating that they, not the Katar were the ones to follow. The next cell was Kaylee's. She hoped the old couple were safe. The combination of the priesthoods and the Katar had made life very dangerous the past few days for all members of the resistance. Kaylee was an old friend. In her mind the old woman would always be the inquisitive little girl who had ignored her shocked mother's admonitions that she leave the mistress alone and no servant girl should be annoying the head of house. She smiled at the memory. A different life. One of many.

A few hours later she arrived. She scouted the house first. No obvious watchers. Just in case she scaled the back wall to the roof, then dropped to the windowsill of one of the second story bedrooms.

"Not bad for an old woman," Kaylee said, lowering the crossbow pointed at her. Larrina laughed as she pulled herself in and hugged and kissed her old friend.

"Your ears have not deteriorated with time."

"Nor your muscles and agility. You could be a thief." Kaylee grinned.

Something in the way she said 'thief.'

"Tsom? You have heard something of him?"

"More, she found me." Tsom stood in the doorway. Larrina's smile froze and then faded. She rushed forward and wrapped her arms around him.

"What have those bastards done to you?" She fought back tears.

"Loosen your grip 'Rina, he is still weak," said Kaylee.

She loosened her grip and looked at the man before her. She recognized the ravages of using *ka* recklessly. His face showed age, but so did his eyes. He had aged greatly in just a few weeks. A Kinel looking thirty meant many more decades of his lifespan had been destroyed. He reached forward with his right arm and she felt a hand on her cheek brushing away a tear. She grabbed his arm fiercely. "Stop. Stop wasting your *ka*!"

She stepped back further, drawing him into the room as she spotted Shara now standing behind him.

"The power to touch without flesh is that of the Tadai family. A family of legend and song. That power hasn't been seen in many Kinel lifetimes." The love song about Tadai she had been singing days before, when packing, returned to her head.

A touch that melted hearts
Or crushed them. For love
Reached across the field of pain
Gave his soul, that we all may gain.

It was lousy poetry, she had always thought, but it had always been one of her favorite songs. It also reminded her of the immense power that the Tadai of the song wielded, before he died.

"What are the limits of your *hands*?"

Tsom shrugged. He sat down, tired already. Shara came in and stood near him. Larrina saw her face. She strode forward and grabbed Shara's left hand and arm. It was pale white and the veins stood out in dark contrast. "Even the damn Katar rings have their price when over-used Shara, as I see you have learned."

She looked deep into Shara's bloodshot eyes and looked at the one cheek that had healed. The obvious hand shape made her turn to Tsom. She held Shara's left hand, which had no ring. Shara's eyes darted to Kaylee. Larrina turned to Kaylee.

"Let her have the ring back, she can be trusted. Shara, put it on your right hand. The whole left hand thing is stupid superstition. Your left hand and arm need to heal. Where is Barin?"

"He is tinkering in the shop, as always. Making adjustments to Tsom's new hands," Kaylee said.

Raised eyebrow was met with a smile. Tsom spoke up.

"They are remarkable, if clumsy."

"You can brief Barin later. No time for resting, but perhaps time for tea while we discuss matters." She fished out a small pouch. "Put some of this in Shara's and Tsom's, it will help."

The tea was wonderful, Tsom thought. It relaxed yet rejuvenated. *Where did the herbs come from*, he wondered again. Was there *ka* involved in her teas?

"Alanar must know by now that we don't have the Sphere. I always thought it too dangerous, but he is more of a risk taker—when the change comes over him—than I." Kaylee looked skeptical at the latter, but kept her mouth shut. "We do need to shut down the gateway between Zethicia and The Cities. As soon as the last wave of Katar go through. We don't want them coming back. I would prefer to destroy it, but even damaging it would suffice."

"What about the one in Zethicia?" asked Shara.

"If we destroy or damage one, then neither side will work," replied Larrina.

Larrina continued, "the Marnoon cell was captured. We don't have enough time to bring in another cell to help. This will have to be done on our own." Kaylee's lips tightened. Larrina knew that the Marnoon family and Kaylee were good friends, but there was no easy way to break the news.

"We have three days to prepare. We know that will be when the Katar have moved most of their forces to Zethicia. Tsom and Shara, you need to recover— as much as possible. Tsom, NO using your hands, or any other action that will drain your *ka*. You need to recover, some of the effect of *ka* loss is temporary. You will not get young again, but your energy and strength will return." She leaned forward and pulled up his shirt where blood was now visible. She examined the bandages on his chest. "Damn, is there no part of your body that is undamaged?" Shara and Tsom both blushed deeply.

Larrina and Kaylee exchanged looks and burst out laughing.

Wiping tears from her eyes Larrina continued. "Needless to say, the gateway is heavily guarded. We don't have the manpower to simply strike, nor the time to coordinate it with the resistance here. All the other cells have other assigned tasks that are crucial. I'm afraid we may have to use Tsom's new powers to disable the gateway."

Chapter 48

Arlec hesitated in front of the gateway. On the other side the streets of Zethicia were clearly visible. Yet, the thought of his next step being a thousand marks away was disconcerting. He had only used the gateway once each way before, as a youth with his father. He noticed the mix of city guards and Katar. They were all watching him. He was sure of it. Gritting his teeth he strode through.

Zethicia was hot. No ocean nearby to moderate the temperatures, and it was closer to the ever hot north pole. There was a sea not too many marks away, but here there was only a river. The smell of dryness hit his nose as he blinked in the sun. He sneezed. It smelled of agriculture. Backwards Zethicia. Hardly worth saving, except it would solidify his power. That and they did provide most of the food for The Cities.

"This way, Lord." The hand touched his elbow lightly. Arlec was ready to display his indignation at the touch, until he saw the ring and the armband. A fellow Katar. Very well.

The escort pointed as they walked. The gateway's location was easy to defend, no buildings nearby and on high ground. The Tarth encampment was visible from the winding road as a dark spot on the sea of green as they made their way down from the gateway. Given the hill they could be over twenty marks away. At least any advance would be easy to spot.

The fall crops had that new green that lasted for a month, ripening for spring harvest. *What a boring life*, Arlec thought. One crop after another with no break in between. The continual warmth of the north seemed like a curse. Arlec gazed at the Tarth encampment, fingered the sphere around his neck, and smiled.

***

The Tarth gathered around Carnel. He was slightly taller than the tallest. Slightly redder than the reddest. The jade sphere hung in plain view on his bare chest. He gestured and a Chimi came forth carrying a black bag. Be Na Tarth grabbed the bag and in his melodic voice began to speak. All were silent.

"Five hundred and fifty." He held the bag up. "On each five souls of our brethren bound to serve the Katar. Five Tarth destroyed to create each abomination. Each ring has the true death of one of our family attached to it. All to aid the power lust of the Katar and mankind." A soft moan went through the group.

"It has been five thousand years for mankind, but only one hundred for us. They have forgotten the power of the Tarth. They have lost their allies of old, destroyed them in their lust for power and continuous population growth. They are vermin that multiply without thought for the future. They are now losing their power—" he poured the rings on the stone dais in front of him. He stooped and grabbed the enormous hammer of stone next to the dais. With a small grunt his enormous muscles bulged. The hammer weighed as much as two horses. With a crash it struck the rings. "—*forever.*" A cheer went up amongst the Tarth. The *ka* of their ancestors washed over them. Be Na Tarth held back the siphoning power of the jade sphere. The *ka* of his race would not be used in such a profane way. The Tarth cheered and wept. Many would dream of lost family from those wars. One hundred years was not so long ago for the Tarth. Many wished it had been five thousand years ago for them also. After mankind had been destroyed for five thousand years, then maybe they would forget.

***

The Chimi commander, Tzless, had been surprised at Be Na Tarth's suggestion. Try to bribe a Human rather than killing or torturing? Yet, it had worked. In a short while, Be Na Tarth had a minor group of spies. He promised them power and their lives after the war. They could rule over any of mankind that was spared. They would get eternal youth from the *ka* of their own kind. Or simply wealth. The bribes differed, yet the result was the same. A few he told that the Tarth were not *daemons*, but gods and he was the ruler of them all. Those that believed, were the best spies of all.

It was one of the latter that was in front of him now. He would have to play his part. Be Na Tarth nodded to Tzless with a wink that the Human could not see. Be Na Tarth towered over the Human. Deepening his already deep voice, he intoned.

"Rise mortal."

The man rose, visibly shaking. Mingled with the fear was a mixture of awe and greed. "My Lord I am honored to come face to face with you. I have news that you will need to win your war against the unholy Katar and their false gods."

"Indeed. You feel that I and the Tarth *need* your help to win our righteous cause?" He glared and caused his red skin to flare redder still.

The coward cringed, but did not crumble. He knew something. He was confident in his knowledge. He could smell it. Fear and confidence, two smells that rarely combined.

"My Lord, of course you will be victorious, but my knowledge will aid you and prevent additional harm from coming to your chosen minions." He looked around at the two Chimi still flanking him.

"Speak and your reward will fit your words."

"Lord," he licked his lips and lowered his voice, "the Katar have an old talisman. The Sphere of Banishment. They mean to use it against you."

Be Na Tarth refused to show emotion, but Tzless knew his master well and tensed. This was devastating news, Tzless knew, without knowing the meaning of this Sphere. The table before Be Na Tarth groaned as he clenched it. Indentations in the strong wood were visible under his fingers.

"The talisman was destroyed five thousand of your years ago. We destroyed it as it was used. The man the Hrýll call *Death* died using it! I was there." Be Na Tarth glared at the Human, his teeth showing. Tzless almost felt pity for the Human. His lord was close to killing.

The man shrank back. The Chimi closed in behind him.

"No my Lord. I know it to be true. It exists. The Katar known as Arlec has it. Arlec of the Karn family."

"I know the Karn." The table splintered. Two inch thick wood crumbled as if it were rotted paper. "How do you come by this knowledge?"

"I am the *loyal* servant of the Lord Priest of Nu Arr. I was with him as the Katar informed him of their find." The man drew himself up tall and looked important, until he noticed that Be Na Tarth did not seem to know who the god of luck was. Tzless stepped forward and spoke to Be Na Tarth in common tongue for the benefit of the visitor.

"Nu Arr is one of the false *gods* that arose immediately after the banishment of the Tarth. It was he who convinced the gods and the Katar to cooperate. He is called the god of luck. The same cowardly gods who try and attack from a distance because they are afraid of the Tarth." Tzless nodded towards Be Na Tarth's chest and the jade sphere. The man looked at it with the same mix of awe and greed that he seemed to have for everything.

"Yes, the so called gods. They were of the First. The First crossers of planes. They had little power then and they fooled the Kinel, the Hrýll, and the Srýll into helping them. gods?" He spat on the ground, the impact creating a small cloud of dust "Your gods are parasites that suck the *ka* out of their own kind. Mankind is their source of power. But, I do not know this Nu Arr specifically.

Luck. It is a strange thing to worship. Luck is fickle. It is chance. What sort of a power is that? Better to worship *me* my little priest. Worship *Destruction*!" With that he brought his fists down upon the damaged table, which exploded with the force of his blow. The *loyal* priest of the god of luck glanced at the fragments of wood and noticed that the wood was smoldering. Tzless smiled at the reaction. All Tarth could generate heat for brief moments, in five thousand years Humans must have forgotten that. The priest nodded vigorously and smiled weakly.

"My thoughts exactly my Lord. Lord of Destruction!"

***

Lanos watched Oonie approach as they mounted. Lanos softly called for his horse to halt and it did. Alanar had selected their horses from the small herd that Oonie had left at their disposal. He had studied them and touched each briefly. Then he had smiled and laid a hand on an older mare. A *mare*. Lanos did not like mares. They were small and unpredictable. Worse, this one was walking with a limp! It was the last horse he would have chosen. At the time he thought Alanar was not serious. But if he was, then Lanos was going to play along. As soon as the mare was saddled the limp disappeared. Alanar smiled and patted her neck. "She is wily. The limp was fake. Don't let her get away with anything."

Oonie held out his hand with a small leather bag in it. "For your woman. She will understand." Lanos opened it. Inside was a small cutting of a Bantri tree, wrapped in more leather.

"But, it will die before I see her."

"No, not if she is the one. The Bantri tree is delicate, but has hidden strength. Under the right circumstances it can live forever. Stranger still, while it grows incredibly slowly, it is extremely easy to make a cutting from. It roots almost immediately. If you love her, then give it to her. She will know what to do with it. She is Kinel."

"Thank you my friend. I will see you at the final battle."

"There is never a final battle. I will see you at the battle we have planned."

Lanos turned and was about to nudge the horse forward to catch up with Alanar, when she trotted off in Alanar's direction on her own.

***

Barnus forced himself to focus on the conversation. He kept thinking of his son, his dead son. Dead forever. The *daemons* were killing everything with true death. It was hard to fully comprehend. How does one mourn forever?

Barnus did not worship the gods. Yet, he believed in the Sea of Souls and rebirth. It was the very basis of society. Bad enough that the Katar meted out their punishment of true death to the worst of criminals, but now a war was taking place where those that died were gone forever. He was thankful that his wife had died a natural death not long ago. She would not have to deal with the knowledge that their youngest was gone—truly gone.

The conversation was with a new Katar leader. The new head of the Karn family. Barnus was not impressed.

"Sit down ..." Arlec began.

Arlec looked to the man on his left who almost rolled his eyes, but caught himself and responded "This is Barnus, *Sir*, the head of the Zethicia army." Arlec looked as if he would lash out at the sarcastic young man who had spoken. Had Arlec not been briefed, or was his memory simply weak?

"... Yes, Barnus, yes, sit down, Barnus. We have a new set of plans we need to finalize."

Barnus sat down with the governor, the heads of the Katar families, and the head of the Yanín. He noted the absence of the priests. Evidently the gods would not be helping, or the Katar were keeping the priests out. Everyone gave the Yanín wide birth, who sat expressionless with his arms bent at impossible angles. The plan was not good, if the expressions of the rest at the table were accurate. Governor Courie looked ill. The other Katar looked slightly disgusted. Barnus did not attempt to read the Yanín.

"I was just filling in the rest of the group on the treason of the Hrýll. They will be properly punished when this is over. They are supplying us with intentionally defective weapon talismans." *He certainly does not look devastated over the news.* Barnus wondered what Arlec's agenda was. *I trust this Katar even less than the others.*

"However, all is not lost. We have an ancient weapon, the Sphere of Banishment, which was used on the Tarth before. To successfully use it we must force the Tarth into a massive battle, where they concentrate all their strength." Arlec gestured and an aid unrolled a large map of the area onto the large table. "The Zethician army and the Yanín will attack here. As the Tarth surround you the Katar will surround the Tarth. Then we will use the Sphere and banish the Tarth once again."

Something was not right, besides the obvious—that his army would be vulnerable until the Katar came. He looked at the governor. She was slumped in her chair. The lines in her face were deep. She looked years older than a few weeks ago. The responsibility of her city state was more than she could handle. She had been elected in peace time, when the biggest issue was how to remain independent from the Katar and The Cities. Now they were at war, and under the Katar thumb just to survive. He looked again at the other Katar. The young man from the Sho family was there. He had not yet developed the arrogance of the older Katar. He looked decidedly pale and guilty. He would not meet Barnus's eyes.

Barnus leaned forward. "How does the Sphere work?"

Arlec smiled, as if smiling at a child. "It is simple. It is keyed for the Tarth. When activated properly all Tarth within its sphere of influence will be shifted to another plane. Hell, the 95th plane, one presumes—obviously I did not visit myself to verify this. That is where they were banished to before. After the Tarth are banished we mop up their servants, these Chimi, and any of those Maite dogs that remain."

"Who activates the sphere?"

"That's the beauty of it. We don't have to worry about someone failing at the last moment. There is a timer mechanism on it. I will go to the site hours before the battle and set it up, hidden from view. You bring in your army, lure them to the spot, and keep them occupied for a few minutes at most and then it is all over."

"May I see this sphere?"

Arlec scowled. Slowly he pulled out a sphere from under his loose shirt.

It looked like a simple glass sphere, yet everyone in the room shivered as if it were cold in the room. Even the Yanín looked uncomfortable. Arlec stroked it. It was clear that he would not let any of the others actually touch the sphere. Barnus looked to Courie for guidance. She slowly nodded.

They got down to planning the details and the precise timing of the battle with the Tarth. Barnus could not help thinking that they were sketching out their own demise as much as the Tarth's. When Katar looked guilty, you knew you were doomed.

Chapter 49

Shara was playing with her ring, which felt unfamiliar on her right hand. She stood on the small balcony and stared out to the river visible from the second floor. Where had that cat obtained it? She understood that coincidences happened and that with Tsom they might happen more frequently, but this seemed unusual. Cats carrying rings around was no coincidence. No, it had been fastened to the cat's collar.

"The rings were wrought out of pain and suffering. I don't know if that makes them inherently evil, but I never trusted them."

Shara turned to face Larrina. "What do you mean wrought of pain and suffering?"

"Each of the white diamonds is the essence of a Tarth soul. Their entire *ka* captured into the diamond. I don't suppose they teach you that in the Katar academy."

Shara shook her head and gazed in slight horror at the ring on her finger.

"What about the black diamond? Is that a soul too?"

"No, it is the controller of the ring, which is really a talisman after all. It draws upon the *ka* of the white diamonds and draws upon living *ka* to recharge the diamonds as needed."

"How do you know so much about the rings that Katar do not?"

"Some of the Katar still know these things. They no longer share it with all the Katar, knowing that perhaps not all of you would approve."

Larrina held out her hand, which Shara took. She then led Shara back into the house and to a couch where they sat next to each other. The resistance was certainly well funded, or families of wealth were part of it. The size of this house and Larrina's house had surprised Shara. Even as part of the resistance, she had little knowledge of its entire infrastructure. She had been a conduit for information and Lanos had been simply a code name. The more she learned, the more she knew that the time of the Katar was over. This wealth had added to her growing conviction that the hold of the Katar really was not benign— when even the wealthy back a revolution, then something is wrong. She sat curled on the soft couch. Its smooth cloth cool against her skin she stroked it absently as she listened to Larrina.

"We told you before that you were part Kinel, if only a small part. The rings are attuned to Kinel, not to Katar. The Katar have so little Kinel blood that they must wear the ring on their finger to use the it."

She held her hand above Shara's left hand, a foot above it. She closed her eyes and the ring began to glow, very lightly, much as she had demonstrated before, a week, or was it two, ago. Larrina opened her eyes and gazed at Shara.

"I am the last pureblood Kinel that I know of. Yet, you have seen Tsom do the same from a great distance. He is only half Kinel, but when I see him I believe he is some sort of throwback to pure Kinel. His is the power of old. Before my time. Not just Kinel, but old blood."

She grabbed Shara's right hand in both her hands.

"I know you care for Tsom. Maybe even love him. You must know that he is likely to destroy himself with the way he recklessly uses his *ka* to achieve things. Sometimes he uses *ka* without knowing it—it comes too easily for him. He could also destroy those near him. Those without enough Kinel blood to defend themselves."

And yet you want to use him for your upcoming plan to destroy the gateway, thought Shara.

"But, can't he use the ring instead of his own *ka*? You said it has a store of *ka* and it recharges itself from those around it."

"Yes. He could. I have told him not to. I believe that to be immoral. No one should lose their life force without consent. Not even criminals. He agrees."

Shara was taken aback. Was Larrina calling her evil? It was only a small amount of *ka,* she was sure of it. Nothing that anyone would notice. It did not take long for her to admit to herself that was a lie. What of her escape from the family compound? The Katar lived so much longer than others. Was that part of the reason? Between the gods and Katar was mankind losing real years of their lives? She had wanted to believe what she had been taught, that using the ring simply caused pain to others. She twisted the ring on her finger.

It was hard to think. Her life was a wreck. Her family betrayed her. She loved a Kinel, a race that she had been taught were evil and a threat to all mankind. Now this—her source of power just a ring that stole from others.

"It is an end justifies the means question, isn't it. Do you think that the loss of life caused by the revolution will justify its end result? You still have not really told me how you know so much about these rings." Shara looked demandingly at Larrina. She twisted the ring on her finger back and forth.

"It was before even my time. Someone called *Gleyas* in the old Kinel tongue wreaked a terrible vengeance on the Tarth. He and his armies defeated them in battle, before the coming of mankind. They had killed his wife. He said that his wife was worth twenty-five thousand of the Tarth. He destroyed forever the souls of twenty-five thousand beings to create the white diamonds of the Katar. With the help of the Kinel he forged the rings. The army of Kinel was to bring everlasting peace to Nakana. That was before mankind. That was before the Tarth came back to fight mankind—the first time. Those Kinel found that they were sterile from use of the rings. Kinel were never fertile to start with. They interbred with humans. Soon, the Kinel army were Katar."

Larrina took a breath and looked off into the distance, her eyes unfocused. She was obviously troubled and her hand was resting on her short sword that seemed a part of her now. She continued.

"I have contemplated your question on ends and means for many of your lifetimes Shara. I never thought I would kill again, yet I have only recently. The only thing I am sure of is that my actions are not motivated by revenge. When I examine the situation with revenge removed I still come to the same conclusion. The Katar cannot make the right decision on their own anymore. They are part of the rings and the rings are part of them. They cannot see what they are doing and will rationalize mankind's slow slavery and demise as necessary. The gods and their priests make the same rationalization, but at least they do not overtly take. I do know that entire races have ceased to exist because of the Katar and that our actions pale in comparison."

She stopped. Silence. Shara did not know what to say in response. She twisted the ring again and again and suddenly pulled it off. Taking Larrina's hand she dropped it in the hand and then pushed it away.

"Alright, there goes the last of my Katar ties. Mankind should indeed be free of the rings on the hands of the Katar," Shara's voice trembled, but she was not sure if it was because of the loss of the ring, or the guilt over having used it.

***

Lanos kept up with Alanar more easily than the last time they had traveled on horseback, on their way to the Hrýll. Letting Alanar choose the horse was proving worthwhile. They were cutting cross country, avoiding the roads for a host of reasons, including that no road led from the Hrýll to Zethicia directly and going back through The Cities was death. There were paths, almost roads, and stretches of wilderness that kept Lanos uneasy. He longed for civilization.

Larrina preyed on his mind. She was in the thick of it in The Cities, with Katar and city guards no doubt searching for her. Tsom may or may not be alive. No Sphere of Banishment in the resistance's hands. The plan to overthrow the Katar was looking wilder and wilder the more he thought about it.

Even with the Katar divided, how long could they hold The Cities before the Katar finished off the Tarth and then returned to destroy the rebellion.

Truthfully, he did not understand why they were even trying to reach Zethicia. Alanar acted as if it were just a few days journey, but this was thirteen hundred marks cross country. Two months travel. The war would be over by then. The Cities was where they should be headed. To help with the rebellion. Alanar had insisted. "Trust me, Lanos, trust me."

He moved his horse closer to Alanar to express his concerns.

"Our original plan was to let the Katar and the Tarth fight it out until both were weakened. If the Tarth win, we use the Sphere of Banishment and ensure no Katar remain to regain control. If the Katar win, they are so weakened and cut off from The Cities that our rebels can force them to give up. Worst case the Sphere is used on the Katar themselves."

"Correct."

"Obviously, that plan is no longer valid as we do not have the Sphere. Yet, Larrina will still try and destroy the gateway and the Katar and the Tarth will still battle. The only reason I can think of for heading to Zethicia is you are assuming we win in The Cities and it is important for you to be in Zethicia to negotiate with the Katar. If the Tarth are close to winning you can negotiate your knowledge of the Sphere. If the Katar are winning we can assess our chances and direct the rebels accordingly."

"Your summary is not wildly different than my thinking."

"Yet the messenger told you that Larrina had information that the Katar would battle the Tarth very soon. She made the decision to accelerate the destruction of the gateway in just a day or two, given the time it took for the message."

Alanar's eyes widened a bit. Lanos pushed on.

"Your spies are used to reporting to me, Alanar. I caught up with one as he left and received a full briefing. We will never make it to Zethicia in time for any negotiations. By the time we reach Zethicia, the Katar will have used the Sphere and returned to destroy the rebellion. Larrina and the others will have wasted their efforts closing the gateway. Perhaps dying in the effort. Do their lives mean nothing to you?"

"I plan on being in Zethicia in a timely manner."

"Really? How do you shorten two month's travel time, pushing the horses, to one week or less?" Lanos let his own impatience show.

"There is a way … if I can remember. Oonie felt I should know."

"Remember?"

"It was such a long time ago, whispered Alanar.

"Painful times. I should never have done it. They would not be so vengeful now. She was so beautiful. She loved me. They killed her."

"What are you talking about?" Lanos began to wonder if the change that had made Alanar youthful had destroyed his mind.

"There are only two of us. I might be able to do two of us," replied Alanar.

"Alanar, are you feeling alright? You make no sense. We should turn south and head for The Cities."

"These mountains we are now in, they are called the Web of God by the Hrýll."

"So I have heard. Yet, they do not worship any god."

"They worship the Sea, the interconnectedness of all things. All things are interconnected. Woven together. A web. Our very existence is just a perception. The danger is getting caught, or lost, in that web. Stay close. Control your horse. Keep a weapon at hand."

Lanos felt like riding off alone, leaving Alanar to his insane ramblings, but then Alanar began to sing in a strange language. Similar to when he had removed the bond on Lanos earlier. Lanos could feel the air changing. So could the horses, their ears were rotating wildly and their eyes were rolling back dangerously. The air smelled moist. It felt hotter. Lanos felt dizzy. It felt like he was spinning after a wild drunken night. Suddenly, it was as if the ground disappeared. He felt nauseated and barely contained himself from throwing up, which was good as his horse went into a full panic gallop.

Normally he would have let the horse wear itself out before trying to control it, but Alanar had told him to control the horse and he had learned that if Alanar bothered to say something, it was important—except for the recent ravings. He pulled the horse into a circle, so that running was harder and he would not go too far. He almost pulled too hard, the horse stumbled once, but made the turn and slowed to a canter, then a trot. He pulled up next to Alanar who looked exhausted, but whose horse was completely under control.

Only then did he look around. Everything was wrong.

The sun was near the horizon almost as if it was going to set, but it was nowhere near time for sunset. This far north the sun almost did not set. The trees were different, large broad leafed and dripping with moisture. It was hot and humid, very humid. The air smelled fecund. It sounded the same, rich with activity. Life was everywhere, moving through the branches of the trees, on the ground shadows moved, in the air birds were circling. The horses kept dancing and their ears stayed moving. Lanos fought to maintain his control and looked to Alanar.

"Where are we? What happened?"

"We are taking a shortcut."

"And?"

"We are on Hell."

Chapter 50

Tiar laid a hand on Ooni's shoulder as he watched Alanar and Lanos ride off.

"They are headed for Zethicia?" she asked.

"Yes."

"They will not make it to be of any use. It is foolish. They should go south, to The Cities," she said, puzzled.

"Perhaps."

"You are concerned for the old one. Alanar. Even with your memories of him in a past life?"

"We were friends before we were enemies. My taste for vengeance is not as strong as his … was."

"Was? He is out to destroy the Katar out of vengeance," her hand tightened slightly.

"Maybe. It may be out of guilt and to right an imbalance that he had a hand in," Oonie fingered her hand on his shoulder.

"Either way. He would destroy the Katar and possibly the gods themselves, if he could."

"True he has wanted to destroy the Katar for a long time, but the *why* is important. The why may have changed. He may have changed. He seems almost Human this time," Oonie replied. Turning away from the now vanished men, he faced his wife. "For whom is it important? Do we care, as long as he destroys the Katar and their hold over the Hrýll?"

"He has power. Knowledge of things ancient. If anyone can help defeat the Katar and mankind's gods it may be him. But, I don't trust him. There is always a price when he is involved. The price is death. Is he to be trusted more than the Katar? The Hrýll helped the gods once before. Our payback has been mankind's growth and their destruction of all that they cannot control," she turned to Oonie, facing him directly.

She wasn't sure why she was getting so worked up, but she did not like that Oonie had become so friendly with Alanar. If Oonie was right, Alanar was really Talanas. The traveler. The guide. The avenger. The gods had betrayed him, but it was said that all who befriended him ultimately died—died the true death. She almost shivered.

"The motivations for one's actions are as important as the actions themselves. They do not always justify the action, but they are important. Alanar has changed. He is no longer Talanas. Perhaps, he has lost enough of his memory over the years. Each time he changes he loses more. Those might be the same memories that contain his power, so he may not be as powerful as he was either. A fair trade, don't you think? Perhaps he has healed. If he has grown a conscience, I hope he can live with his new memories and what remains of his old ones," he said. Oonie stared unfocused at the horizon, then turned and went to their home.

Tiar stood and gazed at the distant trees where Lanos and Alanar had disappeared. She licked her lips nervously. Her eyes looked cat-like as she stared. He was only one man, but he should be dead. Only gods lived that long and living as long as a god, she knew, could drive you insane. It was insanity to be in love with a mortal and wish success to a legend known sometimes as death. She laughed and followed her husband.

Chapter 51

Tsom felt he had interrupted something important when he walked into the sitting room with Shara and Larrina. He turned to leave, but Larrina called him back.

"Stay. We should discuss the plans for shutting down the gateway."

"Shouldn't we get Kaylee and Barin?" Tsom asked.

"No, they have other missions. I am afraid this will be just you and I."

Shara jumped in her seat, sitting forward. Larrina placed a finger over her mouth before she could speak. "You are wanted, well known, and will have a difficult time disguising yourself. Tsom and I can disguise ourselves. We both have our chameleon effect." Tsom nodded as he sat down across from them in the comfortable wooden chair. The arms of the chair helped him get in and out without the use of hands.

Without thinking, he manifested a hand, pulled out a nart, and placed it in his mouth. Larrina scowled at him. "I told you not to waste your *ka* on trivial things!"

Tsom looked only slightly abashed as he struck a match and lit the nart. "Barin is still modifying my mechanical hands," the pain was evident in his voice, "and I am not going to be a cripple every moment." He inhaled deeply. The slight relaxing, pain killing effect coursed through him. Always that background pain in his hands, or where his hands should be. It was distracting and wearing.

Shara looked simultaneously sad for Tsom and angry that she was being pushed out of the plan.

"After all this you leave me out of the action? No. I can dress as a man and as a commoner. I will be as hard to recognize as either of you."

Larrina paused to consider.

"Perhaps. Certainly your training and fighting skills are not trivial. We will assess your disguise later and make a decision then."

The angry look disappeared from Shara's face. Satisfied she turned to Tsom.

"Larrina is right. You will burn yourself out using your powers all the time."

Tsom smiled at her. "It comes easier each time. I use much less power to do it now than before. It is like a muscle that has built up or something."

Larrina pursed her lips, slightly squinting her eyes, but nodding as if this did not surprise her.

"Perhaps. It is not that I don't want you to use your power when you have to, just not all the time and not so close to so many traumas. I'm afraid that I will be asking you to use your power more than you should as it is."

She stood, leaned over and took the nart from Tsom's mouth. She took a drag off of it.

"Be careful not to smoke too much of these tomorrow. It will make you too relaxed and careless." Still holding the nart she walked to the window, standing fifteen feet away from Tsom.

"Try manifesting your hand and reaching for this—from where you are now." She held out the nart, waiting.

Tsom raised an eyebrow, but knew what she meant. Why constrain his thinking to hands the shape and size of his old physical hands. He had already thought along the same lines. He manifested his hand easily. He reached. Nothing. He thought of his hand, his arm growing longer. He could feel it, but it was heavy. Such a long arm was too heavy. Wait, what was he thinking of. It is not really there. It is a light arm. Light as a feather … and it was. He reached and grabbed the nart and pulled it back to his lips.

Larrina smiled. Shara looked pale and walked up to Tsom. She cupped his face in her hands. Looking carefully at his face, she traced the lines around his eyes with her thumbs. Tsom smiled and keeping his hand present he tousled her hair.

"Don't worry, it did not tire me out," he lied. Not too much. It would get easier over time, he was sure.

Larrina went to the desk in the room, pulled out some paper and brought it back to the couch. She spread the paper on the table between the couch and the chair Tsom was sitting at. "Good. I just wanted to make sure you could do that. Now we know you can. Don't practice, it will wear you out. Save your energy."

She then proceeded to sketch out a map of the area around the gate. As she drew, she gave them an overview of the gateway, its guards, latest intelligence, and her thinking. Tsom listened intently as much of this was new to him. Most citizens of The Cities knew the gateway only from stories.

The gateway between Zethicia and The Cities was the spinal cord between the two civilizations. Key products and people traveled through the gateway. Traffic in common goods and the flow of commoners was by road, but the news and information traveled by gate. The action and reaction of the rulers of

218

each civilization was by gateway. The Katar controlled the gateway utterly. It was through the sacrifices of many souls that it had been formed and the Katar had gathered those souls. Through their control, they had a strong hold over even outlying areas and influence over any race that traded with mankind.

Darnel Telsha was the head guard of the gateway. Normally, something as mundane as guarding would be left to the guard police of The Cities, not to the Katar. The gateway was different. Darnel was from a minor Katar family, loosely related to the Telem family and thus under its aegis. Telem's family controlled the qenar mines. The qenar fueled the talismans. The qenar fueled the gateway.

Larrina paused in her explanations and drawing, wriggled her fingers and took a deep swallow of tea.

The gateway stood as a massive stone archway, twenty feet across and almost twenty feet tall at the center, where it rose slightly. Gold and silver bands held the stones in place.

"Darnel will know little of the workings of the arch, other than the gold and silver have special properties when both were used with jade, but beyond this vague knowledge he knows nothing about the manufacture of talismans." Larrina smiled ironically, "It was done by Hrýll, why bother to learn. On either outer side, as part of the archway, is a small alcove three feet off the ground. Both alcoves were filled with qenar laden jade."

"It's an equilateral arch, that is why it is not as high as it is wide," muttered Shara. Tsom and Larrina both looked at her in surprise, Tsom felt a small surge of pride.

Larrina finished her half history lesson half briefing. Qenar was always found bound to jade, which must be in physical contact with the talisman to fuel it. The bright green of the jade fades to a dull brown as the qenar was used up. The brown jade was brittle and generally ground and used as part of a mortar mixture. The rich used it for construction as it was believed that the residual qenar would protect them and give them longer life.

Larrina pushed the map away from her and looked at Tsom and Shara.

"This is a clandestine operation, not an attack. We have only one goal, the long term shut down of the gateway. No heroics, no killing, just sabotage," Larrina looked at Shara, who nodded. "Tsom is the key, with his *hands*. I'm afraid you aren't going to get any younger Tsom."

He nodded grimly, rubbing his hands together, not even noticing that he had manifested them.

Chapter 52

Darnel's job included ensuring that no one stole the unspent jade, and that the gateway always remained open. The sister gateway existed in Zethicia. It was guarded by Darnel's brother, Tarin.

In the two hundred years that the gateway had been working there had only been one attempt to shut it down. The *ka* from those who attempted it had been used to create the massive glow globes that now lit the area. Unlike most glow globes, these did not need refueling, as only with draining to true death could permanent talismans be created. It was rumored that some Katar had similar globes in their compounds, created from the *ka* of the poor or homeless. Darnel did not believe such rumors, as his family had no such talismans, glow globe or other. Katar were protectors of the weak.

It was an hour past dinner and Darnel decided on one more round of the square and the qenar storehouses before letting his cousin Sarc take over for the night shift. The war in Zethicia and rumors of rebels in The Cities had him on edge. If he had more Katar to spare for guarding and patrols, he would, but as it was he had to use City Guard. Keep the access controlled. One way in, one way out. No weapons allowed, or at least nothing that was not packed away. Except, of course, small knives and daggers and decorative weaponry that the nobles wore.

The traffic through the gateway was steady, with nobles from Zethicia continuing to flee; accompanied by their entourages of servants and valuables. The twenty guard police were scattered throughout the square, primarily focused on the main entrance to the square, scanning the crowd. In Zethicia, according to Tarin, there were over fifty guards and ten Katar, due to the refugee crush. Darnel focused on anything unusual. The city guards were competent enough; Darnel did not have the usual Katar disdain for all military not part of the Katar. They carried repeating crossbows, lousy at any distance, but a skilled user could get twenty quarrels out in as many seconds. Firing into a crowd, they were extremely effective. Darnel rubbed his ring. As long as he had it on, he felt secure that he could stop anyone intent on mischief, as long as he saw them in time. Realistically, what could a few rebels do? The gateway's primary defense was its massiveness. It was not as if someone would sneak a battering ram into the square. Still, he was on edge.

He approached the square's gate and stopped. The young man talking with the guard looked familiar. Something in his mannerisms more than his features. He watched without approaching. There, the way he rubbed his left hand. The way all Katar tended to rub their rings. Just as he had moments before. The young man, almost a boy, had vaguely Katar features. Which family was he from? Too young to have a ring already, yet he had the habit. He put his hand on his sword and moved forward.

~~~

Shara looked up from her discussion with the guard. Atem's luck, it was Darnel. Darnel had been in charge of training her father's own guard when she was a child. He was good. When did he start guarding the gateway? Did he recognize her? She had cut her hair extremely short and was wearing a hard leather corset that flattened her breasts rather than emphasized them. She had tried rubbing a light coating of dirt on her face to rough up her face. She rubbed her left hand nervously and snapped at the guard. "As you can see my papers are in order. I am bringing important documents to my master in Zethicia and he will not be pleased if I am delayed."

The guard yawned and looked at the papers one more time. He glanced at the young man and down at the true image embedded on the papers. Expensive. He nodded. "Alright cappa, calm down. You may go." He waved her through.

"You, wait there one moment."

Shara pretended not to hear and moved away from the guard and the rapidly approaching Darnel. The guard looked up and also started toward her also. Shara's hand went to the sword that was not there. She bolted.

Looking back she saw Darnel running toward her and then suddenly he tripped and fell flat on his face. Dancing rapidly into the crowd she looked back once again and caught Tsom in the distance, grinning. His hat lifted off his head on its own an inch and then settled back down. Shara smiled and melted into the crowd.

~~~

"Careful. They are all a bit jumpy as it is." Larrina grabbed Tsom's elbow and guided him toward the gateway. Even knowing that she was influencing her image, Tsom had a hard time seeing through her illusion. She really was the image of a noblewoman. Maybe it was because she had already had the bearing of one, only now it was enhanced. He assumed that he would appear as a servant to all who saw her, a shadow in her flame, even without his own illusion in place to enhance that effect. Alanar was right, the chameleon effect of the Kinel was useful in these situations.

Barin's wooden hands were strapped in place. Even without his influencing what people saw, most would not have noticed that the hands were not real. Barin was a true craftsman. Given time, Tsom felt sure he could manipulate the hands well enough. There was no time and so he cheated. He hoped Larrina would not sense his use of his virtual hands manipulating the carved wooden and metal ones.

He had not told Larrina, but the more he used his virtual hands the more he seemed aware of everyone's *ka*. He could sense Larrina from a distance. She was filled with *ka,* more than anyone he had encountered since first discovering this feeling yesterday. Shara was strong, or stronger than most Humans. The Katar he had just tripped had also been strong relative to the pureblood Humans, but weaker than Shara.

As they brushed against the crowd he felt the whisper of *ka* from an old man. Near death, was his guess. When he momentarily dropped his virtual hands, as movement was not needed, he realized this new sensation was tied to the manifestation of the hands. It was as if he was touching the *ka* of all those around him with his hands.

The crowd let Larrina pass. She was both beautiful and imperious. The gateway drew near.

"We must actually damage the gateway. The bands of gold and silver are not just there for decoration, nor to truly hold the stones in place. They are part of the talisman that is the gateway. If we damage those sufficiently, then the gateway is destroyed. At least until the Katar kill enough souls and coerce the Hrýll into repairing it. I will be distracting the guards by the gateway itself. Shara will be doing her best on the other side of the square. We must try then to break the bands at the top of the archway, which are the weakest. If you can extend your hands to the top, it will be out of sight and we have a chance of not being noticed. You remember how to do it?"

Tsom winced at that very memory. This was going to be painful, but it was necessary. They had only practiced once and that was enough. Enough for his body to tense in anticipation of the pain to come. He wished he had a nart right now, or some of Alanar's Hrýll brandy. Tsom nodded and drifted away from Larrina.

Larrina moved over to the richest looking man near her. She then reached over and slapped him hard across the face. He staggered backward, almost falling.

"You bastard. You lying cheating bastard. You are off to see your mistress again and leave me behind during a war?!" She slapped him again. The flow of people started jamming up around them. A man reached out to restrain Larrina, but she pulled out a wicked, but elegant looking dagger. "You dare touch me? Are you insane? You dare touch the Lady Karnia?" The man backed off. Two of the four guards by the gateway moved toward her. The other two looked on with slight smiles on their faces, but the earlier bored look was gone. They looked for Darnel. Not seeing him, the senior guard signaled to several of the guards wandering the square. Just in case, they put their crossbows at the ready.

"Torrell, get the crowd moving, this will be causing havoc on the Zethicia side," the senior guard said. "Everyone keep moving. Those waiting to go to Zethicia, back up please. You don't start for another twenty minutes. Arnty, get that … woman under control, I don't care if she is the high priestess of Inlas, she is obstructing an asset of the Katar. Remind her of that. Gently," he added, not really wanting to face the wrath of a noble family.

Tsom eased through the crowd on the left side of the gateway, his skill at moving through a crowd had not been dulled by the loss of his hands. He didn't have to be right next to the gateway, just close enough. Manifesting his hands he sent them out. He made himself believe his arms had no weight. His long hands and arm extensions had no weight. He felt along the top of the gateway for the bands. Yes, there they were.

Larrina was keeping the two guards at bay and kicking the poor man she had chosen for the ploy. The guards were loath to injure a noble woman, but loath to let her keep kicking the man. Neither had pulled a sword, rather they worked on keeping the crowd away and moving.

Tsom backed up to get a better glimpse of the top of the archway and where the gold and silver bands were. Larrina said go for the gold. He rested his hands, waiting for Shara.

Larrina stopped kicking just as the guards moved in and yelled. "I am going home. You had better be there instead with your slut." With raised chin she strode off towards the main gate to the square. The crowd gave her wide birth.

Where was the fire? Tsom fretted. Shara should have been able to start it by now. He would have to risk it, fire or no fire. He let his hand flow through the gold then he made it solid. There was a pop as the gold band on top exploded. He used his other hand to catch as much of the small rubble that the melding of his hand and gold had created. He also gasped as the pain of what felt like a rod crushing part of his hand coursed through him. It subsided quickly as he dropped the manifestation.

The dropping of the gateway severed a number of people. Body parts fell to the ground. Larrina hadn't warned him about that, nor had it occurred to him what the consequence of shutting down the gate while it was so crowded would do. Screams soon arose. He concentrated on not being noticed. *He was supposed to be here. I am part of the square and always have been,* he concentrated. The guard's gaze slid past him without a flicker as he searched for the cause of the gateway failure.

Looking away from the chaos by the gate he scanned the crowd for Shara. Something was wrong. He stretched his *hand* out long. Longer. To the edge of the square. Then he moved it through the people, the buildings, and the animals. He could feel each person as he passed his hand through them. He was looking for Shara's *ka.* Her distinct essence. There. There it was, but it was wrong. Very wrong. Her *ka* faint, it was slipping away! She was dying. Tsom broke into a full run, not bothering to be subtle.

~~~

Shara pulled out of the crowd as soon as she was sure that Darnel was not following. She would have to scold Tsom later for wasting his *ka* on her like that, but she felt a little warm that he had risked both his energy and being seen to help her. It felt good to have someone want to help her and to be capable of it.

She approached the qenar store house. It would be heavily guarded due to its value. There was enough qenar in there to fuel hundreds of floaters and thousands of glow globes for years. Many had died mining it. Prisoners for crimes she was no longer sure that all committed. Even if they did commit the crimes, was it justice for them to pay so heavily? She had never given it much thought before meeting Larrina and Tsom. Tsom was a thief and could easily be one of the souls used to create the gate if he had been born a thousand years ago; or one of the souls used for countless other necessary projects the Katar had in progress right now.

The noise of the crowd was lower here. She heard the two guardsmen speaking and froze. Flattening herself to the side of the building she breathed deeply to slow her breathing and calm her trembling. She knew that voice. She had sworn to remember that voice. Of all places, he was here. A small shiver went through her. She shook it off angrily. She was Katar. She was of the Karn family. No simple woman who could not defend herself. She reached for her sword. The dirty rapist would pay for violating a Katar woman. No sword. She forgot that all large weapons were forbidden in the square, unless packed away for transport. She pulled her small thin blade from her back sheath. Slowly she peered around the corner of the building, lowering herself to below eye level.

She was staring straight into a male groin inches from her face. Without thinking she slammed her blade into it and rolled sideways. The guard fell to the ground with a half scream, half gurgle which went unheard by the crowd on the other side of the building, as they were focused on Larrina and her theatrics. The other guard rushed with his sword drawn, yelling to the inside of the storehouse. This was her man. It was his voice she was after. She silently apologized to the other guard writhing on the ground.

She concentrated on her ring. Damn. No ring! She could not depend on the enhanced speed of a Katar ring to help her. She dropped into the stance they trained for Katar fighting Katar. Without her ring she would be as any Human, well she hoped she was better trained. The guard slowed his charge at her stance, his eyes darting to his fallen comrade. He started to circle, still yelling. Shara charged, not waiting to see if anyone was in the storehouse. At the last moment, as he swung his sword to attack, she intentionally tripped over her own foot, tucking herself into a tight roll and coming up on his right side—his sword arm. She jabbed the thin blade between his ribs and leapt backwards, again dropping to a roll. Springing up she assessed her strike.

Three quarrels hit her in the chest. Her thick leather tunic slowed them down enough that they did not go clean through. Startled Shara looked down at the three bolts protruding from her chest and then up at the three guards with crossbows. She reversed the thin blade and threw it. It embedded itself in his leg. She turned to run and fell to the ground. Part of her was surprised at how easily she had been taken.

Chapter 53

Lanos knew they were not going to make it to Zethicia in time, Hell or no Hell as a short cut.

Without Alanar to command the rebel forces, either the Katar won in Zethicia and then returned to crush resistance in The Cities, or the Tarth destroyed the Katar, then Zethicia, then moved on to The Cities. Either way, Alanar's memories, ravings and behavior was worrying. Perhaps it was best that he was stuck here, possibly on Hell, while the war and rebellion waged on. Lanos shook his head, not liking any of the options.

The Tarth worried him. He understood Katar, but *daemons* was something he had no experience with. One talisman, ancient or not, could certainly not be all that it took to win against the Tarth. Maybe the rebellion could negotiate with the Katar. Join forces, defeat the Tarth and ...?

From what Oonie and Alanar said, Alanar knew how the Tarth fought. That could be valuable in the war. Finally, Lanos could stand the silence of their ride no more.

"You said this was a shortcut, that we would step from Hrýll, to here—wherever here is—to Zethicia. We need to get to Zethicia. We have the two new talismans from the Hrýll, they may be needed to defeat the Tarth. Where is this next gateway to Zethicia?"

Alanar smiled, "soon, my friend, soon."

There was no trail to speak of, but Alanar would occasionally stop, look around, close his eyes, and then nod—occasionally muttering, "This way."

They wound their way up the strange mountainside, whose name was unknown by either of them, until they reached the end of the trail. It ended with a drop off that caused Lanos to sway, the ravine below shrouded in fog, with tree tops decorating the gray like cake decorations.

"Where to now?" Lanos asked, a bit sarcastically, recalling all the "don't worries" of the past hours.

"We jump," said Alanar, grabbing Lanos' horse's reins and whispering something into his own horse's ears. The horse neighed and bolted, causing his own horse to follow as they leapt off the edge of the cliff.

They landed a few feet down on the grassy slope of a hill nestled among a set of rolling hills.

Both horses' nostrils flared and their ears swiveled frantically as they prepared to bolt again, but Alanar whispered into his horse's ear again and patted him … as it calmed down, so did Lanos' horse. Until the scream washed across them.

The scream was the call of some wild animal, but Lanos did not recognize it. Neither did he recognize where they were. Everything was wrong. The sun, no moons, it was all wrong.

"What?" Lanos muttered as he yanked his sword out.

Alanar shrugged as he pulled his sword. The sounds of creatures drawing closer were evident. Both of them wiped the sweat from their foreheads. Although the sun was not visible, it was hot. "I don't exactly know. As we were riding I remembered that there was a place near where we were that was weak between the planes. I weakened it some more and we stepped through."

This was a *shortcut,* to what, death?

"If you can move us across planes … how about moving us now?"

"I cannot explain, but there is no path here. We are stuck where we are, until we find another path."

The conversation was interrupted by another roar, or scream. A large death cat bound forward out of the trees. It was larger than any death cat Lanos had seen. Death cats were notoriously fierce, but this one made the ones he had seen before seem like a house cat. The dark tan fur shimmered with a metallic silver undercoat. Its eyes were deep red and large. Small ears were pinned back and teeth the size of knives gleamed as it roared.

Lanos and even Alanar fought to keep the horses from bolting; Lanos lost the battle. As Lanos's horse ran the cat bounded after, latching on to the rear and bringing the horse down. Lanos leapt free, sword in hand. Alanar spurred his horse and charged the cat, sword swinging. He yelled to Lanos. "Careful, they are intelligent. As intelligent as a man."

As if to prove Alanar's point, the cat dodged to the side and kept out of sword range. It then leapt toward the rear of Alanar's horse. Alanar anticipated the cat's movement. He was now sitting on the horse backwards and slashing with the sword. The sword cut deep into the cat's shoulder, which leapt away. Alanar somehow guided his horse sitting backwards to a turn and a stop. As the horse turned he reversed himself in the saddle again, faster than Lanos could follow. The cat backed slowly away from them, watching both Lanos and Alanar. It backed to the crippled horse and killed it, still watching them, then began to drag away the horse.

Lanos was going to let the cat have the horse, but then remembered that besides valuable supplies in the saddlebags, he also had his small bantri tree, the gift from Oonie, for Larrina. He waved his sword, yelled, and approached.

"Let him have the horse Lanos, we don't have time."

"I need my saddlebag."

Alanar considered and then yelled something in a language Lanos did not recognize. The large cat raked its claws across the cinch, severing it, and then continued to drag the horse away.

"What did you say? What language was that?"

"Tarth. I figured if they knew any language it would be that. I told it to leave the saddle and bags and we would not pursue it. We need to get going. All this commotion will attract other predators and scavengers. Not all of them are as gentle as that cat."

Lanos hoped he was joking, but felt he was not, as he scooped up the saddle-bag and jumped behind Alanar on the horse. Alanar pushed the horse as he had when they were pursued not so many weeks ago. Now, as then, he seemed to channel some of his energy to the horse to allow it to keep going past its limit.

"How far is it?" Lanos asked, assuming that if this was a shortcut that Ala-nar had a way back to Nakana and it was fairly near to Zethicia. He racked his brains for the tales he had heard as a child about Hell and the other planes. Until this moment, he had never really believed it all, despite recent evidence of the returning Tarth.

"An hour, if the horse lasts."

And if you last, thought Lanos.

The roar of the cat being challenged by some other creature drifted toward them, followed by the sounds of fierce battle. The horse found new energy.

Chapter 54

"Lord, there is someone to see you."

Be Na Tarth looked up. A Chimi was in the entrance of the tent. "Who? And why do you look so surprised?"

"It is a nar Tarth."

A female Tarth? Here? Impossible. He had not brought any nar with him. Too few females survived to risk it. They could not be risked in this war. As he was about to speak the tent door opened wider and revealed a tall, beautiful, deep red skinned Tarth female. Her hair was white with a touch of blond. Be Na Tarth felt a surge of lust which he quickly quelled. He stood and gestured to the Chimi. "Leave us."

He strode to her. "Who are you? What family? And how did you get here?"

She laughed. A musical, enticing laugh. A laugh that promised more. He thought of his dead wife. Killed by the ravages of Hell. Narina, killed by the banishment of mankind and the Katar. His lust faded further and he stepped back. He looked at the beautiful nar Tarth carefully. She strode closer to him so that he smelled her again. It was intoxicating, yet the vision of his dead wife drained the intoxication. There was something too perfect about this woman. His hand shot out and grabbed her by the neck. His other hand grabbed the jade sphere around his neck. "Who are you?" He whispered tightening his grip around her neck. She grabbed his hand with both of her hands and pulled. Her image wavered and a long legged Human woman stood before him. She hissed like a cat and he could feel the *ka* flowing from her to his sphere as she tried to manipulate it. "Stop—" she croaked through her constrained throat "—we are on the same side. I am here to help you."

He loosened his grip, but did not let go. He could feel the *ka* still flowing and the power within her. This was no Human, she was trying to manipulate *ka* and no small amount. "Who—are—you?" He emphasized each word with a squeeze. Each squeeze would have snapped the neck of a Human yet she simply glared at him. She was as strong as a nar even if she was not really one.

"Some call me Hallam." She waited.

It took him a few moments to process the name. Ah yes, the 'goddess' of nature. The one who did not depend only on Humans for her power. Interesting. Also interesting that she seemed capable of changing her shape, or the illusion of her shape. Wasn't there a 'goddess' of illusion also? Were they the same? Or did these 'gods' have multiple powers. Very like the Kinel, but more powerful. He let go his grip.

"Greetings, 'goddess'. What brings you to my tent?"

Hallam rubbed her neck and glared at his sphere. "I did not think it would work on me. My *ka* is not from mankind. Interesting device you have there, Lord of *Daemons*." She seemed to know enough Tarth to translate his honorific title into common tongue.

He smiled and nodded. "*Ka* is *ka* when it is from life. That is what this works on. Your source is simply larger in quantity, smaller in quality. The result is the same as the other 'gods.' You are all parasites. You simply drain animals instead of mankind." He strode back to his camp desk and chair and sat down. He pulled open a drawer and pulled out a glass decanter. "Some Hrýll brandy? One of many things they make that cannot be imitated."

She smiled and pulled up one of the smaller chairs in the tent and sat opposite him. For a Human, or Human 'god', she was extremely appealing.

"Yes, it is good that neither you, nor I, are out to destroy the Hrýll. But, perhaps we also agree on some other things?"

She raised an eyebrow and leaned forward. He thought he heard a purring, but could not be sure.

Chapter 55

Tsom pushed his way past surprised guards and made his way to the storehouse. The background sounds faded as he concentrated on getting to Shara. He did not remember the guard who blocked his way as he ran. The surprised look on his face as his heart stopped would only come to him later. He did not even notice his *hands* in front of him, feeling for Shara, destroying anything else in his path.

He burst onto the three guards standing over her. One had his foot on her bleeding chest, his sword against her throat. The others were bending down looking at her. The two bending looked up in astonishment as their comrade went flying backward, pulled suddenly by his throat. His neck snapped and he died instantly. They had no time to rise as both of their hearts stopped also.

Tsom leaned over Shara and placed his hands on her. The *ka* was faint and fading. He pulled for energy. He had healed her before, he would do it again. He pulled. He needed energy to heal her. He did not remember that before he had the aid of the Katar ring. He stretched his hands and thought of them as giant hands covering the area. Scooping *ka* for healing. He felt the massive energy. He was strong. Stronger than he had ever felt. Stronger than Larrina. He had infinite *ka*. He pulled. He could not hear the screams and the cries in the background. The energy flowed as he poured it into Shara. She breathed. Her eyes opened.

"Tsom. It is too late. I can feel my soul in the river of life. Don't destroy yourself to try and save me."

Tears were in her eyes. She blinked.

"Katar women should not cry … it's just … that I learned to love you …."

He pulled the quarrels out. He sealed the wounds. He could feel the injuries and he reached in and sealed the wounds. But her *ka*, it was so weak, he could feel it with his *hands* being pulled somewhere. He had to replenish it. He pulled. He strained. More power flowed through him. He needed more still. He could not sense the absolute silence around him.

"Stop."

He felt a hand on his shoulder and he whirled his hands going for the heart instinctively. Yet, he felt resistance, pushing back. Something struck his face.

"Tsom, it's me. Larrina. You must stop. You are killing innocent people. You are draining their *ka* rapidly. You are becoming like Alanar, like the Katar you loath, killing to save what is lost! Stop! She would not want the souls of all these on her conscience. Stop before you kill them all."

Larrina slapped him again.

He hesitated. He looked around and saw the writhing bodies in the distance. Three Katar were entering the area. Their rings were glowing brightly. They were straining with each step. Their faces drawn, eyes bloodshot, moving in slow motion. Struggling against the unseen drain on their power, the rings conduits to him, not them. Why should he stop? They were the cause of all this. The Katar needed to die. He reached out to one and pulled. Not on his heart, on his *ka*. He pulled. The ring glowed too brightly. It exploded. Tsom felt the *ka* release and yanked it and pushed it to Shara. Then his head cracked with a thump.

"I am sorry Tsom, but you must not do this. She would not want it."

He turned and focused on Larrina. She was trying to stop him. She was the enemy. He reached and squeezed. He met resistance. She staggered back.

"Tsom, stop, you are killing me. Stop. You don't know what you are doing."

She reached blindly behind her. The jeweled sword came out and she sliced in front of her. Searing pain. His right hand was on fire. He blindly struck her with his other virtual hand, trying to ignore the pain in the one she had somehow injured. She went flying and hit the building with a thud. He did not look to see if she survived. He had to save Shara before her soul was gone, he could still feel it. It was not here, but far away, but with a thread still attached to her body. He could pull it back, if he had enough power.

Tsom turned back to Shara. Ignoring the pain he now felt in his right hand he reached again. The remaining two Katar who were so near died in two explosions. He pulled and channeled the energy. *Ka*. Huge amounts of *ka* flowed. Shara stirred again. He could feel her draw a ragged new breath. Then another. Her head lifted and she looked with love at him. Then she looked around in horror.

"Tsom, what have you done?"

His head started to clear with her voice and he looked around. The square was nearly lifeless. A few miserable bodies moved slowly, across the square toward the gates in feeble attempts in fleeing. Katar and guards lay strewn, dead. The gateway was lifeless, the qenar laden jade gone from green to brown. The silver and gold bands shattered. The trees were blackened. Hundreds of bodies, dead and dying, all looking old and emaciated. He looked back at her, tears flowing down his cheeks.

"I had to. I had to, to save you."

She looked at him with sadness, knowledge in her eyes. Her hand grasped his arm. She pulled him close and held him tightly. She shook her head. Her body spasmed in his arms and before he could react he knew she was gone. Gone beyond his power.

Chapter 56

The horse stumbled and fell to the ground. Both Lanos and Alanar leapt off before it rolled on their legs. Alanar knelt beside it and rested his hand on its trembling neck. "Peace," he said and the horse stopped struggling, lay its head down, and died. He picked up his saddlebag and started walking briskly, although he was obviously tired from his earlier efforts at channeling energy to the horse. Lanos followed, his eyes and head moving in much the same manner as the horse's had—fear. There were noises all around. Unfamiliar noises. The sounds of large animals and a myriad of small ones. He guessed that they had been at full gallop for almost forty-five minutes. Without Alanar's ministrations the horse would have died after the first ten at the rate they had been going.

"On foot, how much longer?" He asked.

"I think we are very close, the horse was stronger than I thought."

The thick forest thinned and soon they were on a mountain plain. Rolling hills and tall grass, it looked very peaceful and inviting after the jungle. Unconsciously, Lanos slowed his pace.

"Don't slow down. The plains on Hell are as dangerous as anywhere else." Alanar pointed up. Lanos looked and saw a bird circling. A large eagle perhaps. He looked at Alanar quizzically.

"It is very high up. Thirty foot wing span. It has already spotted us, but may have already fed."

Lanos increased his pace.

The terrain was looking very familiar. "This reminds me of the Muglanth Plains, near Zethicia?"

Alanar nodded. "Yes, we are close to another thinning between the planes of Hell and Nakana. This is where the Tarth army came through, I hope."

They topped one of the rolling hills and both of them dropped to the ground quickly. Below them was a huge encampment. Thousands of Tarth and Chimi soldiers and support personnel.

Lanos, peering over the edge of the hill, turned to Alanar. "Let me guess, down there is where we cross planes?"

Alanar nodded.

Chapter 57

The noise outside of the Katar war room startled all of them. Arlec held his right hand over his sphere and reached for his sword with the left. All of the Katar rings were glowing. The door swung open and Djarn, Lord Priest of the god of luck strode in as if nothing was the matter. The two Katar guards outside the door rushed in after him. They began to apologize, but Jern smiled grimly and spoke. "It's alright, we understand that you could not stop him from entering. Go back to your posts."

Djarn waited for the invitation and then sat down. Jern took the lead again, much to Arlec's displeasure. "To what do we owe this particular visit Djarn? The gods have already made it clear that they will not interfere in the battle with the Tarth. They are afraid. gods who are cowards."

Djarn grimaced. Briefly a look that told he had thought the same thing passed across his face. Then he leaned forward as if not hearing the insult. "The gods act in ways that do not always make sense to us mortals. Yet, we priests are willing to help in your righteous war against the Tarth. We have the blessings of the gods in this."

Arlec was suspicious. Could the priests help enough that his aid would be diminished? He leaned forward. "If the gods are unwilling to help then what good are the priests?"

Djarn looked at him disdainfully. "We are vessels of the gods' power. We know much that you do not and we know much that you think we do not. I know that you have the ancient Sphere of Banishment, Arlec."

Did he know more? Arlec fought for calm. No, how could he. No one knew. Only Pé, if he really existed, could know more. If the god of souls actually tended the Rivers of Life and Death, what were the odds that he noticed the old man's soul? Obviously the priests had spies within the ranks. Even some of the Katar were known to worship the gods. Fools.

Jern watched Arlec for a moment then interjected. "Even with your staffs of power, what can the priesthood do? You are like the Katar, dependent on *ka* to augment your powers. Against Be Na Tarth the rings of Katar are useless and so are your staffs. It then comes down to standard war practice. Brute fighting force, strategy, and tactics. And the Sphere of Banishment. This is a matter for soldiers, not for priests."

Djarn visibly fought to retain his temper. "True, we are not fighters, but we can influence the events around your fighting forces. Especially the battles away from Be Na Tarth and his cursed power drain. The battles on the outskirts, where his power is weak. The weather. The animals. Even the plants. All these can be influenced. If we coordinate we can help tip the balance."

Jern nodded. Arlec relaxed. Peripheral help. He was still the most important part. Too bad there was no easy way to lure the priests to work with Barnus and his force. When the Sphere was triggered they would all be cast to Hell, assuming that the sphere sent its victims to the same plane each time. Any plane the Tarth ended up on would be Hell by definition, he thought. Then the Katar would be in complete power. The people would see that the gods had been of trivial help. Already, confidence in the gods was waning.

The war council agreed and the other Lord Priests were summoned to join in the planning. The major battle was planned for five days from now. They needed a few more supplies and the last of the Yanín—both of which should be arriving through the gateway soon. Once the threat of the Tarth was over, they could concentrate on the rebels that were springing up in The Cities, and Arlec could finish up with his sister Shara and that damned thief who was so hard to kill. Next time he would have him killed outright, true death or not. They were an annoyance, but nothing more. He had been too easily swayed by the fear of the families' reaction to killing his sister and the need for public revenge on the thief. The priests were cowards, just as the gods were, and the boy was a simple thief—nothing more. Arlec smiled and caressed the Sphere.

~~~

Tsom held Shara in his arms and wept. He wept as he had when his mother had died. The loss was more than he expected. He had been so sure he could save her. He had saved her before. He had more power now. More skill. How could she have died? He sat there weeping. He felt tired. Exhausted. Drained.

Slowly the rage crept in. The Katar. They destroyed Shara. They destroyed his mother. They destroyed everything they touched. The Katar. The rage helped. He stood and slung Shara over his shoulder. She was light. Lighter than he remembered.

Again he look around. The blackened trees and plants. The shriveled bodies and the almost dead crawling away from him. Away from his deadly need for *ka*.

Larrina.

He set Shara down and went to Larrina's still body. He touched her. He manifested his right hand and then dropped the manifestation. The hand hurt. The sword Larrina had used had somehow injured his non-corporeal hand. He switched to his left hand and felt for her *ka*. She was alive. The touch seemed to awaken her. Her eyes opened. He flinched at the look in her eyes. It faded to be filled with one of sadness, which hurt even more.

Larrina slowly rose, rubbing her head. She sheathed her short sword. "We must leave. The Katar for marks around will have felt this. Their rings will have been burning their hands trying to protect them, but they will be shocked at the pain that you still inflicted."

Tsom went to Shara and picked her up again.

"Leave her. She will slow us down and will make us easy to spot," said Larrina.

"No, I will not leave her here to be picked up by the Katar. She is no longer Katar."

Larrina stared at him for a long period. "Men. You cannot let go. You have these foolish notions of love. She is dead, her body has no meaning. Her soul survived, you felt it slip away."

He scowled and strode off ignoring her. She shook her head and quickly caught up with him.

"You will run out of energy soon. Give her to me and I will carry her."

He shook his head no and continued. He tried not to look at the few still living in the square. He could not help them now. He was the cause of their death and pain. *But only because of the Katar*, he told himself. They must pay. The revolution must exterminate them, not just overthrow them.

"How can we get to Zethicia and help Alanar thwart Arlec and his use of the Sphere?" he asked.

Larrina considered. "The gateway is beyond easy repair, possibly beyond any repair after what you did, which is what we wanted. By road it is months away, even on floater. Without a gateway there is no way to get there in time."

"What if I made a gateway?"

"You do not know how. Even if you did, where would you get the *ka*?"

He looked away guiltily.

"Larrina, you are Kinel. You have lived many lifetimes compared to me. You must know something about the way the gateway works. We need to help Alanar. If Arlec defeats the Tarth he then unites the Katar around him and the revolution will be crushed. The Katar will be more powerful than ever! We must do something. Are you willing to stand by and let more races be destroyed by the Katar? Let mankind be permanent slaves to their rule?" *I must be there to destroy them*, he thought.

They made their way out of the square, not encountering anyone. Everyone who could flee had.

"I see in you a rage I have seen in another. I am loath to trust you with that rage."

Tsom felt a wave of guilt. He would never hurt Larrina, but he had. He had tried to kill her, for a second or two. But, now it would be different. He would make sure Larrina was not near. He saw that Larrina knew something. Had some idea.

"I cannot take back what I did. I regret the innocent lives. You know that with my powers I could help Alanar at a crucial time. Despite all that has happened the Katar must still be defeated. To do that, they must lose their fight with the Tarth. Tell me what you know Larrina. If not for me then for Alanar and Lanos."

He hoped he was not hitting too hard with the last statement. But, he felt she loved at least one of them and love drove one to strange behavior.

"I know the principle behind the Hrýll talisman; the gateway. The idea is that many places are closer to each other than would appear. Like a crumpled piece of paper. If you punch a hole through the paper you go from two spots that are very distant very quickly. It is said that one can even cross between planes where they touch in this manner."

She paused in her walk and placed a hand on his shoulder, stopping him. "Your use of your hands has expanded as you have recently demonstrated." He grimaced. She continued. "I have injured you badly with my sword. That wound will never heal. No wound from that sword ever heals. I am surprised that you even can manifest your right hand at all. I don't think it matters that it was not flesh that I injured, although I have never fought against someone like you before."

Tsom shook his head as if to rid himself of this thought of losing his hand once again. *Yet, it was only just,* he thought. *I was hurting my friend. One of my few friends.* She nodded as if reading his thoughts. "It will be a constant reminder of your power and its danger."

"You have an idea Larrina. Tell me what it is."

Chapter 58

"Turn around slowly." Alanar whispered to Lanos. They turned and faced ten Tarth. Two had enormous longbows, arrows nocked and aimed appropriately. No man could have strung those bows. The leader, somewhat shorter than the rest, had a massive chest and light pink skin instead of the darker red of the others. He spoke, but Lanos could not understand any of it. He looked to Alanar for translation.

"Greetings Humans. Welcome to Hell." Alanar translated. "It is hard to properly convey the sarcasm that he is implying." He added, with a wry smile. "I would not try anything with this group. The Tarth make the Yanín look like amateurs."

Alanar returned the greeting. The Tarth looked astonished. Then angry. Then he laughed out loud and seemed to relax. "What did you tell him?" asked Lanos

"I returned his greeting and said how flattered we were to be escorted by this honor guard to see their leader. I used some carefully chosen words which have double and triple meanings. He seemed to appreciate the subtlety."

The Tarth said something more and gestured for them to arise. He also indicated that they should not try anything. Lanos needed no translation. They moved down toward the encampment.

Their presence caused quite a stir. The outskirts were populated by Chimi, the fur covered companions of the Tarth. They moved closer to the center, where more of the residents were Tarth. "No women," noted Lanos.

"I noticed also. The Tarth women are as skilled warriors as the men, perhaps even better as they lose their temper less often." After a moment he spoke in Tarth to the leader. The leader scowled and his face grew as red as his companions. He growled a reply.

"The women have mostly died. It seems that there is something on Hell that affects primarily women." Alanar looked troubled. He looked around the encampment. Lanos followed his gaze. Eventually it struck him. None of the soldiers appeared young. They were all over forty, or what looked like forty on a Tarth. The Tarth were a dying race. No wonder they wanted to get off of Hell. Well, the creatures they saw in the past hour were enough reason, but now Lanos thought of an entire race going extinct.

The tent they were shown into was marginally larger than the others. Two of their guard, along with the short Tarth, accompanied them. The cool shade was welcome after the oppressive heat. The tent was sparsely furnished with a cot, table, and a number of chairs. Small windows from the shady side of the tent were open, allowing indirect light inside. No glow globes. The dark red Tarth behind the table had the normal white blond hair of his race but with a streak of red. His voice was more musical and sing-song than the short one.

Alanar answered his question. The Tarth asked another, directed at La-nos. Alanar answered that one also. The Tarth frowned slightly. Then in slow words, as if translating them in his head first, he spoke again to Lanos in common tongue.

"You are Human?"

Lanos nodded.

"How came you to Hell?"

Lanos glanced at Alanar for guidance. The glance was not lost on the Tarth. Alanar nodded. "We came through a weak spot between the planes."

The Tarth looked at both them. "Then you will take us back to Nakana."

Alanar replied in Tarth and the Tarth erupted in rage. The two guards backed up a bit, but Alanar seemed unfazed. He repeated what he had said earlier. The Tarth calmed down a bit and began walking back and forth. He fired off several more questions. None of Alanar's responses seemed to make him happy.

"What are you talking about?" Lanos spoke in the dialect of Arbeneth, on the off chance that this Tarth did not know that.

"He is threatening us. If I don't transport him and the army to Nakana he says he will kill us. I explained that I can only take one other; that is why there are only two of us. He threatened some more and tried bribing me."

The Tarth gestured to the two guards and said something. They grabbed Alanar and Lanos and pulled them out of the tent. Lanos thought his bone was going to break. Alanar said something softly and the guards loosened their grip slightly.

"They are taking us to the area where the women and children are kept. Evidently it is the best guarded area and they are not afraid of us doing anything to harm the women." Alanar smiled ruefully. "As I said the women are actually better fighters than the men."

The series of tents in this new area were interconnected. They were thrown into one tent with an old Tarth woman. Their saddlebags, thoroughly searched, were thrown in after them. Lanos glance inside his to see what they had left.

The woman looked up from her pile of swords that she was sharpening. She looked ancient. Her hair was thin and her eyes sunken. Her skin had a pink look to it, almost unhealthy compared to the red of the others. She still had all her teeth, or perhaps some sort of false teeth as they looked almost perfect. She looked closely at them both. With surprising speed and grace she was on her feet with a sword in her hand, the tip against Alanar's throat. Lanos had seen Alanar's muscles twitch as she had started to move, but he did nothing to block the blade.

She said something in a beautiful young woman's voice. He could not understand anything, but heard the word 'Talanas.' The name Oonie had once used for Alanar.

She knew him. That seemed impossible. He knew that Alanar was ancient, but from what he knew of the Tarth, they had been banished thousands, not hundreds of years ago. Many thousands. Five thousand was the legend. Of course, Alanar might have traveled here recently. That must be the explanation.

Alanar spoke. The old woman spoke again. Her name was Venicia from what he could gather. She seemed looking for an excuse to plunge the sword home. Alanar responded, slightly more heatedly. Venicia's muscles tightened. Lanos tensed himself, though for fight, or flight, or death he was not sure. Slowly she lowered her sword and grabbed Alanar's arm and led him away, her back to Lanos. She seemed to ignore him totally.

"Don't try anything Lanos, she may be old, but she is better than you." Lanos eyed the stack of swords wistfully and then followed them.

They went from tent to tent connected by covered walkways. Occasionally there was a female Tarth who would jump up and bow briefly to the old woman. They entered a largish tent and inside were twenty or so children playing. Small Tarth. *They almost look cute*, Lanos thought. The old woman pointed and said something. Alanar looked shocked and saddened. He spoke softly to the old woman and she replied, along with a gesture that seemed to indicate the area they were in. Alanar shook his head as in disbelief. He spoke to the woman, gesturing to Lanos and then the encampment. He spoke for a considerable period of time. He seemed to be trying to persuade the old woman of something. She replied, often angrily and pointing to Alanar, then the small group of children, or to herself. She frequently waved the sword and yet Alanar never defended himself and she would pull back at the last instant.

She was better than I am, thought Lanos, maybe better than Alanar, *but he always seems to rise to the level of his opponent.*

After some time Venicia seemed to be wavering. She issued a statement, pointing with her finger, instead of the sword, this time.

Alanar bowed his head, either in shame, or in thought, Lanos could not tell which.

Venicia returned them to her tent. Calling, a Tarth woman stuck her head in Venicia's tent. Venicia spoke and the younger woman shook her head in fear and surprise. Venicia's voice took on an edge and the younger woman bowed and disappeared.

"What's happening?"

"I am being tried for my crimes."

"What crimes?"

"For banishing the Tarth. For exterminating the race."

"You? But that was ... I mean ..."

"For these Tarth it was only a hundred years ago. This encampment is all that remain of the race."

"But it is large, there must be tens of thousands."

"Yes, but there were millions a hundred years ago. The Tarth do not reproduce quickly. Those children we saw, twenty, are the last generation."

"But, it was not just you, it was war. It was you or them."

"Perhaps. I no longer remember it all. It was so long ago. My memory is fractured. It has been through many ... changes. But, I never intended to destroy an entire race."

The younger Tarth woman returned and handed Venicia a jade chain with two tiny jade daggers, almost needles, at each end. She looked questioningly to Venicia, who spoke. The younger Tarth turned and called, two female Tarth and two male Tarth entered the tent, making it feel cramped. Their eyes widened at the sight of the jade chain. At Venicia's command they sat down.

Venicia spoke to Alanar who sat and gestured for Lanos to do the same.

Suddenly, lightning fast, she plunged one of the tiny jade daggers into Alanar's forehead. Lanos leapt to his feet, or rather tried to. The hand of one of the male Tarth kept him in place. Alanar blinked, but held still. Venicia plunged the other tiny dagger into her own forehead.

The Tarth in the tent all began to hum. It was an eerie sound that made his very bones vibrate. Both Alanar and Venicia were still. Soon, Alanar began to weep.

Lanos could not tell how long the humming lasted. His legs were cramped and his throat was dry, but time lost meaning. Suddenly it stopped. Alanar collapsed and the jade dagger slid out of his forehead. There was no wound, no blood, but he lay unconscious. Venicia sagged forward and two of the Tarth women caught her and pulled the other dagger out of her forehead. She slowly sat straight and the two women let her go. She spoke to Alanar, who stirred and pushed himself back to a sitting position also.

"What happened? Are you all right?" Lanos asked.

"No, but the damage is not to my body. A moment, Lanos." He then spoke to Venicia in Tarth. She replied and waited.

"Well?" asked Lanos.

"She has asked me to determine my punishment."

"You determine your own punishment? How about a slap on the wrist and letting us go?"

Alanar stared at Venicia for a long time, then he turned to Lanos.

"Your saddle bag. After removing the Hrýll talismans, they left the rest of your supplies inside?"

"Yes."

Alanar went to Lanos's bag and pulled out the bantri tree cutting. He knelt and held out the tree to her. She looked at it and him in obvious astonishment. Lanos restrained his instinct to grab it from Alanar. He was obviously up to something. She smiled half at the joke and half out of sadness. She spoke a few words solemnly and accepted the tiny tree cutting. She then walked outside and plunged the tree into the earth. They all followed. Before his eyes it quivered and grew a lush green with a small growth sprout appearing on one of its branches.

Venicia laughed a musical laugh. She called out and several more Tarth women came in a rush. She spoke and pointed to Alanar and the tree. They looked in astonishment and smiled strange smiles. Several left, but Lanos could hear the ripple of word of mouth traveling out from them, like a stone cast into a pool of Tarth. The news made its way outward.

"Now tell me what in the world you just did?" He demanded.

"I married her."

Silence.

"What?!"

"She is the oldest living Tarth. She knows me, or the me of five thousand years ago. I have lived her life, felt her pain, seen what I have done to the Tarth. I have seen the world through her eyes and I have lived the evil I have done, through her. More, I have lived the lives of each of the women before her that held the jade chain. It links each generation to the next. The woman of her position, I have no translation for it, has a collective memory. I cannot remember it all, it is too much, but I know that I was wrong. The Tarth are not evil. I cannot use them as I planned to, the Tarth already on Nakana. We cannot let them stay on Hell, or the race will die; and I will not be the destroyer of races … again. My punishment is to become a Tarth, in some sense."

He paused and Lanos wondered if the Tarth had altered his friend, taken control of him. Become a Tarth? Save them? They were *daemons* intent on wiping out mankind, what was he talking about? Alanar continued to explain.

"The oath of the bantri tree is one that the Tarth take very seriously. When the Tarth get married the male swears to obey the woman and protect her and all she holds dear. The tree in effect binds that oath. It is said that as long as the tree lives, the oath cannot be broken. Myth perhaps, but the Tarth take it very seriously."

Lanos was speechless. Alanar married to that old woman? What of Larrina. Of course he had thought he would have to vie for Larrina with Alanar. Now what? How seriously did Alanar take this vow? He remembered the time difference between this plane called Hell and Nakana. They had to get going, or the battle between the Tarth and mankind would be over.

"Will they let us go now?"

"Perhaps. But I must think if there is a way to bring them back with us."

"Why? The army of Tarth is already too strong on Nakana. They will destroy all of mankind if we let them. I thought our plan was to help push the balance just long enough to defeat the Katar and then defeat the Tarth with the Sphere of Banishment ourselves."

"It was. Not is."

"What? I will not let you betray all of mankind. Better to be stuck here then let you bring more of these *daemons* back with us."

Alanar smiled and gestured to Venicia.

"She speaks the common tongue very well my friend, she simply chose not to use it. Be careful you don't insult my wife so badly that I am forced to defend her honor."

Lanos scowled. This was absurd. Was Alanar taking this marriage farce seriously?

"Of all races, I thought the Tarth would have prospered and tamed this plane. I was terribly wrong. They thirst for revenge only out of a need to survive. They have been punished enough for sins both real and imaginary. I think we can make peace with them and together force the Katar to give up their power. There is room for both the Tarth and Mankind on Nakana, I understand them now in a way I never could. I had burned it out of my mind, but the reason I had helped banish the Tarth was they killed my wife. But, you see, I killed Venicia's husband. The irony and the punishment is complete."

Lanos shook his head.

"The Katar will never give up their power. You of all people should know that. We have always sworn to destroy them utterly. And allowing the Tarth to exist is equally dangerous."

"No, I think we can make peace with the Tarth. I know Venicia. *Know* her.

She has suffered as much as any of us. Her taste for revenge is gone … and it has only been 100 years for her." The latter part a whisper that Lanos barely heard. "The banishment of the Tarth was too harsh. I should never have let it happen. Hell is worse than I imagined and my past thirst for revenge too high."

Lanos could not believe what he was hearing. Maybe it was part of an elaborate trick and this was being said for Venicia's benefit. They would get back to Nakana and the old Alanar would be back.

"I will not be responsible for the extinction of an entire race," Alanar said softly.

"But if the Tarth truly win you will be responsible for the extinction of mankind!"

"No. Mankind is too prolific, and I believe Venicia when she says she can convince Be Na Tarth to settle for peace. She is his mother and he will listen to her. "

"I guess that makes you his father-in-law." Lanos muttered, unconvinced, but realizing that for now he had to let this play out. They had to get back to Nakana now and Alanar was his only way back.

"We must move swiftly. We have been on Hell for almost four hours. That is a hundred hours on Nakana."

"I thought the ratio was one hundred to one?" Had it been only four hours? It felt like days.

"No, the added time for Be Na Tarth was due to his gateway, he did not go from Hell to Nakana directly, he did not know how. It is amazing he made it through at all. I will be opening the way directly."

"I thought you said you could only take two people?"

"The Tarth have consented to each of them sharing a little of their *ka* with me. With their added power I think I can shift the entire group if they move fast enough, I will stand in one place as a bridge between Hell and Nakana."

"Ten thousand beings? Have you ever done anything like that before?"

"No. I don't think so, but as with most of my life, I don't remember." Alanar smiled.

The encampment was breaking quickly. They had rehearsed this before, only they had expected the call to come from Be Na Tarth, after his sphere had been charged sufficiently with the souls of mankind. Venicia was directing the Tarth. The male Tarth who had interrogated them earlier was arguing with her. She was yelling back and pointing at Alanar. He turned, redder than his normal already deep red. His huge muscles bulging with rage. He turned and stormed away. *They would have to watch out for him*, Lanos thought.

He spotted one of the women carrying a newly potted bantri tree. He thought of Larrina. Was she still alive? Much more time had passed for her than for him. Had she disabled the gateway between Zethicia and The Cities?

They were ready.

Alanar stood at the center of the mass and they started walking. He started singing in that language that Lanos had heard when they first shifted over to Hell and when Alanar had released his bond on him weeks ago, it seemed to somehow aid him while manipulating *ka*. This time Lanos felt weak and nauseated. He stumbled as did many of the Tarth. He had a hard time focusing on the terrain: The scene blurred as if two paintings of the same image from different angles where layered on top of each other, then their surroundings sharpened as they walked.

The mass of Tarth flowed past Alanar ten on either side as he stood singing. Lanos was forced to march with them. As he looked back he saw Alanar already looking drawn, older, thinner, yet his voice rang with strength and conviction, and as Lanos continued the march with twenty thousand Tarth and twice as many Chimi, Alanar winked out of sight. Turning forward once again Lanos gazed at the encampment in front of him. More Tarth.

They were on the Muglanth Plains of Nakana, near Zethicia. Lanos glanced around at the river of Tarth and Chimi spilling into the small sea of their companions waiting for them.

Mankind is doomed, he thought.

Chapter 59

The house of Kaylee and Barin felt warm and safe. A haven. A false sense of security. Tsom sank into the couch after they had buried Shara out in the fenced back yard in a small grove of trees, away from prying eyes. The rebels would be attacking the Katar family compounds soon, now that the gateway was destroyed. The civil war had begun.

Larrina disappeared into the kitchen and returned with one of her teas. Tsom sipped it gratefully, knowing that she probably put something in it to numb his pain and dull his senses. He was right. The smell of cinnamon stirred memories of Shara, but the hot, almost sweet fluid spread a warming numbness throughout his body. He could almost forget Shara was dead, that he had nearly killed Larrina, and that hundreds of innocent people were dead by his hand.

"So tell me. What is your idea? The one I see you hesitating to tell me."

Larrina had a look of sadness on her face as she looked at him. As if he was dying or going to die. Tsom knew, by the look in her face that he must look terrible. Had he aged so much again? He resisted the temptation to find a mirror and look at himself. What did it matter? He had one goal now: the destruction of the Katar. Nothing else mattered.

"I think you might be able to pull yourself there."

He looked at her and tilted his head.

"You already can stretch your hands across a fair distance. Try not thinking of the distance as you normally would, but as the crumpled piece of paper I described. Try reaching with your hands through the paper to the other side."

"But, I have never been to Zethicia. How do I know where to reach?"

"True, but you have met Arlec. You know him. He is at Zethicia with the Sphere. Don't reach for the Sphere, but for him. Reach for him to get a bearing, then move off to the side. You don't want to be right next to him." They both smiled a joyless smile. "Then, try pulling yourself through. I have heard of such a thing long ago when the Kinel were numerous and careless. It can be done. At a cost."

She then unbuckled her short sword—the one that had so recently injured him—and handed it to him hilt first. "It will drain you to pull yourself through great distances. Do not do it frivolously. Use this if you have to. It is my family's sword, from generations before the time of mankind and before the time of gods. It is dangerous, as you already know. As with the Katar rings, it can only be used by one with Kinel blood."

He nodded and buckled it to his back, as Larrina had done. He looked at her. No disguise hiding her Kinel markings. She was tired and worn. Worn in no small part due to fending him off earlier. Yet, her beauty remained. He hoped that she found happiness with either Alanar or Lanos. She deserved that.

No sense in waiting. Time was short. He manifested both his hands with ease. The right one flared with pain. The invisible wound on his invisible hand causing him to momentarily wince. Then he cast out in a manner similar to what he did to find Shara. This time he concentrated on Arlec, the brother of Shara. Their *ka* must be similar and he knew Arlec. He did not think of Arlec in Zethicia. He concentrated on finding him as close as possible. Reaching and sensing. Still it was far. He kept reaching, his direction instinctive. Unconsciously he kept thinking of Shara. Within his mind he wept.

There. There it—he—was. Arlec. He could feel his hands and arms stretched thin. Tenuous strands with the right one on fire with pain. Now that he had a location he felt that there was indeed a shorter path. He shifted his destination by focusing on the *ka* of someone, he knew not whom, that seemed not too far, nor too close. He pulled himself there. He felt his body flying through something as it tried to join his hands. He could no longer breath. No sounds reached him. His hands/arms felt weak. He kept pulling.

Cold. Black. Tiring.

He was there. Here. He opened his eyes and breathed. It was a street similar to hundreds of other streets, but he immediately knew that he was not in The Cities. He glanced at the people passing by giving him strange looks. He focused on looking like them. Dark skin. Blond hair. Slightly frightened. He blended in, as he always did.

~~~

It did not take long for word to reach the war council that the Tarth forces had multiplied, by factor of three. Arlec was nervous. His plans were straining and fraying at the edges. The gateway to The Cities had failed. It had never failed. Some speculated that it was rebels, others that it was the Hrýll, still others thought the Tarth somehow had something to do with it. For a moment he wished his father were still alive. The old man knew more about complex military matters and politics then he did.

He had no idea what the limits on the Sphere were, but this definitely changed their plans. If Barnus and his Zethician forces, even augmented by the Yanín, went in against the now huge Tarth forces then they would fall too quickly. The Sphere would not be activated at the optimal time. Even worse, he now doubted that the Sphere was the answer to their problems. If more Tarth had come through from Hell, then they had solved how to get past the banishment. The spies had been wrong, and Be Na Tarth did not need many more souls within his own strange jade talisman-sphere. What could he do? What could any of them do? It was hopeless, banishing them to where they could simply return from was a waste.

Jern noticed that Arlec was losing control and called the council to order himself. He laid out what they knew. The Lord Priests were now part of the council. The Yanín representative was there. Barnus and Courie the Governor was there. All except the Yanín looked worried, but with Yanín it was impossible to tell.

"The new count of the forces is fifteen thousand Tarth and over fifty thousand Chimi. The gateway is definitely dead with no hope of repair on our side. We have sent messenger pigeons, boats, and riders to The Cities, but it will be weeks before any word from the pigeons, if they make it through. They will most likely verify what we already have discovered through other means.

"There are a few Hrýll here that we trust. They tell us that the gateway here is fully operational, so it must be the other side. The Priests tell us that they have had contact from the temples in The Cities. There is a full-fledged rebellion in progress. The Katar and even the temples are under attack."

The Katar present all noticed the smallest twitch on the corners of Barnus's mouth, but chose to ignore it. Arlec had a sinking feeling. They had to succeed here so that he could return home and crush any rebellion in Arbeneth. The other family heads had looks that said the same thing.

"Arlec, your Sphere would appear to be of no true use to us, unless to delay the Tarth by sending them back, only to return."

Arlec frowned and kept silent. His power play would have to wait. First they must defeat the Tarth, then quell the rebellion. Without the gateway the latter would not be easy. Without the former the latter was moot. The Sphere would have other uses—the Tarth may know how to return from Hell, but others did not.

Djarn, Lord Priest of the god of luck, spoke.

"Perhaps not."

The group turned to him expectantly. He waited dramatically and then continued. "I have had a vision from Nu Arr." Several of the Katar groaned aloud. Even the diplomatic Jern rolled his eyes. "Please Djarn! We know enough of the gods that you need not add the layers on. Save it for your ignorant worshippers."

Djarn scowled. "Nu Arr remembers the Sphere of Banishment. It was created not as a banishment device, but as a transport device. From before the time of the gods. It was the man called Talanas who set it for Hell and banished the Tarth. It can be set for other destinations. Perhaps the Tarth cannot escape these other planes as easily as Hell."

Arlec pulled out the sphere from hanging around his neck. "How?"

Djarn held out his hand. Arlec held the sphere and glared at him.

"So if it is a transportation device, how is it set to transport only Tarth?" asked Barnus.

Djarn looked at him puzzled.. "It is not. It transports all living creatures within its radius. It is indiscriminate."

Barnus's look of rage was mirrored on several of the other members. The Yanín turned its head and stared wordlessly at Arlec. He backed away from the table, eyes darting from side to side.

"I did not know that. My father's notes indicated that it was only the Tarth."

Looking around he knew that no one believed him. He thought about bolting for the door. He even briefly thought about using the Sphere. Take them all with him. But, watching them, he realized that he was not in immediate danger. They would not punish him now. They still needed him, or rather the Sphere. He pulled out the Sphere and with a show of magnanimity handed the Sphere to Djarn.

The Katar fingered their rings nervously as Djarn held the sphere. He consulted notes that he pulled out of his pocket. Gingerly, he pressed several places on the sphere simultaneously and rotated the sphere's timer. Arlec jumped. "You just set the timer!"

"No, it has ninety nine settings. Hell was the ninety-fifth. I set it for ninety-nine. If Hell is bad, I am assuming that ninety-nine is even worse. My vision … ah … Nu Arr indicated that the ninety-ninth plane is impossible to leave. Now, if we activate it properly we can send all the Tarth to a place that they will not know how to get off of. Or it will take them another five thousand years to do so."

Barnus, looking at Arlec with a grim smile, leaned forward. "Now all we have to do is figure out a way to put that in the center of the Tarth forces and activate it—without taking all of us with them."

Chapter 60

Lanos was left out of the negotiations between Alanar and Be Na Tarth. It was all conducted in Tarth and there seemed no need for him to be directly involved. As the companion to Alanar, husband of Venicia, matriarch of the Tarth, he was given free rein to wander the encampment.

The Chimi looked at him curiously, but with no malice. There were now enough Human spies and others that were allowed into the camp that he did not even cause much attention. It gave Lanos time to think.

The smells of the camp were strong. Strange smells to even an old military man. The Maite dogs smelled of meat and humid carnivore breath. The Tarth had a unique smell of dry leather and the Chimi smelled vaguely of horses. Despite the smells, the general structure or the encampment was something he was familiar with. He had fought battles before.

The original force of Tarth had been dangerous enough to bring the majority of Katar to Zethicia, leaving The Cities open for revolution. Alanar had been convinced that the Tarth and the Katar would virtually wipe each other out and that had been with the smaller Tarth forces. The faulty Hrýll talismans were to further weaken the Katar and the Hrýll with their last true talismans were to join forces with the rebels in The Cities to mop up any Katar resistance. Leaving mankind and the Hrýll free of the Katar. Alanar had felt that once the balance was clear the priesthoods would actually aid the rebels as they resented the Katar power—as long as mankind itself was not in danger.

Lanos and Alanar had argued over the priesthoods, but Alanar felt they were the lesser of two evils right now. The Hrýll, of course, did not care about the priesthoods as they did not worship mankind's gods. It had been an imperfect plan, but at least it had been sane.

Now this. Thousands more Tarth were suddenly on Nakana. The delicate balance of power that was key to the original plan was broken. Alanar and Venicia may have agreed to put revenge in the past, but wandering the encampment it was clear to Lanos that the rest of the Tarth did not feel that way. He had spoken to some of the Human traitors in the camp. They told stories of how the Tarth had destroyed entire villages, to the last living creature, including babies. They even told stories of the Tarth eating the dead, but Lanos wasn't sure he believed that.

Tarth, *daemons* of old, free on Nakana to wreak havoc as they had in the past? It seemed incredible that Alanar was willing to let that happen. What had that jade chain and daggers done to Alanar's mind? Was it possible he was under Venicia's control? Was his brain damaged? In most ways, Alanar was acting normal, or as normal as he had been for the past few weeks. He looked older and tired. Maybe that change had been more than physical. Alanar was losing his objectivity. His own sins were not those of mankind as a whole. If the priesthoods were the lesser of two evils, than the Katar were definitely the lesser evil between Tarth and Katar.

He stepped around the sleeping bodies of a group of Chimi. From what he had heard they bred quickly. They too were a threat—a new threat. Mankind's advantage over the Old Races had been one of proliferation. He knew that as well as the Hrýll. How would they fare with this new race on Nakana? With the Tarth backing them, he feared they would be a strong threat to mankind. Had Alanar factored this in? No. Alanar was acting on faith and the promises of a few Tarth, of one old woman. Could Alanar be persuaded of his folly in time? Lanos doubted he could be persuaded at all. He was acting like a Tarth now, not a Human.

The gateway should be destroyed by now and The Cities in the middle of civil war. No, Alanar would not change his mind. He had made up his mind and nothing would change it. He had that air of self-righteousness about him now. Before he had been focused on destroying the Katar, now he was focused on saving the Tarth. Lanos preferred the vengeful Alanar to the self-righteous one.

He made his way to the periphery of the camp. Still no one stopped him. Word of him must have spread quickly, because they Tarth and Chimi alike glanced at him and occasionally nodded. He nodded back, it seemed the prudent thing to do.

Lanos had made up his mind. He must contact the resistance in Zethicia and have them join the army. He was known as Alanar's right hand. The network could also warn the military planners, probably Katar, of the situation, including that Alanar was helping them. Alanar had gone insane. Perhaps the network had news of Larrina and Tsom. They would trust him almost as much as Alanar or Larrina and he would be there in person. He could point to the Tarth encampment. This was no wild story. Perhaps they could gain concessions from the Katar by joining forces. A partial victory for rights, some freedom from the Katar. Maybe Zethicia could remain a haven from the Katar and free movement of people would be allowed.

He would have to persuade Larrina, but if the gateway was destroyed, she could wait. Then there was Tsom. Alanar had felt that he was a catalyst for change and as a Kinel he had power that few others did, more than Larrina. Maybe he could contact Tsom and, by persuading him things had changed, trigger events that might thwart Alanar and the Tarth. Maybe there was some strange Kinel power that could be used against the Tarth. Understanding Tsom's power was elusive, but his talent for survival and the ability to deal with Katar rings was something he could understand. If he or Larrina were in Zethicia, they could help—or hinder.

He rubbed his chin. Larrina. Did she love Alanar? He would have to be careful what she learned in the aftermath of all of this. If Alanar died, would she forgive him?

He made his way into the fields and grasslands at the outskirts of the encampment. When he was sure no one was watching, he dropped and, moving slowly, made his way to Zethicia, less than a day away. Alanar might be better in fighting, but Lanos was not sure anyone was better at moving silently alone.

Chapter 61

Tsom staggered into the tavern. He did not even try to actively blend in anymore and depended solely on his low level instinctive chameleon effect. Maybe his fatigue would be mistaken for drunkenness. He felt like the octopus that the fishermen beat alive when caught, to keep them tender. Every muscle was going limp. He assumed it was the after effects of pulling himself through from The Cities to Zethicia.

He sat and tried to get his vision to clear. The tavern owner came up to him to see what he wanted and grunted in disgust at the order of tea.

He drank using his left mechanical hand and manipulating the fingers with his virtual hand. His right hand was too painful to use. Even the act of manifesting it hurt. The weak bitter brew they served him was still welcome. A small part of his brain reacted to tea now with comfort and warmth. He remembered Larrina's sad look as he had left. Her pained and saddened expression of betrayal when she had fought him as he had tried to save Shara. He hoped she did not hate him.

He sipped and sat back in his corner of the tavern. Sleep was tempting him, but he knew he needed to find Lanos and Alanar, who should be here in Zethicia somewhere near—if they had followed their original plan. He had contemplated trying to find them with his hands and transport to them, but any additional travel after pulling through the folds—as he thought of it—would have been devastating in his current state. Larrina had told him where several of the rebel cells were, but she was not sure that they would be available with the war effort. Leaning further back into the shadows he cast out for Lanos and Alanar. At least he could see if they were within Zethicia. Just locate them.

As his giant virtual hand touched the citizens of Zethicia he could feel the fear, the anxiety, and the fatigue of all that he touched. He avoided touching the Katar, their rings would react. There, he found Lanos. Alone, not too far from here. Although he could not be sure, it seemed that it was at one of the locations that Larrina had given him.

Pushing himself up, he almost fell. The muscles were still liquid. The short use of his hand had made things worse. He felt nauseated and dizzy. He moved slowly to the tavern's privy. There, thankfully alone, he threw up his tea and anything else that remained in his stomach. It did not really help, but at least he would not be throwing up in the street. The privy had a mirror. Tsom gazed at the reflection. It was bad, even worse than he had imagined. He did not see what his chameleon effect had on others, only his raw reflection. The man he had become was emaciated. The mechanical hands were strangely strong looking on his thin arms. His eyes were sunken with the golden glow still there. His Kinel skin coloring was mottled with white splotches. There were pain lines all around his eyes. Deep and permanent looking. He looked like someone whose age was impossible to guess, but young was not the word that came to mind.

He opened the water valve and let the slow gravity fed water pour over his hands and splashed his face. He shut the valve and slowly walked out. Maybe the outdoor air would at least help the nausea.

It took an hour to get to the location where Lanos was, or where he thought he was. He did not recheck if Lanos was there as he was afraid what it would cost him. The city was a blur of scared faces. The smell of fear mingled with blood and rotted food. Occasionally he would lose his concept of where and when and thought he was back in the cell in Arlec's personal dungeon. Then he stumbled and would jar himself back to the present. Get to Lanos and tell him what had happened. He had to help Alanar and Lanos. It did not occur to him that right now he looked more like he needed help rather than giving it.

Finally, when he was sure he was at the right house, he manifested his uninjured hand. Yes, Lanos was here. He knocked on the building's door, remembering to use the code knock. The door opened and he passed out.

He awoke to see Lanos's face. Lanos was wiping his face with a damp cloth. The look in his eyes reminded him of Larrina. *I know what I look like. It's not that bad! Was it?*

"You have a bad habit of collapsing when we are around each other," said Lanos.

"I seem to run into problems," Tsom said waving his stumps in front of Lanos.

Lanos grimaced and lost his humor. "You were out for some time, so I had a chance to absorb your loss." He rested a heavy hand on Tsom's shoulder. Lanos looked older than the last time. "Was it the Katar? Torture?"

"I suppose one was my own fault," he waved the right arm, "the other was Arlec's."

"What news of the resistance?" asked Lanos, his hand still resting on Tsom's shoulder.

"She was fine when I left her earlier today—in The Cities," replied Tsom, anticipating what was really on his mind and telling him where Larrina was.

"So the gateway is still open?" Surprise in his voice.

"No. I came another way."

Lanos did not ask the next question and Tsom was too tired to explain it. His nausea was fading, but still there. "Do you have any Hrýll brandy, or at least tea? Something to ease pain and nausea?"

Lanos turned and faced someone out of sight who evidently nodded as Lanos nodded after a moment.

While the tea was brewing, Lanos briefed Tsom on the events surrounding Alanar and his marriage, and how Lanos had left the Tarth camp. Haltingly Tsom did the same. When he came to Shara, Tsom's voice trailed off. He simply said, "Shara is dead." Lanos seemed to see the pain in his eyes and left it alone.

"Will you help us defeat the Tarth now that things have changed?" asked Lanos.

"Not if it means saving the Katar. I am here to help destroy the Katar!" He coughed weakly on the last emphasis. "The Katar leadership is here. That is why I came. To destroy them. Destroy Arlec."

"But mankind could be wiped out. The Katar might be the only thing to save us, despite their dominance on all of Nakana. You are half Human Tsom. Your father was Human. Shara was Katar. If we aid the Katar, perhaps we can strike a deal with them. Get some more freedoms for them."

"What of the Hrýll and the Kinel—or Kinel half breeds. Larrina is Kinel and you love her. Will you let her be killed by the Katar? They don't even care for their own. They killed Shara. What of Alanar, Lanos? Will you betray him? Larrina trusts him. He does not have the fear you have. You served him and worked with him for decades. Now you would betray him?"

Lanos bent his head and whispered through clenched teeth. "I do not betray mankind. Friendship, or love for one person—does that count for more than an entire race, *our* race? You're half Human. We have no time. Alanar may be under Tarth control, I have no way of knowing what that device did when it connected him with that female Tarth. Alanar has hated the Katar for decades, maybe even centuries if what Larrina has hinted at is true. Do you believe that Alanar would have changed so easily? He will wreak revenge on the Katar, not matter the price! He believes peace can be negotiated between the Mankind and Tarth. Can we risk it? Can we risk all of mankind on the ability of one man to negotiate with *daemons*—after they have destroyed mankind's only weapon, the Katar?"

Tsom tried to absorb the new information. He had three friends in the world left alive. One was asking him to betray another. Would Larrina say the same thing? What would Shara have said? Tsom shook his head in frustration.

Lanos leaned forward his face close to Tsom's.

"When the Tarth met Alanar, they seemed to know him, Tsom. Know him. No man can live that long. Do gods even live that long? The Hrýll spoke of reincarnation as if they know it to be true. What if Alanar is some reincarnation that the Tarth know. What if he has changed completely with the talisman the Tarth used on him? I tell you no man loses the thirst for revenge that easily. Something is wrong."

"Yet, I have that same thirst for revenge and you are asking me to give it up, Lanos. I need to talk to Alanar. I cannot believe he would sacrifice mankind simply to destroy the Katar."

"I told you, he thinks he can reason with the Tarth. Reason with them? Don't you recall the legends? The stories of the Tarth destroying everything in their path? Look at what they did to the villages and towns here. It's too dangerous a weapon he wields now—the entire Tarth race. The Tarth must be sent back or destroyed. They will never willingly go back, for good reason. I was there, it is worse than the childhood stories we heard. They must be destroyed for our own survival. They will destroy us for their survival."

"What can I really do? I came for my revenge against the Katar and to help the last of my people. Just to do my part. To get Arlec and make him pay for his sister and my hand. I think I can get him and maybe two or three of the Katar leadership from a distance." He slumped back onto the cot, exhausted. "There is really nothing more I can do." He whispered and fell asleep, dreaming of revenge and reliving Shara's death over and over.

"How are you holding up?" Asked Lanos.

"I am better than I probably look," replied Tsom. He was better, at least his nausea was gone and he had some of his physical strength back. But, he was older. He could feel it. He must look like a wreck.

Why were they here, near the military garrison? This was a dangerous place for a rebel to be. Lanos had insisted that he see something. He seemed to have some old connections to the military here. Soon they were in the garrison itself. Tsom concentrated on being unnoticed. Lanos glanced at him once and jumped back a bit.

"I forgot that you can do that." He shook his head slightly disbelieving. "I took you for an old Zethician veteran for a moment. He whispered something to one of the guards and they strode into what Tsom soon discovered was an infirmary. Lanos guided him by the elbow as they strode through. This section held the survivors of the Maite dogs. One out of a hundred survived. The next section was for those who survived the Chimi soldiers. They had fared somewhat better; physically. Finally, they came upon a few men who were in body casts. Lanos approached one of those who did not have their jaws broken.

"Afternoon soldier." Lanos spoke softly to the man in the cot.

"Sir."

"I know you have been over this before, but can you briefly recount your encounter with the Tarth?"

The soldier began to speak, his voice trembling slightly and his eyes blinking a few times. "We came upon one of them that was alone. Twenty of us."

Lanos waited patiently, resting a hand on the soldier's shoulder. After a moment the soldier continued, as if in a trance.

"We no longer had any arrows, so we attacked five at a time. The Tarth ripped the leg off of the first to reach him. Bilji was his name. I didn't know him well. He ripped his leg off without killing him outright. Then he bludgeoned the other four with the leg, knocking aside their swords as if they were sticks. Five more of us were attacking by now and the Tarth laughed with pleasure. He killed the next five by reaching into their bellies and pulling out their intestines." Pause. "The next five were dead more cleanly. I was in the last five. The bodies were getting in our way and the Tarth's. Yet, he still laughed at us. He crushed the head of Lylee and reached into the skull and threw the brains in our faces. In broken common tongue it said 'You are the beginning of the end. We will destroy your entire race like the sick cattle that you are.' Just then five Katar came over the small hill and charged the Tarth. He screamed in rage, picked me up like a small sack and threw me thirty feet into one of the Katar. That is the last I remember."

Later, Lanos took Tsom to other areas of the city. The refugees from one of the few villages that had not been totally wiped out. The descriptions of the burning, the destruction of every living thing were augmented by the small child without parents who cringed at every sound and the nearby mother who lost all three of her children to the Maite dogs.

"These are the allies that Alanar is choosing. These are the allies that Alanar has brought thousands more over from Hell to join the forces here. Twenty men were no match for one Tarth. Five Katar merely pissed him off into running. Tsom, we made a mistake thinking we could use even the initial force of Tarth as a weapon! It is insanity to deal with them all. They fear nothing, not even the gods. The Yanín take only a few more seconds for one of the Tarth to kill them.

Tsom absorbed the devastation. It ground into his psyche rubbing the raw wounds of Shara's death and his own circle of destruction. Everyone seemed to be in pain, or dying, or afraid. Shara had been Katar. Shara had given up her ring and its parasitic power. She was part Human. His father had been Human. Were the Tarth a greater threat? If one Katar could change, couldn't more? He pushed away from Lanos and the world of waste. Lanos tried to follow him and Tsom, without thinking, manifested a hand, knocked him back, and held him there until he was out of sight. He had to think. Alone.

~~~

Lanos stood before the astonished war council. He might not have made it past the first sentry, but Barnus had halted the guards who were ready to haul him away. "Lanos. I know this name. A Lanos once saved the life of my now dead son." He looked Lanos up and down, studying his face and his bearing. "My son described you well." Turning to the guard, "Let him inside."

The guard hesitated. Barnus was not Katar. "Do I need to have you disciplined by Jern in front of the entire guard? Let him through." The guard looked Lanos over, checked for any weapons, and let him through.

Lanos told them little which they did not know. Djarn, the Lord Priest, seemed disturbed by the name Talanas that Lanos mentioned during his story. They probed for information on Tsom, especially the Lord Priest, but he led them to believe that Tsom was dead. Arlec looked both pleased and skeptical.

After considerable discourse, the true nature of the Sphere was revealed to Lanos.

"Let me have it."

They looked at him with a great deal more surprise than when he had first entered.

"I alone can get back to the Tarth encampment. They trust me. I can get the Sphere inside, activate it, and hide it."

This was not wildly different from their current plan, except that they had not figured out how to get the sphere into the camp safely. Yet, how could they trust him, Barnus asked.

Arlec spoke for the first time in a long time since giving up the sphere. "Mind scan him." He smiled as if he had just suggested a tasty after dinner drink. Several of the Katar, remembering how his father had used the same technique on Arlec, looked away. Jern did not. He looked directly at Arlec. "Do you have the mind scanning talisman with you?"

Arlec's grin broadened.

"Are *you* willing to use it?" asked Jern.

His grin disappeared.

Lanos understood. The rape of the mind was not easy. The talisman facilitated the act, but it had the potential of harming not only the target mind, but the user. It was, he thought, in some ways similar to the device Alanar had used with Venicia. It was illegal and even owning the talisman was illegal, but these were, after all, Katar. Was he willing to allow a mind scan? By Arlec? No. Not by him. For one thing, he would probe after Tsom. He looked around the room.

"Barnus. I will only allow it to be done by Barnus."

They all turned to Barnus. White faced, with beads of perspiration on his forehead, Barnus nodded; as did Arlec, relief written on his face.

***

Carnel considered Alanar's words. His mother had intervened when he had tried to kill him on their initial meeting. She had anticipated his reaction. So had Alanar. It had been a shock that Alanar had both dodged his blow and had actually caused him no small amount of pain. His mother was still stronger than she looked and she too knocked him back as he had attacked Alanar. After a time the words of both his mother and Alanar had started to make sense. Occasionally he would glance at Alanar and wonder. *He is puny as any other Human, yet this man has killed more than I would ever want to. He does not look like death, nor does he feel like a god.* In fact, he could feel no *ka* from this man, as if he did not exist.

Peace, at a price. Nakana was a large world. The Tarth were long lived and strong, but slow breeders. Alanar was proposing that they live in peace in the mountains to the west. They leave the other races alone, unless actually attacked by them. They work out a peace with mankind on the condition that the Katar no longer rule mankind.

The latter part seemed the hardest to swallow. The Katar were worse than Talanas, or Alanar as he called himself now. Alanar had acted out of revenge in the past. Revenge was something Be Na Tarth understood. But Alanar had never been cruel, just indiscriminate and massive in his destruction. The Katar had been cruel. The Katar were a group, not an individual. The Katar had not married his mother. He clenched and unclenched his jaw.

"Very well. We will try this peace of yours, if you can convince mankind's spokesmen and we can both convince the Katar."

Narlan, the short, lighter skinned Tarth that had originally captured Alanar, objected. "We are all here now. We are more powerful. Let us destroy them all and make Nakana ours as it was before! Destroy the Katar and mankind's gods and then consider whether to destroy mankind or simply enslave them. Our spies tell us the gateway to The Cities is broken—we can destroy Zethicia and almost all the Katar without the millions of The Cities to worry about."

Several of the other Tarth leaders agreed. One of the recently arrived spoke up. "We are grateful that Talanas brought us back. With his marriage to Venicia he has pledged to protect all of what is hers. We forgive his past sins with this in mind, but there can never be peace between the Tarth and the Katar and mankind, who are simply Katar slaves." Several more nodded.

Be Na Tarth was not used to being challenged, but he kept his temper. He understood their arguments. Yet, his mother was wise and she trusted her new *husband*. She had used the Chain of Melding with him and both had survived. A male and a female melded, it had never occurred before. She would know if Alanar was planning a betrayal. Her new husband, if legend was accurate, was older than his mother would ever be and felt that mankind could live in peace with the Tarth, if only without the Katar ruling them. The Katar, would they ever give up their power? He thought not, but why not try. If they refused, then kill them all.

"We will give this peace a chance. We give up nothing by trying. We gain the help of Talanas by trying. He knows more about the Katar, their rings, and the Sphere of Banishment than anyone. He is a useful ally."

Alanar looked uncomfortable at the description and Narlan stormed out of the tent, along with several others, including a nar Tarth, which Carnel did not recognize. She had strangely cat like eyes.

The female Tarth with the strangely cat like eyes spoke at length with Narlan, just outside the tent. They both nodded and went their own way.

Chapter 62

The knock at the door caused Tsom to start. He was alone. Too weak to help the rebels; he had told them to leave him alone. He struggled to his feet and pulled out the sword that Larrina had given him, holding it awkwardly in his mechanical hands. The knock was harder.

"Enter" His yell was more of a croak.

A man followed by four guardsmen entered. He held up an empty hand and signaled for the others not to draw their weapons. "Tsom, my name is Barnus. You must come with me, or you will be discovered soon. Lanos sent me."

Tsom swayed back and forth. He manifested his left hand and reached. Yes, the man's *ka* felt as if he were telling the truth. Another skill he had developed recently. He had tried it on Lanos and the soldiers during his tour of devastation. They had all been telling the truth also. He dropped the manifestation and sank to his knees. Slowly he tried to sheath the sword. One of the guards stepped forward to help him, but he waved them back. "No, no, I must sheath it. Do not touch it."

"Where are you taking me?" He asked after finally sheathing Larrina's sword.

"To watch and see if Lanos succeeds. He felt it was important for you to see."

They made their way to the lookout. The disc of seeing was focused on the now huge Tarth encampment. Through it, Tsom was amazed to see that he could discern Lanos making his way to the center of the encampment. He was in the open and unchallenged.

Suddenly, the sky turned black. Tsom looked up and saw not clouds but thousands, hundreds of thousands, millions of birds. The birds descended upon Zethicia destroying themselves upon the inhabitants. Several small finches hit Tsom and almost knocked him down in his weakened state, causing the disc of seeing to move. Gazing through it as he pulled himself back to his feet Tsom cried out. "An attack! The Tarth are attacking from the north!"

The winds started picking up and the birds were soon struggling against the winds. Barnus rushed off the lookout to his troops, leaving Tsom alone on the tower. Fighting the wind and the occasional bird he moved the disc from view to view. To the south masses of animals large and small were smashing the walls of the outer city. Lightning was striking a small percentage of the animals, but there were so many that the impact was nominal. He moved the view back to Lanos. Lanos was standing holding what looked like a sphere in his hands. Suddenly a pale pink Tarth was behind him with his sword drawn. Tsom called out instinctively. He was too late. Lanos sensed the movement but seemed determined to do something with the sphere first and did not dodge well. The blow aimed at severing his neck hit him at the waist. The effect was the same.

The pain was almost physical. Lanos, the mighty warrior who had saved both Tsom and Shara, was dead with one simple blow. Lanos who loved Larrina. Lanos who had shown the first bit of compassion when presenting him to Alanar. Dead by a Tarth. Dead by Alanar's mistaken trust in the Tarth. Betrayed.

Tsom now knew what the sphere was, he should have guessed immediately, but it was so hard to stay focused, his head throbbed.

The attack from the north proved that Lanos had been right, the Tarth could not be trusted. Alanar was wrong to trust these *daemons*. They had some sort of control over animals too. Lanos would not die in vain. He hated the Katar, but Lanos was right—the timing of the revolution was wrong, the cost too high. He reached. The pain in his right hand and the energy consumption was enormous. He needed *ka*. He began to draw upon those nearby. He thought of all the Katar in the city and their rings. He was becoming like them, he thought. A parasite willing to use other's *ka* for his own purpose. He thought of Shara and Larrina, both begging him to stop. Do not become like them. Do not use others wantonly. He dropped the hold he felt on those nearby and reached within himself and tapped the reserves of *ka* he found there and then reached for the Sphere.

As he touched the Sphere he felt the presence of Alanar next to it. He grabbed the sphere with his left hand, manifested his right, and reached with that, through the wall of pain. More energy flowing along his virtual arms and hands. The pain in his right unbearable, worse than when Larrina had first injured him. Each time he used his right hand it seemed worse. He reached and tried to pull Alanar to him. *You made a mistake my friend, but I can still save you.* He touched Alanar and screamed in pain. His *ka* was like fire, death, ice. It was strange. It was not Human. It felt like it would suck his essence into its own, almost a negative *ka*. He let go and touching the sphere with both hands he thought of it as a lock. Instinctively, he found what seemed the obvious thing to push and did.

The area grew blurry and dark. The encampment seemed to fall into a dark, moonlit haze. Suddenly, all the Tarth, Chimi, and Alanar were gone. With the last of his strength Tsom took the sphere and focused on Larrina. He pushed the sphere to her, between the folds in the paper. He felt the folds give way and felt Larrina's presence. He dropped the sphere in her hand.

Then, he passed out.

Chapter 63

"You have betrayed us Talanas! Once again you are death to my people," Be Na Tarth was trembling with fear, anger, and guilt.

"No, I did not. I tried to stop the device from going off. I did not know that Lanos carried it. Someone else triggered the Sphere, from a distance. This is not even Hell, but some other plane, a plane I have never been to."

"There was no one else! I was a fool to trust you, somehow you deceived my mother and fooled even the Chain of Melding. You must die, once and forever." Be Na Tarth lifted his huge arm holding a fat bladed scimitar. The dull moonlight of the strange world reflected off of its blade. So complete was his rage that he was unable to stop as his mother burst through the crowd, throwing herself in front of Alanar. The sword, made for fighting Tarth in a time when Tarth fought amongst themselves, cleaved through her and Alanar simultaneously. Alanar, who had tried to push Venicia aside had no time to pull his own weapon. Their blood flowed together as one.

Be Na Tarth dropped his scimitar and rushed forward. The fallen body of Alanar moved! It pushed Be Na Tarth aside as if he were a child and grabbed the body of Venicia. The gaping area of his chest and shoulder seeming to reseal itself. Truly he was not Human, or any other race Be Na Tarth knew of. There was a look of unseeing in the moving corpse of Alanar, who he still called in his mind by his old name, Talanas. Unseeing rage. The eyes gold on gold with blue flecks. Be Na Tarth felt his sphere full of *ka* drain almost instantly, he felt his own *ka* touched. The ground around them blackened. The other Tarth began to flee. Then sight returned to the eyes of this creature who had fooled his mother and betrayed the Tarth. It gazed at Venicia's body and at Be Na Tarth. "This time I did not betray you, or my wife. I kept my vow and will keep it. I will keep the one final vow I gave her and the wishes of another whose spirit is similar to your mother's." He bowed his head, Be Na Tarth felt the drain on his own *ka* subside and his strength return. "I have changed. I have changed. All for naught. The burden of this is on you, Carnel. You will live with guilt similar to my own."

There was a look of immense pity in his eyes as he gazed at Be Na Tarth. His wounds opened up again and the last of his blood spilled forth. The creature that the Tarth had called Death thousands of years ago died. Carnel, the Lord of *Daemons*, wept as he lifted his mother's body and strode into his doomed people now gathering around.

Chapter 64

Larrina walked the empty Tarth encampment with Tsom, who moved slowly. It was just a few days since the Sphere had been used. The encampment had not yet been looted and stripped. Barnus had protected Tsom after Arlec refused to acknowledge that Tsom deserved a full pardon for his efforts. Now the Katar were in full march back to the cities, where the rebels had taken Argn and were attacking Qenaril. The rebels hoped by controlling the qenar they would be in a position of power by the time the Katar arrived. Larrina was not sure it would be sufficient. The Katar would not give up generations of power easily and even with their numbers reduced, too many of them and their rings survived. Once the Katar arrived, she was not sure that the rebellion would be able to shake off the legacy of fear that thousands of years of Katar rule had produced. Alanar had been right in that respect, the Katar needed to be destroyed, or broken, for mankind to be free. She did not know if the price would have been worthwhile, but she knew he had been right about this.

Larrina was here reluctantly. Tsom had pulled her through today with his *hands*. He claimed it was becoming easier, as all new skills were. Larrina quietly showed him a mirror and asked if he could afford even easier uses of his *ka*.

Larrina suddenly stopped and knelt by a dying bantri tree, laying fallen in its small pot by a large Tarth tent. Its small branch was brown and lifeless.

"What is it?" asked Tsom.

Larrina was silent. She touched her lips to her finger and touched the dead branch of the tree. Then she stood, brushing a tear away. "Nothing." They kept walking slowly.

Glossary

Alanar Tonshon—leader of the rebellion. Talanas—another of the names for Alanar. An ancient name, possibly from a prior incarnation of Alanar.

Arbeneth—One of the five cities. The main port city, with an island in the center of the river. It controls both riverbanks and the sea.

Ague—god of seas

Alam—as in Festival of Alam. Alam is one of the seasons in Northern Nakana, which is a permanent sub-tropical area due to the tilt of the planet's axis, making the seasons subtly different, generally accented by wind movements from the south. The southern portion of the planet is much colder.

Arlec—Katar guard, member of the Karn family

Argn—Northwest city, partially agricultural, of the five cities it gives the most rights to women. Known for its colors and meaning behind every color scheme.

Artifact—see *Iribansu*

Askatasuna—an old name for the resistance, meaning Freedom. While not used in common discussion, everyone in the resistance knows this label.

Atem's luck—An expression of being fooled into thinking something is good when it is not. Atem is a person from legend whose good luck always turned into something bad.

Ba—*ka* is the energy that fuels life. *Ba* is the soul, the essence of an individual. Total destruction of the *ku* destroys the *ba*, the soul. The *ba* needs some ka to return to the Sea of Souls. *Ba* and *ka* are Hrýll and Srýll words.

Barnus Erras—head of the guard/army of Zethicia

Be Na Tarth—Literally *First of Tarth* , sometimes referred to as Lord of the *Daemons* An honorific name/title. His given name is Carnel. The titles among the Tarth are also used as names. Tarth itself has multiple meanings, meaning both the race and the people and even the family. Ruling is hereditary, so First of the Tarth is both a title and a reference to the family that is claiming to be descended from the very first of the race and it is reference to first as in first among equals. No one but a close friend, family, or someone wanting to insult would refer to him as Carnel. It should always be Be Na Tarth. Even his mother would often refer to him that way.

Barin—husband of Kaylee. A craftsman.

Brontriste—a Katar and advisor to Devon. Age unknown, but quite old.

Cappa—a cadet or young untrained person.

Chimi—the companion race to the *daemons*. They have short fur, more dog-like than the Hrýll, with very Human faces.

Cities, The—The Cities are six cities so close to each other that most people refer to them as a single unit. **Arbeneth** the southernmost is the main port city spanning both sides of the Darnen river as it spilled into the Nýlyr sea. Just North, on the Western shore, is **Slurne**. Across from it lies **Vranin**. East of Vranin lies **Qenaril**, so named because of its proximity to the qenar mines to the North. West of Slurne is both **Bronin** and **Argn**, the city states with an agricultural base surrounding them. The total population of The Cities is nearly 20 million, accounting for over 80% of the Human population on Nakana.

Courie Marcone—Governor of Zethicia, which has a partially elected government.

Darnen river—major river of Arbeneth

Djarn—Lord Priest of Nu Arr, god of luck

Devon Karn—head of the Karn clan

Farnlaran—the largest city of the Hrýll. Some view it as the capital, but Hrýll governance is not the same as Human, or others, and not centralized.

Flana Showa—young noblewoman, object of romantic interest from Arlec. Timon is her father, a noble and powerful merchant.

Gink—Small rodent, similar to a mouse, but very destructive to crops.

Gnali—Pickled fish, batter dipped and deep fried.

Governor Courie—governor of the Zethicia region, including the main city. A lifelong appointment, but not hereditary.

Hallam, Lady—goddess of nature.

Hrýll and **Srýll**—two of the old races: They are Humanoid, but covered in a fine light fur, or hair. Not heavy or shaggy, but still enough to protect the skin somewhat. Most have brownish hair, but there is a variety of colors analogous to hair color of Humans.

Inlas—goddess of illusions

Iribansu—an artifact, usually from early Hrýll history. A talisman with no need for qenar as additional fuel.

Jern Tanec—Katar. Head of the Tanec family

Ka—the energy of life. Total destruction of the *ka* destroys the *ba*, the soul. The *ba* needs some ka to return to the Sea of Souls. *Ba* and *ka* are Hrýll and Srýll words.

Karn family—one of the five families forming the Katar. Arlec and Shara are Karn.

Katar—Katar are Human with traces of Kinel blood. They have ruled mankind for ten thousand years, with most of their power and abuse taking place in the past five thousand.

Five ruling Katar Families, by family head and city they rule:

Jern [Argn - Tanec Family: Crissa and Mia daughters]

Devon, later **Arlec** [Arbeneth - Karn Family]

Telem [Qenaril and Vranin—Sho family (second most powerful of the families)]

Wara [Bronin—Terrel family]

Jahone [Slurne - Katir family]

Katraniara (Kate)—Tsom's mother

Kaylee—wife of Barin—Human—member of the resistance.

Kinel—an old race that was long lived when they did not abuse their use of *ka*. While they were not one of the 'old ones' they were one of the earliest races to arrive in Nakana, according to their own legends. They were hunted to extinction by the Katar.

Larra and **Piea**—older sisters of Arlec. Larra is the oldest and the natural leader. Both have dark hair and are often confused for each other.

Larrina—Last of the Kinel. Old ally of Alanar, perhaps one time lover. Age unknown.

Lord Priest Farlam—All heads of the priesthoods are called Lord Priest. Farlam is head of the god of luck, Nu Arr.

Maite dogs—Tarth war dogs. Size of horses.

Mark—a mark is a unit of distance. Based on a horse running a full speed, each mark is a minute of local time (100 seconds). One mark = 6600 feet (a little over a mile).

Met—god of weather

Moons—Five Moons circle Nakana, not all in the same plane of orbit. Two moons are usually visible during the day (Naka and Saryll), while three are usually visible at night. The orbits are such that eclipses are extremely common, with one, two, or even three moons. Once every ten thousand years the five moons eclipse each other and the sun. The moons are: Naka, Saryll, Farthul, Taril, Torin.

Muglanth Plains—vast plains near Zethicia. Very fertile.

Nart—a mildly intoxicating leaf, rolled and smoked. The rolled version also called a nart.

Nar Tarth—female *daemon*. An honorific address.

Ne Na—cult that does not believe that the gods are gods.

Nu Arr—god of luck. There is some tie to Nu Arr's history and the birth of gods and rise of mankind, all which took place circa the eclipse of the five moons, ten thousand years ago. His power is one of synchronicity in the Jungian sense.

Oonie—'Unchya' translated to common tongue as 'First of the Tea Family'

Piea and **Larra**—older sisters of Arlec. See *Larra and Piea*

Pintar—one sixtieth of a sintar.

Pé—'soul' god. Guardian of the rivers of life and death.

Qenar—generally found in jade, qenar is an inanimate form of *ka*. It can fuel many talismans, but cannot be used to create a talisman, which requires *ka*. It is the fuel of 'technology' on Nakana and only one source is known.

Qenaril—the city that controls the qenar mines.

Riconé—one of the old races—banished the *daemons* with the Kinel.

Saman—another Human population center. Smaller than Zethicia.

Sar—honorific used for both male and female. Acknowledges high birth.

Shara—younger sister of Arlec

Shenar—'judge'

Shela—woman on the docks that Tsom was close to, who gave him the coin for the resistance.

Sintar—Unit of currency

Slurne—one of The Cities

Sphere of Banishment—*San Par'eh Shante* in old Kinel is an ancient artifact that does not require power from *ka* nor qenar. Its origins are not clear.

Srýll—one of the old races.

Talanas—another of the names for Alanar. An ancient name.

Talisman—fueled by Qenar, to create a talisman requires *ka*.

Tanec—family—Katar of Argn

Tarth—Hrýll name for the old *daemons*.

Tarth river—river of Argn, flows into the Darnen

Tiar—Oonie's wife. A Hrýll. [Also the goddess of illusion posing as mortal]

Timon Showa—Flana's father.

Tsom—When not using his chameleon effect his description is: Gold eyes both the iris and pupil. His skin dark, except for parts of his face. The dark skin covered his neck, all of his jaw, but narrowed to a point at the top of his forehead. His hair was white blond.

Tsunon tea—a heavily caffeinated tea with other stimulant herbs added. Like most teas, this is from the Hrýll.

Venicia—mother to Be Na Tarth. Oldest of the Tarth. Former queen of the Tarth.

Vranin—one of the five cities.

YanÃn—warrior race. Reduced to mercenaries for centuries. Their joints are all double jointed and they have a partial exoskeleton which acts as an armor. They one weakness is a tendency to drink too much. To reproduce three of them must mate together—which is a rare occurrence, but their population is stable at a small number. Like the Tarth, they cannot interbreed with Humans.

Yarm—dead mentor of Tsom

Zethicia—large geographically, mostly agricultural, with several million in population. It is the largest population center outside of The Cities which contains tens of millions. It is on the main continent. There are small towns scattered around Zethicia, for ranching and farming. There are also numerous towns between Zethicia and The Cities, following the main trade route. There are other pockets of mankind on Zethicia, which are not part of this story.

New Libri Press is a small independent press dedicated to publishing new authors and independent authors in both eBook and traditional formats.

We choose our manuscripts not based on what large publishers have sold in the recent past, but on what we think the independent reader would enjoy.

- Our model includes releasing all our works first in eBook form, followed by print.
- Our model includes accepting manuscripts directly from authors.
- Our model includes hands on editing.
- Our model includes asking all of our authors to help choose additional authors.

We would love to hear more from you! Tell us your thoughts and what you like to read! Feel free to send us an email at *printreader@newlibri.com*

Visit our website at: www.NewLibri.com

www.ingramcontent.com/pod-product-compliance
Lightning Source LLC
Chambersburg PA
CBHW060308260626
47160CB00007B/2537